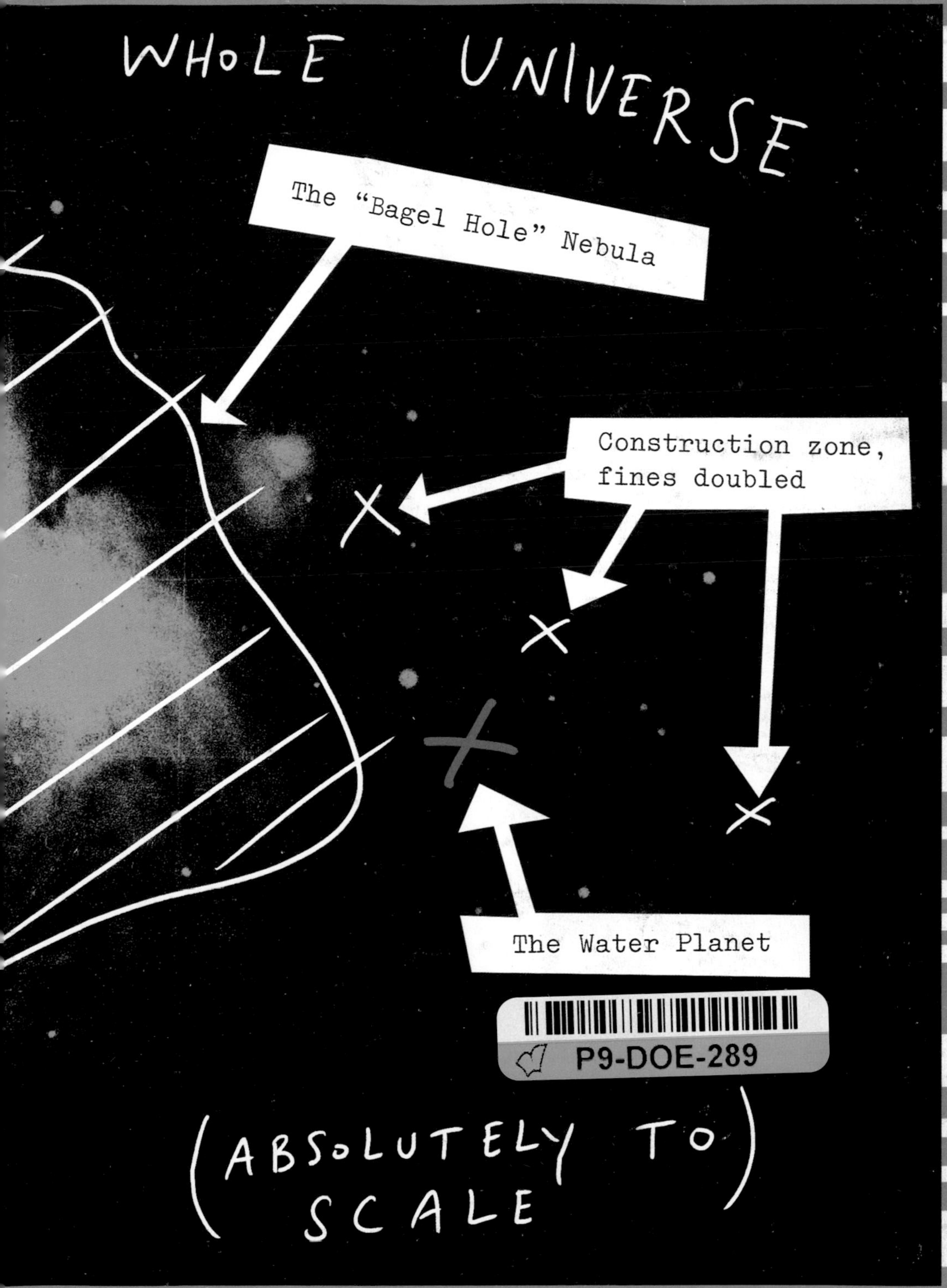
WHOLE UNIVERSE
The "Bagel Hole" Nebula
Construction zone, fines doubled
The Water Planet
(ABSOLUTELY TO SCALE)

ASTRO-NUTS

Mission Two: The Water Planet

By Jon Scieszka

Illustrated by Steven Weinberg

chronicle books · san francisco

NNASA!

Many thanks to the Rijksmuseum for the use of art featured throughout the book. Command Escape, Earth, Mount Rushmore, and the work of Ernst Haeckel are all collaged from images in the public domain.
More information on all of this is available at AstroNuts.space.

For Felix —J.S. and S.W.

Text copyright © 2020 by JRS Worldwide LLC.
Illustrations copyright © 2020 by Steven Weinberg.

Library of Congress Cataloging-in-Publication Data:

Names: Scieszka, Jon, author. | Weinberg, Steven, 1984- illustrator.

Title: The water planet / by Jon Scieszka ; illustrated by Steven Weinberg.

Description: San Francisco : Chronicle Books, [2020] | Series: AstroNuts; mission 2 | Audience: Ages 6-9. | Audience: Grades 2-3. | Summary: On their second mission to find another habitable planet, the four mutant animals, LaserShark, AstroWolf, SmartHawk, and StinkBug, splash land on the Water Planet, run by some suspiciously friendly clams, who are very eager to swap planets—and if the AstroNuts can stop arguing among themselves they may find out why before it is too late.

Identifiers: LCCN 2019042569 | ISBN 9781452171203 (hardcover)

Subjects: LCSH: Life on other planets—Juvenile fiction. | Extrasolar planets—Discovery and exploration—Juvenile fiction. | Astronauts—Juvenile fiction. | Genetic engineering—Juvenile fiction. | Pollution—Juvenile fiction. | Science fiction. | Humorous stories. | CYAC: Life on other planets—Fiction. | Extrasolar planets—Fiction. | Astronauts—Fiction. | Genetic engineering—Fiction. | Pollution—Fiction. | Science fiction. | Humorous stories. | LCGFT: Science fiction. | Humorous fiction.

Classification: LCC PZ7.S41267 Wat 2020 | DDC 813.54 [Fic]—dc23

LC record available at https://lccn.loc.gov/2019042569

Manufactured in China.

FSC™
MIX
Paper from responsible sources
FSC™ C008047
www.fsc.org

If you are reading this, then you have been selected. Don't look around like that. Act natural. Do not draw attention to yourself. Keep reading. The future of humans on Earth depends on you. Here is your mission—read this book. It will give you all the information you need to know.

Design by Jay Marvel.
Typeset in Freight Micro, Typewriter, and Noyh.

10 9 8 7 6 5 4 3 2 1

Chronicle Books LLC
680 Second Street
San Francisco, California 94107
www.chroniclekids.com.

NNASA!

5

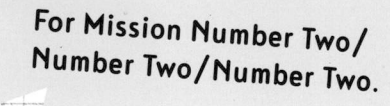

AstroNuts Activate!

For Mission Number Two/
Number Two/Number Two.

NNASA

CMD. esc.

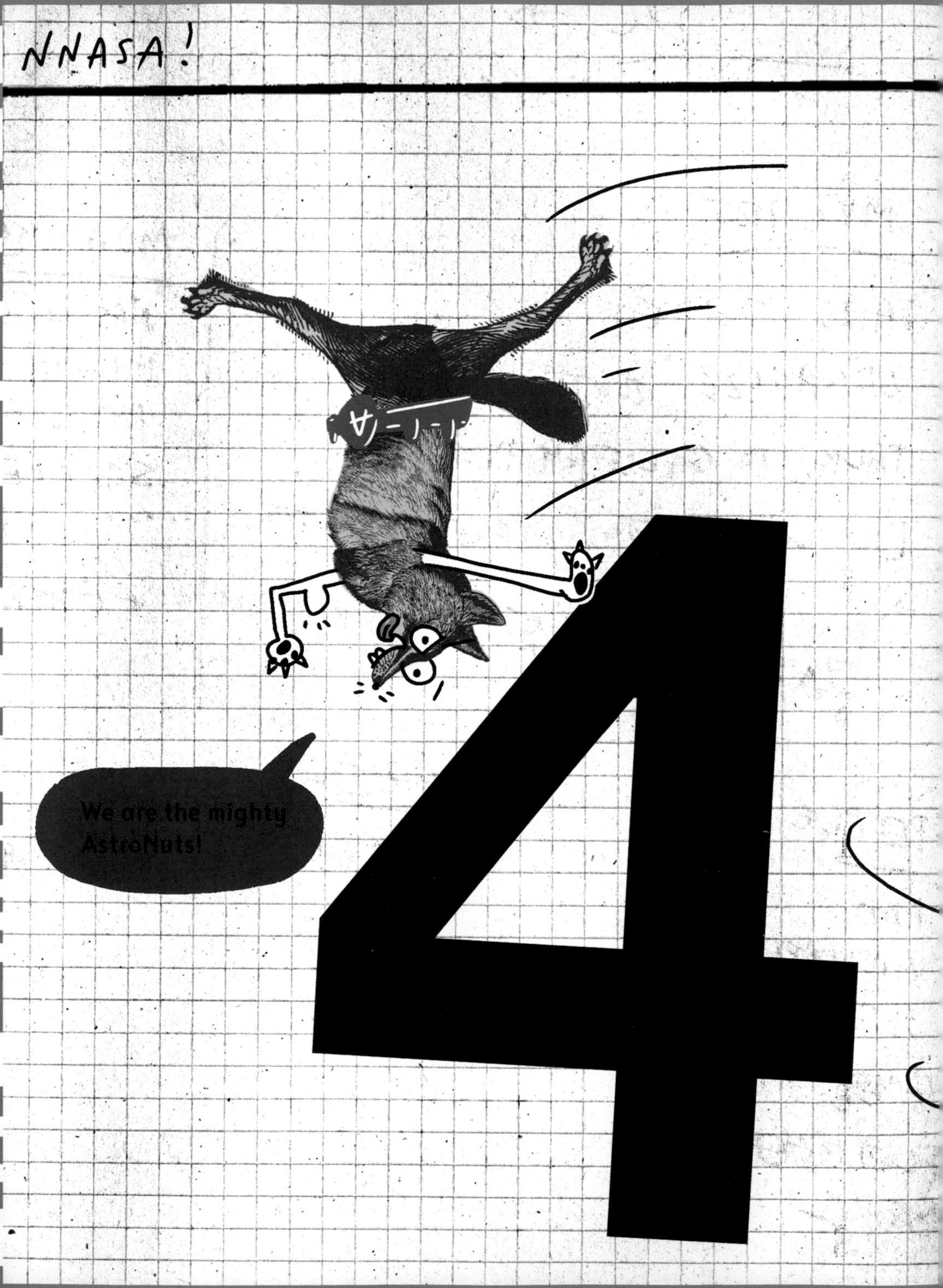
NNASA!
We are the mighty AstroNuts!
4

NNASA!

3

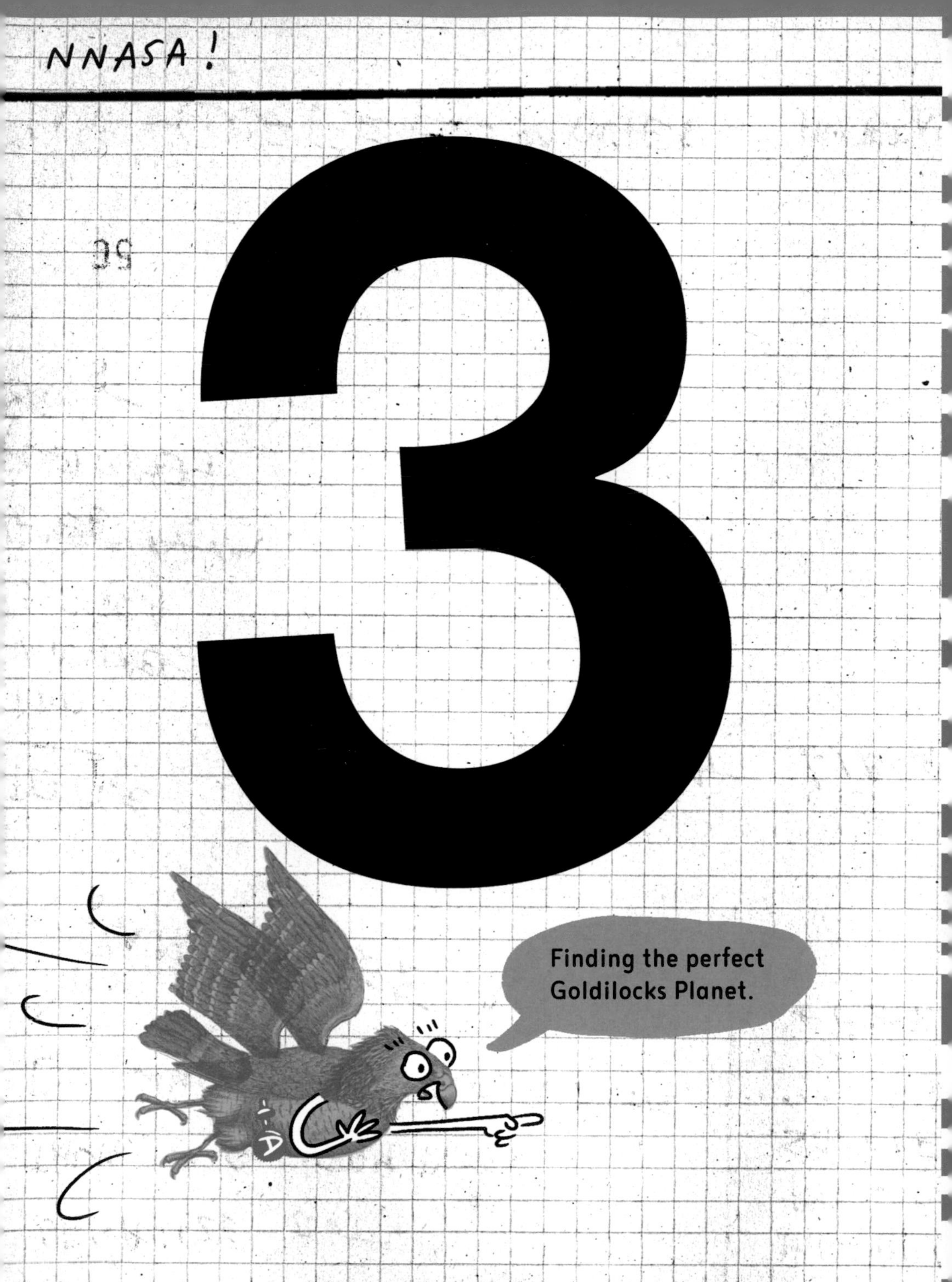
Finding the perfect Goldilocks Planet.

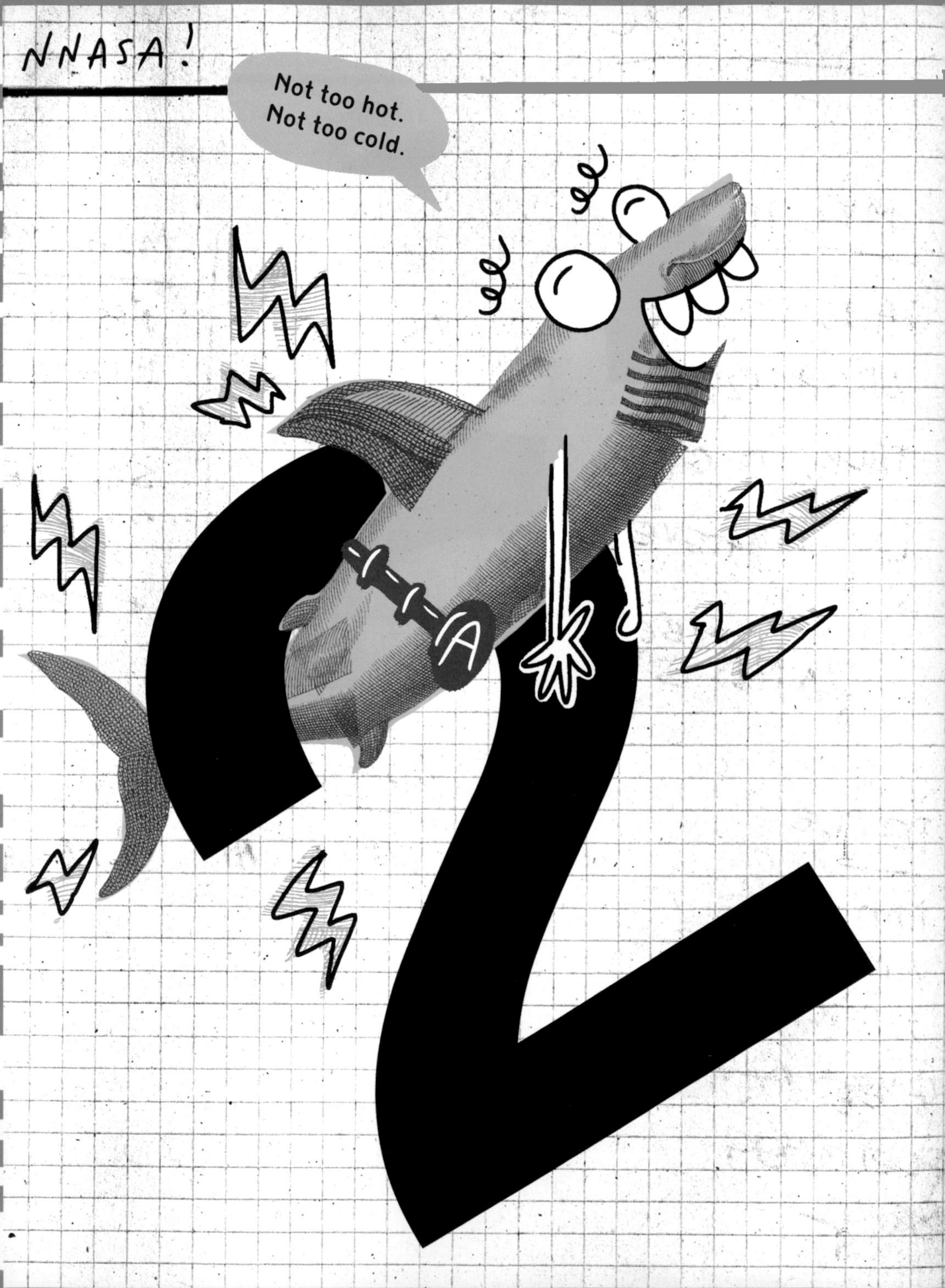
NNASA!
Not too hot.
Not too cold.

NNASA!

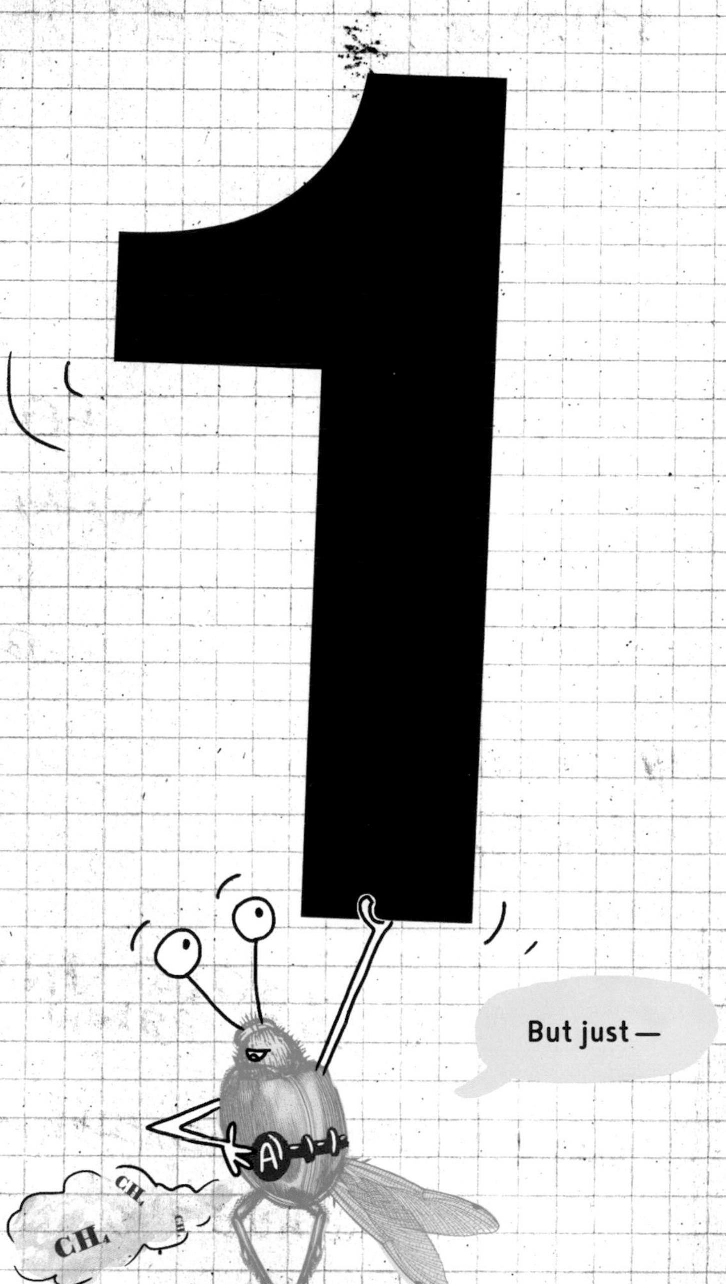

But just —

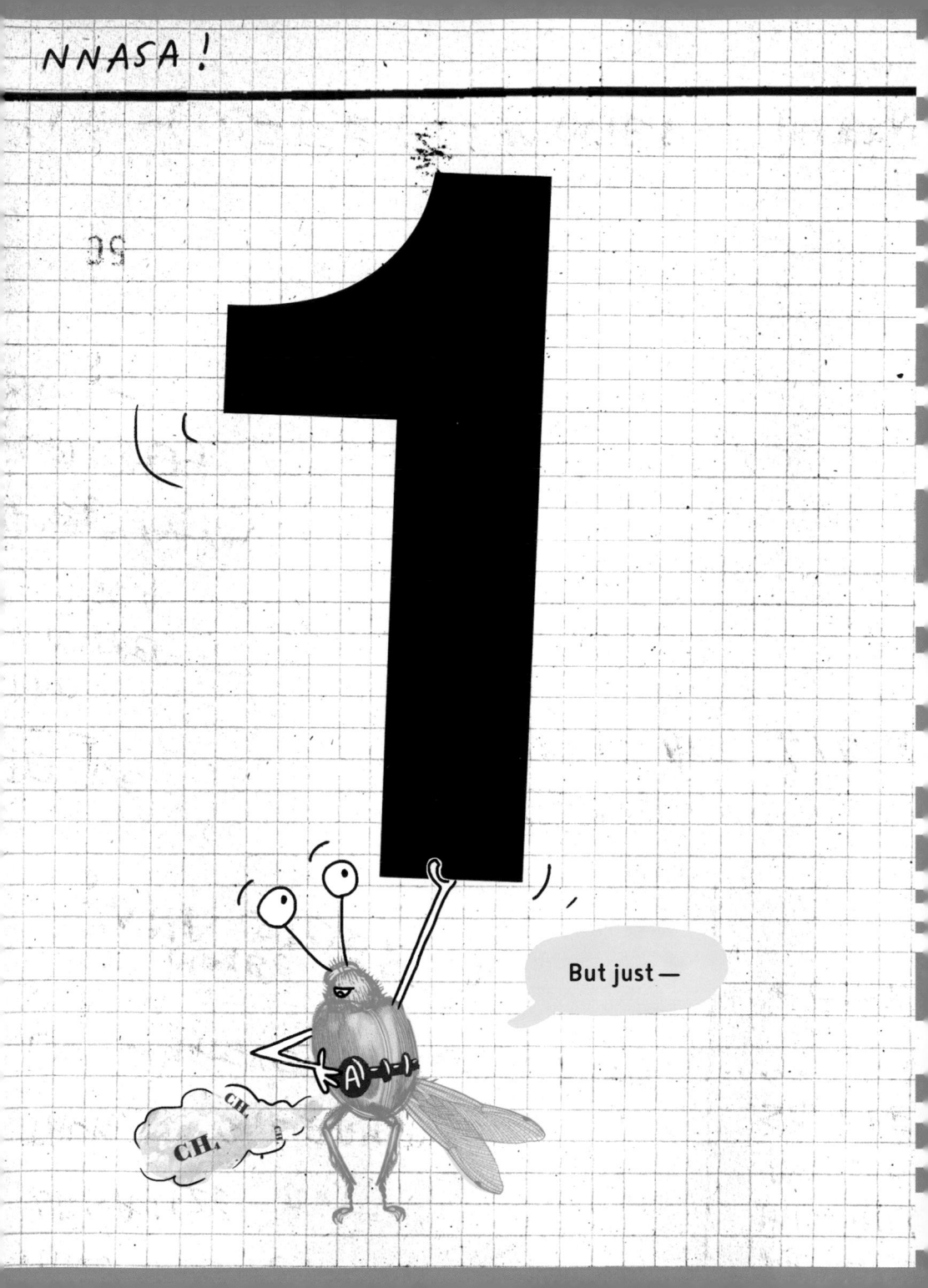

BLAST OFF!!!

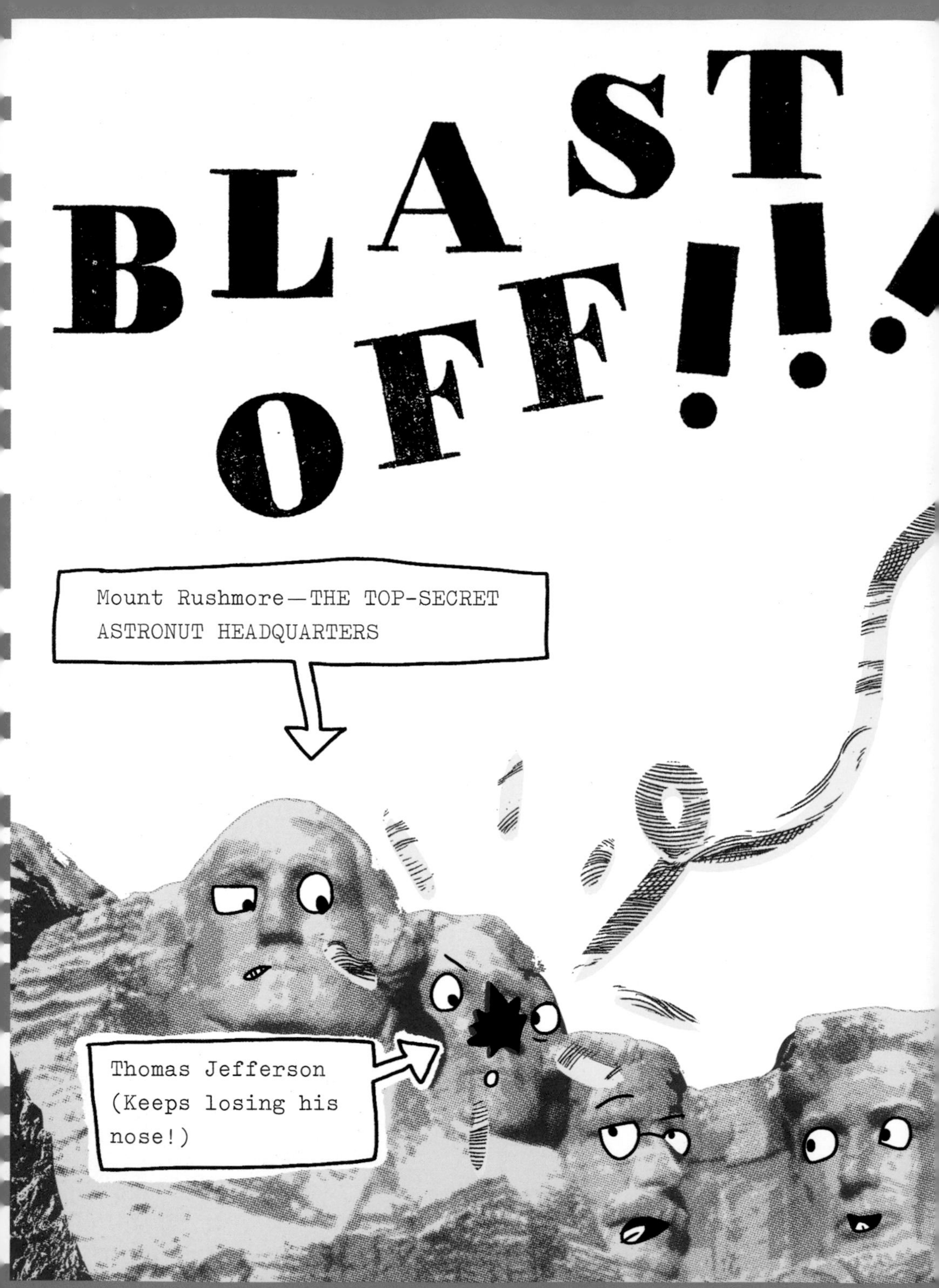
Mount Rushmore—THE TOP-SECRET ASTRONUT HEADQUARTERS
Thomas Jefferson (Keeps losing his nose!)

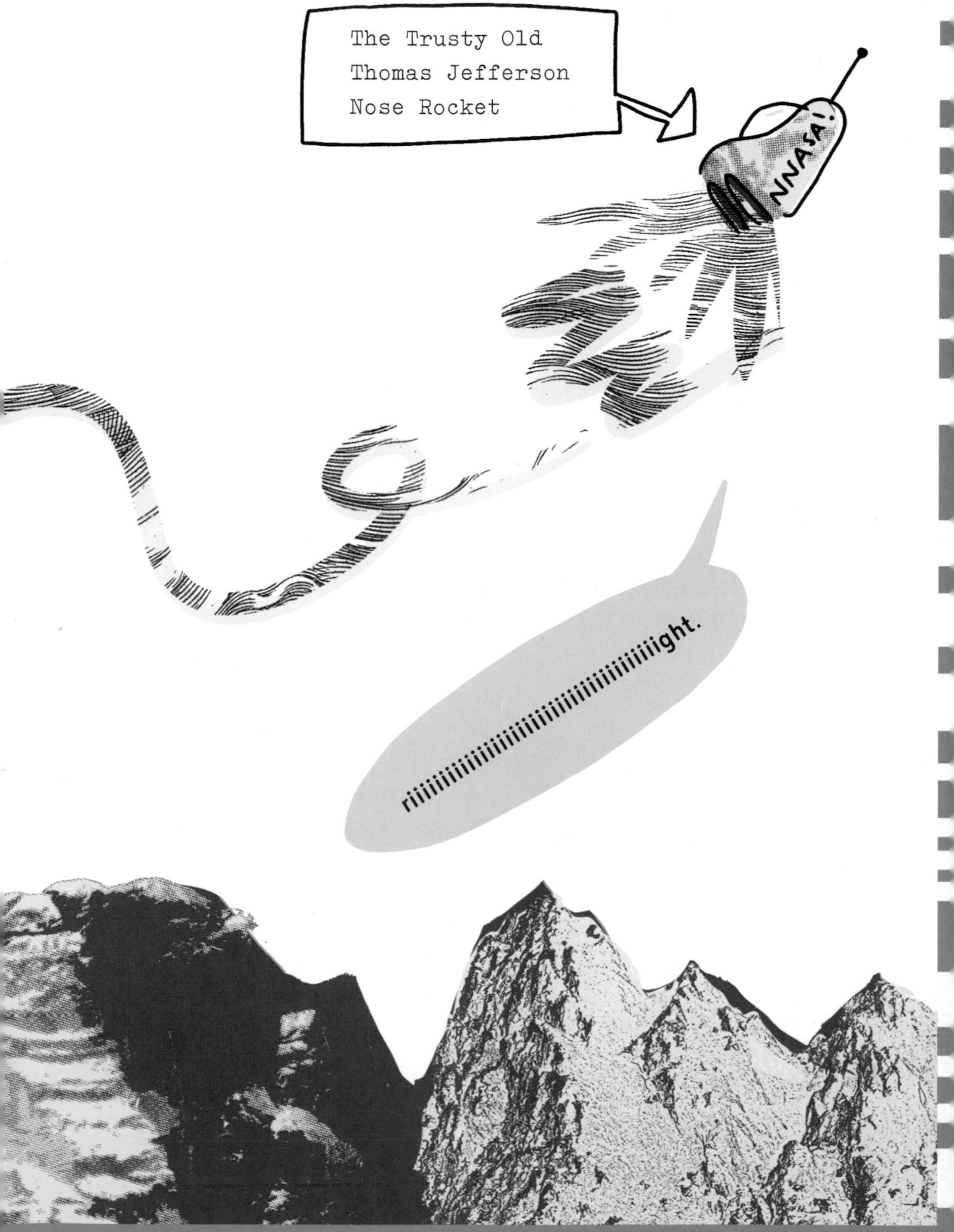
The Trusty Old
Thomas Jefferson
Nose Rocket
NNASA!
riiiiiiiiiiiiiiiiiiiiiiiiiiiiiiiiiiiiiiight.

Oh, boy. Here we go again.

Another day, another secret NNASA mission. Just a typical day in the lives of four superpowered animal astronauts looking for a perfect Goldilocks Planet (not too hot, not too cold, but just right) for humans to move to.

Because I am your planet, Earth, I know that most of you 7.7 billion humans read all about the AstroNuts in Mission #1.

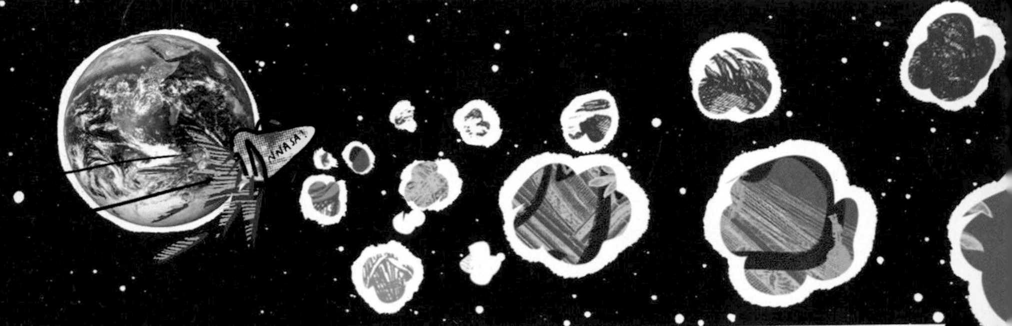
NNASA!

So you know how they blasted off from their secret Mount Rushmore laboratory in their Thomas Jefferson Nose Rocket and arrived to check out the Plant Planet.

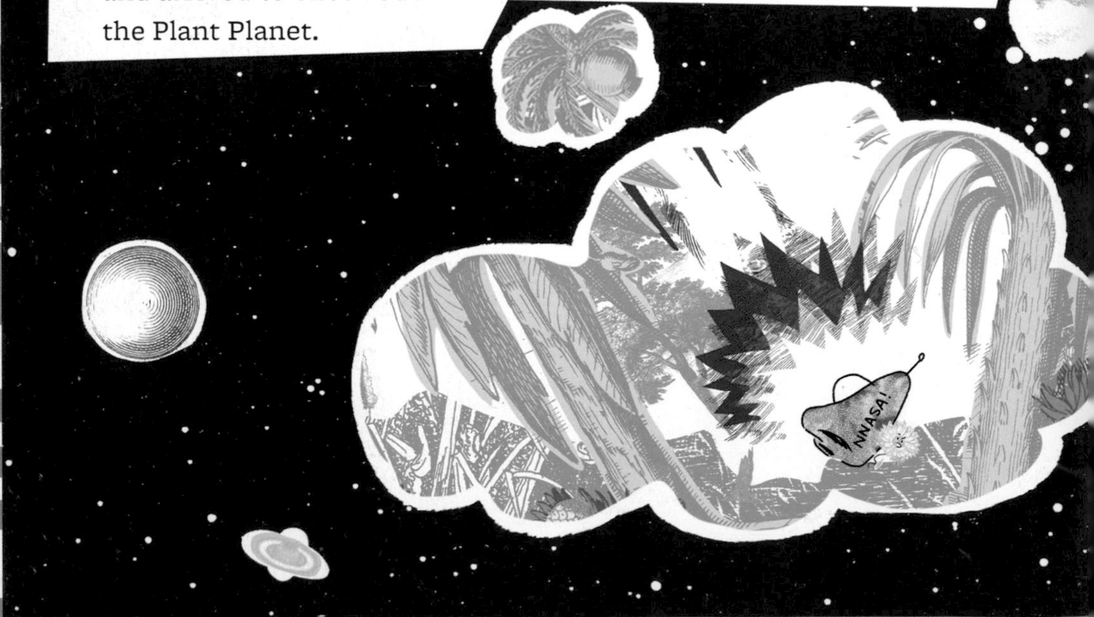
NNASA!

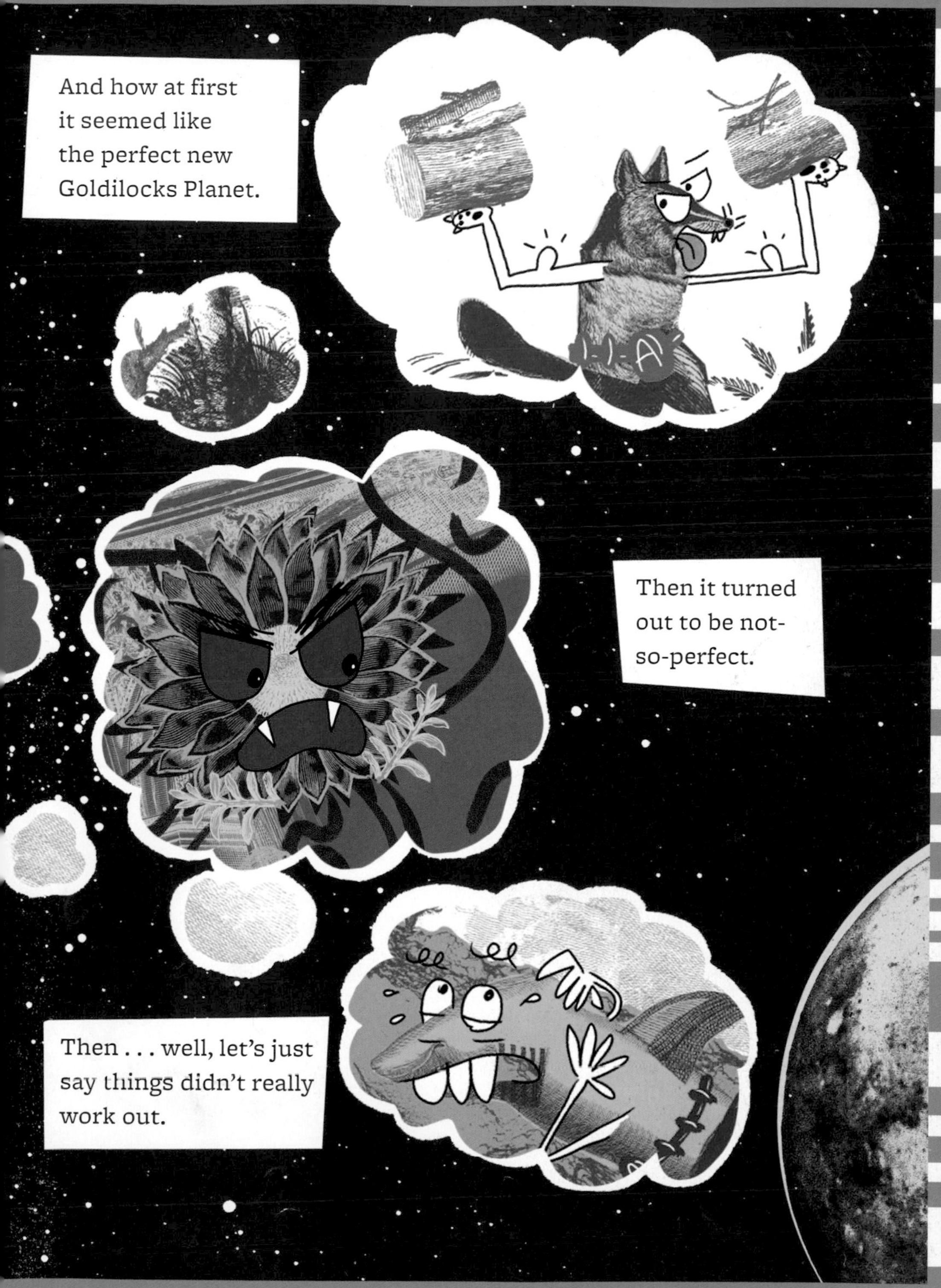
And how at first it seemed like the perfect new Goldilocks Planet.
Then it turned out to be not-so-perfect.
Then . . . well, let's just say things didn't really work out.

So that's how the AstroNuts' mission became even more important.

Time is wasting. And my climate is getting worse.

As your own scientists put it: "Earth's climate is now changing faster than at any point in the history of modern civilization . . . as a result of human activities."

And a lot of your human activities are **messing with my water**, which, as you know, is 71% of my surface.

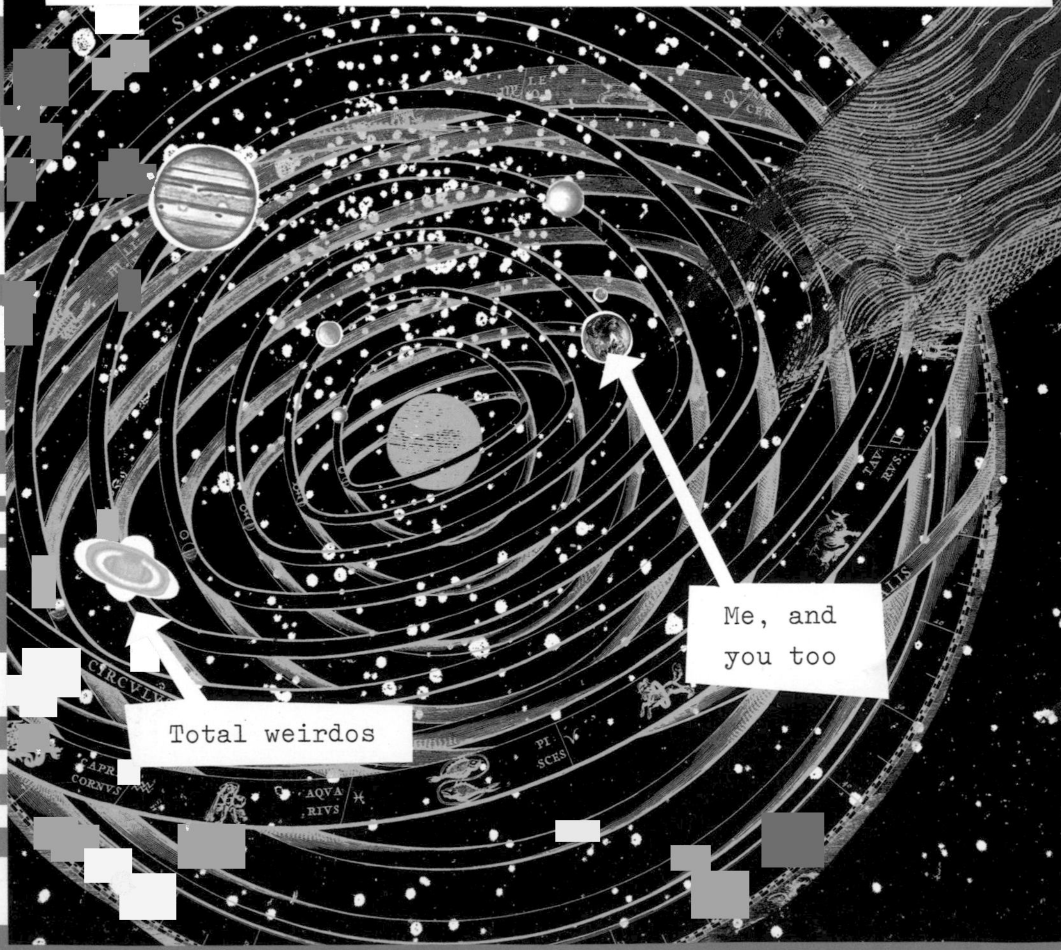
Me, and you too
Total weirdos
CIRCVLVS
CAPR CORNVS
AQVA RIVS
PI SCES
TAV RVS

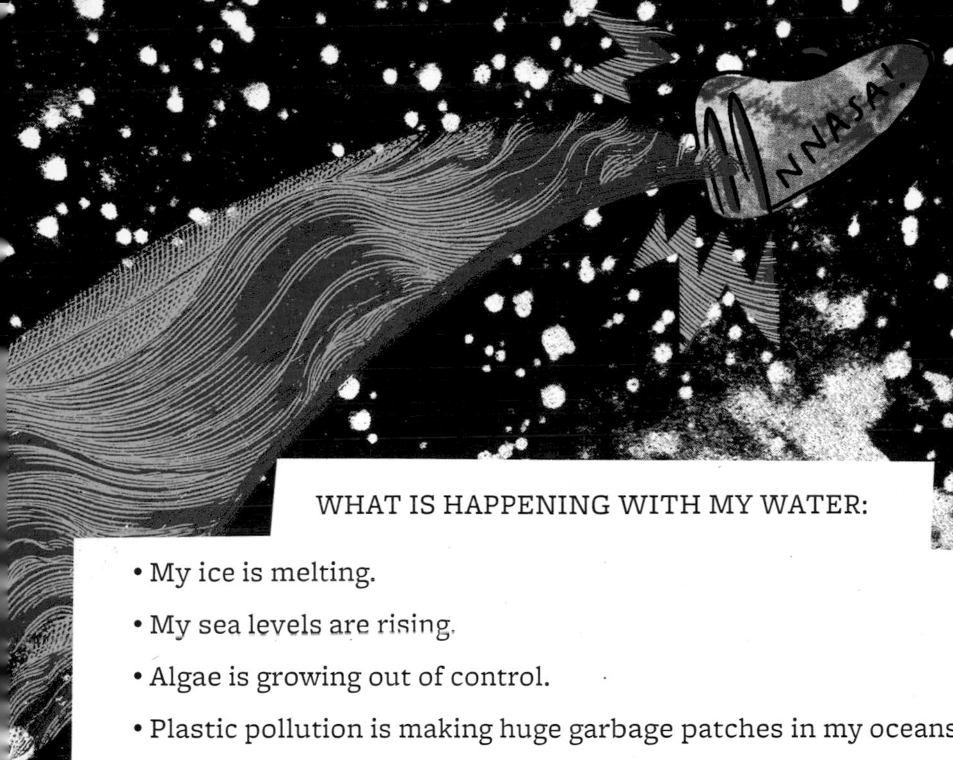
NNASA!

WHAT IS HAPPENING WITH MY WATER:

- My ice is melting.
- My sea levels are rising.
- Algae is growing out of control.
- Plastic pollution is making huge garbage patches in my oceans.
- My oceans are turning more acidic.
- My coral reefs are dying.
- Fish species are going extinct.

If this keeps up, I am going to be called “The Big Polluted Mess” instead of “The Big Blue Marble.”

So I was pretty happy that the AstroNuts were heading out to look at a Water Planet. And I was glad that at least three out of four of them were prepared and wearing seatbelts.

CHAPTER 1: AHHHHHHHHHHH!!!

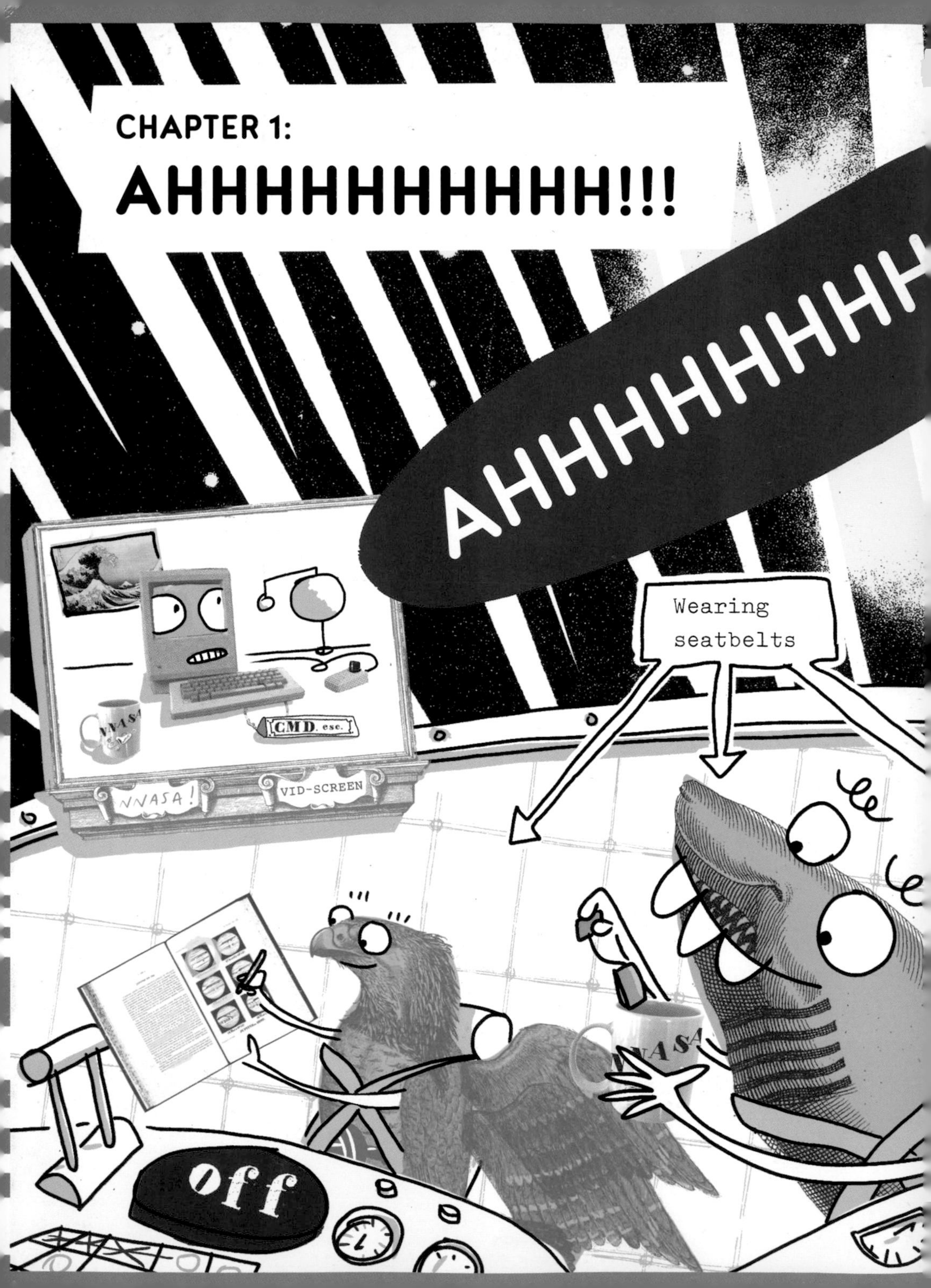

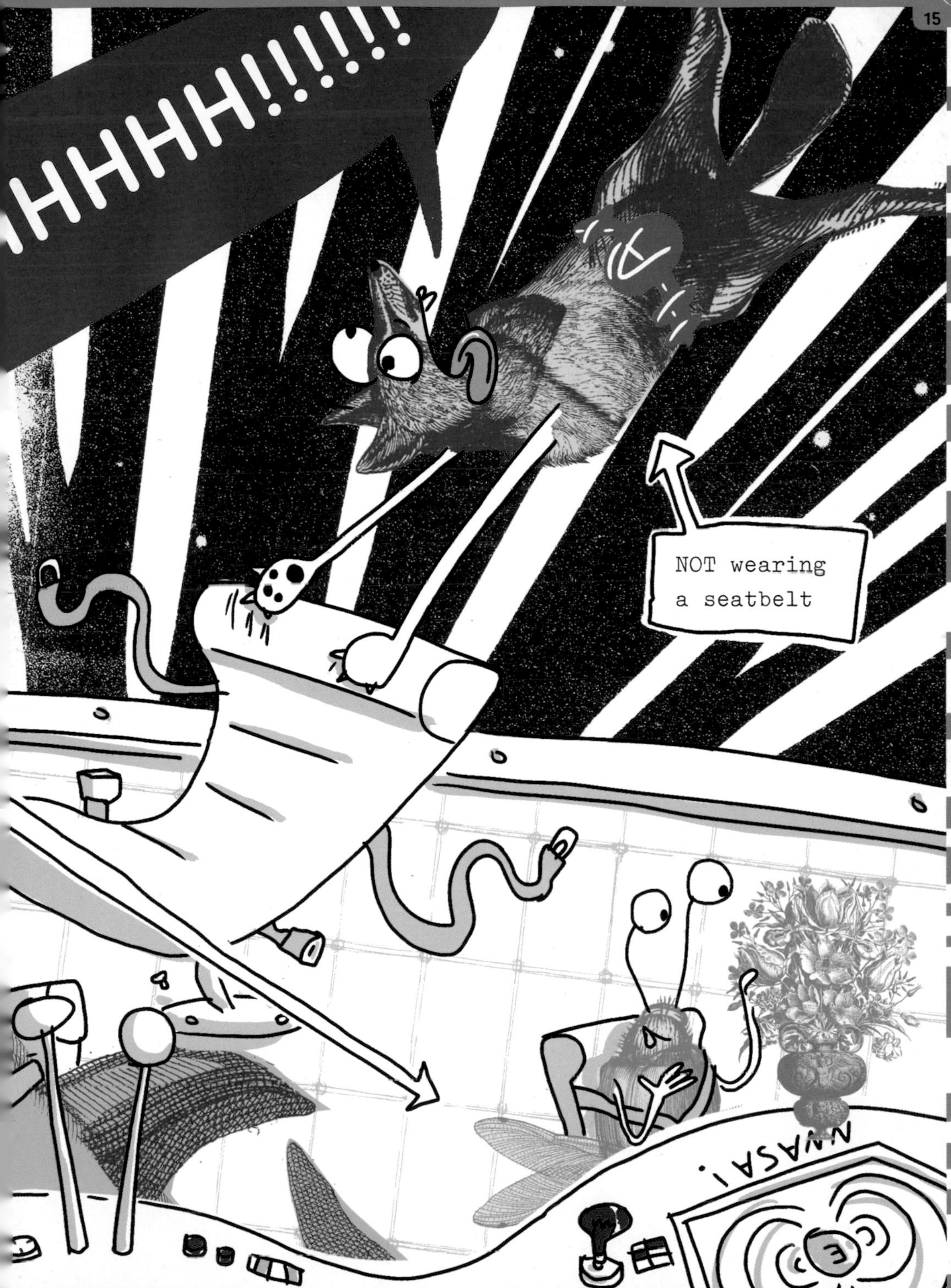
HHHH!!!!!!
NOT wearing a seatbelt
E
NNASA!

Command Escape, the AstroNuts' boss, laid out the mission in his glitchy 1988 computer style.

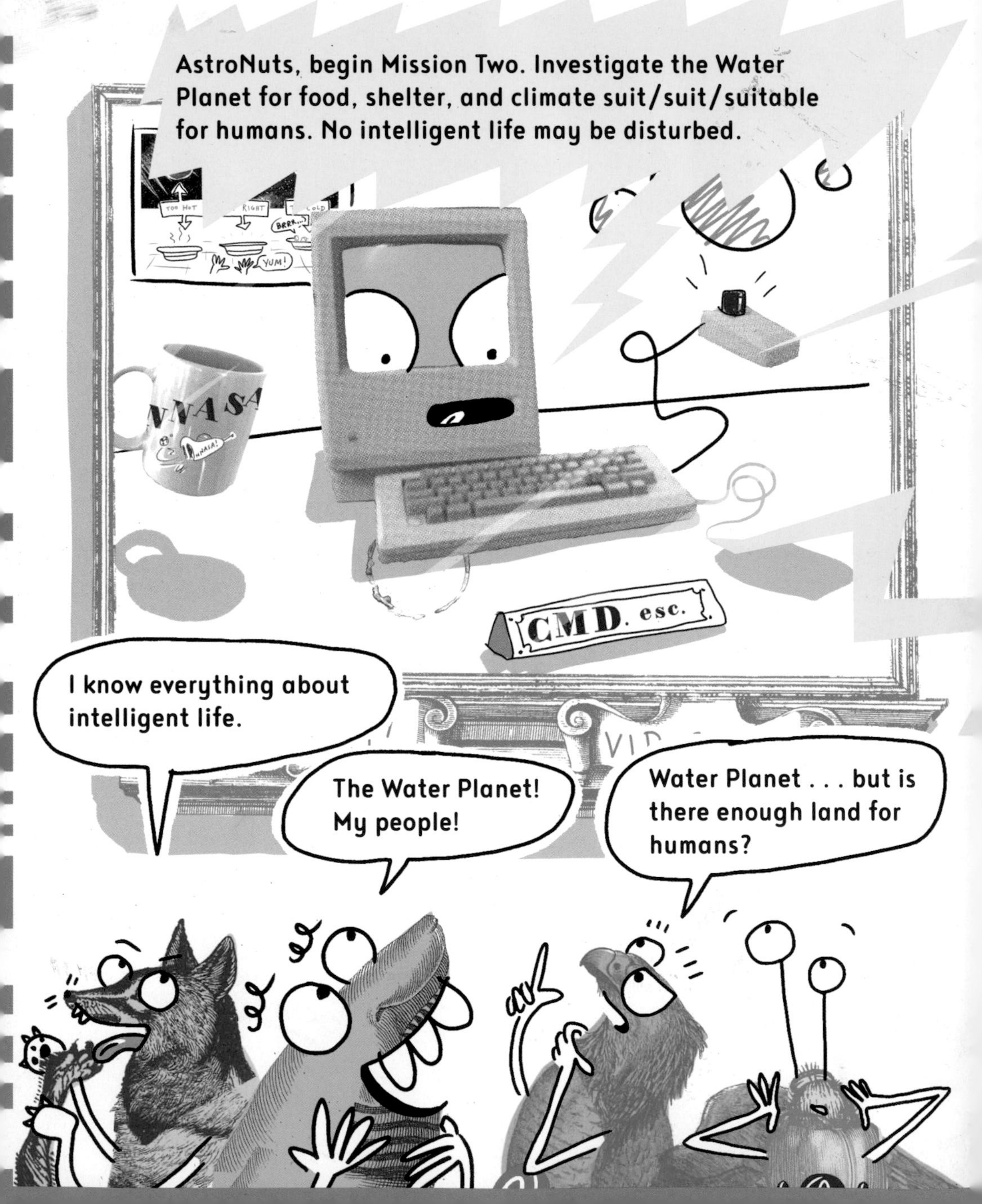
AstroNuts, begin Mission Two. Investigate the Water Planet for food, shelter, and climate suit/suit/suitable for humans. No intelligent life may be disturbed.
TOO HOT
RIGHT
BRRR...
YUM!
NASA
CMD. esc.
I know everything about intelligent life.
The Water Planet! My people!
Water Planet . . . but is there enough land for humans?

Investigate the Goldilocks Planet/Goldilocks Planet/ GoldilocksPlanet/Goldilocks Planet/Goldilocks Planet.

Not too hot. Not too cold. Just right.

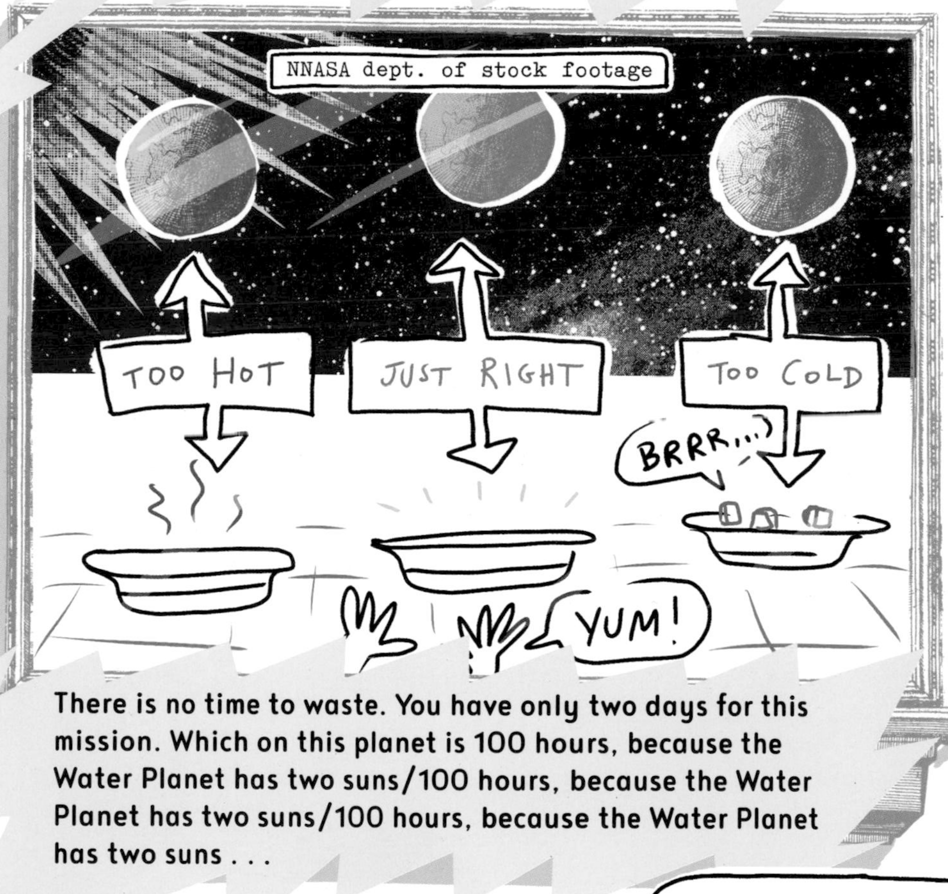
NNASA dept. of stock footage
TOO HOT
JUST RIGHT
TOO COLD
BRRR...
YUM!

There is no time to waste. You have only two days for this mission. Which on this planet is 100 hours, because the Water Planet has two suns/100 hours, because the Water Planet has two suns/100 hours, because the Water Planet has two suns . . .

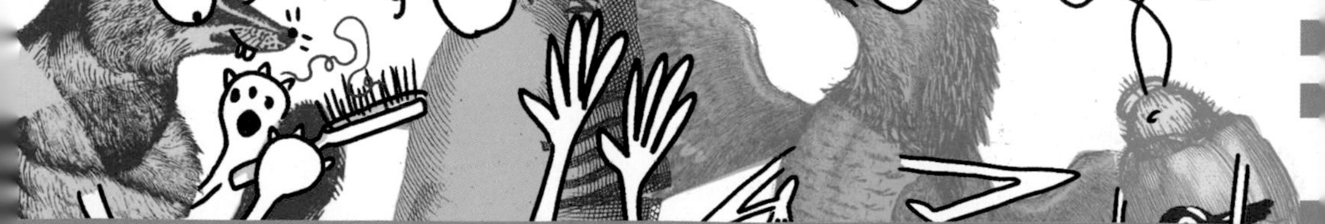
This will be very wet.

///// Official NNASA transcript /////
//// of ASTRONUT MISSION 2 ////

AlphaWolf: Did you get our name fixed back to Astronauts yet?

Command Escape: Yes, it is in progress. I turned in your new rename request.

StinkBug: Which means it will be another eighty-five days.

Command Escape: Actually, standard approval time is seven or eight months/seven or eight months/seven or eight—

—sound of someone pressing a giant OFF button—

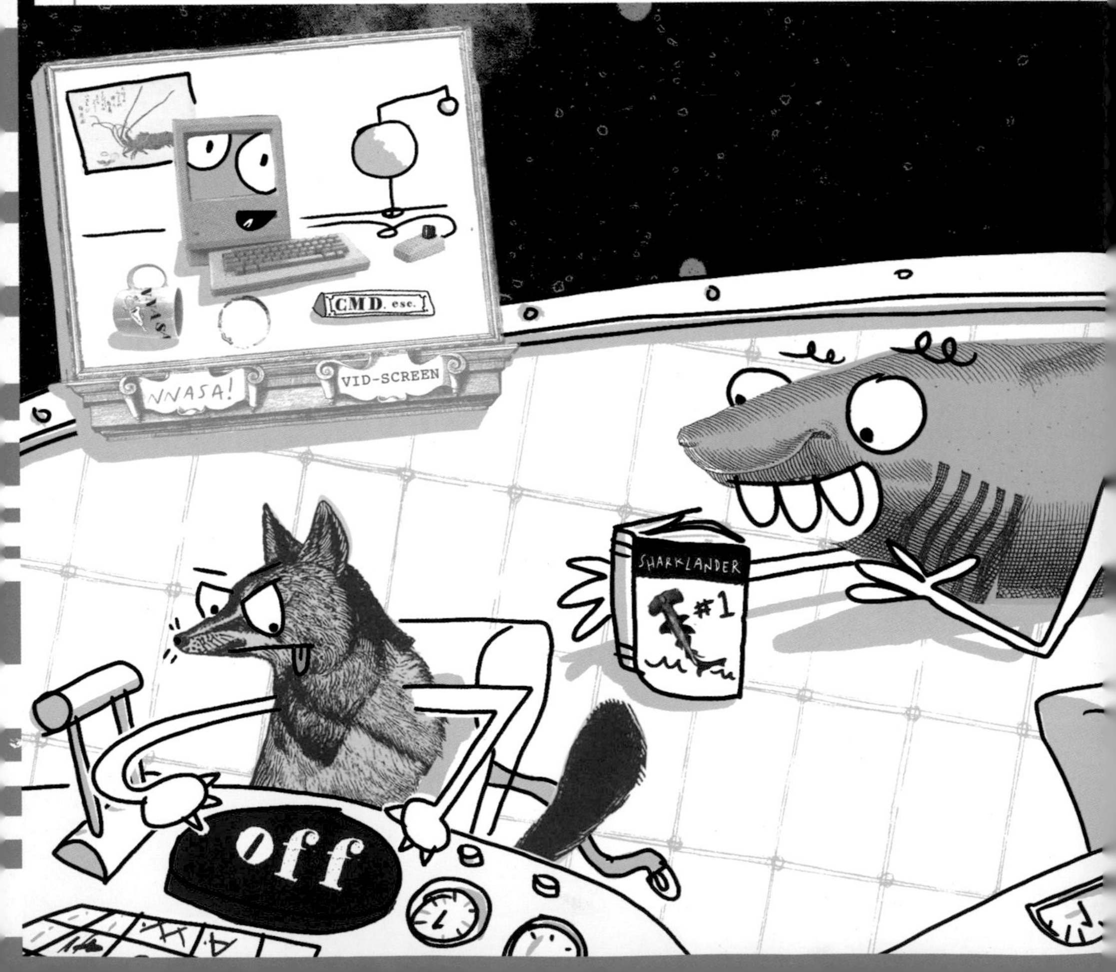
CMD. esc.
NNASA!
VID-SCREEN
SHARKLANDER
#1
off

AlphaWolf: This Water Planet better be good. I've got wolfie things I need to be doing. So let's check this place out quick and get back here pronto.
SmartHawk: The first data that we have on this planet is excellent. There is so much water in the liquid form that humans need.
StinkBug: Which is surprisingly scarce in the universe.
LaserShark: I am so excited for a Water Planet.
StinkBug: I do not really like to get wet.
AlphaWolf: Are we there yet?

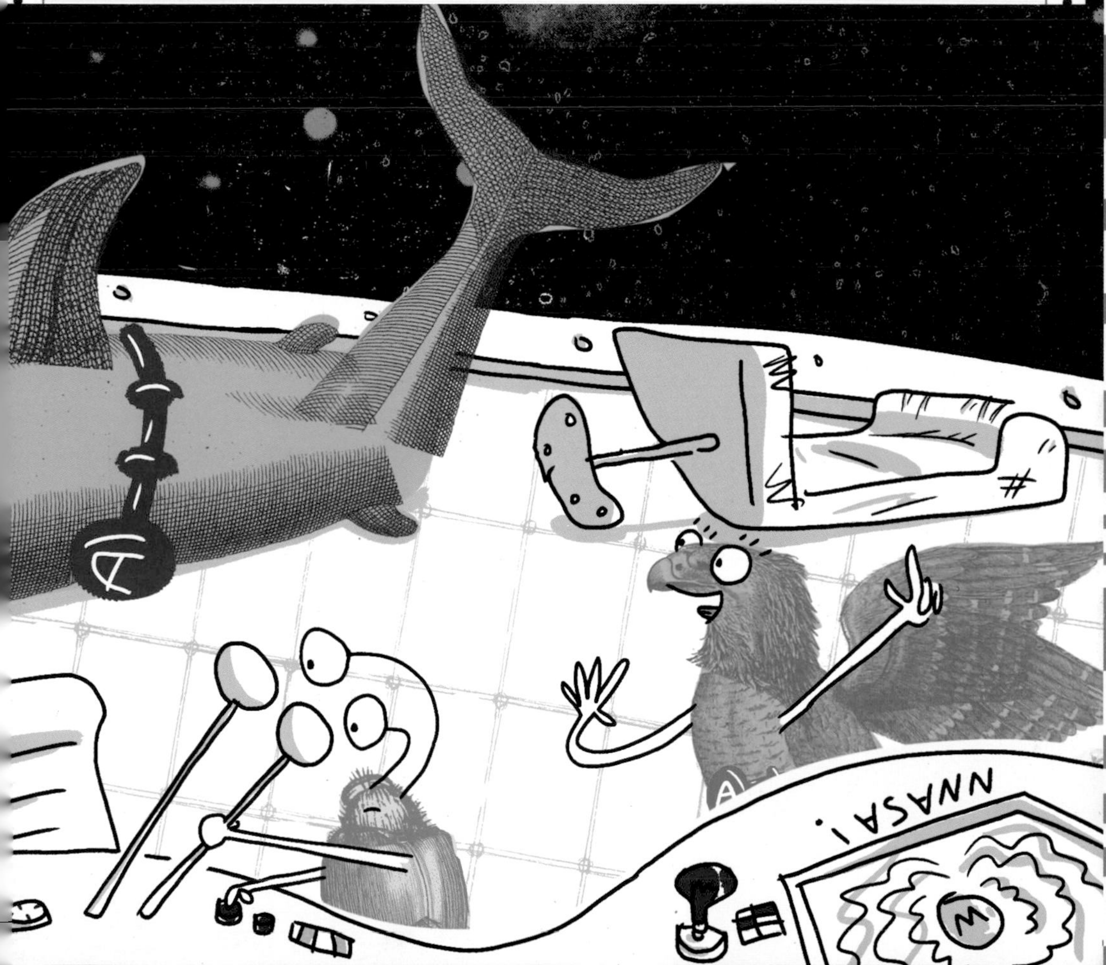
NNASA!

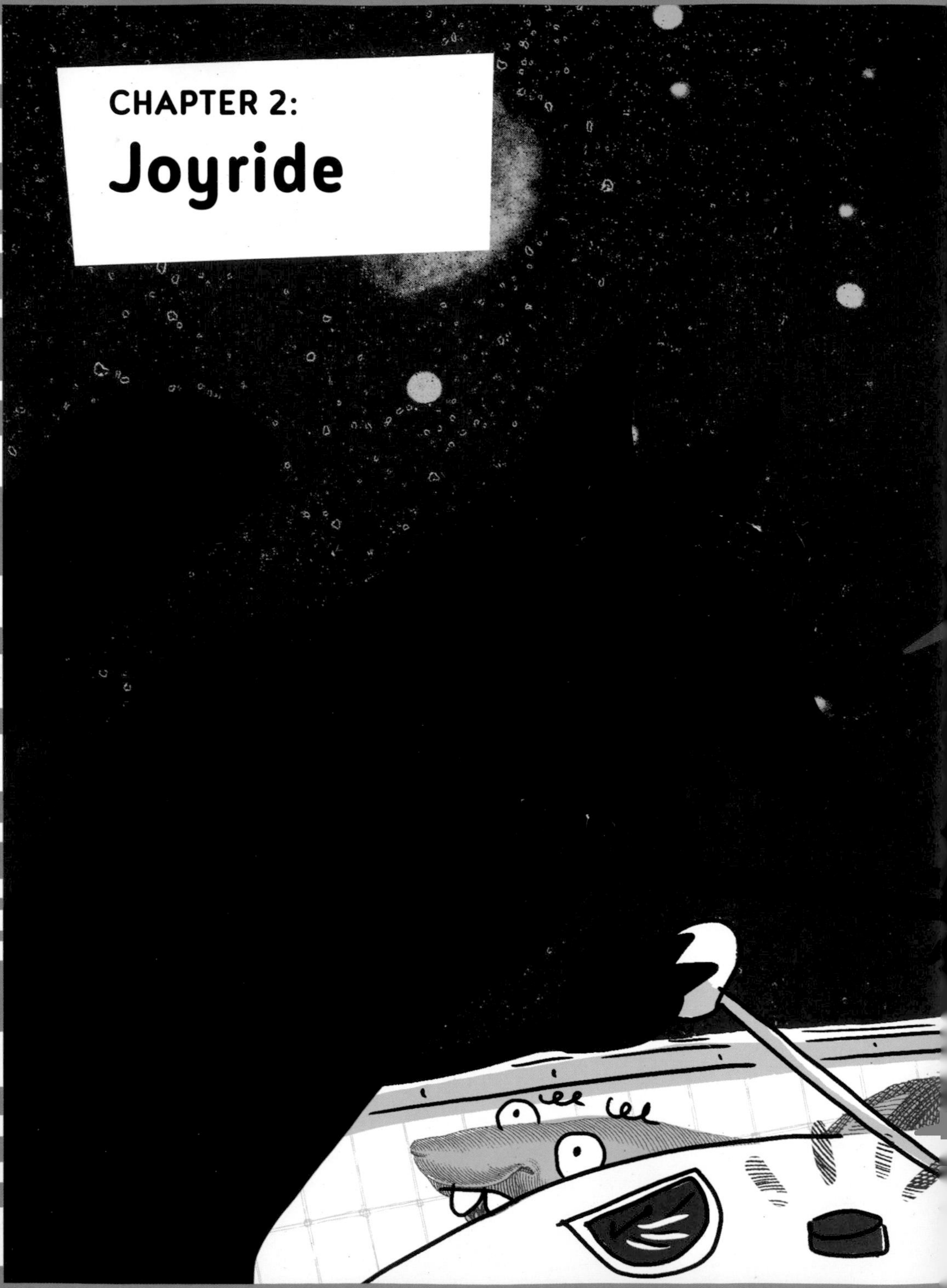
CHAPTER 2:
Joyride

Enough of all this talking.
Time for some action.
Let me show you some really
great AlphaWolf flying skills!

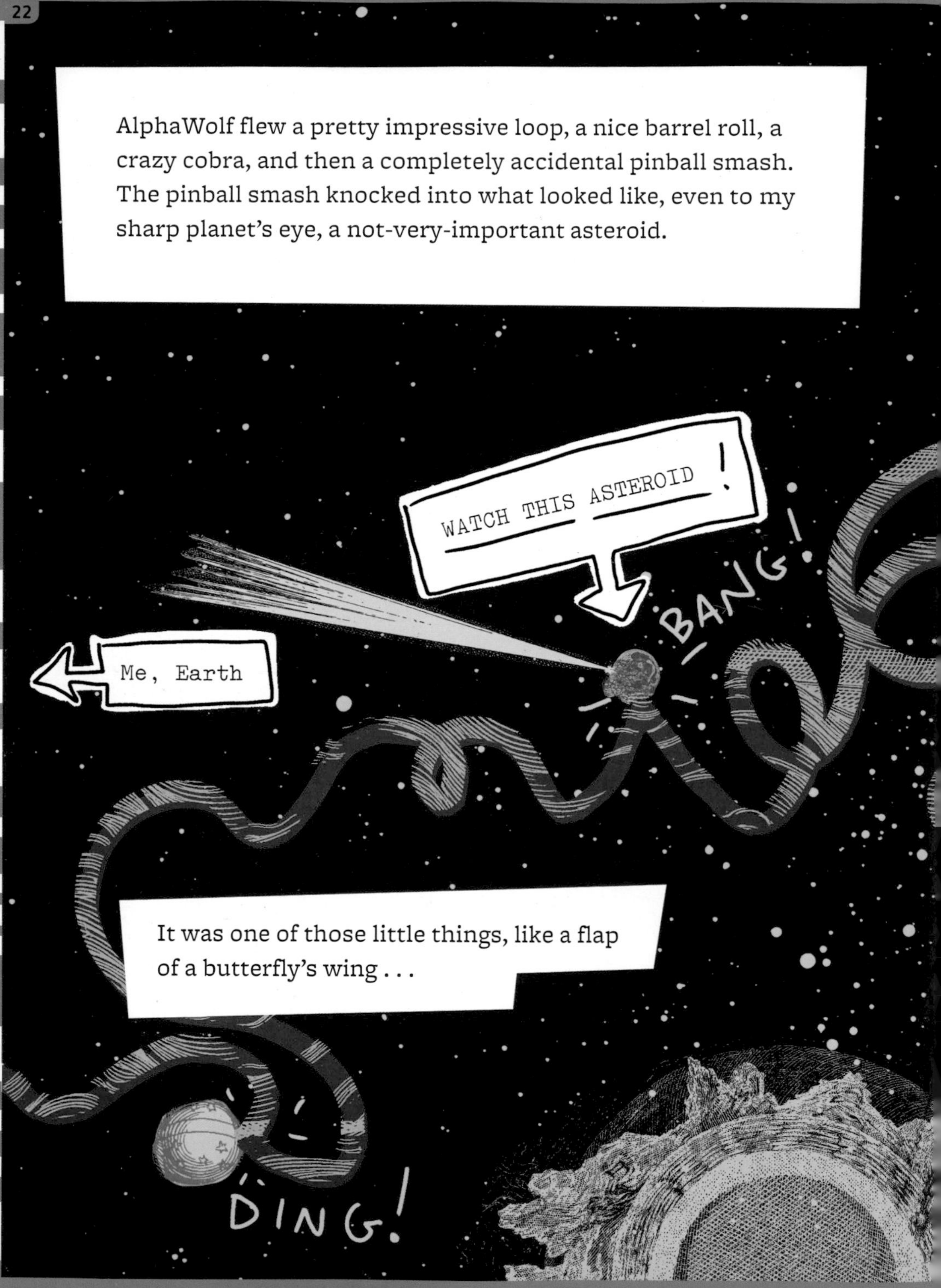
AlphaWolf flew a pretty impressive loop, a nice barrel roll, a crazy cobra, and then a completely accidental pinball smash. The pinball smash knocked into what looked like, even to my sharp planet's eye, a not-very-important asteroid.
WATCH THIS ASTEROID!
BANG!
Me, Earth
It was one of those little things, like a flap of a butterfly's wing . . .
DING!

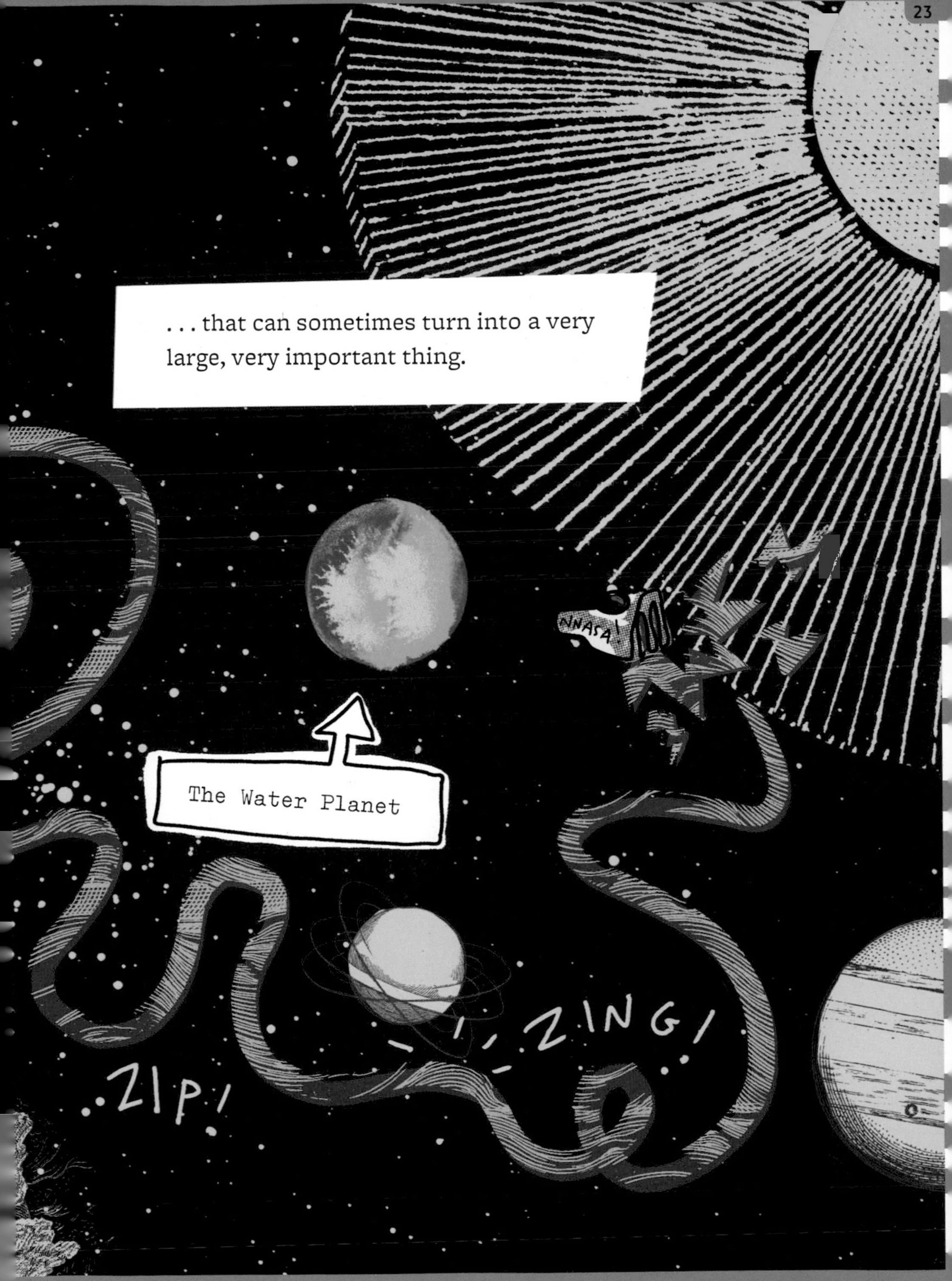

. . . that can sometimes turn into a very large, very important thing.
The Water Planet
NNASA!
ZIP!
ZING!

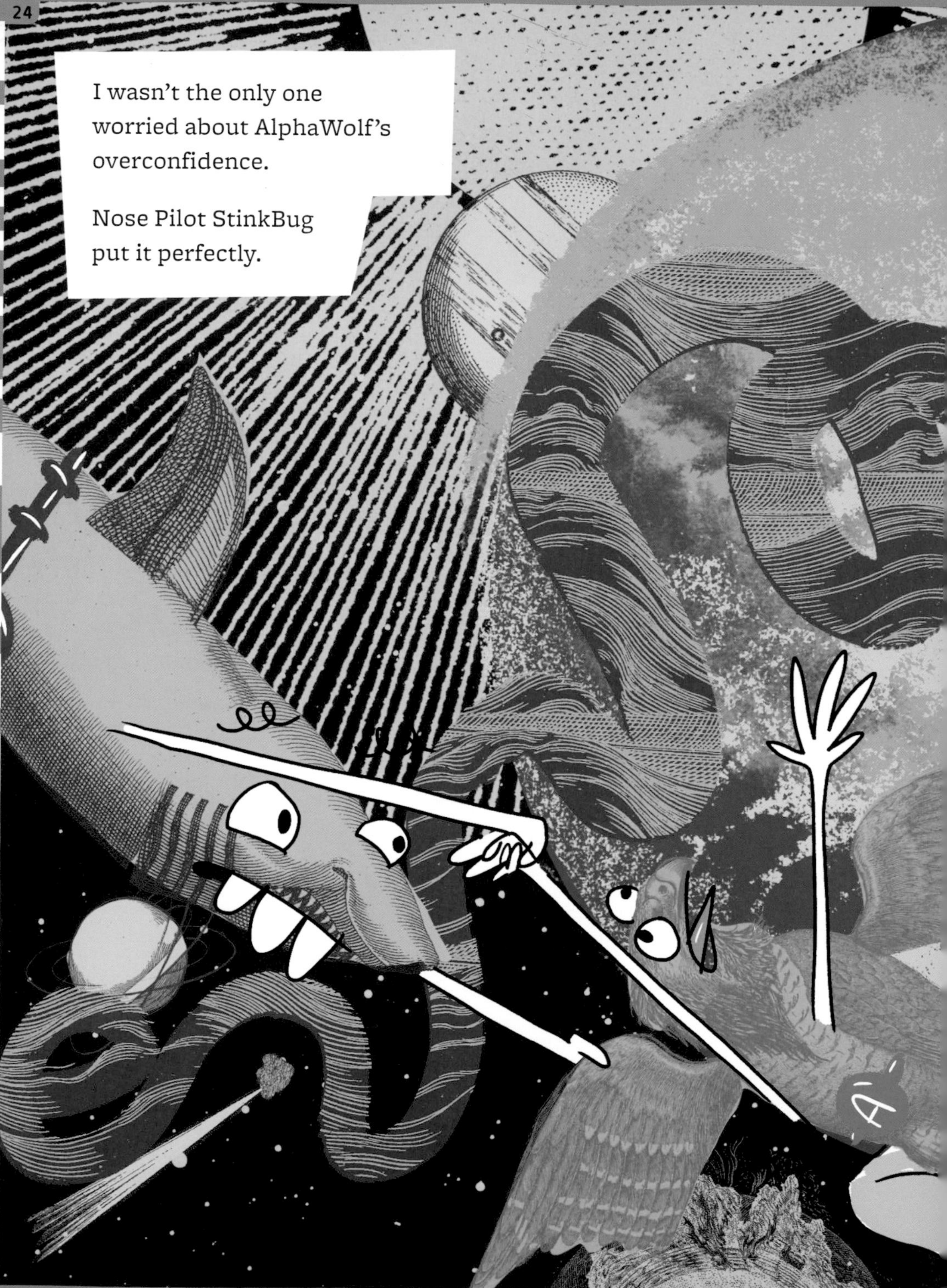
I wasn't the only one worried about AlphaWolf's overconfidence.
Nose Pilot StinkBug put it perfectly.

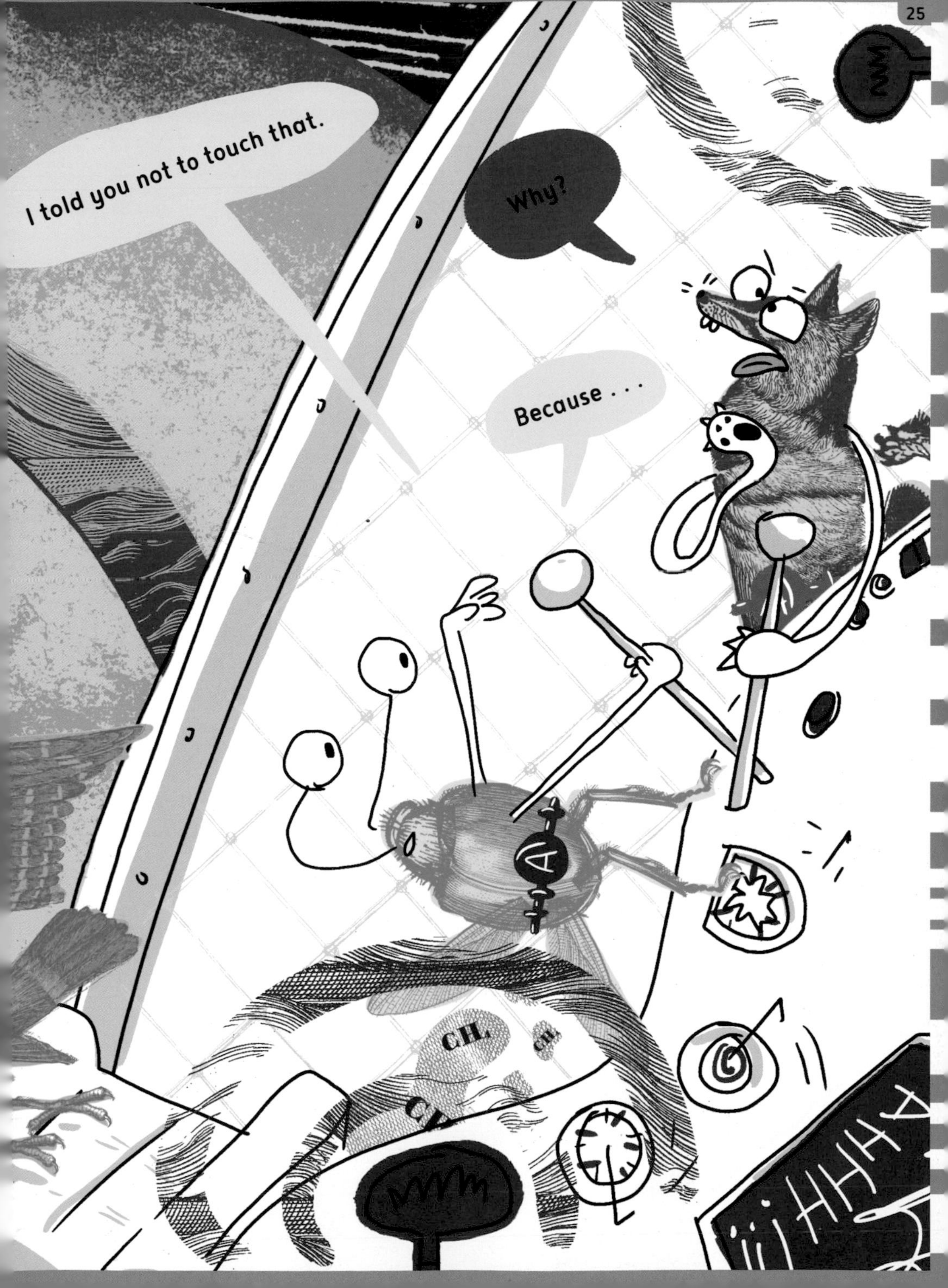
I told you not to touch that.
Why?
Because . . .
MM
CH,
CH,
CH
MMM
AHHH!!!

CHAPTER 3: Splash

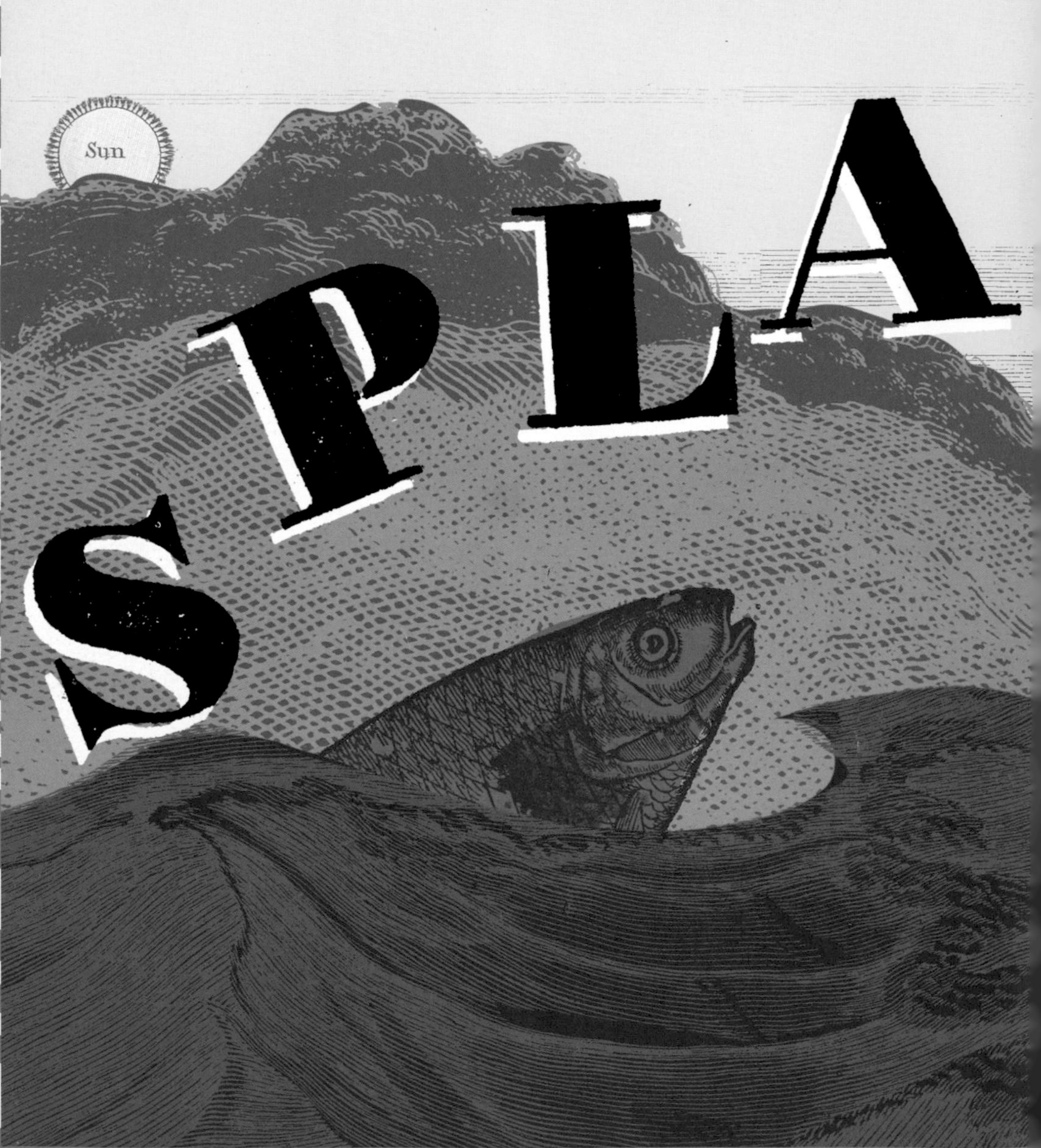
Sun
SPLA

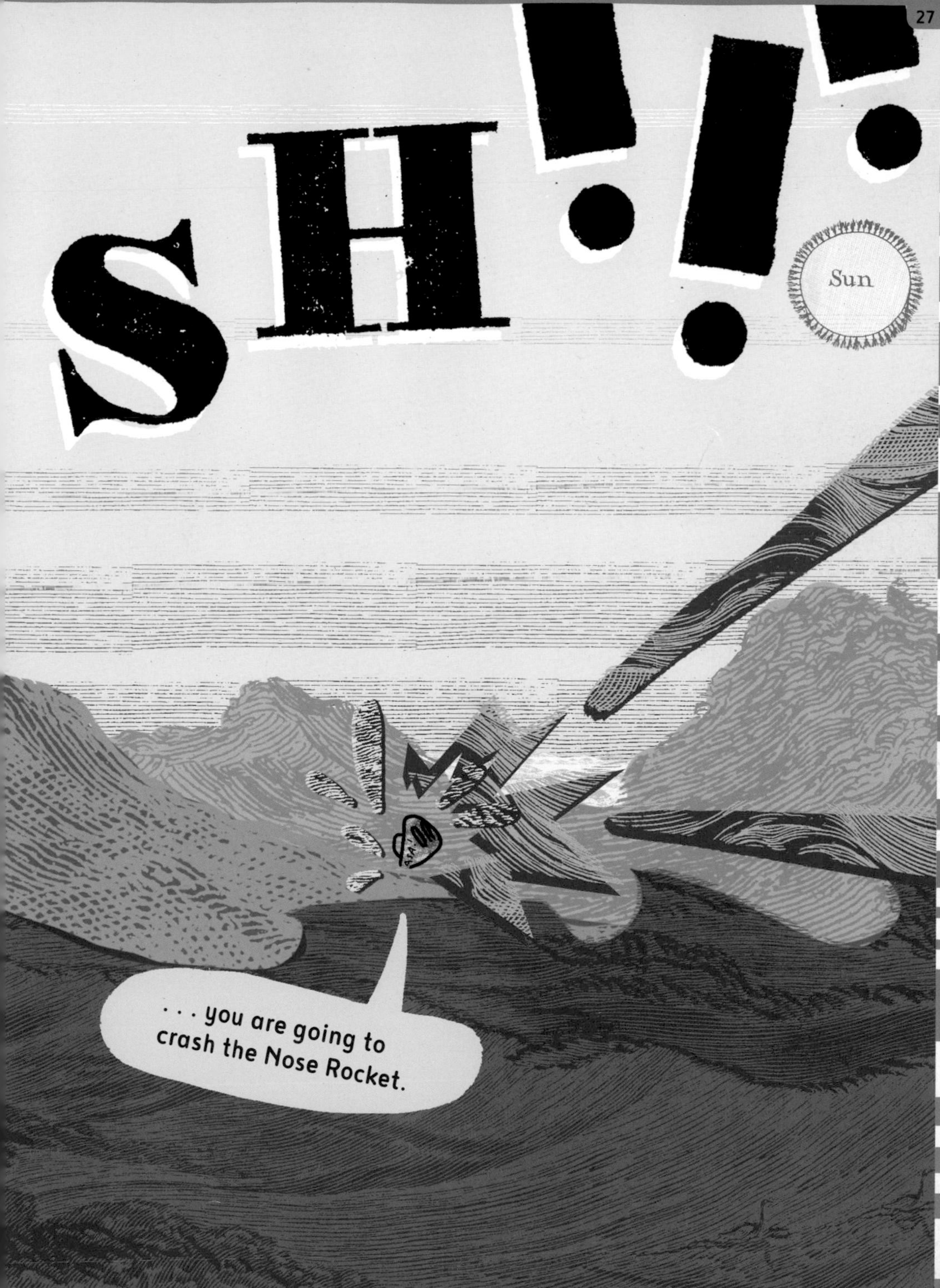
SH!!!
Sun
. . . you are going to
crash the Nose Rocket.

CHAPTER 4:
Mods!

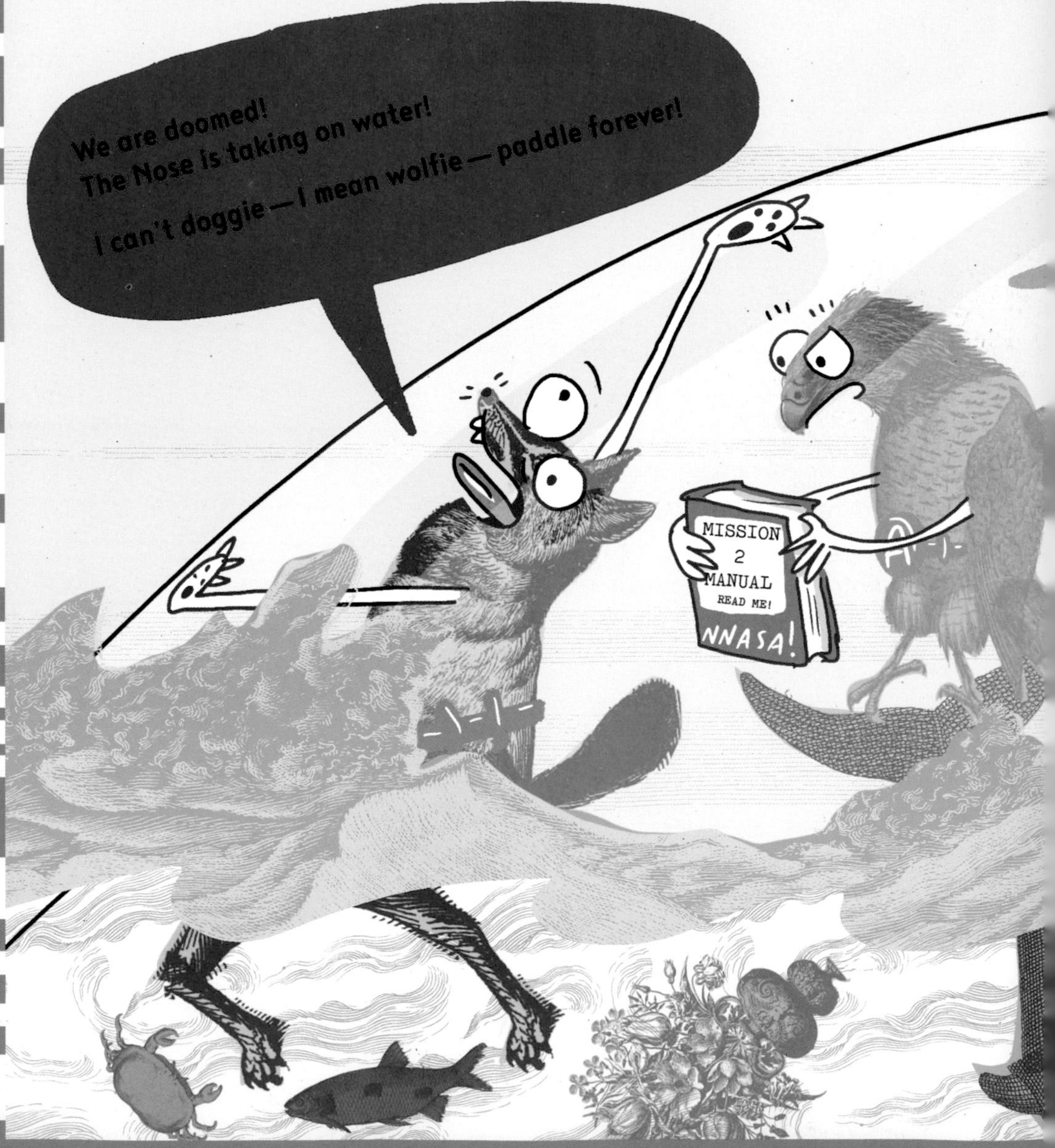
Sun
We are doomed!
The Nose is taking on water!
I can't doggie — I mean wolfie — paddle forever!
MISSION 2 MANUAL
READ ME!
NNASA!

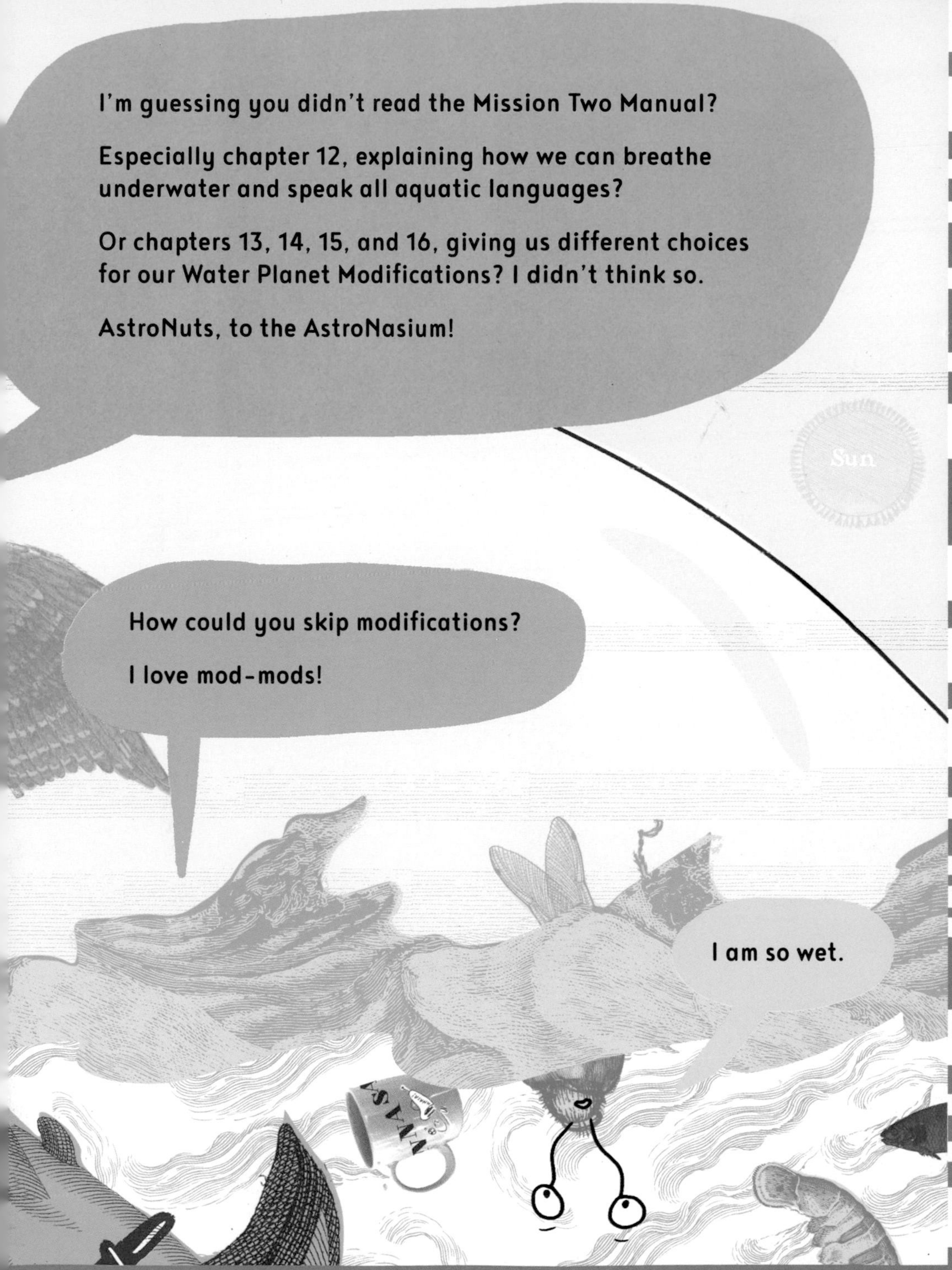
I'm guessing you didn't read the Mission Two Manual?
Especially chapter 12, explaining how we can breathe underwater and speak all aquatic languages?
Or chapters 13, 14, 15, and 16, giving us different choices for our Water Planet Modifications? I didn't think so.
AstroNuts, to the AstroNasium!
Sun
How could you skip modifications?
I love mod-mods!
I am so wet.
NASA

Oh, and if you, like AlphaWolf, didn't get a chance to read chapters 12, 13, 14, 15, and 16 of the Mission Two Manual, "mods," or "mod-mods," are modifications. That's the NNASA word for the new superpower additions the AstroNuts get for each new mission. It's another reason they liked to think of themselves as superheroes.

AlphaWolf chose the dorsal fin of a killer whale because he thought it made him look tough.

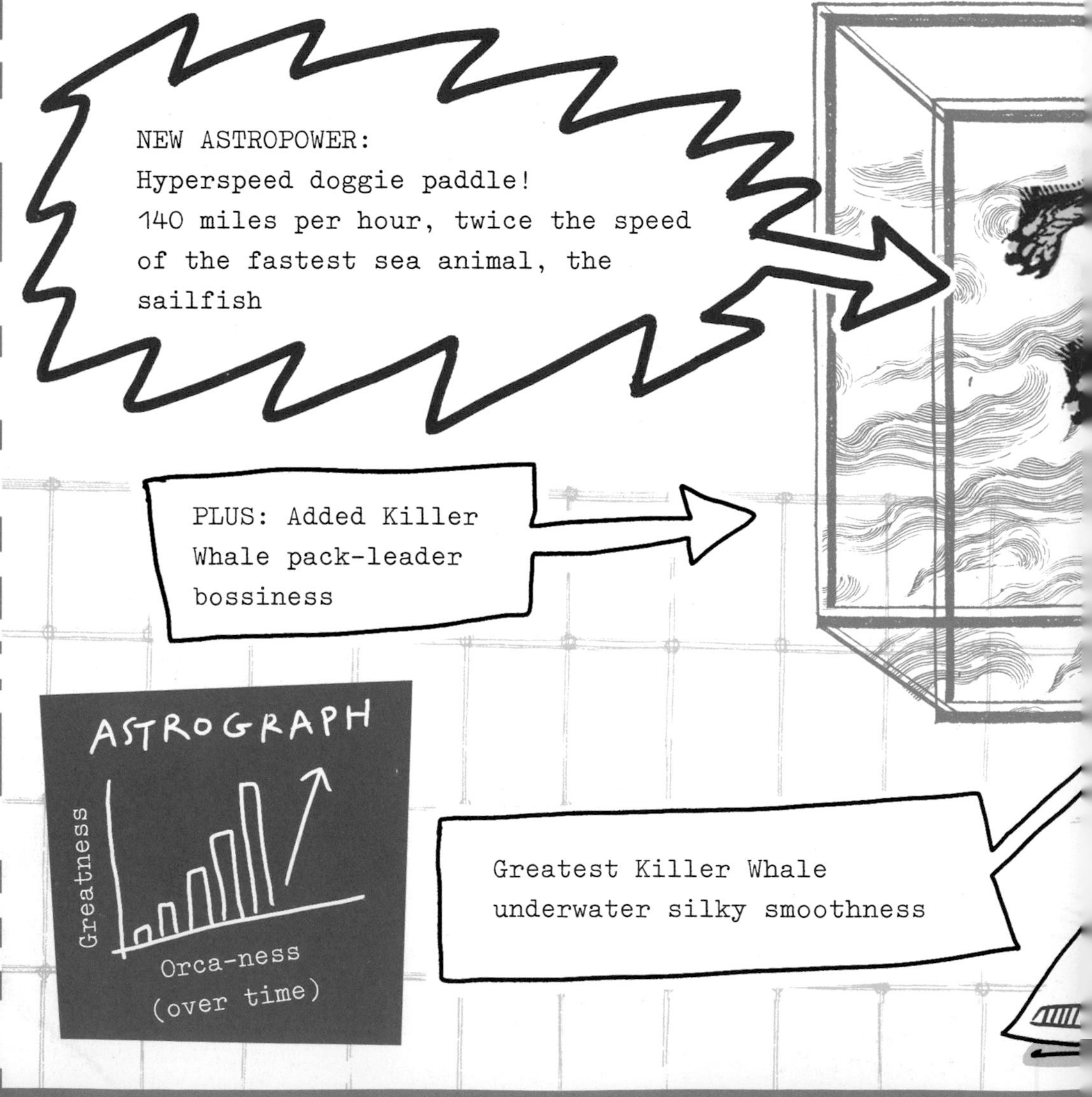
NEW ASTROPOWER:
Hyperspeed doggie paddle!
140 miles per hour, twice the speed of the fastest sea animal, the sailfish
PLUS: Added Killer Whale pack-leader bossiness
ASTROGRAPH
Greatness
Orca-ness (over time)
Greatest Killer Whale underwater silky smoothness

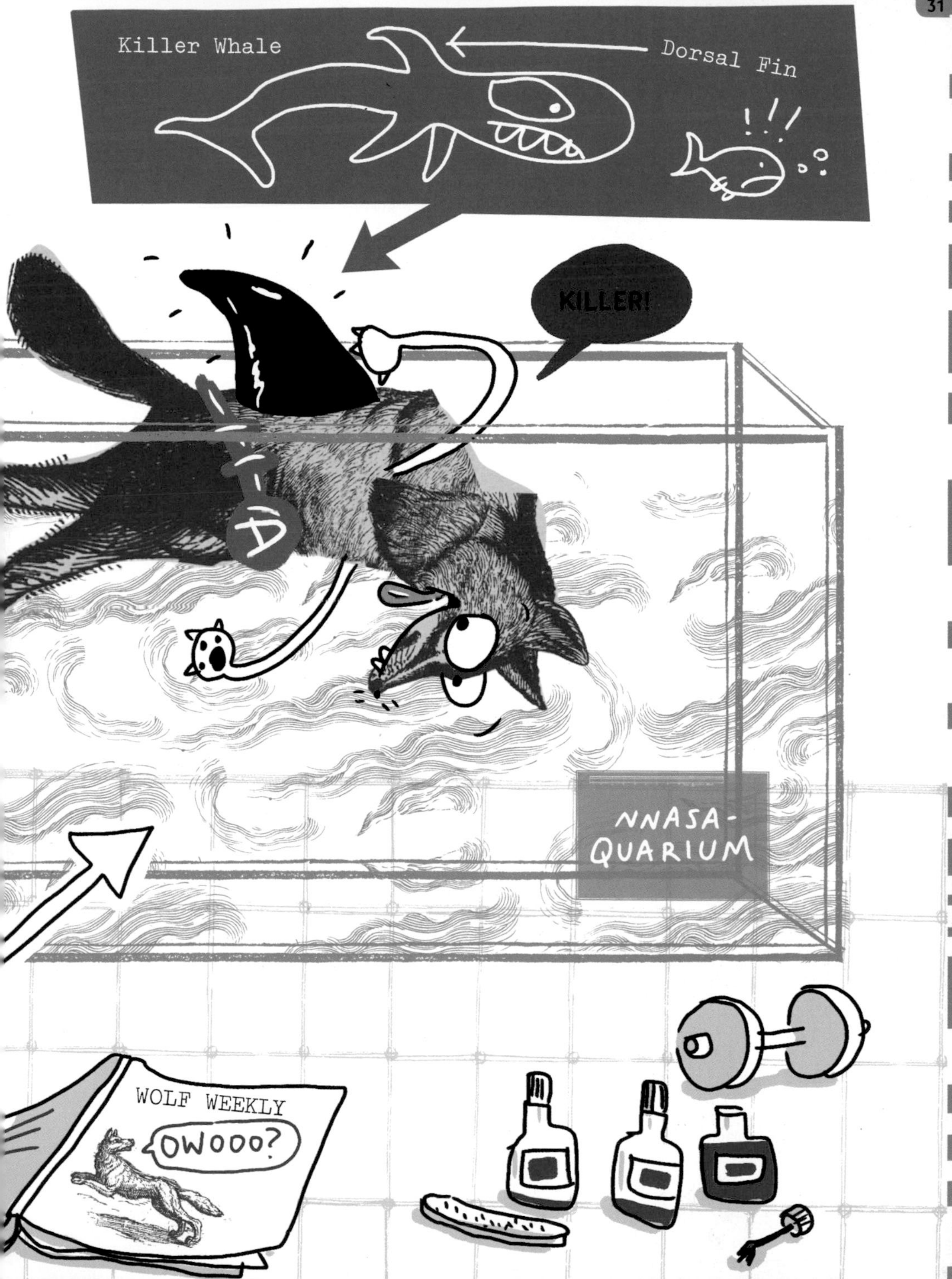
Killer Whale
Dorsal Fin
KILLER!
NNASA-
QUARIUM
WOLF WEEKLY
OWOOO?

LaserShark got the light of an anglerfish for her mod-mod. Because she wanted her smile to be even more dazzling.

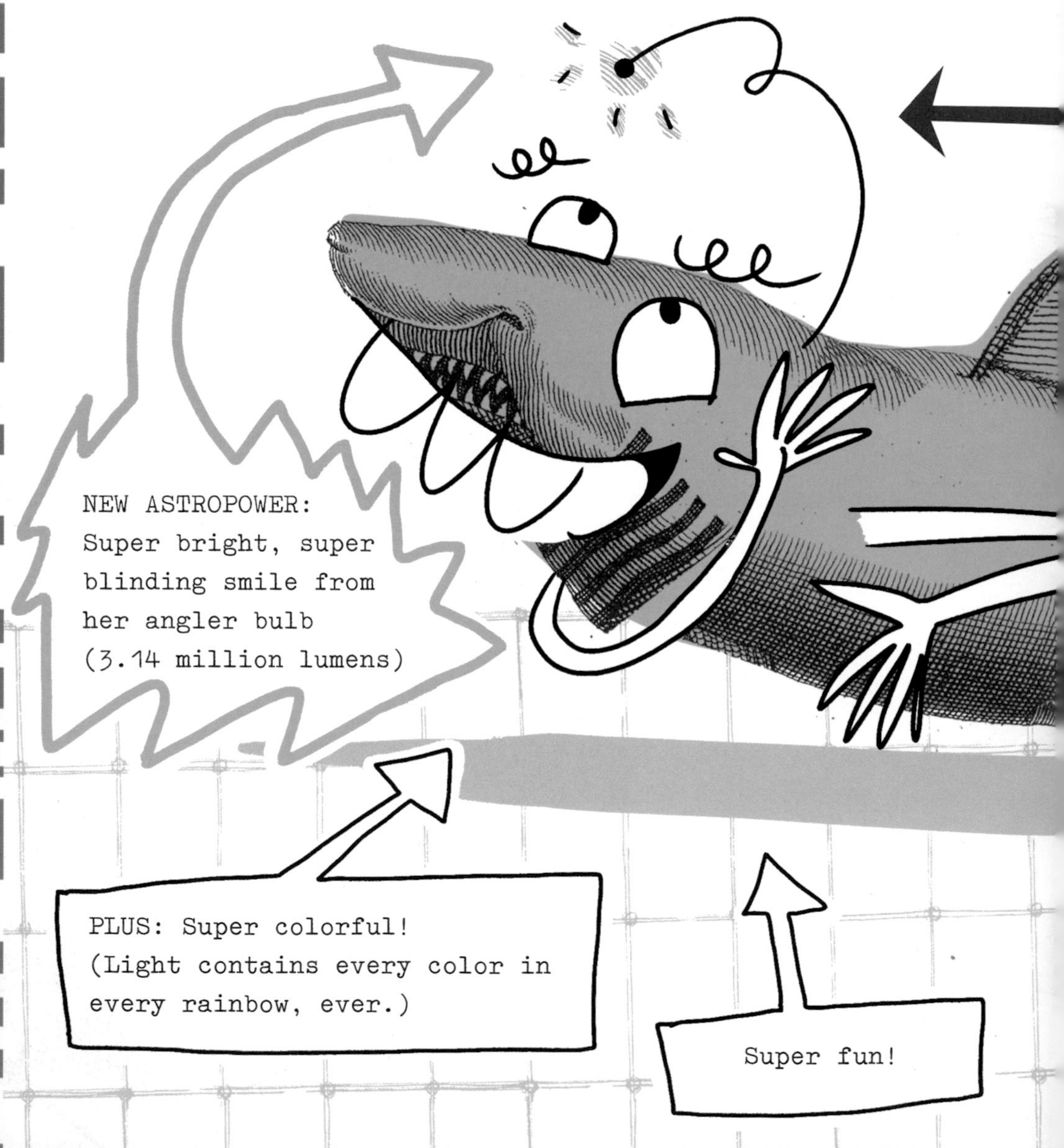
NEW ASTROPOWER:
Super bright, super
blinding smile from
her angler bulb
(3.14 million lumens)
PLUS: Super colorful!
(Light contains every color in
every rainbow, ever.)
Super fun!

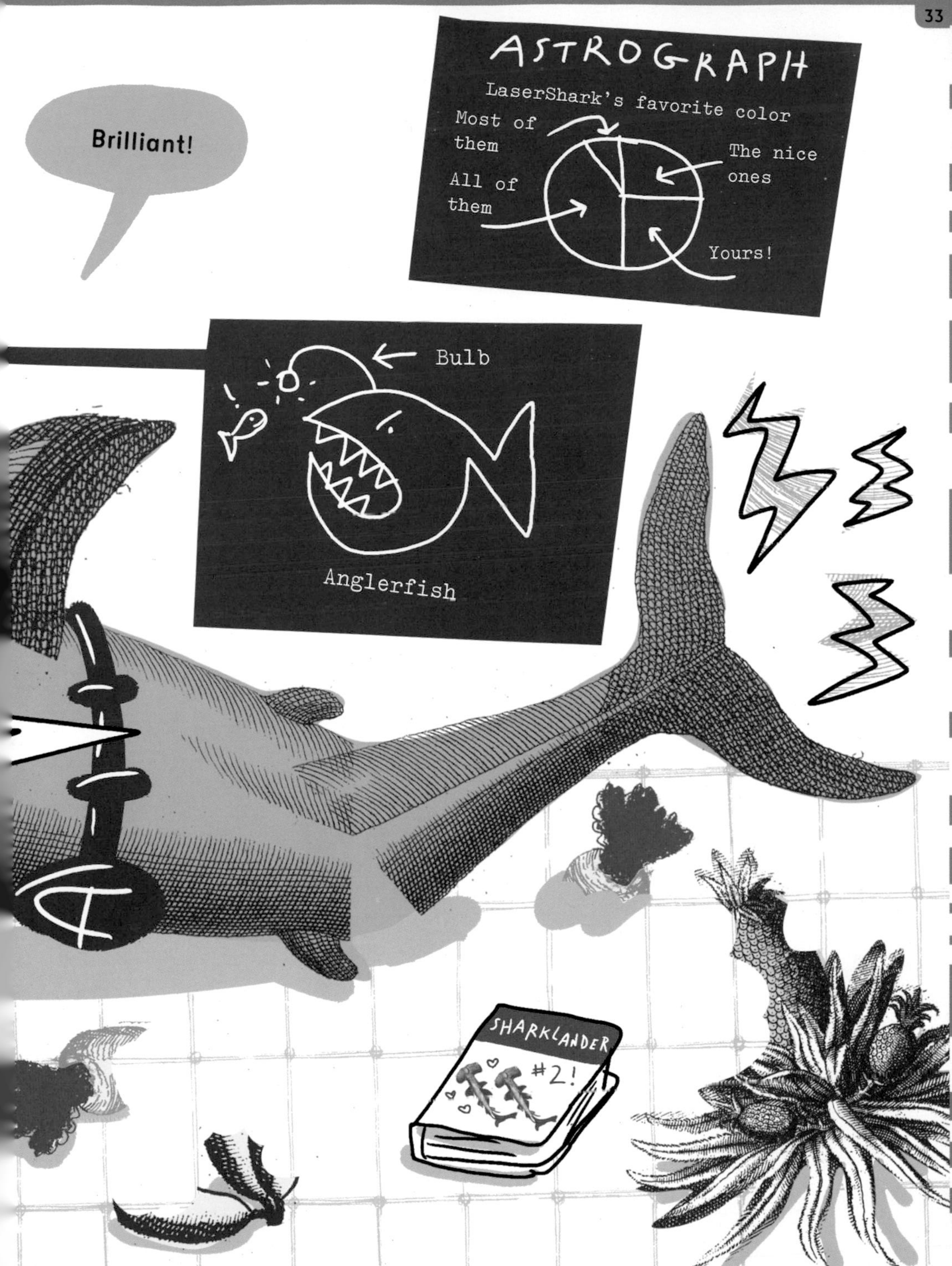
Brilliant!
ASTROGRAPH
LaserShark's favorite color
Most of them
The nice ones
All of them
Yours!
Bulb
Anglerfish
SHARKLANDER
#2!

SmartHawk got duck feet. Yes, duck feet. A good decision.

Trust me, I'm Earth. I know feet. And I know duck feet can come in very handy. Or should I say—footy.

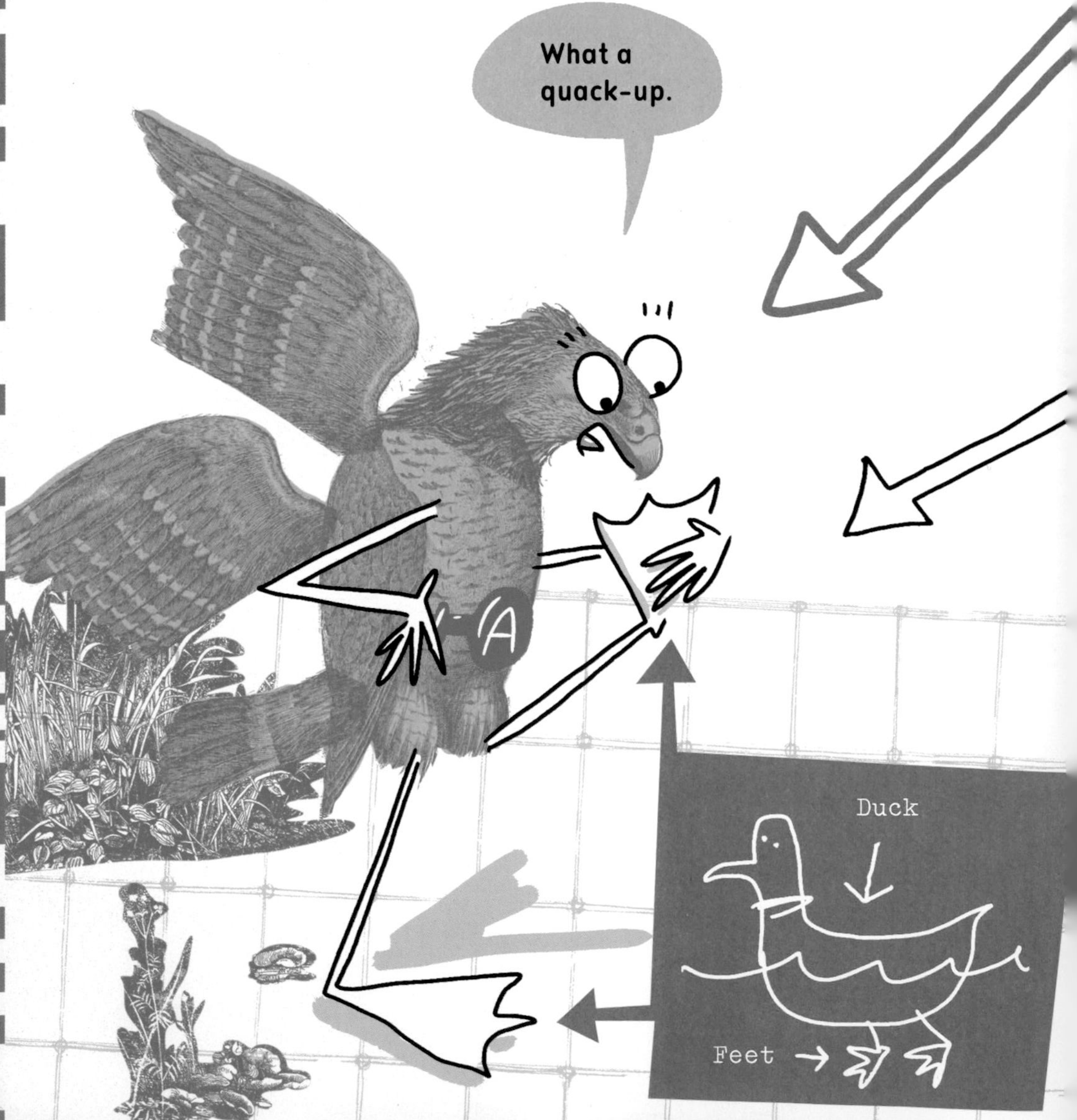
What a quack-up.
Duck
Feet

NEW ASTROPOWER:
Perfect duck feet, dark energy whirlpool power.

PLUS: Perfect propulsion

AND: Perfect slapping sound for walking on dry land

ASTROGRAPH
0
50
100
Duckness

QUACK
QUACK
a memoir
NNASA!

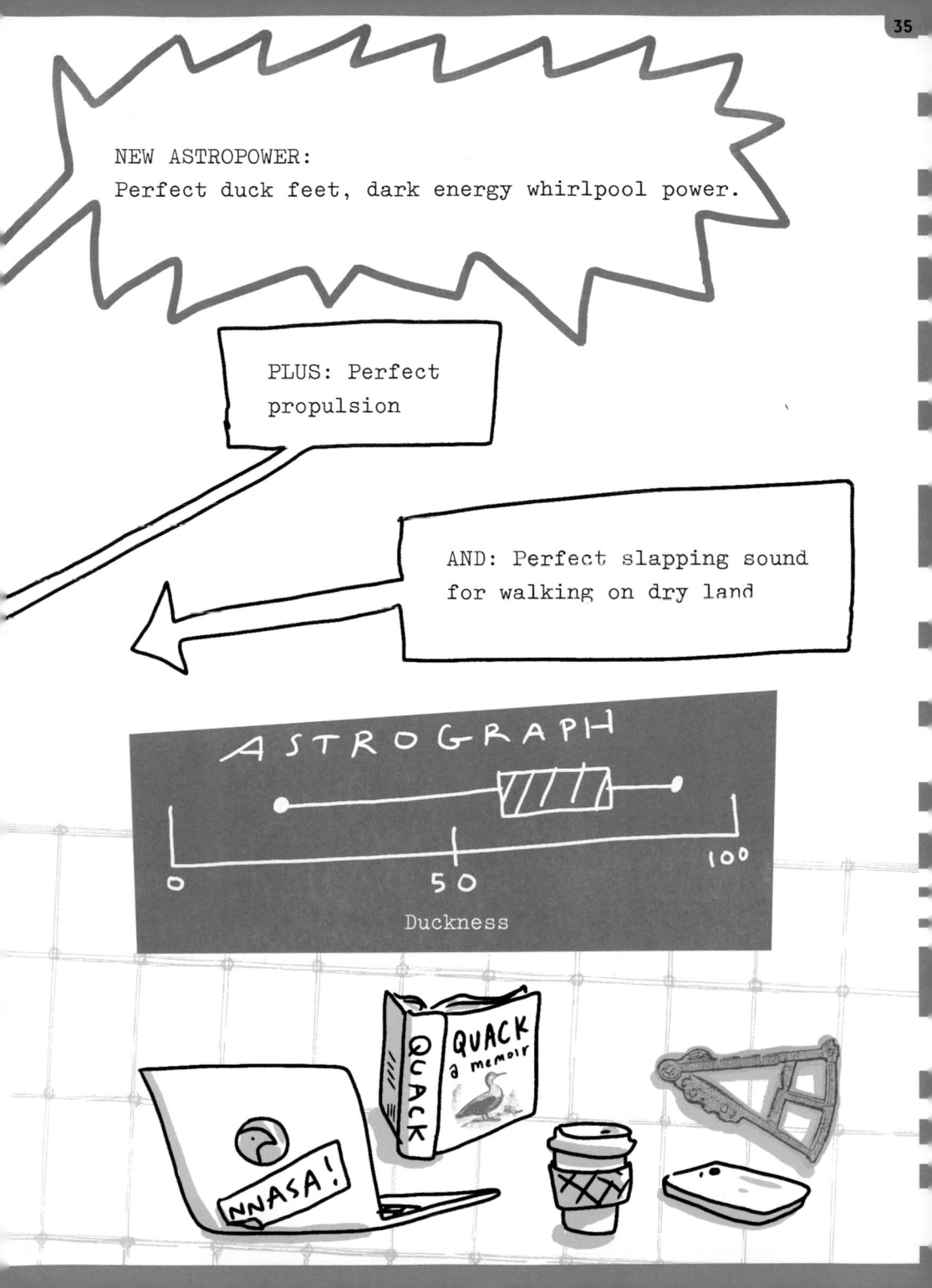

And StinkBug got the most SERIOUS mod-mod of all—squid tentacles, squid water jet propulsion, and squid ink mechanism.

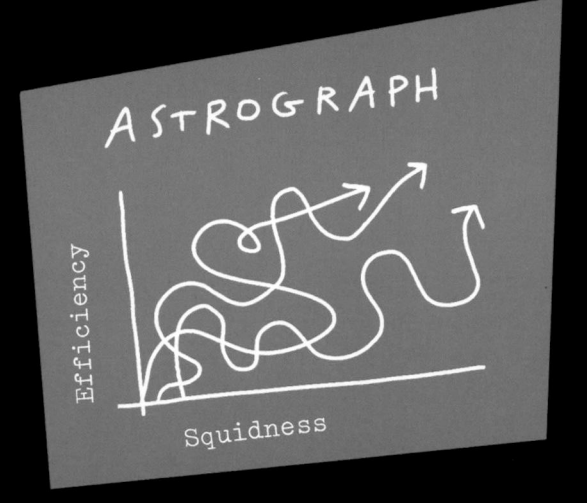

ASTROGRAPH

Efficiency

Squidness

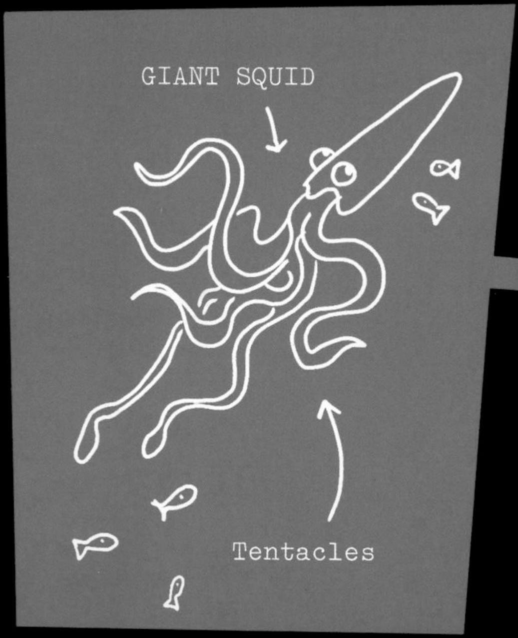

GIANT SQUID

Tentacles

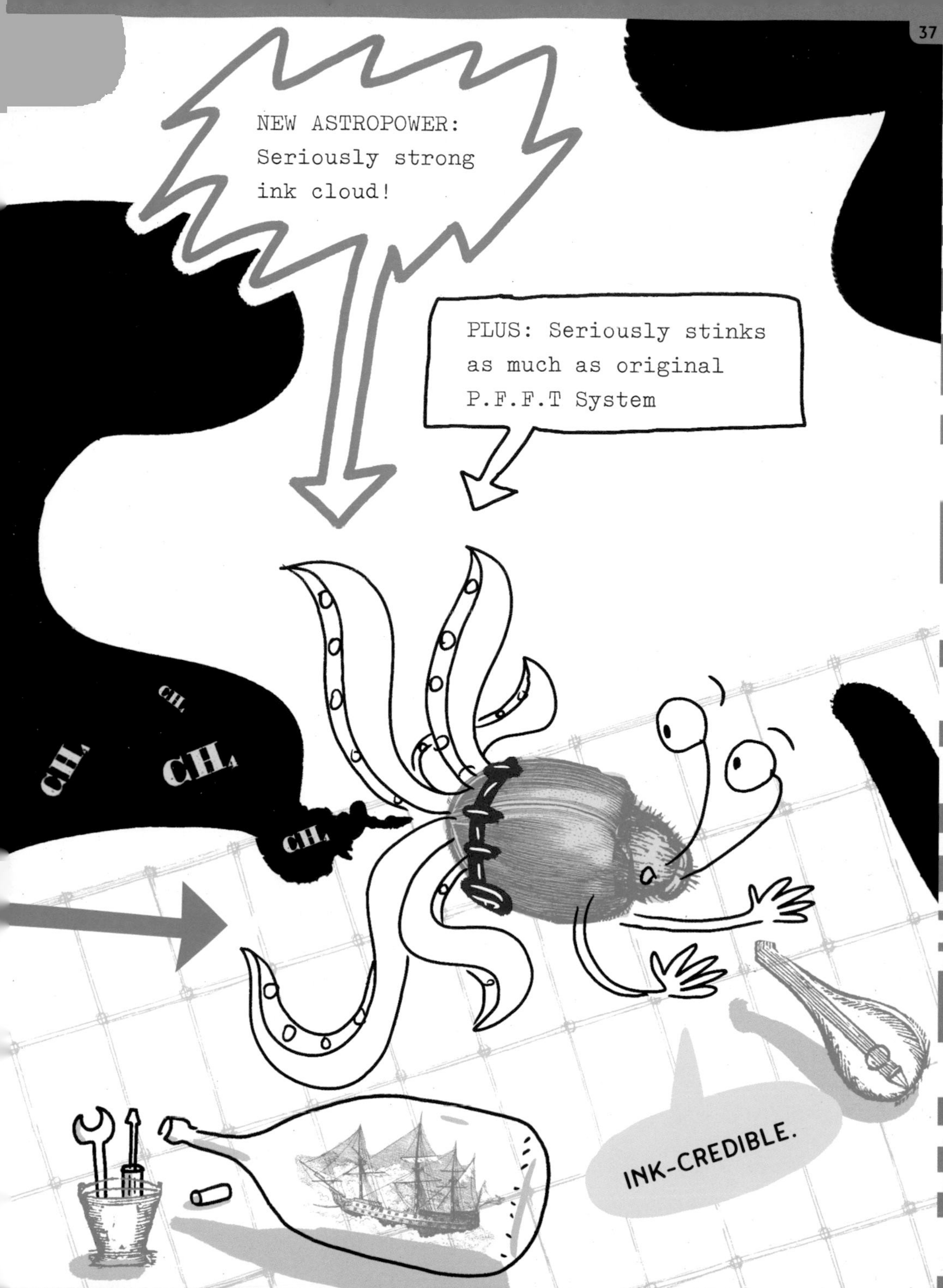
NEW ASTROPOWER:
Seriously strong
ink cloud!
PLUS: Seriously stinks
as much as original
P.F.F.T System
CH4
CH4
CH4
CH4
INK-CREDIBLE.

The AstroNuts met in the AstroPorthole to begin their check of the Water Planet . . . but mostly to admire their new mods.

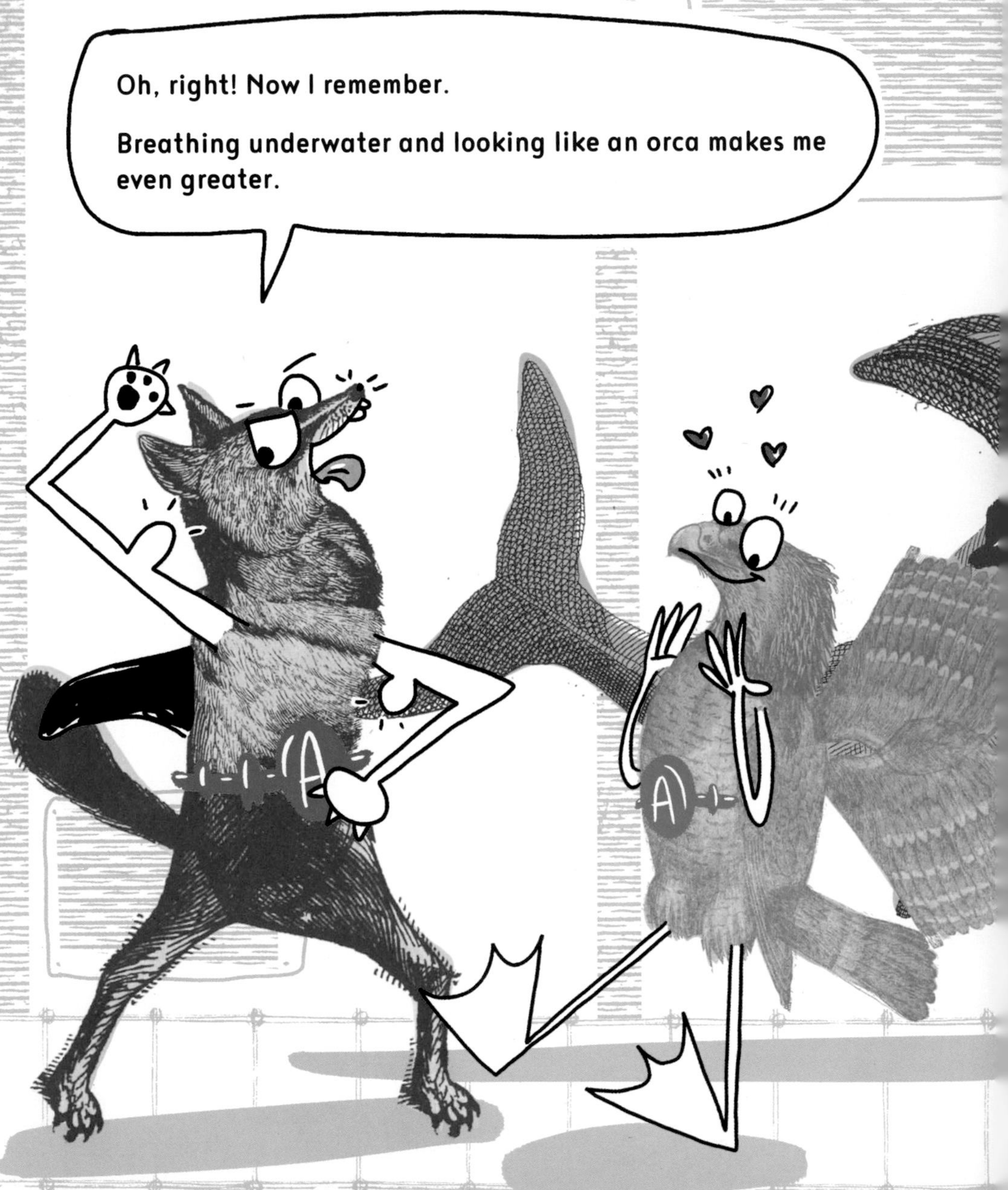
Oh, right! Now I remember.
Breathing underwater and looking like an orca makes me even greater.

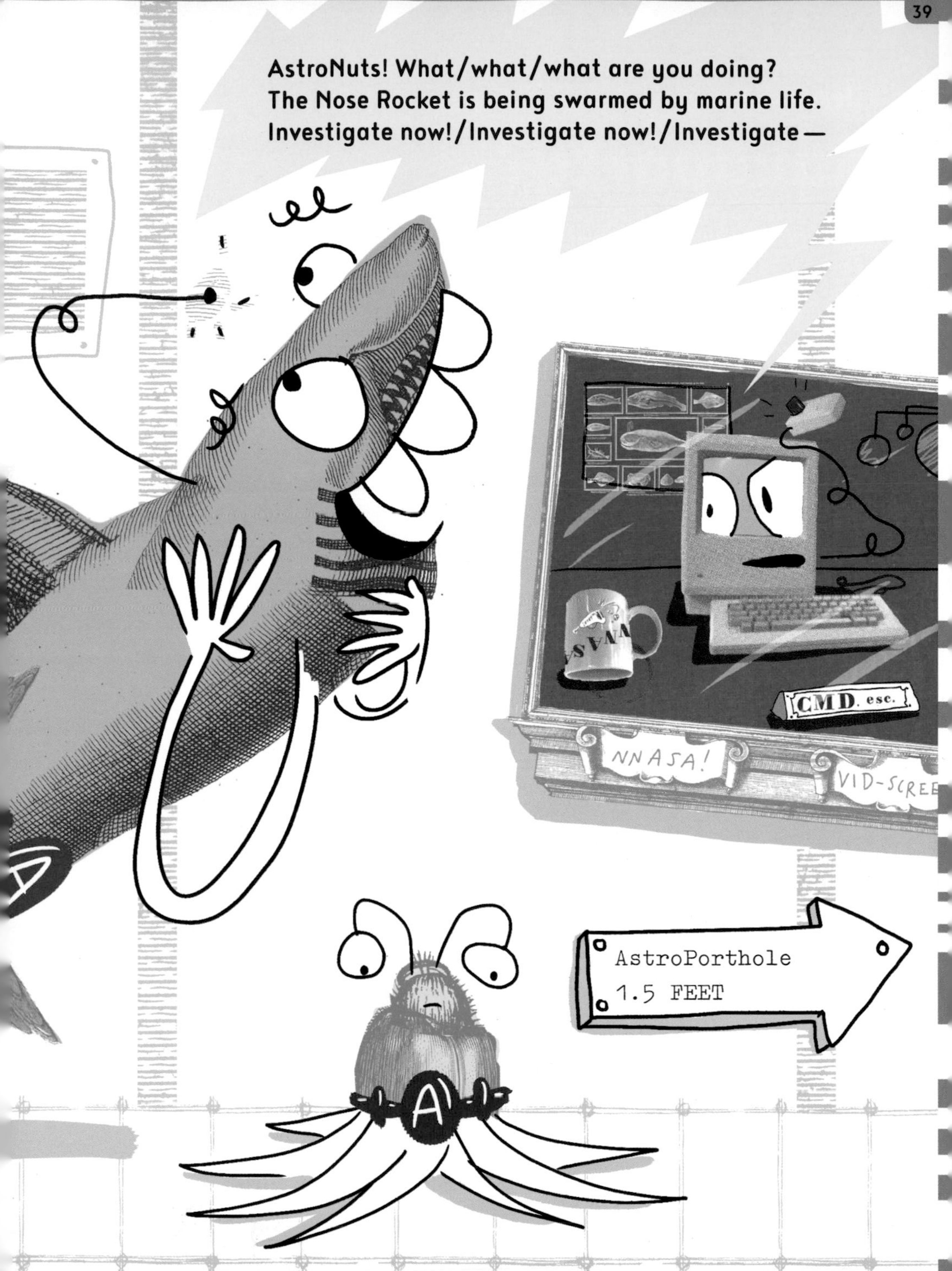
AstroNuts! What/what/what are you doing?
The Nose Rocket is being swarmed by marine life.
Investigate now!/Investigate now!/Investigate—
CMD. esc.
NNASA!
AstroPorthole
1.5 FEET

CHAPTER 5:
Aquaparty?

It was a good thing that at least Command Escape was doing his job. Because he was 100% right. The AstroNuts looked out the Nose Rocket porthole and saw that, yes, the Nose Rocket was being surrounded by marine creatures!

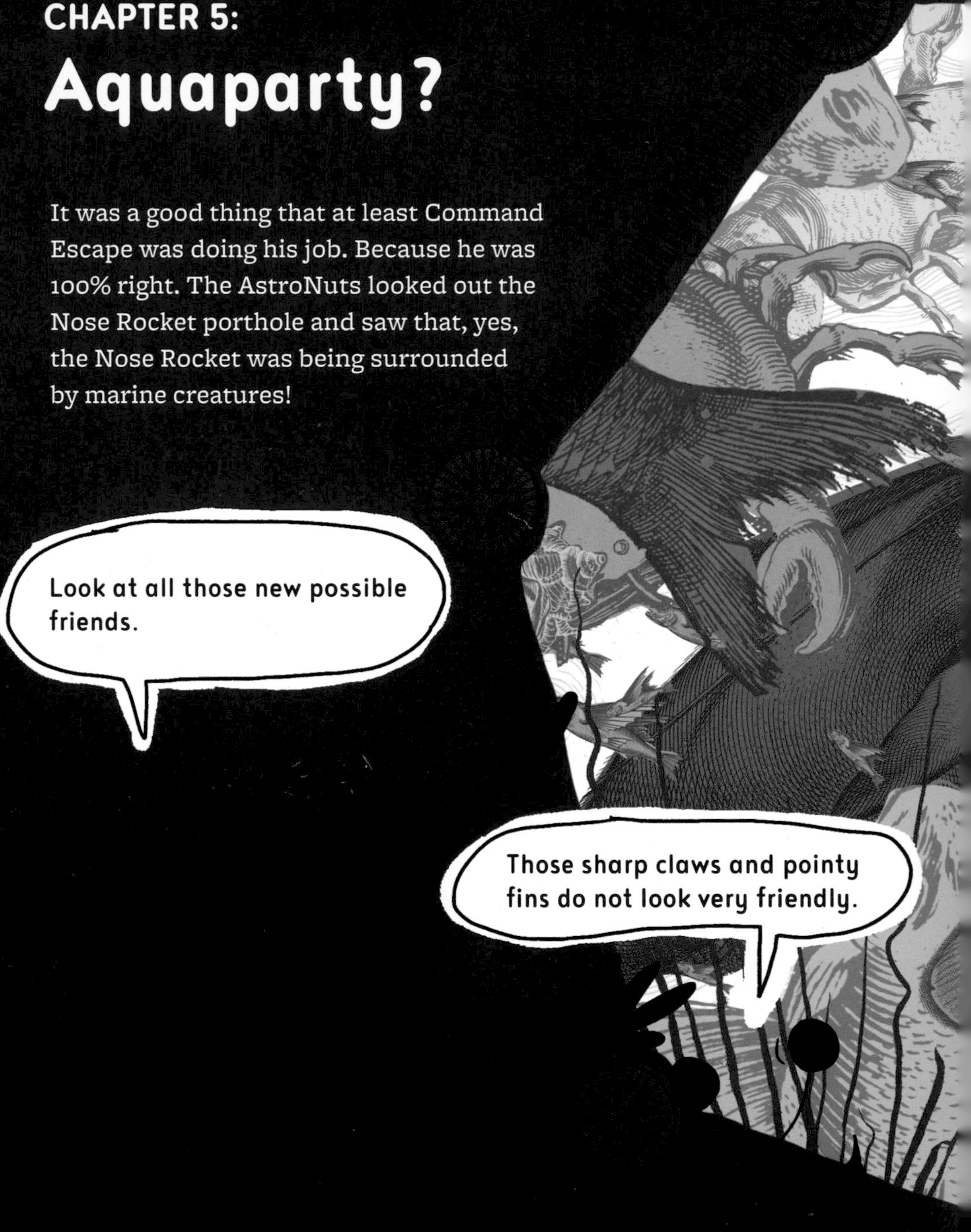

Look at all those new possible friends.
Those sharp claws and pointy fins do not look very friendly.

This is a big moment: first contact.
We should consider all options, and make a careful decision.
WE ARE BEING ATTACKED BY SAVAGE SEA MONSTERS!
We have to get out there and fight!
Mission Leader's orders!

The rest of the AstroNuts weren't really sure AlphaWolf was right. But he was the Mission Leader. So they followed his order and blew out of the Nose Rocket to fight.

Using his new Killer Whale fin Hyperspeed doggie paddle, AlphaWolf attacked.

SmartHawk started stirring a duck-feet whirlpool. StinkBug got ready to shoot his squid ink. LaserShark amped up her angler bulb. The AstroNuts revved up to full AstroBattle mode.

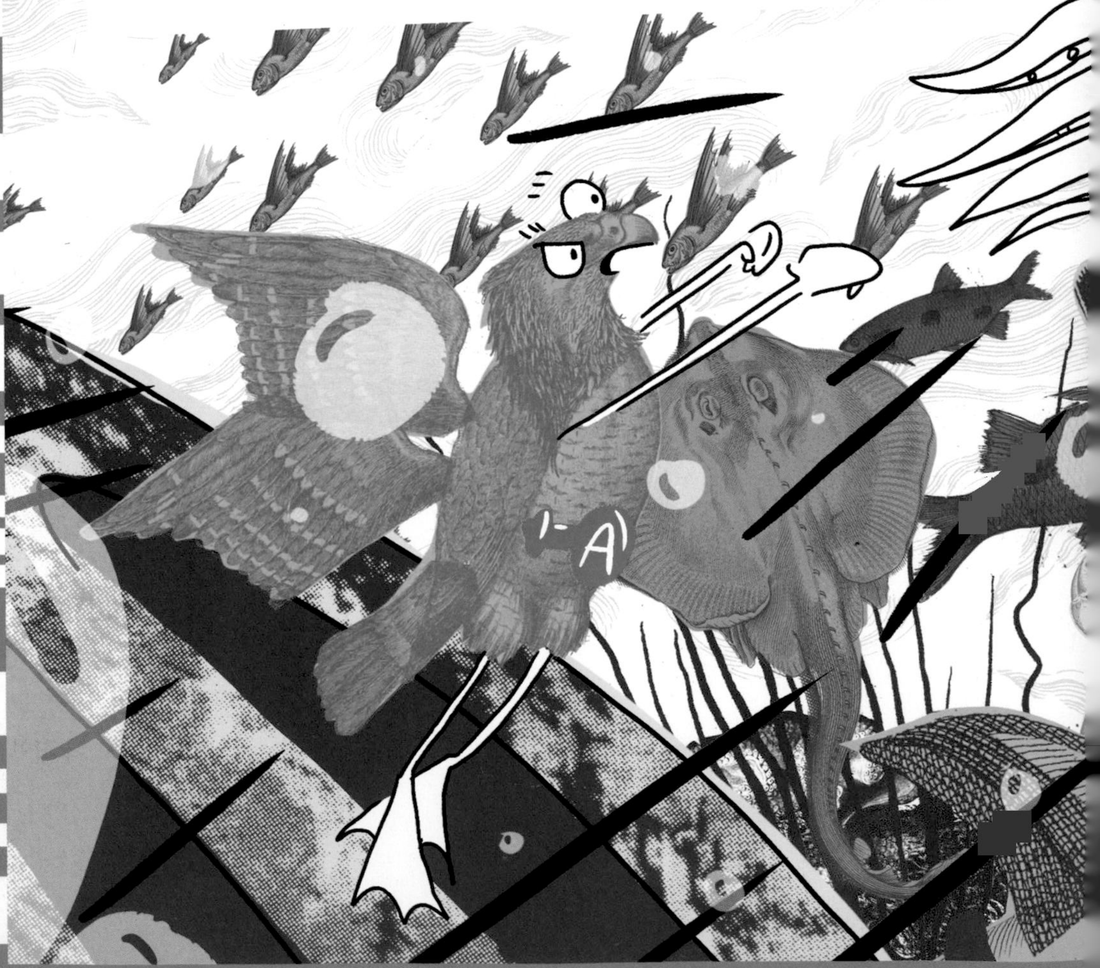

But fortunately for the AstroNuts, LaserShark looked more closely at the sea monster AlphaWolf was fighting. She noticed the sea monster was holding a banner.

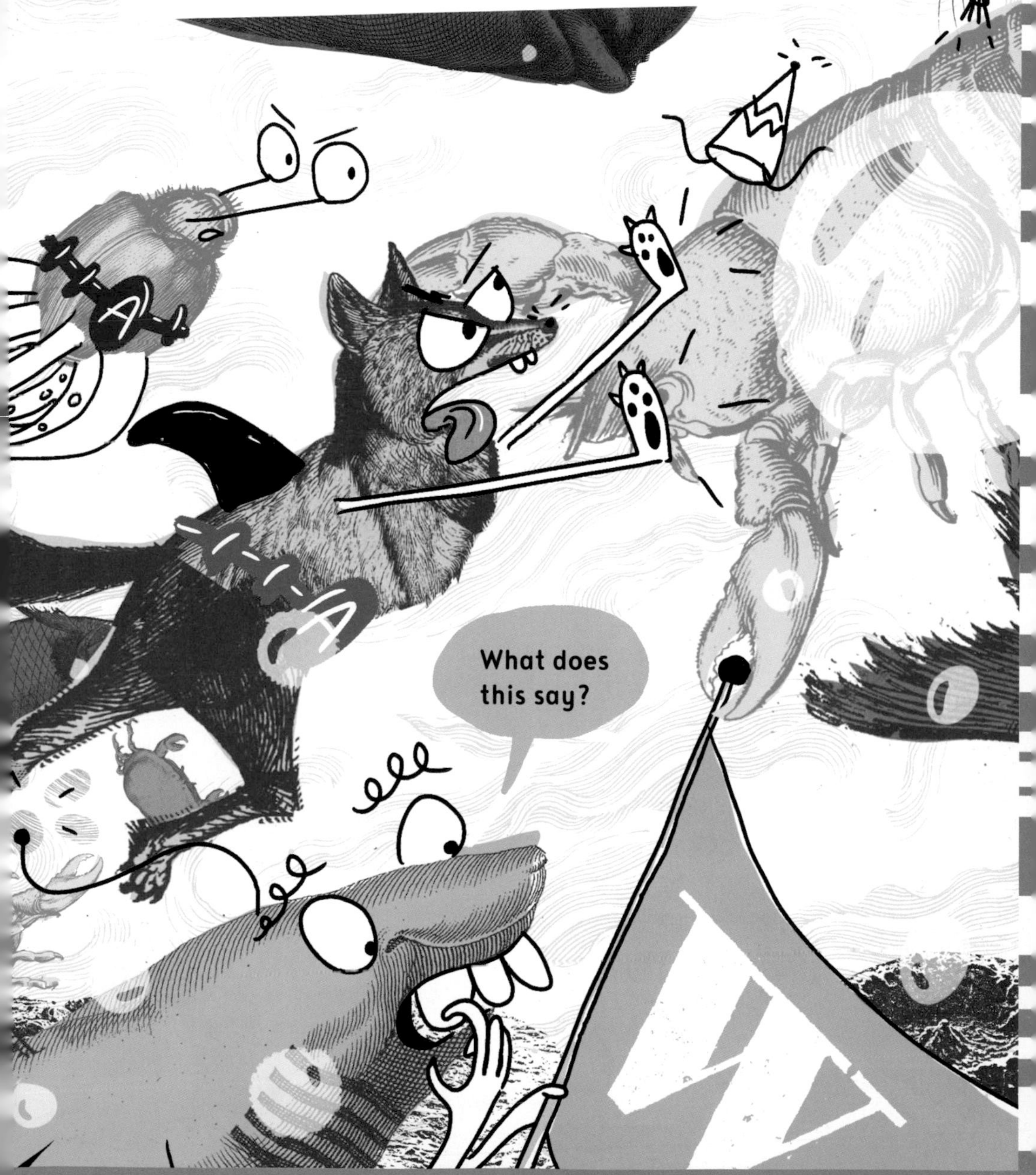
What does this say?

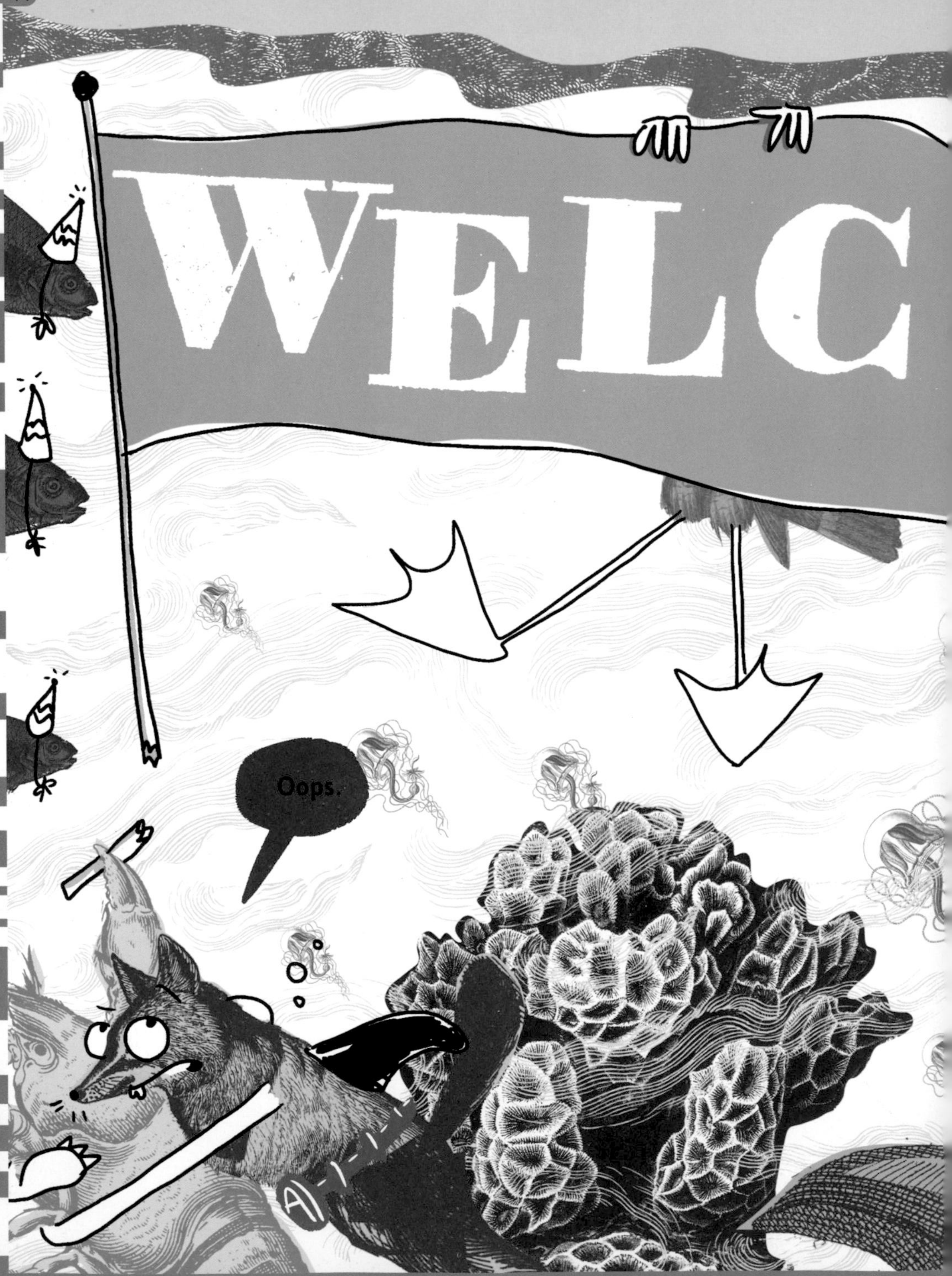
WELC
Oops.

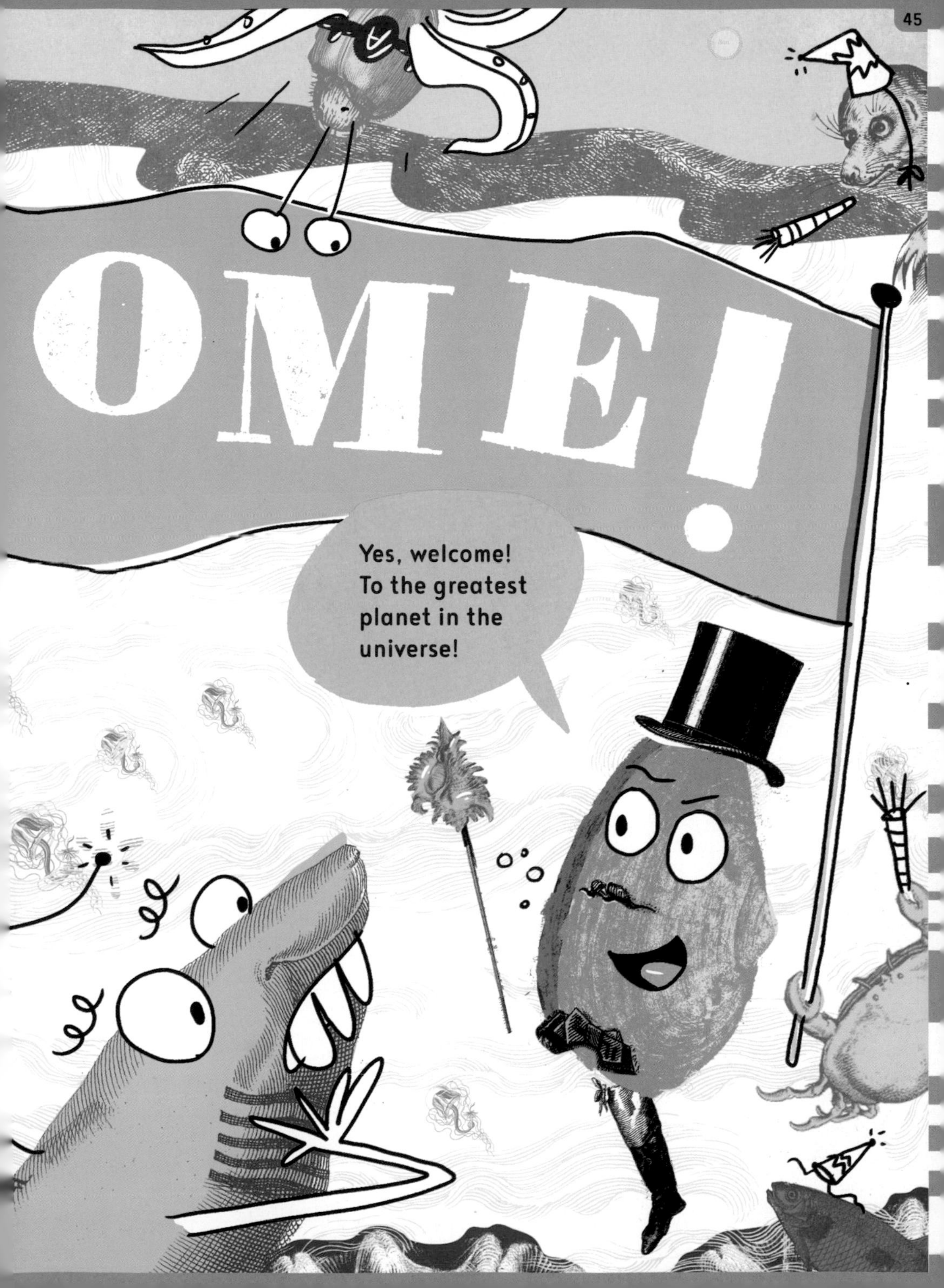
OME!
Yes, welcome! To the greatest planet in the universe!

CHAPTER 6:

Clam You Very Much

So it turned out that it wasn't a Water Planet attack. It was a Water Planet Welcome Parade for the AstroNuts.

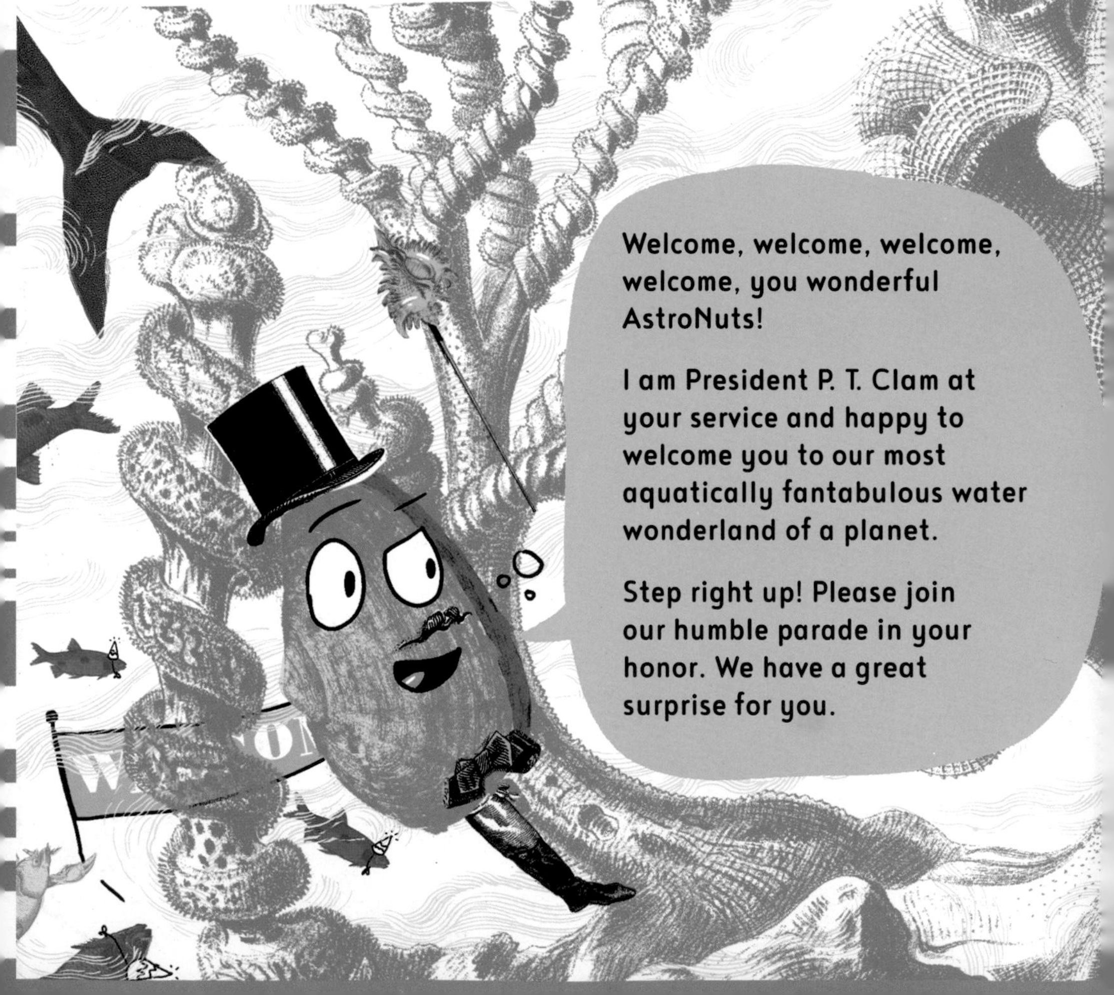
Welcome, welcome, welcome, welcome, you wonderful AstroNuts!
I am President P. T. Clam at your service and happy to welcome you to our most aquatically fantabulous water wonderland of a planet.
Step right up! Please join our humble parade in your honor. We have a great surprise for you.

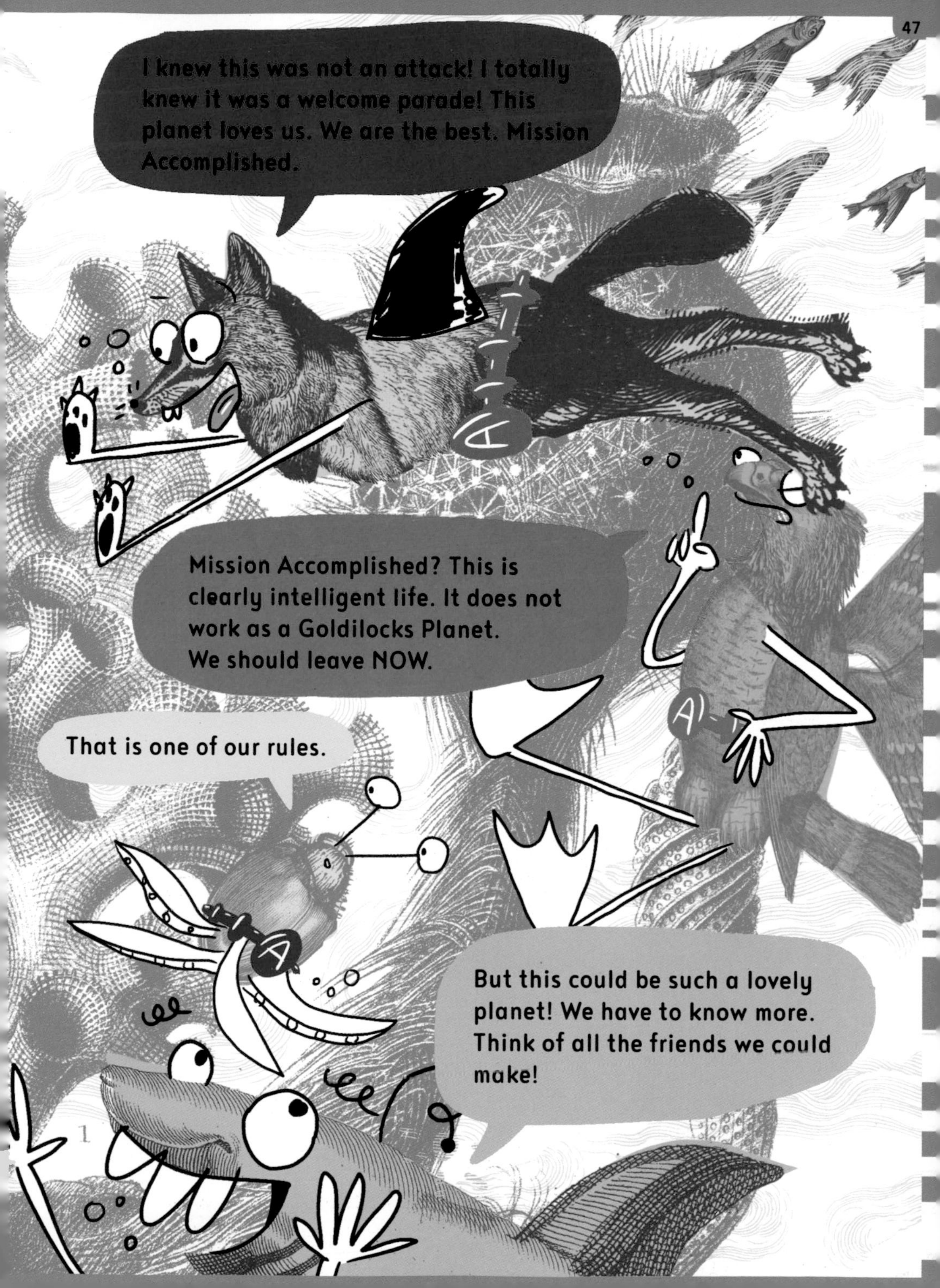
I knew this was not an attack! I totally knew it was a welcome parade! This planet loves us. We are the best. Mission Accomplished.
Mission Accomplished? This is clearly intelligent life. It does not work as a Goldilocks Planet. We should leave NOW.
That is one of our rules.
But this could be such a lovely planet! We have to know more. Think of all the friends we could make!

President P. T. Clam invited Mission Leader AlphaWolf to be the Grand Marshal of his parade. And it was a pretty impressive parade.

Though, word to the wise, when people are really excited to see you, you might want to find out exactly why they are so excited.

All this hoopla reminded me of when humans first started drilling oil out of me. We were all excited. But now look how that has turned out.

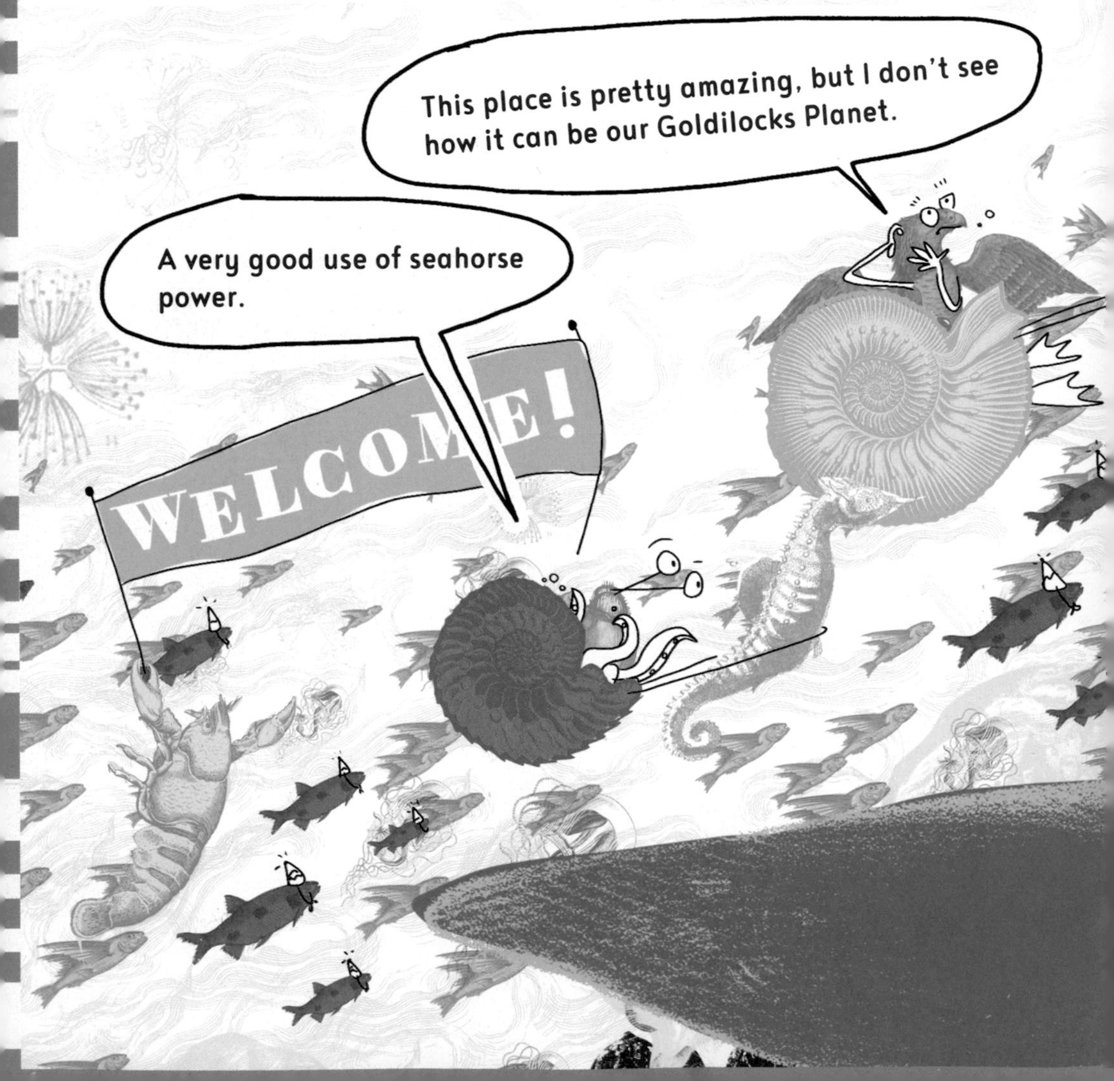
This place is pretty amazing, but I don't see how it can be our Goldilocks Planet.
A very good use of seahorse power.
WELCOME!

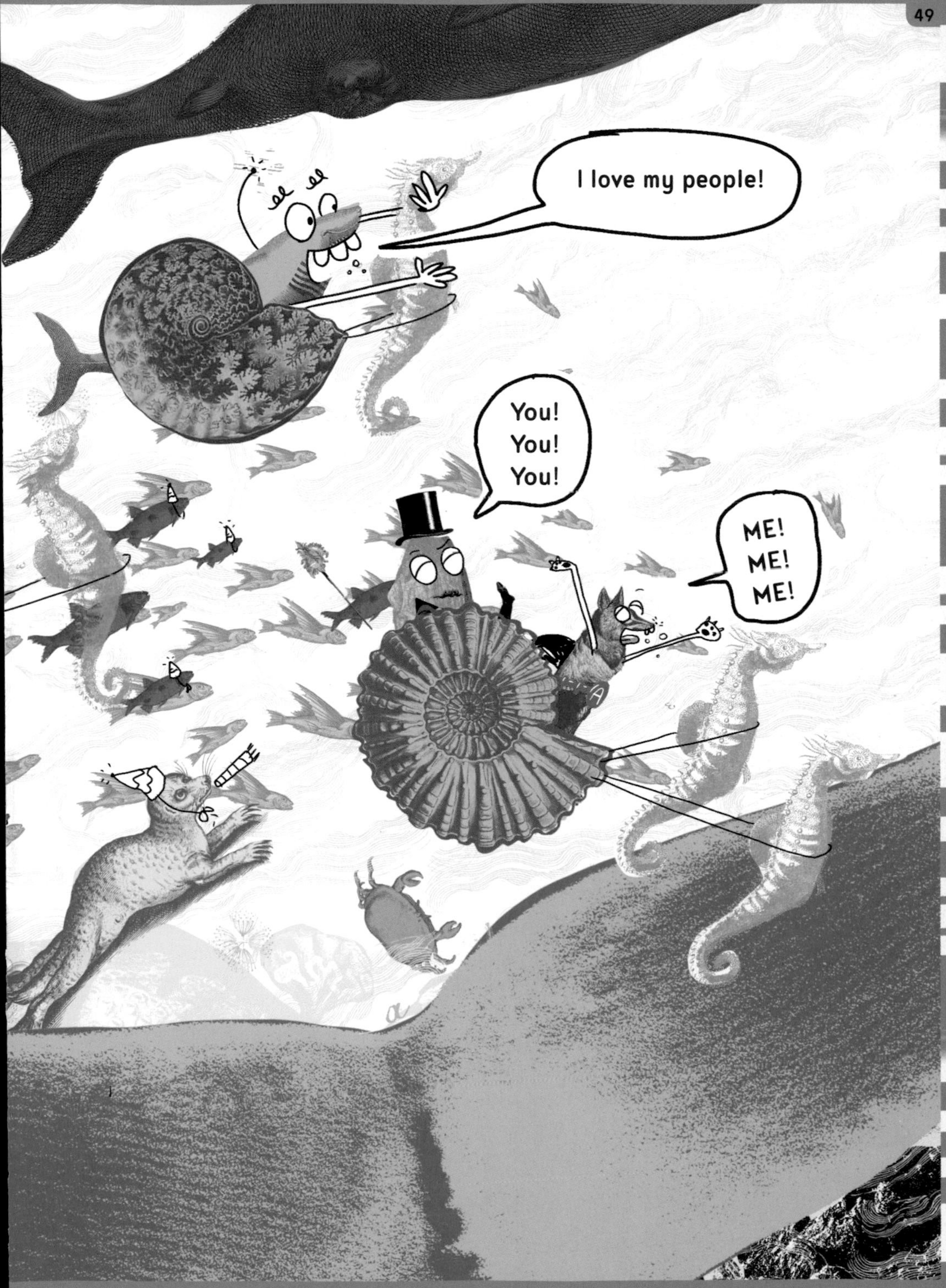
I love my people!
You! You! You!
ME! ME! ME!

After much fanfare and welcome waving, the AstroNuts arrived at President P. T. Clam's surprise.

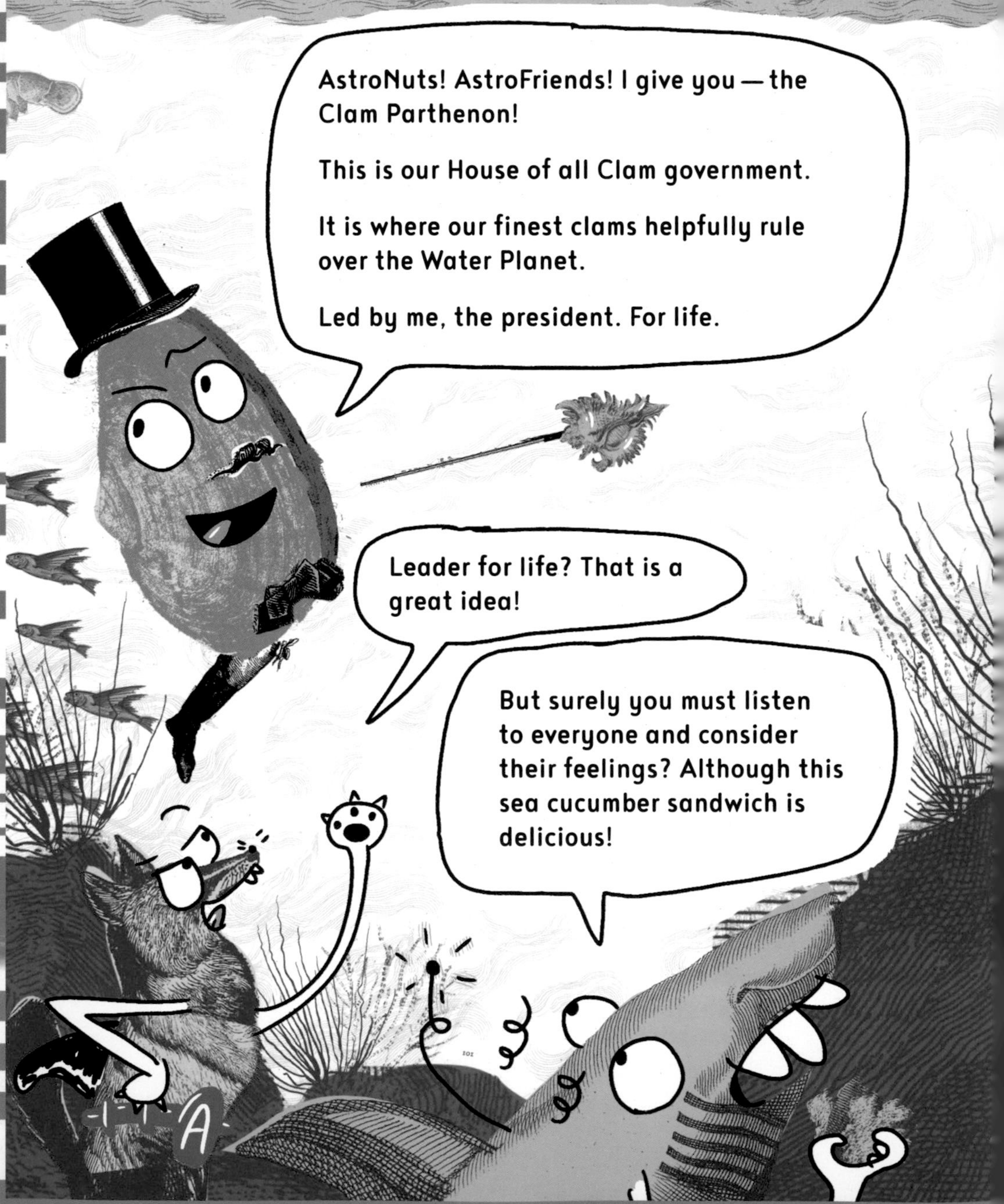
AstroNuts! AstroFriends! I give you — the Clam Parthenon!
This is our House of all Clam government.
It is where our finest clams helpfully rule over the Water Planet.
Led by me, the president. For life.
Leader for life? That is a great idea!
But surely you must listen to everyone and consider their feelings? Although this sea cucumber sandwich is delicious!

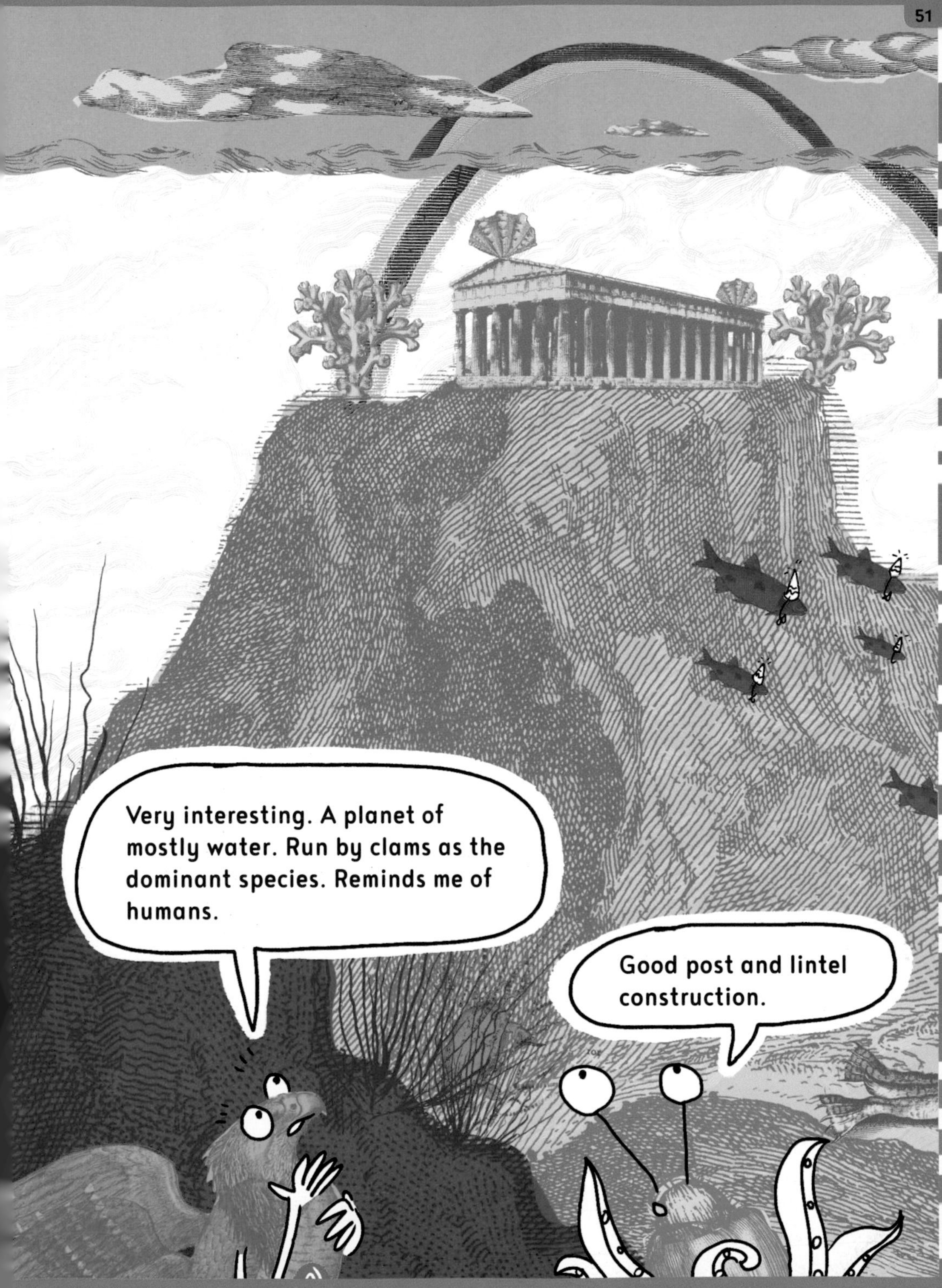
Very interesting. A planet of mostly water. Run by clams as the dominant species. Reminds me of humans.
Good post and lintel construction.

I present to you — the Clam Senate.
We make all the rules. For the good of all clams, and everyone. In a word, it is clamtastic.
CLAMTASTIC?
POWER!
CLAMS.
FRIENDS?

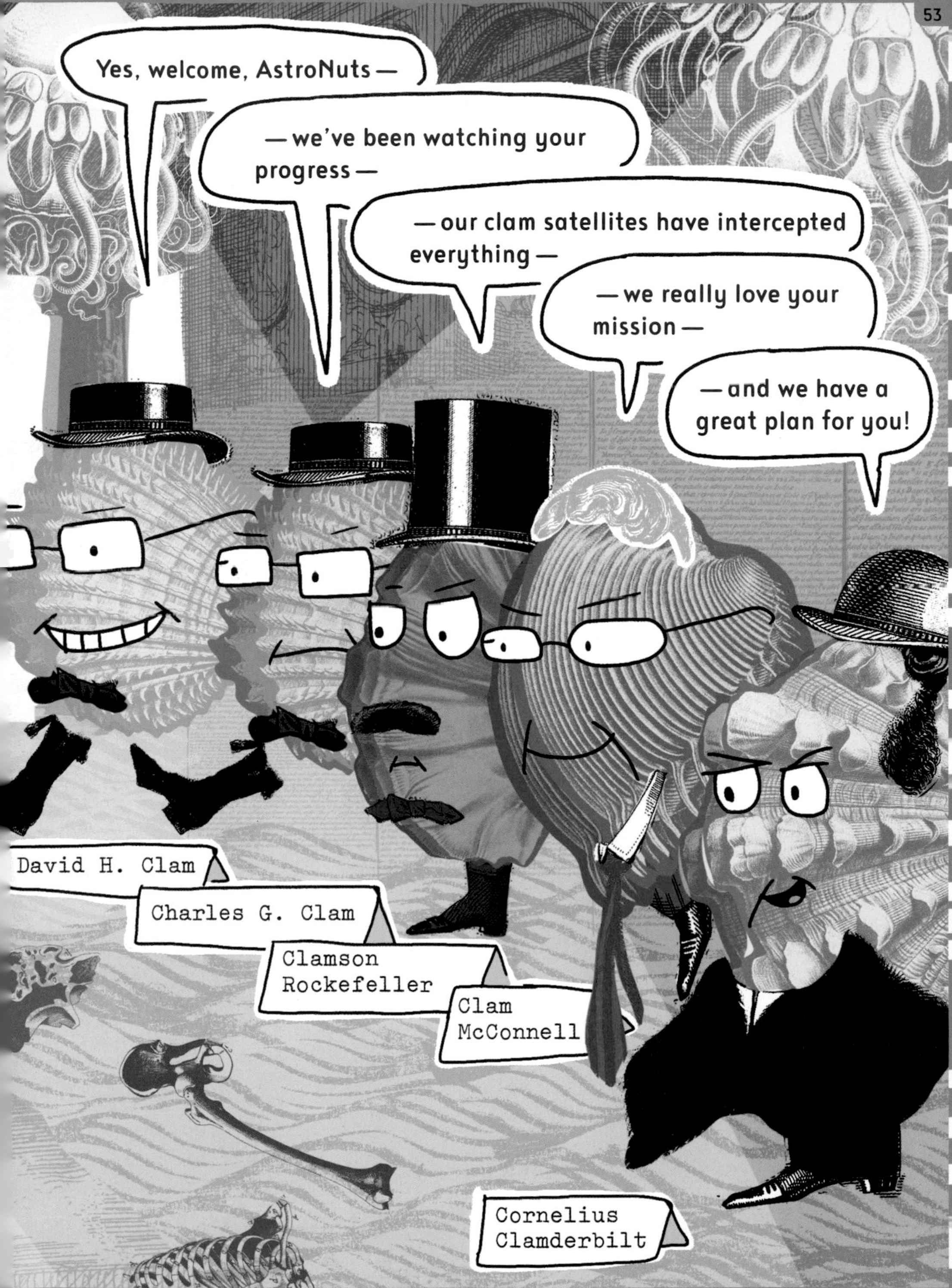
Yes, welcome, AstroNuts —
— we've been watching your progress —
— our clam satellites have intercepted everything —
— we really love your mission —
— and we have a great plan for you!
David H. Clam
Charles G. Clam
Clamson Rockefeller
Clam McConnell
Cornelius Clamderbilt

CHAPTER 7:
The Clamazing Plan

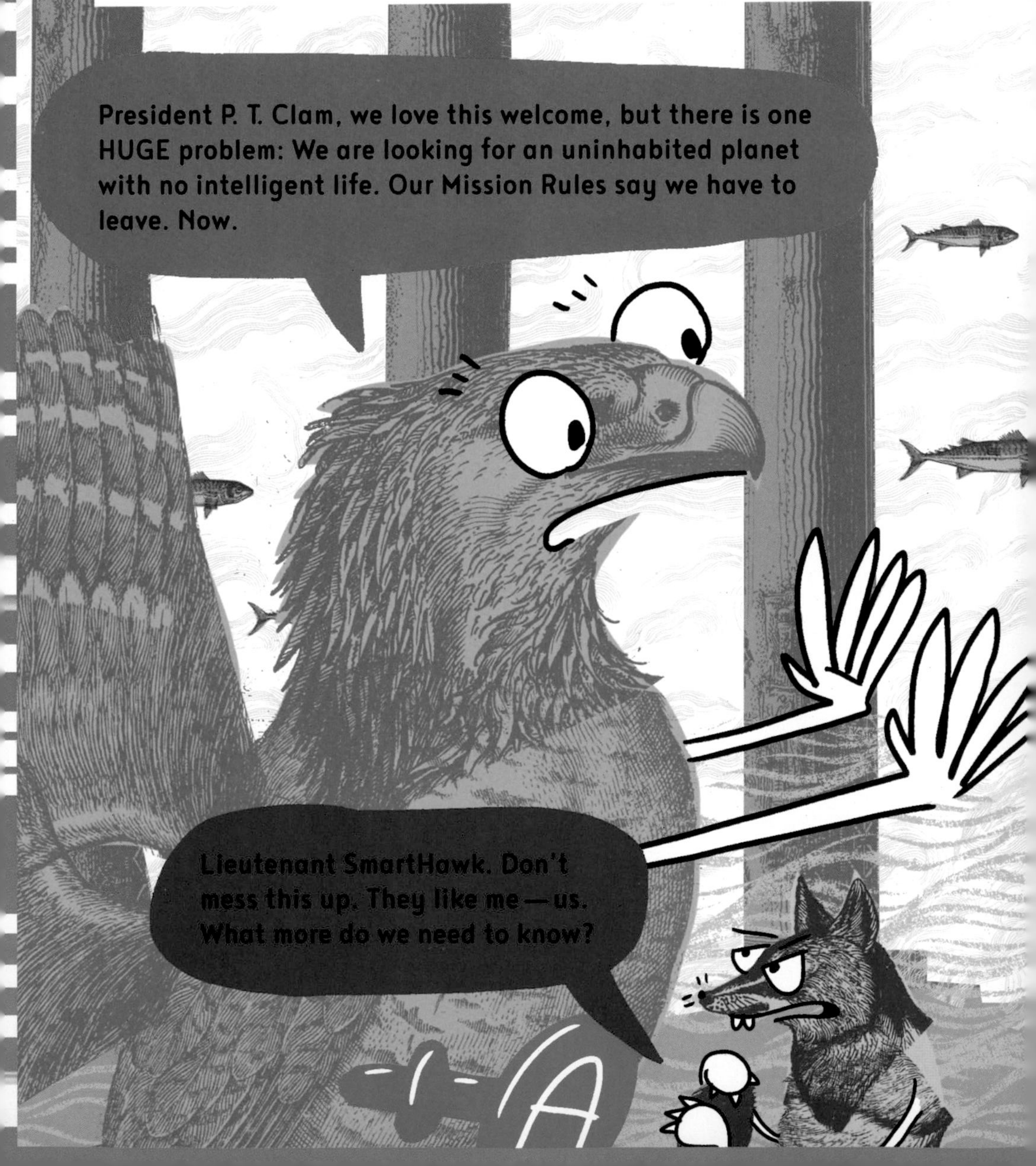

Oh, great barnacles no, Lieutenant SmartHawk! We would never want you to break any rules. Which is why you are going to love our fantastic plan.
Senators, please bring in the display whale.

Have we got a clamazing deal for you.
A never-before, never-again, one-time incredible offer.
So between us we have two planets, right? Yours, Earth, just a terrible mess.
Ours, the Water Planet, the most wonderful aquatic paradise.
EARTH (BAD — TO YOU) (NOT US)
WE
Fig. 1.

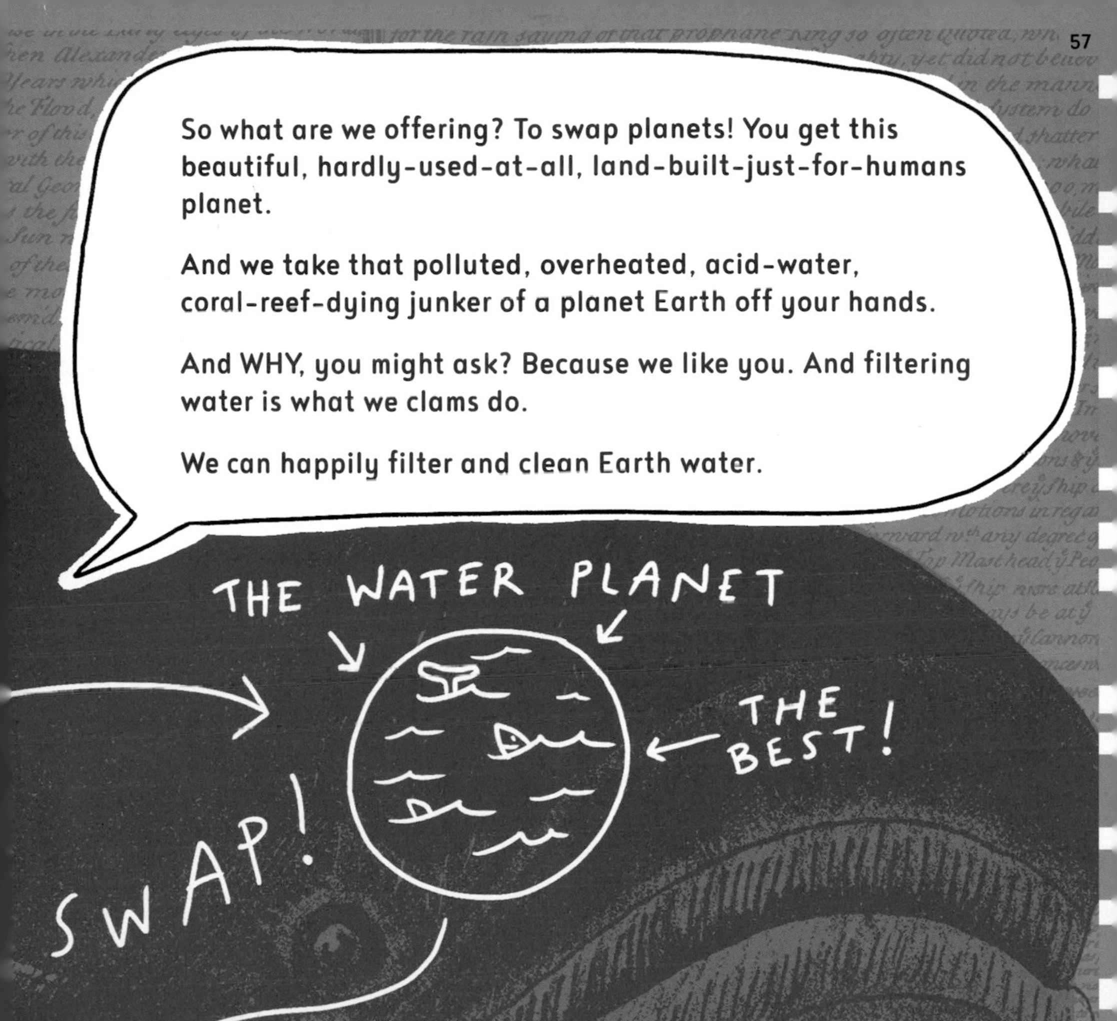
So what are we offering? To swap planets! You get this beautiful, hardly-used-at-all, land-built-just-for-humans planet.
And we take that polluted, overheated, acid-water, coral-reef-dying junker of a planet Earth off your hands.
And WHY, you might ask? Because we like you. And filtering water is what we clams do.
We can happily filter and clean Earth water.
THE WATER PLANET
THE BEST!
SWAP!
CLAMS FOR PROSPERITY
CHALKWHALE ©

It did sound like a great plan. But I have heard a lot of smooth-talking clams. And based on past experience, I've made it a personal policy never to trust a smooth-talking clam. Especially when that clam insults a planet he doesn't think is hearing his insults.

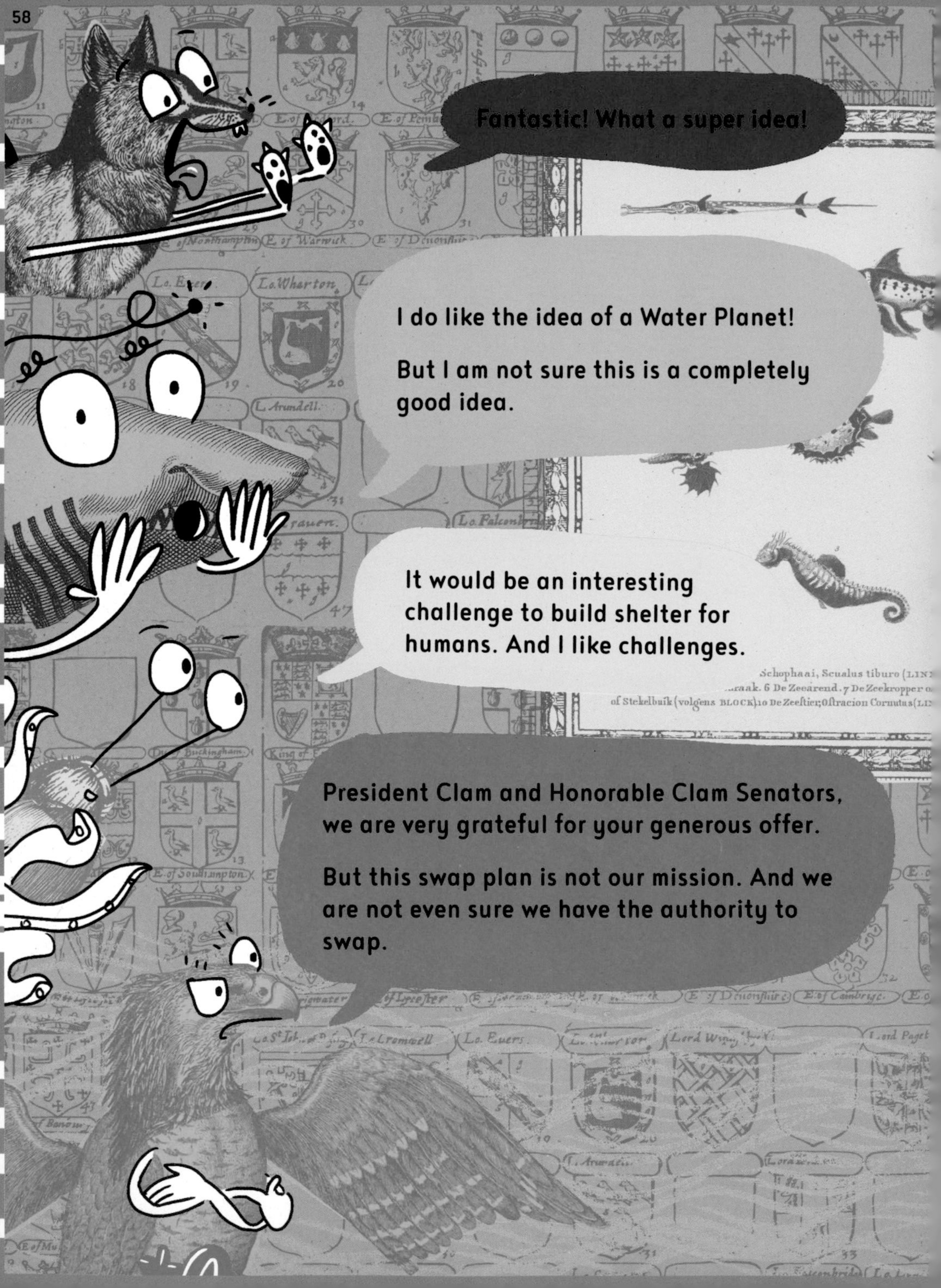
Fantastic! What a super idea!
I do like the idea of a Water Planet!
But I am not sure this is a completely good idea.
It would be an interesting challenge to build shelter for humans. And I like challenges.
President Clam and Honorable Clam Senators, we are very grateful for your generous offer.
But this swap plan is not our mission. And we are not even sure we have the authority to swap.

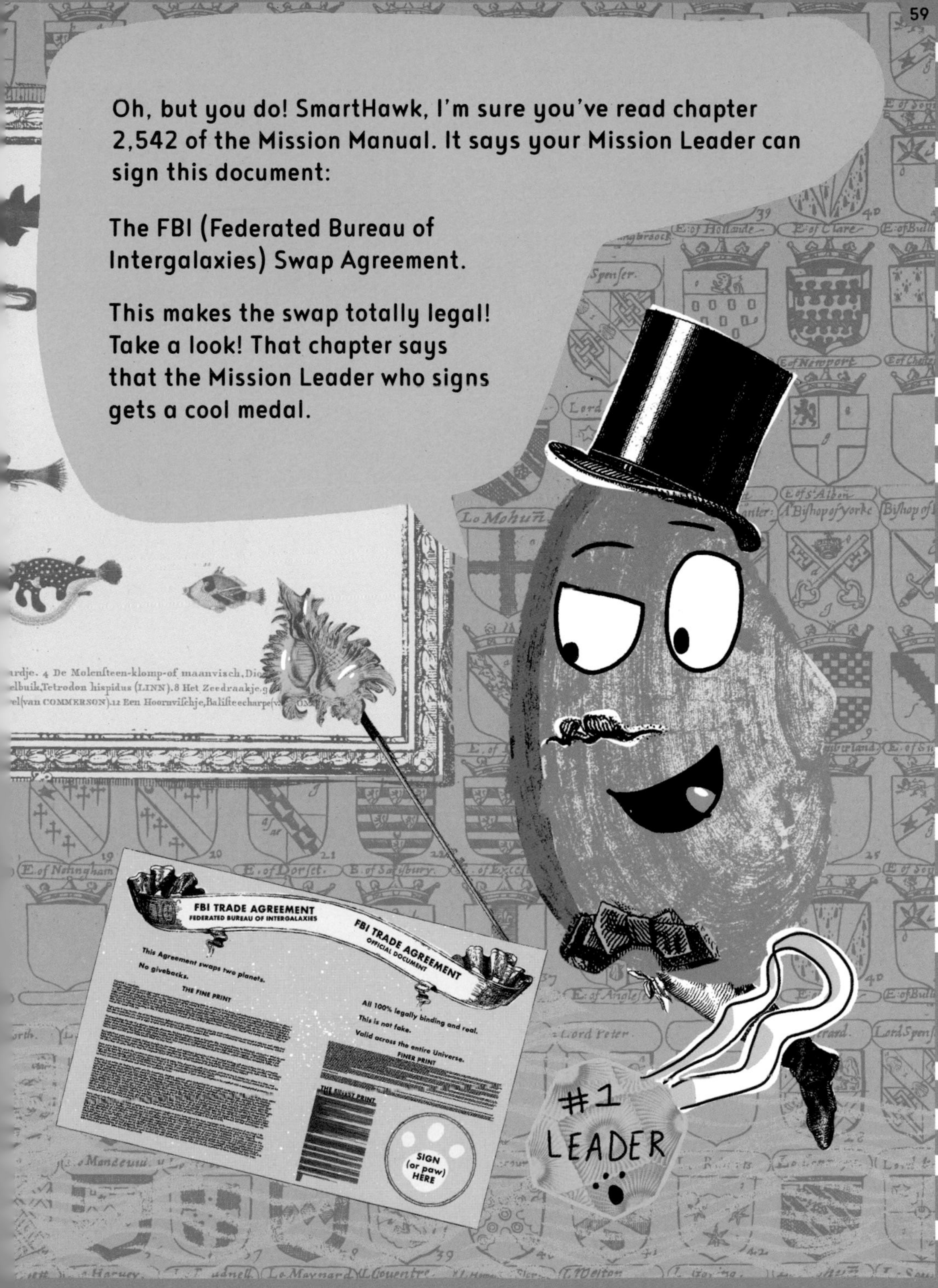
Oh, but you do! SmartHawk, I'm sure you've read chapter 2,542 of the Mission Manual. It says your Mission Leader can sign this document:
The FBI (Federated Bureau of Intergalaxies) Swap Agreement.
This makes the swap totally legal! Take a look! That chapter says that the Mission Leader who signs gets a cool medal.
FBI TRADE AGREEMENT
FEDERATED BUREAU OF INTERGALAXIES
FBI TRADE AGREEMENT
OFFICIAL DOCUMENT
This Agreement swaps two planets.
No givebacks.
THE FINE PRINT
All 100% legally binding and real.
This is not fake.
Valid across the entire Universe.
FINER PRINT
THE FINEST PRINT
SIGN (or paw) HERE
#1 LEADER

FBI TRADE AGREEMENT
FEDERATED BUREAU OF INTERGALAXIES

This Agreement swaps two planets.

No givebacks.

THE FINE PRINT

CHAPTER 1. Loomings.
Call me Ishmael. Some years ago—never mind how long precisely—having little or no money in my purse, and nothing particular to interest me on shore, I thought I would sail about a little and see the watery part of the world. It is a way I have of driving off the spleen and regulating the circulation. Whenever I find myself growing grim about the mouth; whenever it is a damp, drizzly November in my soul; whenever I find myself involuntarily pausing before coffin warehouses, and bringing up the rear of every funeral I meet; and especially whenever my hypos get such an upper hand of me, that it requires a strong moral principle to prevent me from deliberately stepping into the street, and methodically knocking people's hats off—then, I account it high time to get to sea as soon as I can. This is my substitute for pistol and ball. With a philosophical flourish Cato throws himself upon his sword; I quietly take to the ship. There is nothing surprising in this. If they but knew it, almost all men in their degree, some time or other, cherish very nearly the same feelings towards the ocean with me.

There now is your insular city of the Manhattoes, belted round by wharves as Indian isles by coral reefs—commerce surrounds it with her surf. Right and left, the streets take you waterward. Its extreme downtown is the battery, where that noble mole is washed by waves, and cooled by breezes, which a few hours previous were out of sight of land. Look at the crowds of water-gazers there.

Circumambulate the city of a dreamy Sabbath afternoon. Go from Corlears Hook to Coenties Slip, and from thence, by Whitehall, northward. What do you see?—Posted like silent sentinels all around the town, stand thousands upon thousands of mortal men fixed in ocean reveries. Some leaning against the spiles; some seated upon the pier-heads; some looking over the bulwarks of ships from China; some high aloft in the rigging, as if striving to get a still better seaward peep. But these are all landsmen; of week days pent up in lath and plaster—tied to counters, nailed to benches, clinched to desks. How then is this? Are the green fields gone? What do they here?

But look! here come more crowds, pacing straight for the water, and seemingly bound for a dive. Strange! Nothing will content them but the extremest limit of the land; loitering under the shady lee of yonder warehouses will not suffice. No. They must get just as nigh the water as they possibly can without falling in. And there they stand—miles of them—leagues. Inlanders all, they come from lanes and alleys, streets and avenues—north, east, south, and west. Yet here they all unite. Tell me, does the magnetic virtue of the needles of the compasses of all those ships attract them thither?

Once more. Say you are in the country; in some high land of lakes. Take almost any path you please, and ten to one it carries you down in a dale, and leaves you there by a pool in the stream. There is magic in it. Let the most absent-minded of men be plunged in his deepest reveries—stand that man on his legs, set his feet a-going, and he will infallibly lead you to water, if water there be in all that region. Should you ever be athirst in the great American desert, try this experiment, if your caravan happen to be supplied with a metaphysical professor. Yes, as every one knows, meditation and water are wedded for ever.

But here is an artist. He desires to paint you the dreamiest, shadiest, quietest, most enchanting bit of romantic landscape in all the valley of the Saco. What is the chief element he employs? There stand his trees, each with a hollow trunk, as if a hermit and a crucifix were within; and here sleeps his meadow, and there sleep his cattle; and up from yonder cottage goes a sleepy smoke. Deep into distant woodlands winds a mazy way, reaching to overlapping spurs of mountains bathed in their hill-side blue. But though the picture lies thus tranced, and though this pine-tree shakes down its sighs like leaves upon this shepherd's head, yet all were vain, unless the shepherd's eye were fixed upon the magic stream before him. Go visit the Prairies in June, when for scores on scores of miles you wade knee-deep among Tiger-lilies—what is the one charm wanting?—Water—there is not a drop of water there! Were Niagara but a cataract of sand, would you travel your thousand miles to see it? Why did the poor poet of Tennessee, upon suddenly receiving two handfuls of silver, deliberate whether to buy him a coat, which he sadly needed, or invest his money in a pedestrian trip to Rockaway Beach? Why is almost every robust healthy boy with a robust healthy soul in him, at some time or other crazy to go to sea? Why upon your first voyage as a passenger, did you yourself feel such a mystical vibration, when first told that you and your ship were now out of sight of land? Why did the old Persians hold the sea holy? Why did the Greeks give it a separate deity, and own brother of Jove? Surely all this is not without meaning. And still deeper the meaning of that story of Narcissus, who because he could not grasp the tormenting, mild image he saw in the fountain, plunged into it and was drowned. But that same image, we ourselves see in all rivers and oceans. It is the image of the ungraspable phantom of life; and this is the key to it all.

Now, when I say that I am in the habit of going to sea whenever I begin to grow hazy about the eyes, and begin to be over conscious of my lungs, I do not mean to have it inferred that I ever go to sea as a passenger. For to go as a passenger you must needs have a purse, and a purse is but a rag unless you have something in it. Besides, passengers get sea-sick—grow quarrelsome—don't sleep of nights—do not enjoy themselves much, as a general thing;—no, I never go as a passenger; nor, though I am something of a salt, do I ever go to sea as a Commodore, or a Captain, or a Cook. I abandon the glory and distinction of such offices to those who like them. For my part, I abominate all honorable respectable toils, trials, and tribulations of every kind whatsoever. It is quite as much as I can do to take care of myself, without taking care of ships, barques, brigs, schooners, and what not. And as for going as cook,—though I confess there is considerable glory in that, a cook being a sort of officer on ship-board—yet, somehow, I never fancied broiling fowls;—though once broiled, judiciously buttered, and judgmatically salted and peppered, there is no one who will speak more respectfully, not to say reverentially, of a broiled fowl than I will. It is out of the idolatrous dotings of the old Egyptians upon broiled ibis and roasted river horse, that you see the mummies of those creatures in their huge bake-houses the pyramids.

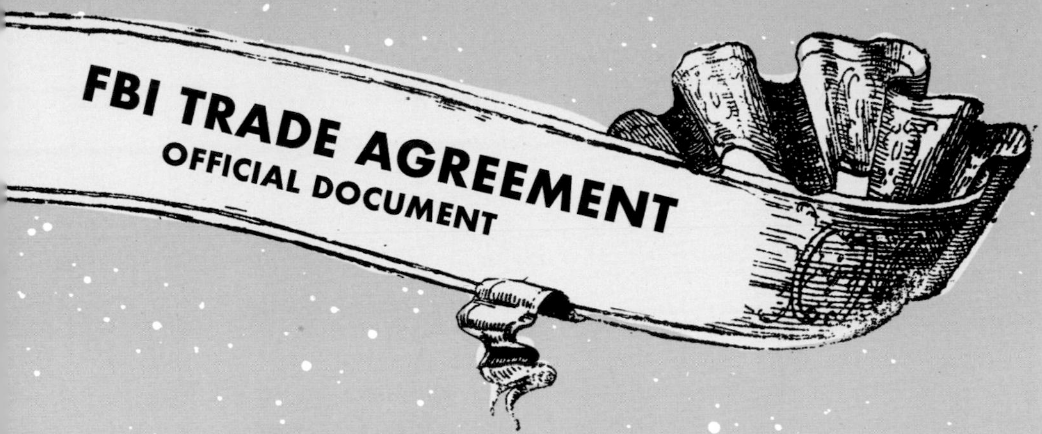
FBI TRADE AGREEMENT
OFFICIAL DOCUMENT

All 100% legally binding and real.

This is not fake.

Valid across the entire Universe.

FINER PRINT

No, when I go to sea, I go as a simple sailor, right before the mast, plumb down into the forecastle, aloft there to the royal mast-head. True, they rather order me about some, and make me jump from spar to spar, like a grasshopper in a May meadow. And at first, this sort of thing is unpleasant enough. It touches one's sense of honor, particularly if you come of an old established family in the land, the Van Rensselaers, or Randolphs, or Hardicanutes. And more than all, if just previous to putting your hand into the tar-pot, you have been lording it as a country schoolmaster, making the tallest boys stand in awe of you. The transition is a keen one, I assure you, from a schoolmaster to a sailor, and requires a strong decoction of Seneca and the Stoics to enable you to grin and bear it. But even this wears off in time.
What of it, if some old hunks of a sea-captain orders me to get a broom and sweep down the decks? What does that indignity amount to, weighed, I mean, in the scales of the New Testament? Do you think the archangel Gabriel thinks anything the less of me, because I promptly and respectfully obey that old hunks in that particular instance? Who ain't a slave? Tell me that. Well, then, however the old sea-captains may order me about—however they may thump and punch me about, I have the satisfaction of knowing that it is all right; that everybody else is one way or other served in much the same way—either in a physical or metaphysical point of view, that is; and so the universal thump is passed round, and all hands should rub each other's shoulder-blades, and be content.
Again, I always go to sea as a sailor, because they make a point of paying me for my trouble, whereas they never pay passengers a single penny that I ever heard of. On the contrary, passengers themselves must pay. And there is all the difference in the world between paying and being paid. The act of paying is perhaps the most uncomfortable infliction that the two orchard thieves entailed upon us. But being paid,—what will compare with it? The urbane activity with which a man receives money is really marvellous, considering that we so earnestly believe money to be the root of all earthly ills, and that on no account can a monied man enter heaven. Ah! how cheerfully we consign ourselves to perdition!
Finally, I always go to sea as a sailor, because of the wholesome exercise and pure air of the fore-castle deck. For as in this world, head winds are far more prevalent than winds from astern (that is, if you never violate the Pythagorean maxim), so for the most part the Commodore on the quarter-deck gets his atmosphere at second hand from the sailors on the forecastle. He thinks he breathes it first; but not so. In much the same way do the commonalty lead their leaders in many other things, at the same time that the leaders little suspect it. But wherefore it was that after having repeatedly smelt the sea as a merchant sailor, I should now take it into my head to go on a whaling voyage; this the invisible police officer of the Fates, who has the constant surveillance of me, and secretly dogs me, and influences me in some unaccountable way—he can better answer than any one else. And, doubtless, my going on this whaling voyage, formed part of the grand programme of Providence that was drawn up a long time ago. It came in as a sort of brief interlude and solo between more extensive performances. I take it that this part of the bill must have run something like this:
"Grand Contested Election for the Presidency of the United States. "WHALING VOYAGE BY ONE ISHMAEL. "BLOODY BATTLE IN AFFGHANISTAN."
Though I cannot tell why it was exactly that those stage managers, the Fates, put me down for this shabby part of a whaling voyage, when others were set down for magnificent parts in high tragedies, and short and easy parts in genteel comedies, and jolly parts in farces—though I cannot tell why this was exactly; yet, now that I recall all the circumstances, I think I can see a little into the springs and motives which being cunningly presented to me under various disguises, induced me to set about performing the part I did, besides cajoling me into the delusion that it was a choice resulting from my own unbiased freewill and discriminating judgment.
Chief among these motives was the overwhelming idea of the great whale himself. Such a portentous and mysterious monster roused all my curiosity. Then the wild and distant seas where he rolled his island bulk; the undeliverable, nameless perils of the whale; these, with all the attending marvels of a thousand Patagonian sights and sounds, helped to sway me to my wish. With other men, perhaps, such things would not have been inducements; but as for me, I am tormented with an everlasting itch for things remote. I love to sail forbidden seas, and land on barbarous coasts. Not ignoring what is good, I am quick to perceive a horror, and could still be social with it—would they let me—since it is but well to be on friendly terms with all the inmates of the place one lodges in.
By reason of these things, then, the whaling voyage was welcome; the great flood-gates of the wonder-world swung open, and in the wild conceits that swayed me to my purpose, two and two there floated into my inmost soul, endless processions of the whale, and, mid most of them all, one grand hooded phantom, like a snow hill in the air.

CHAPTER 2. The Carpet-Bag.

I stuffed a shirt or two into my old carpet-bag, tucked it under my arm, and started for Cape Horn and the Pacific. Quitting the good city of old Manhatto, I duly arrived in New Bedford. It was a Saturday night in December. Much was I disappointed upon learning that the little packet for Nantucket had already sailed, and that no way of reaching that place would offer, till the following Monday.
As most young candidates for the pains and penalties of whaling stop at this same New Bedford, thence to embark on their voyage, it may as well be related that I, for one, had no idea of so doing. For my mind was made up to sail in no other than a Nantucket craft, because there was a fine, boisterous something about everything connected with that famous old island, which amazingly pleased me. Besides though New Bedford has of late been gradually monopolising the business of whaling, and though in this matter poor old Nantucket is now much behind her, yet Nantucket was her great original—the Tyre of this Carthage;—the place where the first dead American whale was stranded. Where else but from Nantucket did those aboriginal whalemen, the Red-Men, first sally out in canoes to give chase to the Leviathan? And where but from Nantucket, too, did that first adventurous little sloop put

THE FINEST PRINT

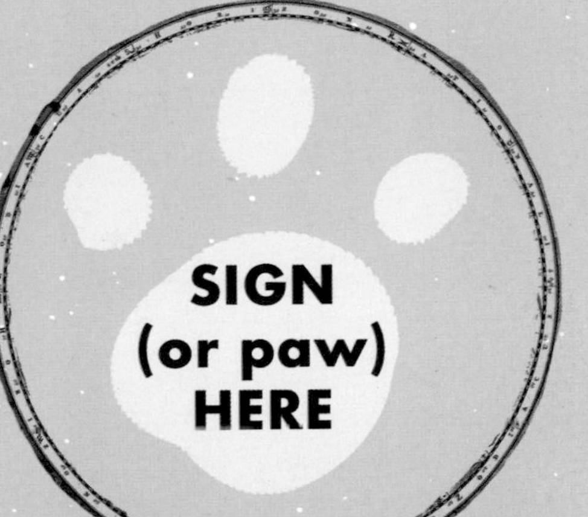
SIGN
(or paw)
HERE

This was heavy stuff. Trading me for another planet on just a signature? That's a big step. It reminds me of the time some fish in my ocean decided to grow legs and live on land. . . . Anyway, three of the AstroNuts decided they should discuss this.

///// Official NNASA transcript /////
//// of ASTRONUT MISSION 2 ////

AlphaWolf: We did it! I have found the Goldilocks Planet! I get a medal!

SmartHawk: Wait, wait, wait. We might be able to do this legally. I guess I missed chapter 2,542. But we'll need to do our NNASA tests first to make sure it's worth the swap.

LaserShark: And it does seem a teeny bit unfair that only one of us gets to decide something so important.

StinkBug: P. T. Clam must be a very good reader. I did not know there were 2,542 chapters in the Mission Manual.

AlphaWolf: Did you guys see that medal?

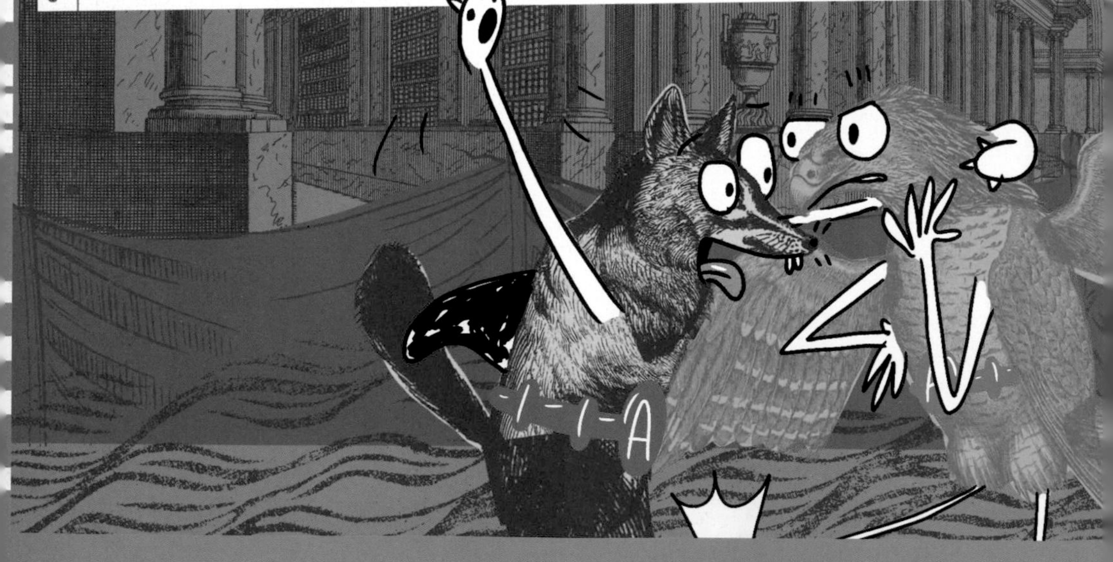

LaserShark: This is about more than a medal, AlphaWolf! Think about everyone else on planet Earth.

AlphaWolf: OK.

—three seconds of silence—

AlphaWolf: I just did. And I'm sure everyone would love this planet. Who doesn't like the beach?

SmartHawk: No, we have to follow ALL of the Mission Rules. We have to run our tests.

StinkBug: And look at this. Chapter 2,543 says to read chapter 2,542 again because it is 100% true.

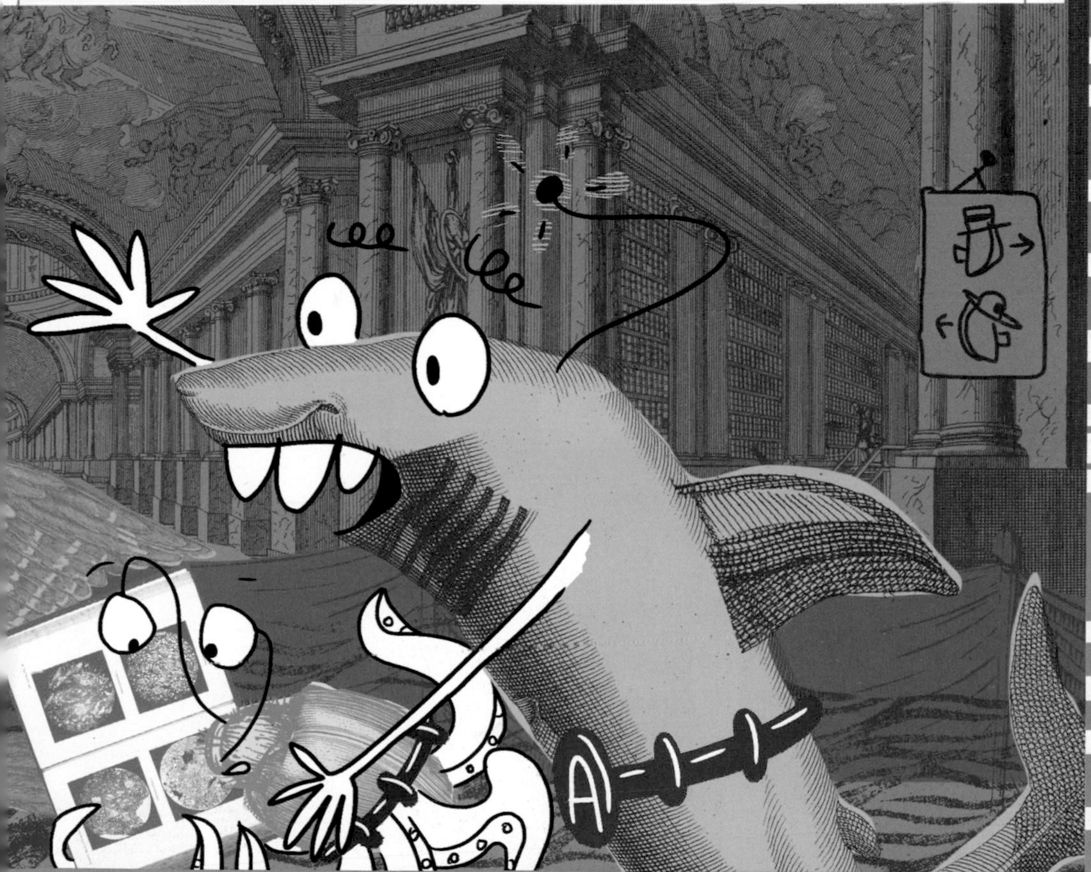

President P. T. Clam did not look like he was liking the way this AstroDiscussion was going. He poked the Clam Senators to make their pitch.

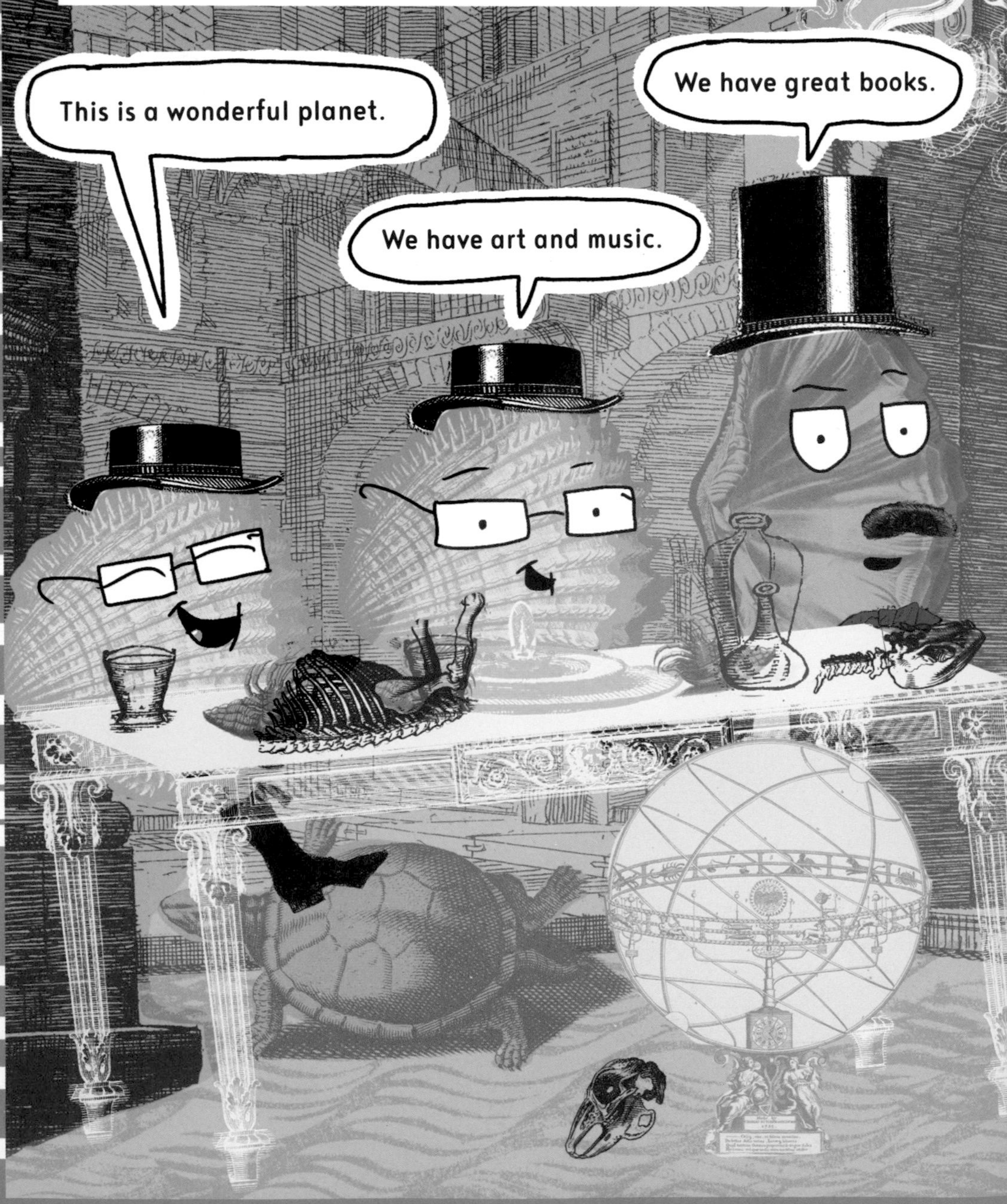
This is a wonderful planet.
We have art and music.
We have great books.

It's a perfectly healthy planet in every way!
Trust us!
We will show you the wonders of this new planet that will be yours.
Then your great Mission Leader can make it official with his beautiful paw print.

CHAPTER 8:

The Clamtastic Tour

And before the AstroNuts could disagree or ask any more questions, President P. T. Clam hustled them off to be amazed by the Seven Wonders of the Water Planet.

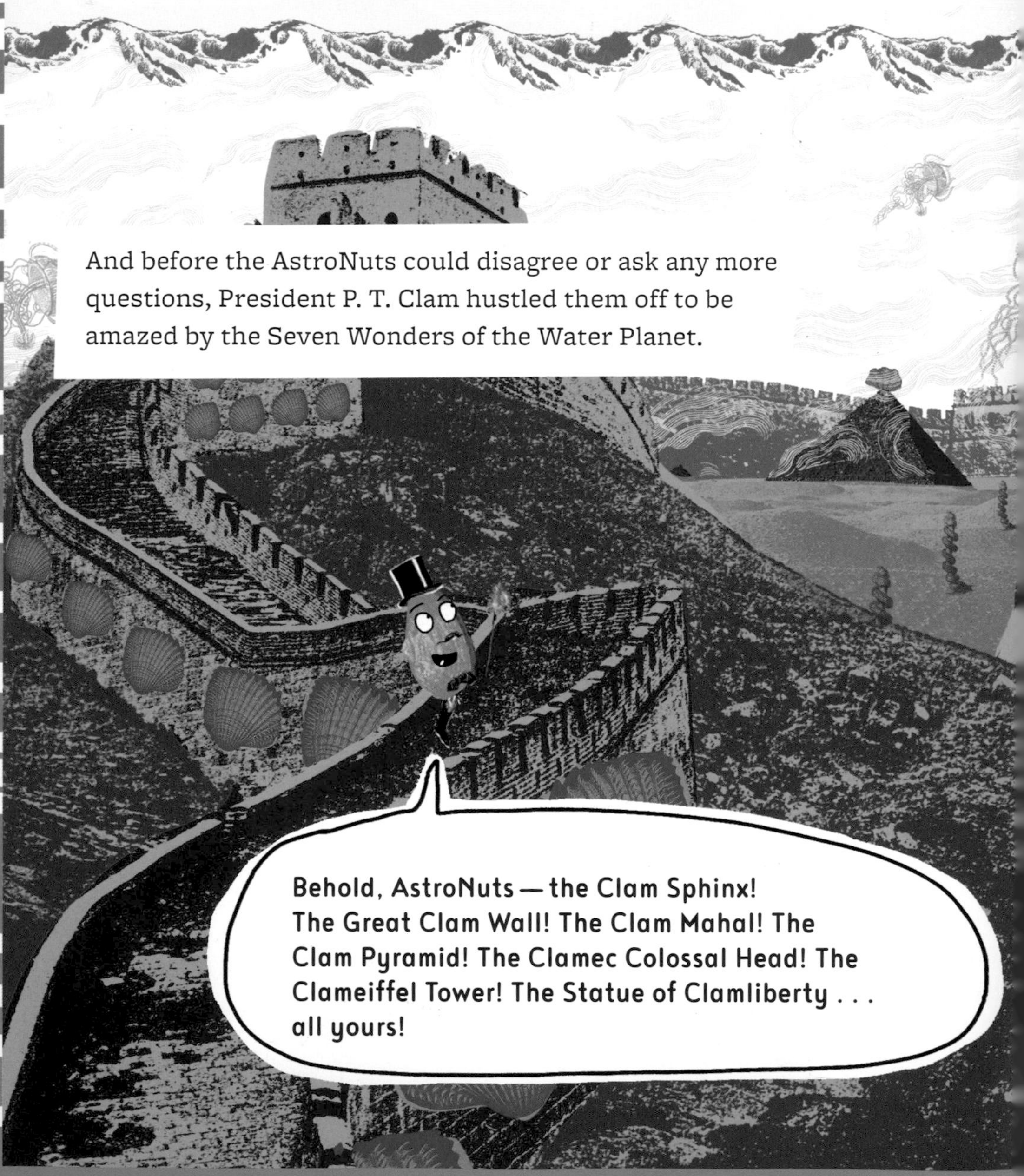
Behold, AstroNuts — the Clam Sphinx! The Great Clam Wall! The Clam Mahal! The Clam Pyramid! The Clamec Colossal Head! The Clameiffel Tower! The Statue of Clamliberty . . . all yours!

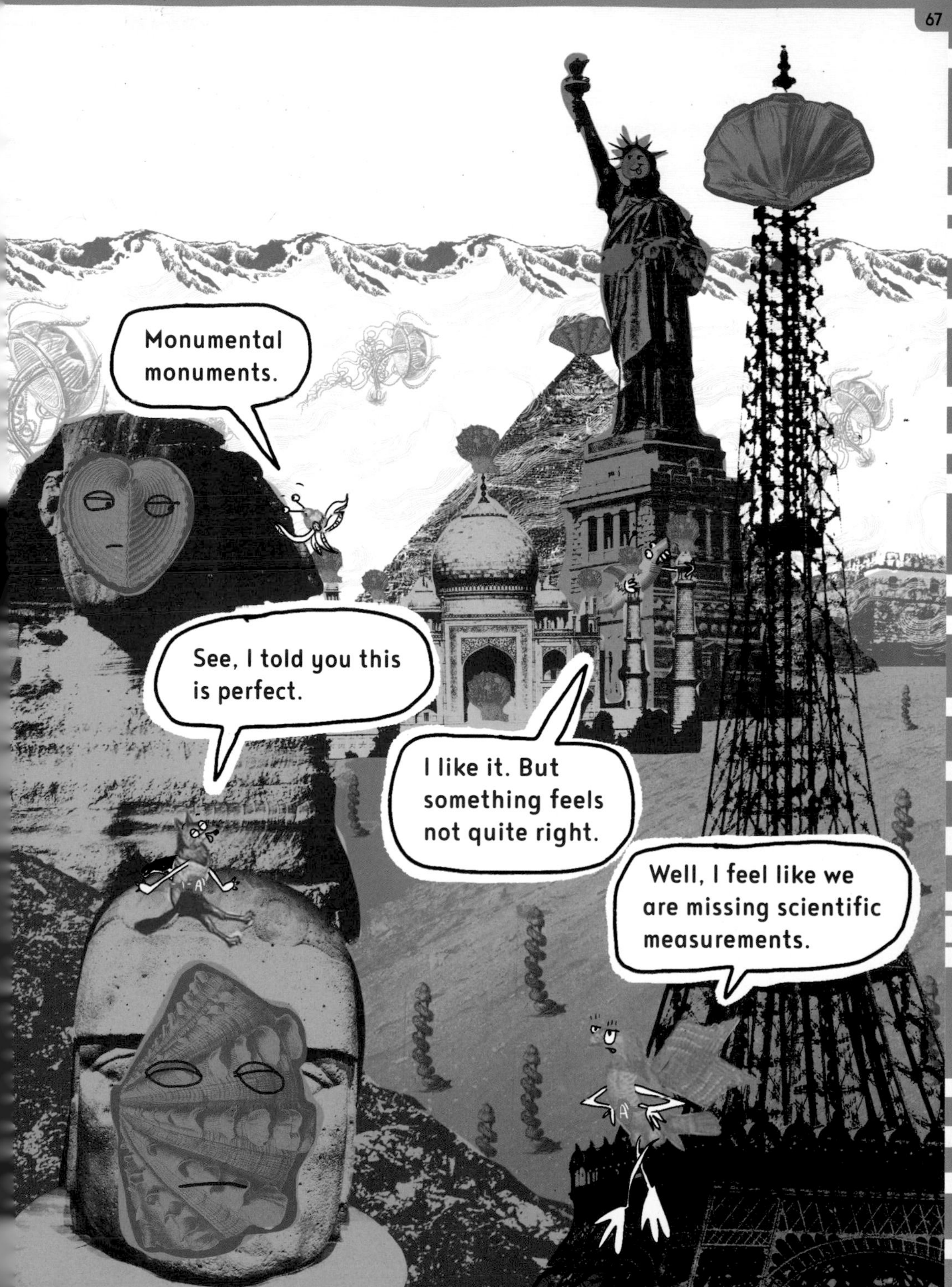
Monumental monuments.
See, I told you this is perfect.
I like it. But something feels not quite right.
Well, I feel like we are missing scientific measurements.

As a fellow planet, I have to say I was pretty impressed by the Water Planet tour. Just like humans had become the one main species on me (by using their big brains and working together), the clams had become the main species on the Water Planet. And they had made some very nice things.

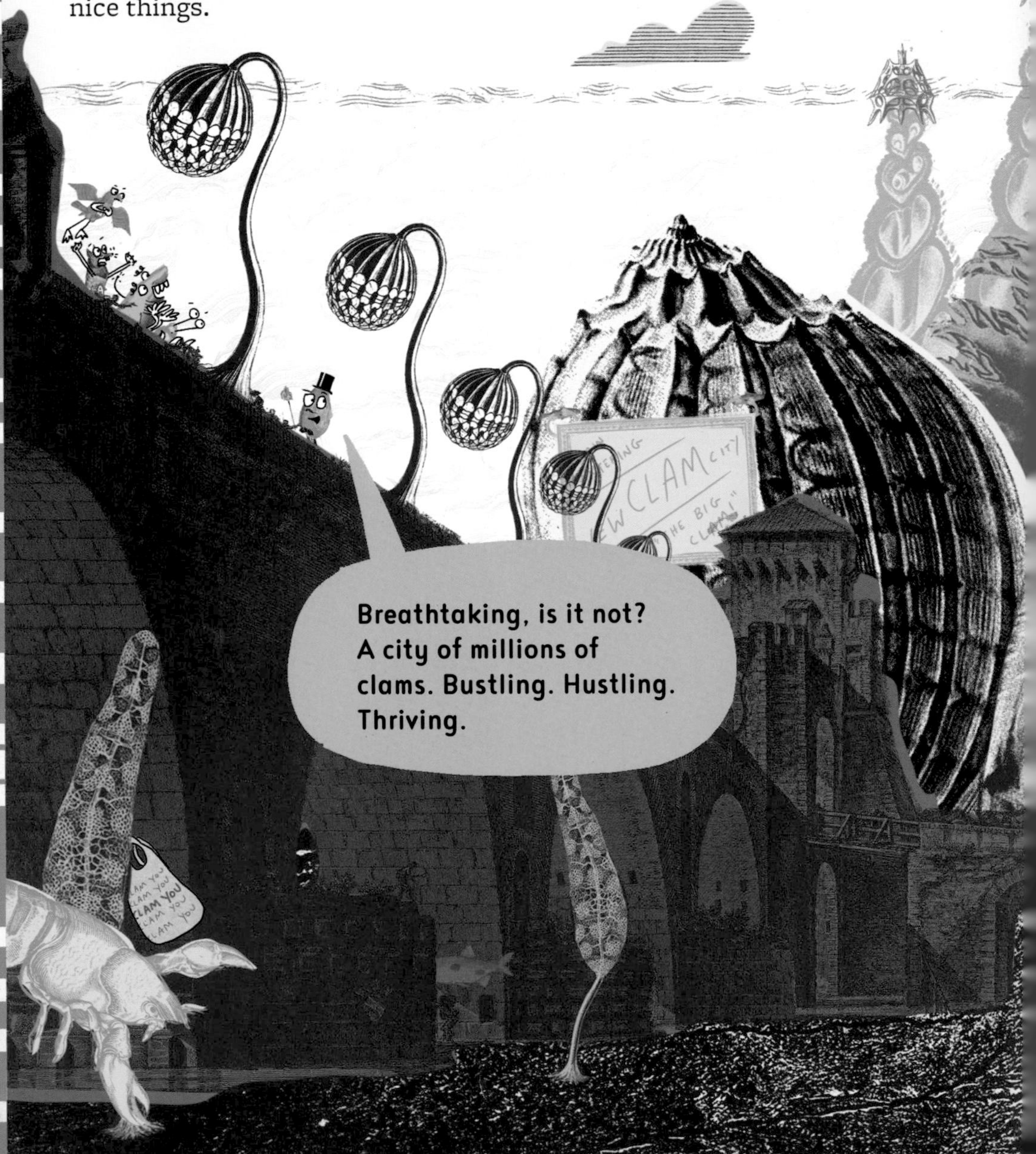
Breathtaking, is it not? A city of millions of clams. Bustling. Hustling. Thriving.

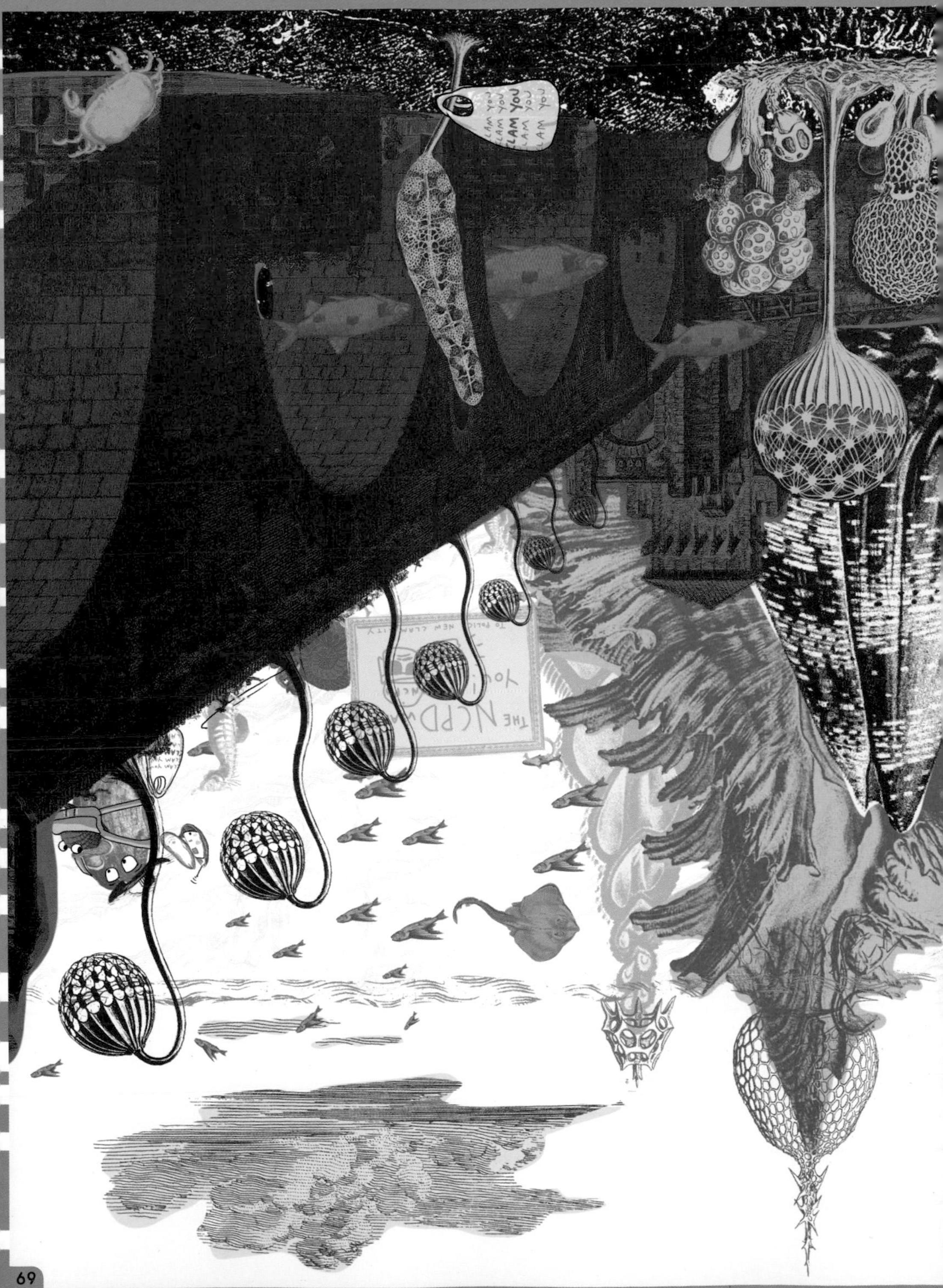

Then again, have you ever had someone try to talk you into something you weren't sure about? And it felt like they were trying too hard? And it felt like this something was too good to be true?

That's what this tour felt like.

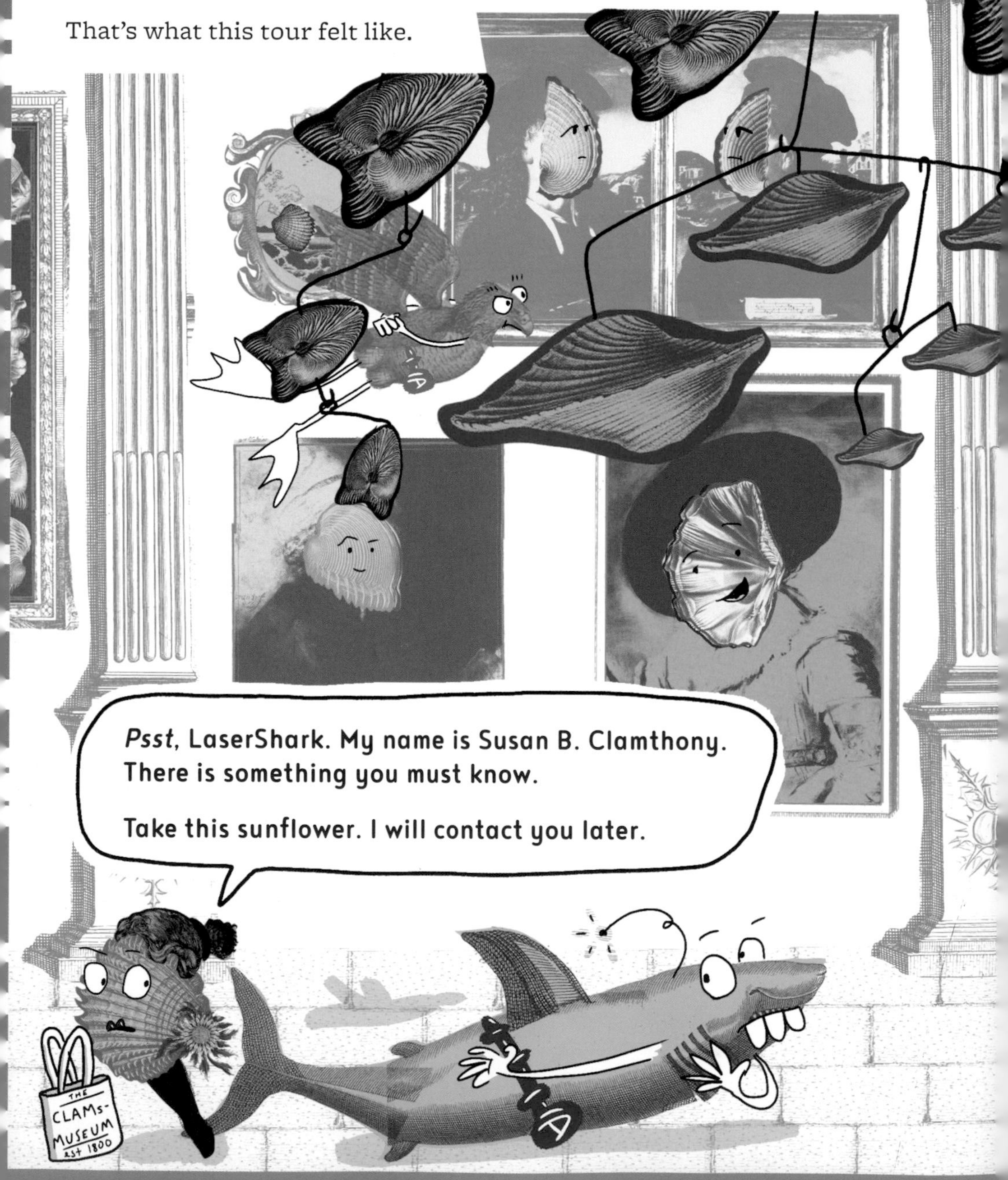
Psst, LaserShark. My name is Susan B. Clamthony. There is something you must know.
Take this sunflower. I will contact you later.
THE CLAMS-MUSEUM
est 1800

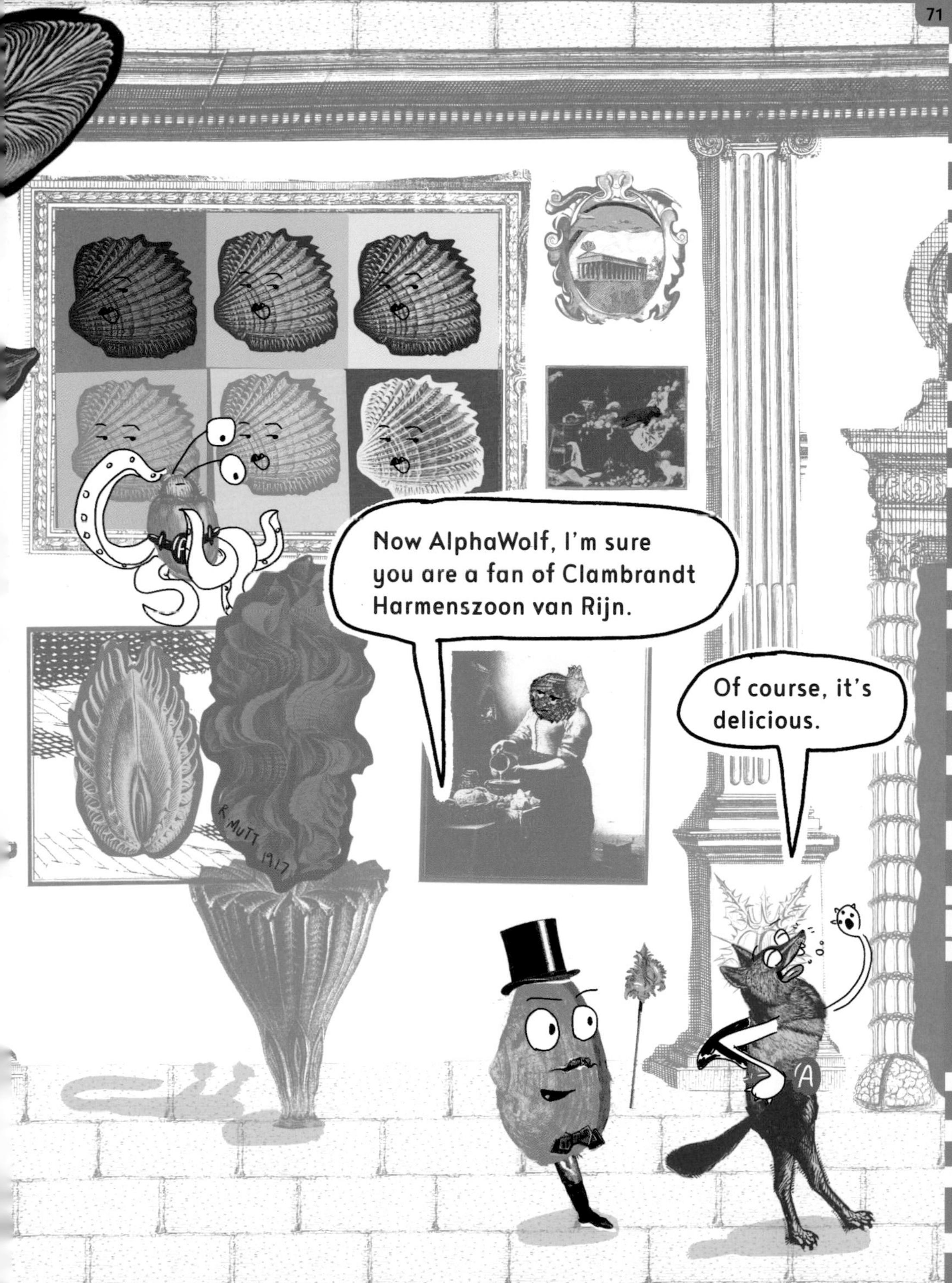
Now AlphaWolf, I'm sure you are a fan of Clambrandt Harmenszoon van Rijn.
Of course, it's delicious.
R. MUTT 1917

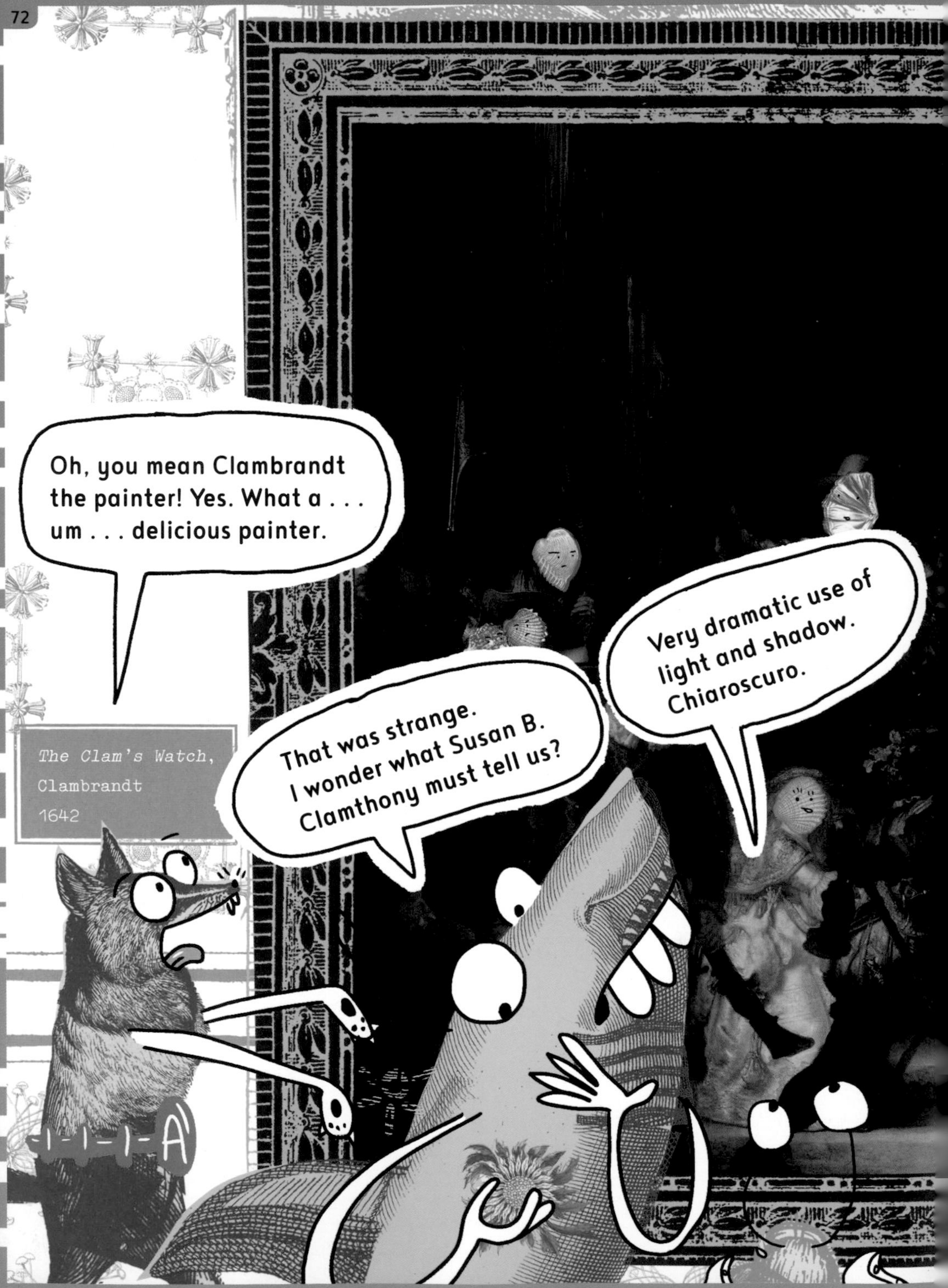
Oh, you mean Clambrandt the painter! Yes. What a . . . um . . . delicious painter.
The Clam's Watch, Clambrandt 1642
That was strange. I wonder what Susan B. Clamthony must tell us?
Very dramatic use of light and shadow. Chiaroscuro.
A-I-I-I-I

This is all wonderful, President Clam. But it doesn't really help us with our scientific investigations.
But of course! Which is why we have arranged a Serious Scientific Look for each one of you, covering each one of your areas of study.
But first . . .

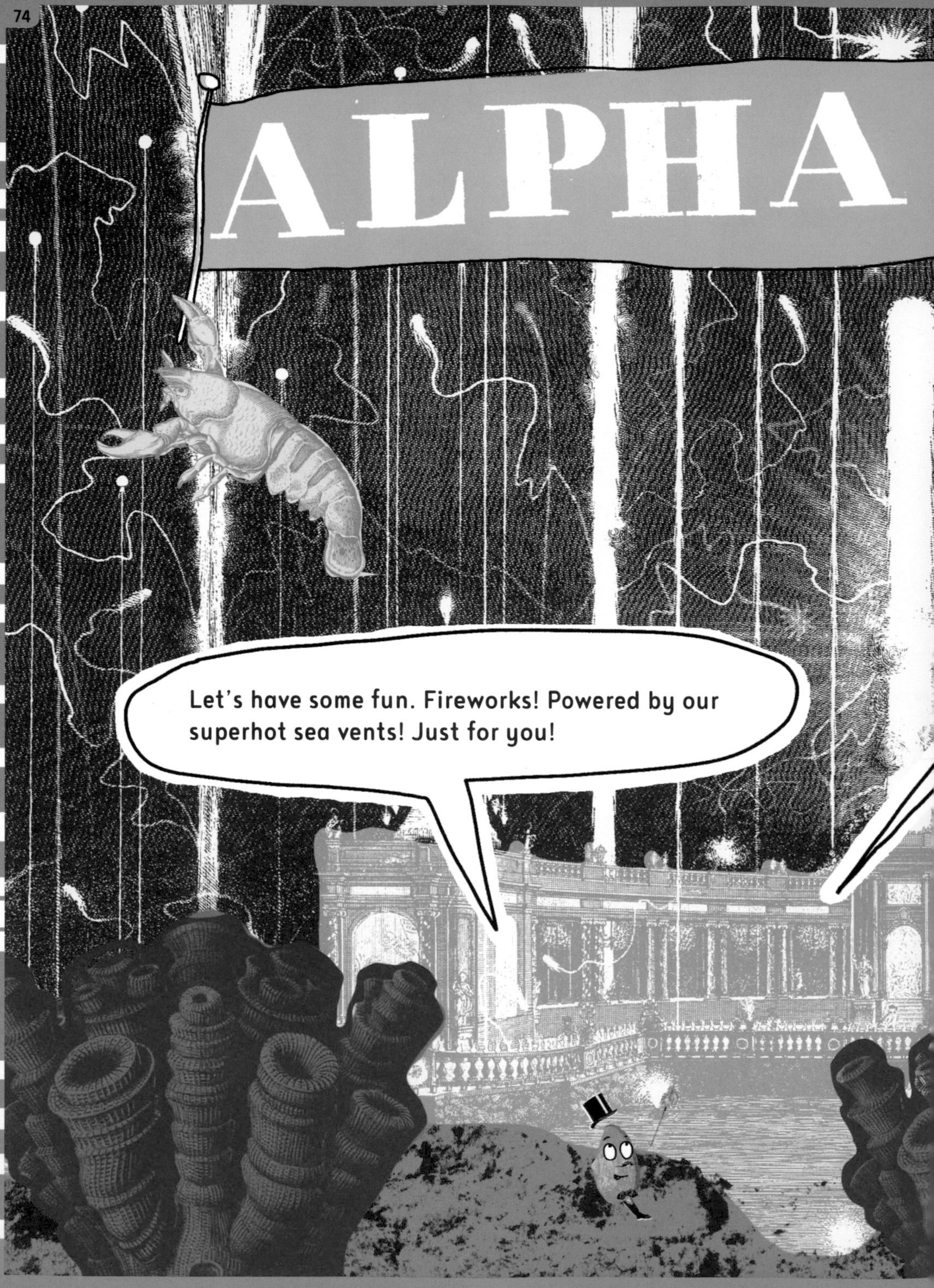
ALPHA
Let's have some fun. Fireworks! Powered by our superhot sea vents! Just for you!

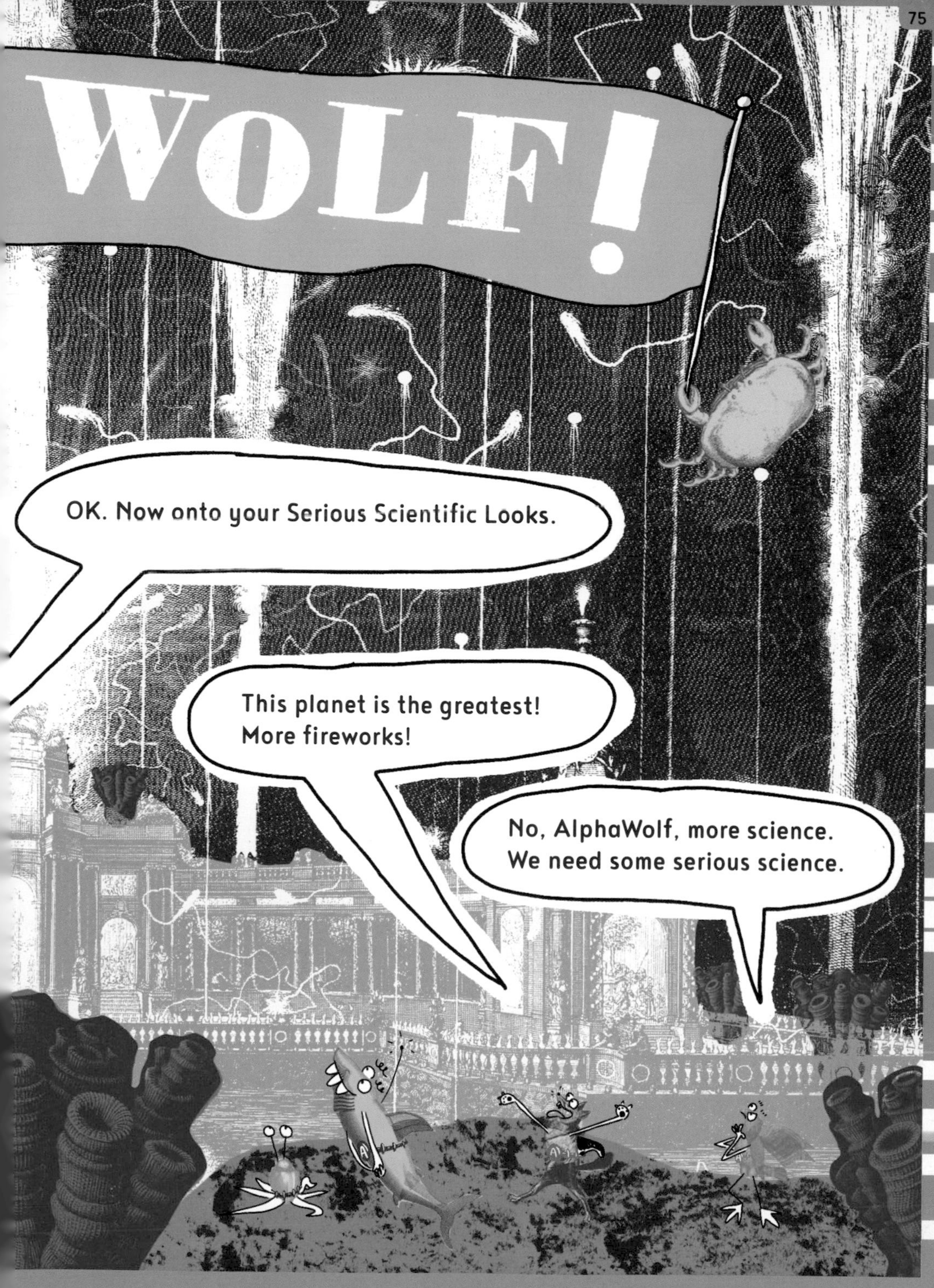
WOLF!
OK. Now onto your Serious Scientific Looks.
This planet is the greatest! More fireworks!
No, AlphaWolf, more science. We need some serious science.

CHAPTER 9:
Aquaculture

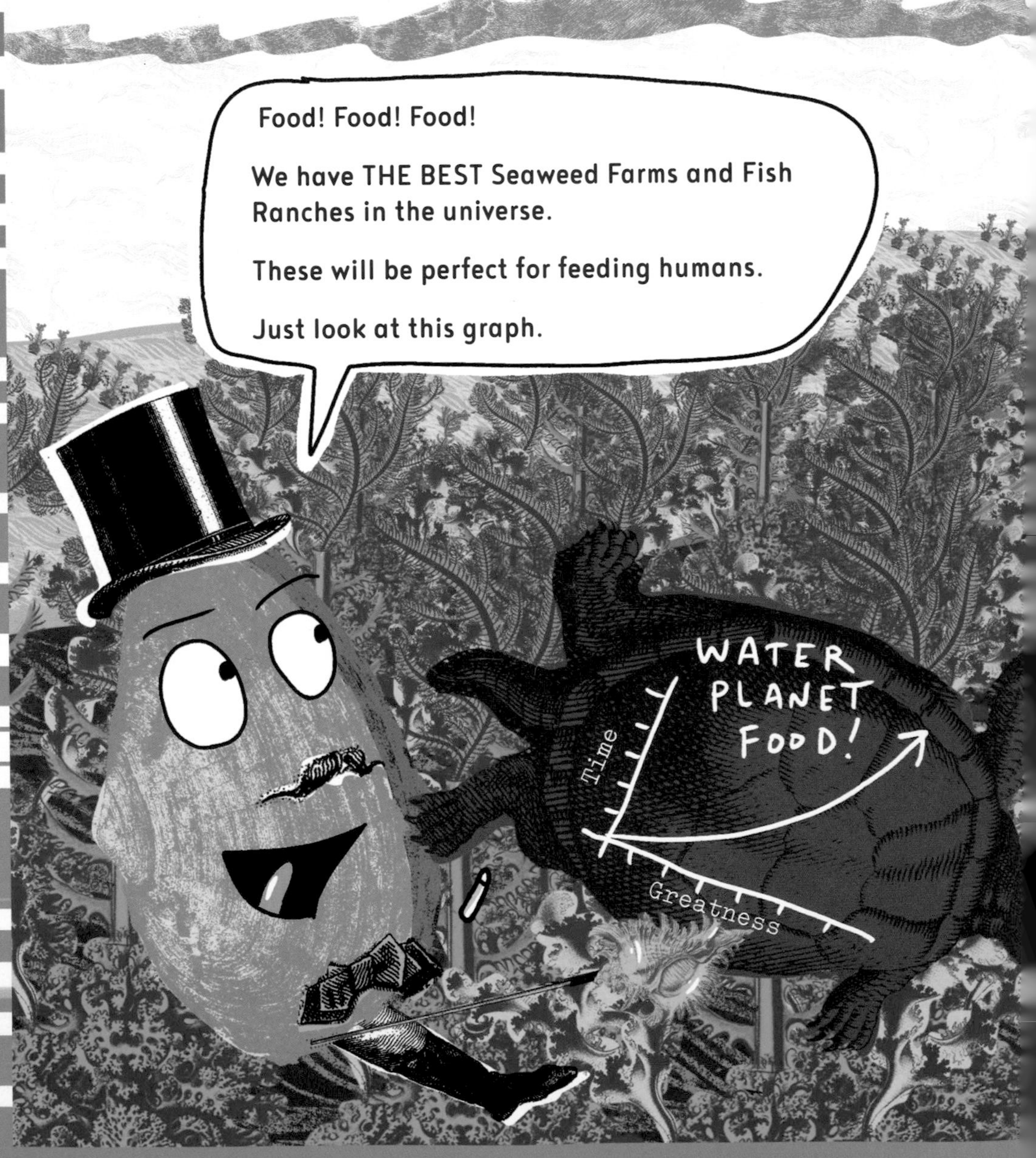
Food! Food! Food!
We have THE BEST Seaweed Farms and Fish Ranches in the universe.
These will be perfect for feeding humans.
Just look at this graph.
WATER PLANET FOOD!
Time
Greatness

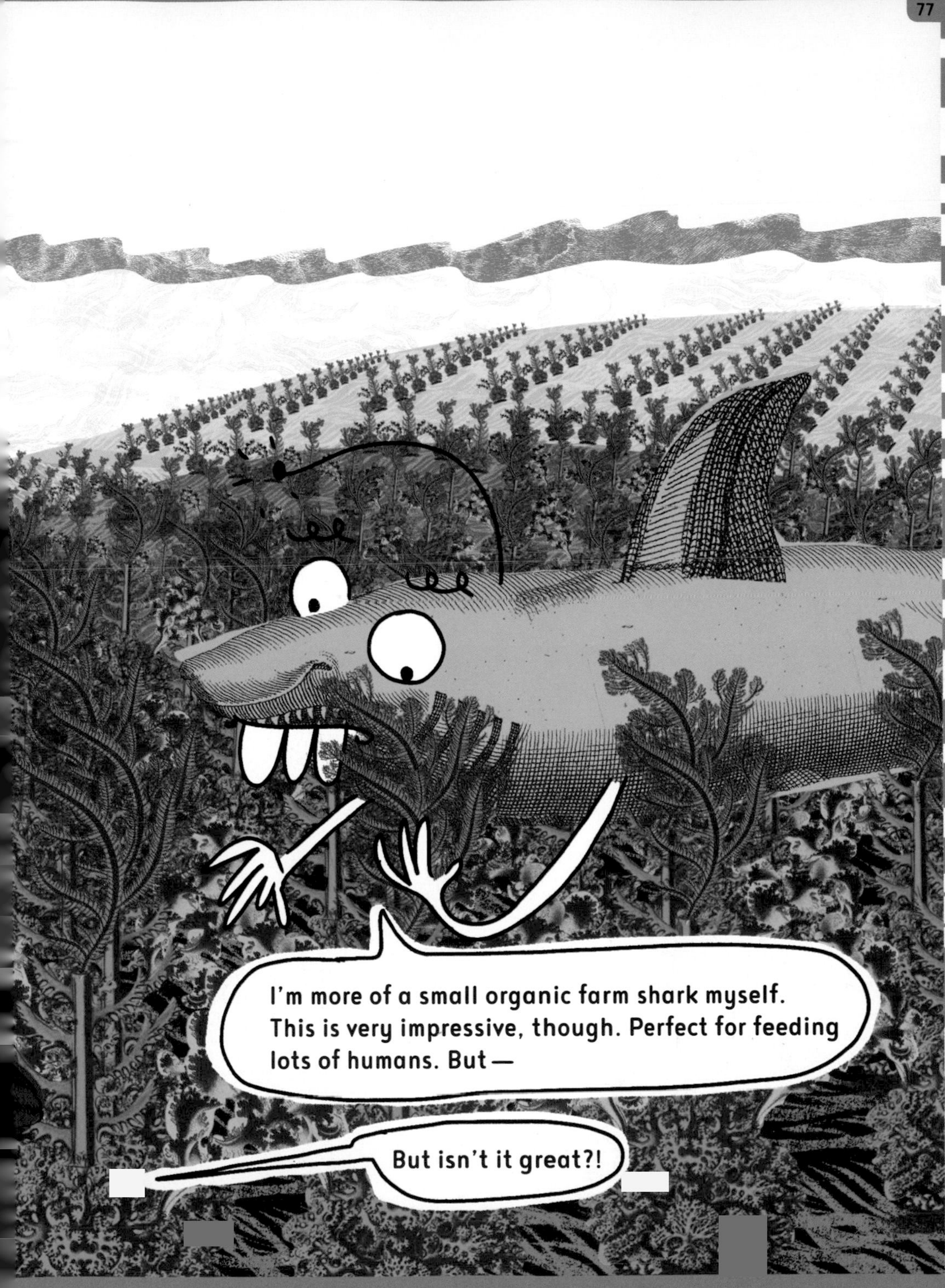
I'm more of a small organic farm shark myself. This is very impressive, though. Perfect for feeding lots of humans. But —
But isn't it great?!

CHAPTER 10:

Coral Condos

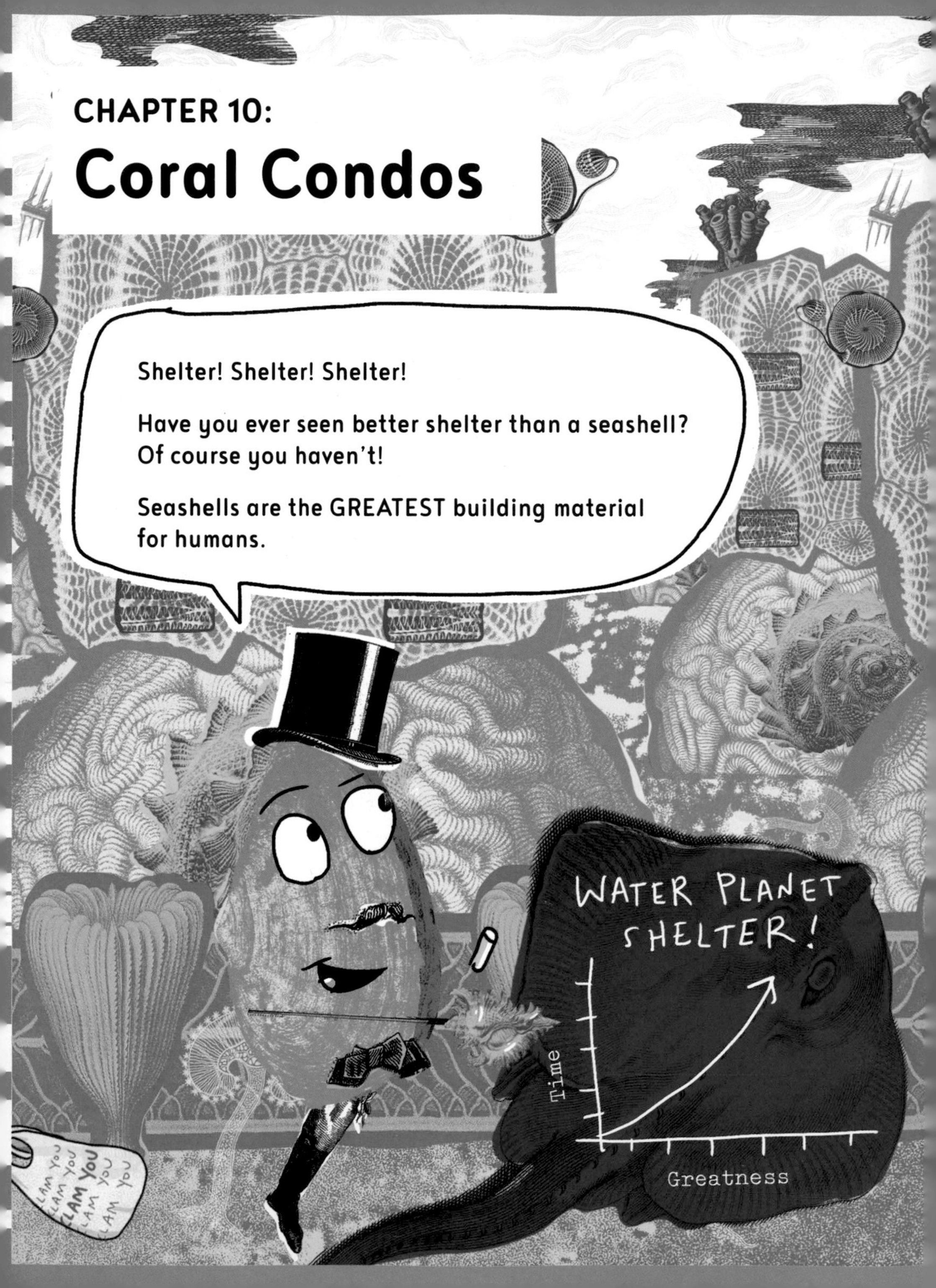
Shelter! Shelter! Shelter!
Have you ever seen better shelter than a seashell? Of course you haven't!
Seashells are the GREATEST building material for humans.
WATER PLANET SHELTER!
Time
Greatness
CLAM YOU CLAM YOU CLAM YOU CLAM YOU CLAM YOU

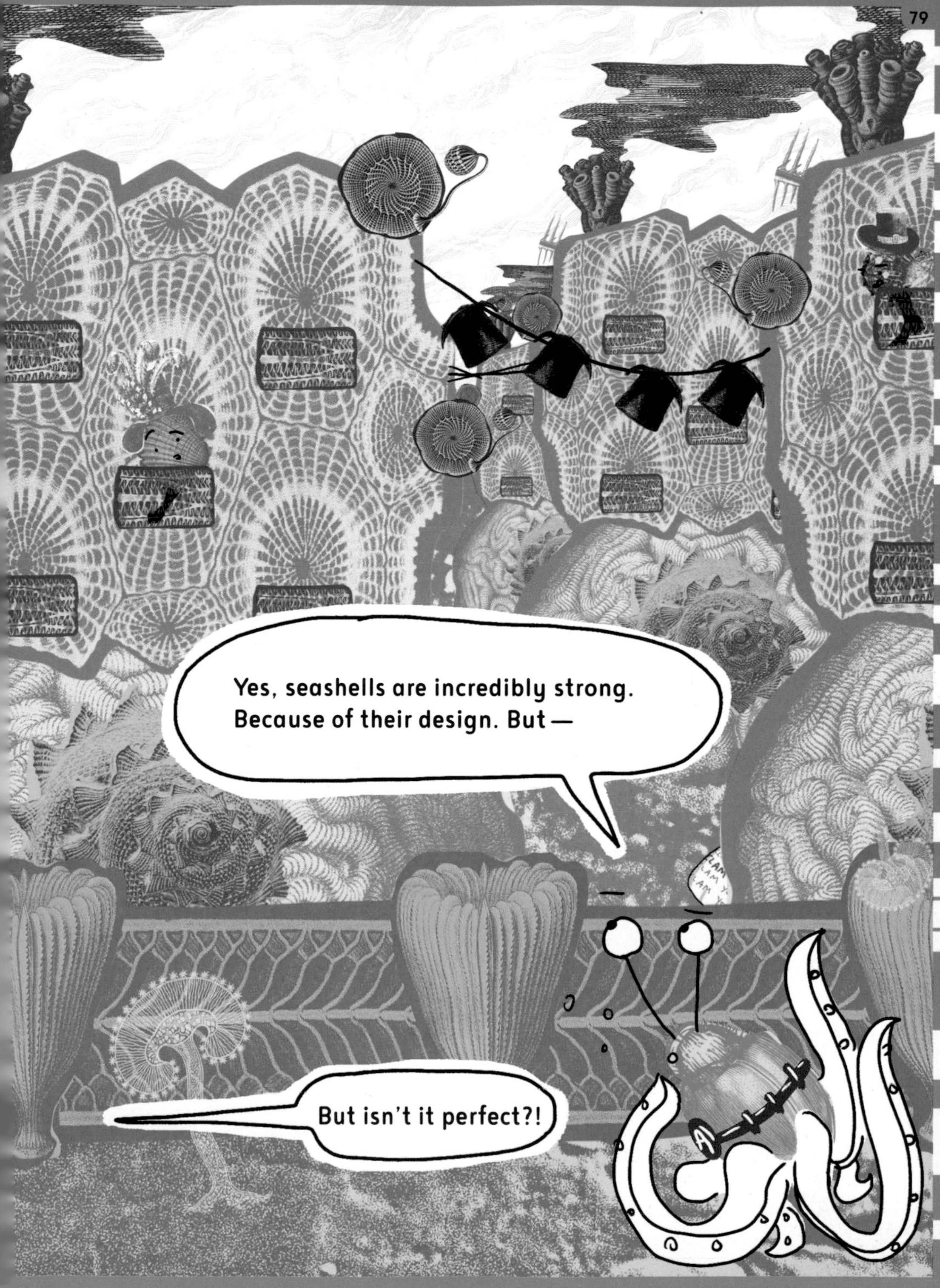
Yes, seashells are incredibly strong. Because of their design. But —
But isn't it perfect?!

CHAPTER 11: Mount Clam Fuji

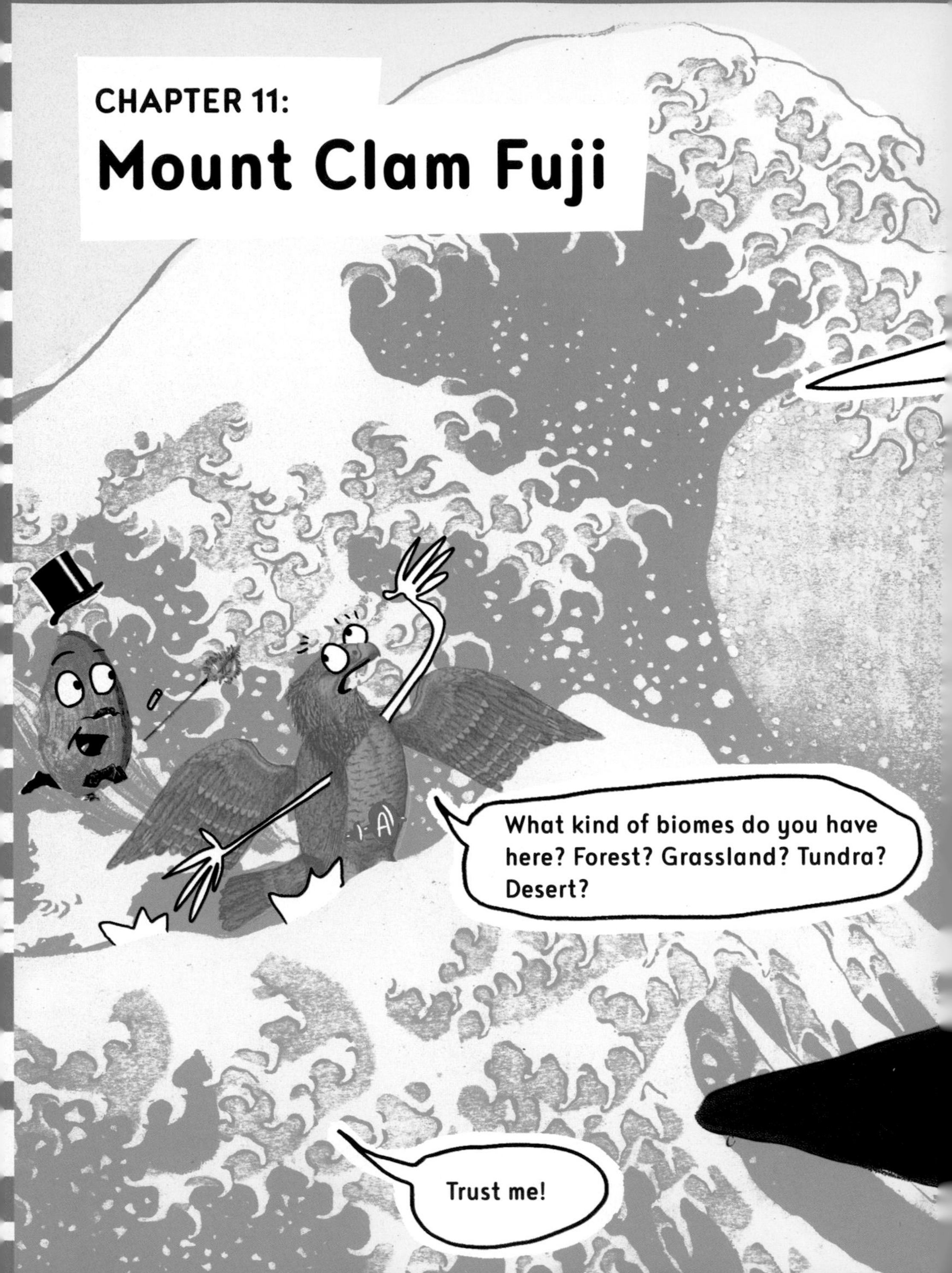
What kind of biomes do you have here? Forest? Grassland? Tundra? Desert?
Trust me!

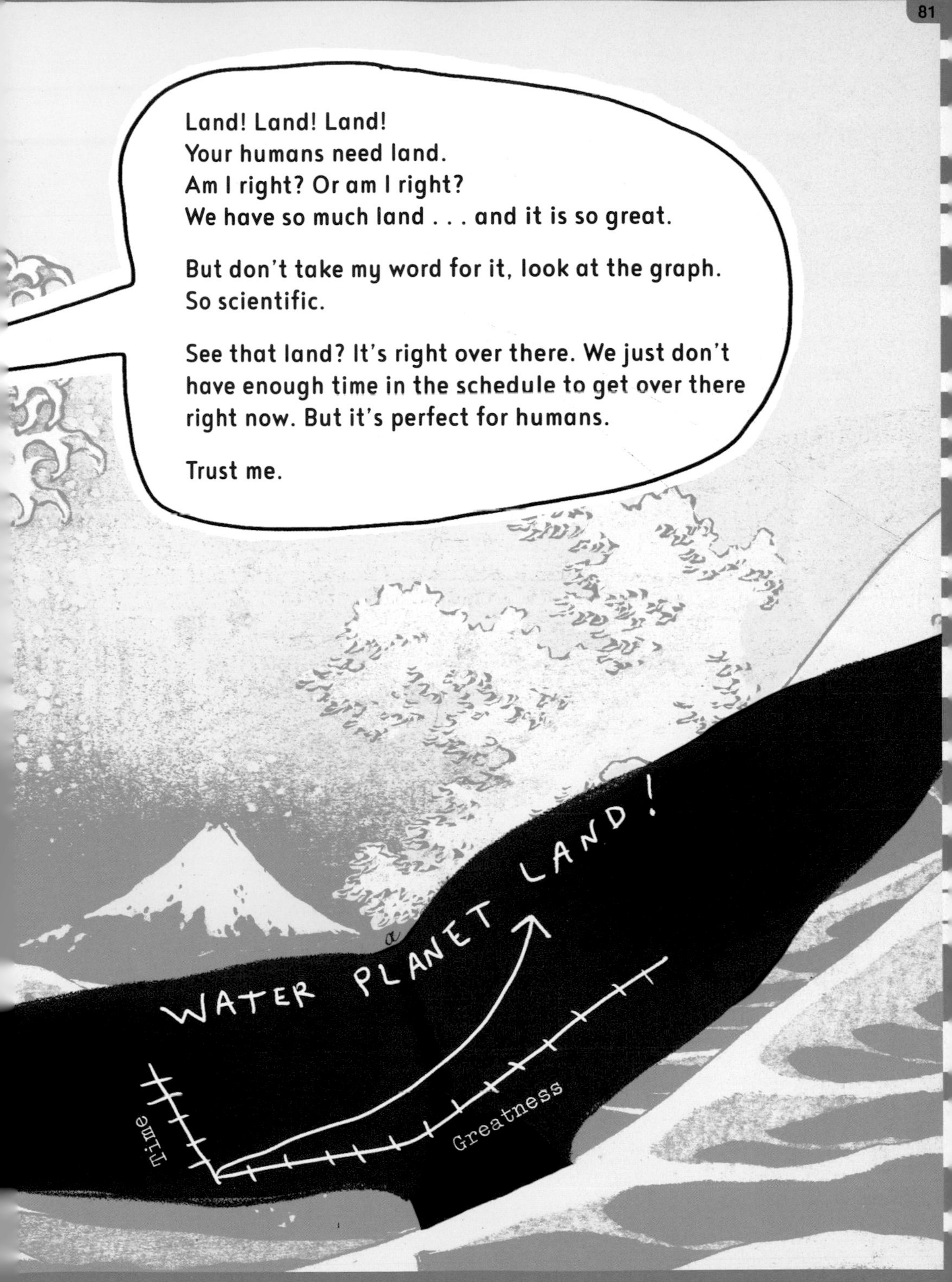
Land! Land! Land!
Your humans need land.
Am I right? Or am I right?
We have so much land . . . and it is so great.
But don't take my word for it, look at the graph.
So scientific.
See that land? It's right over there. We just don't have enough time in the schedule to get over there right now. But it's perfect for humans.
Trust me.
WATER PLANET LAND!
Time
Greatness

CHAPTER 12: Sold!

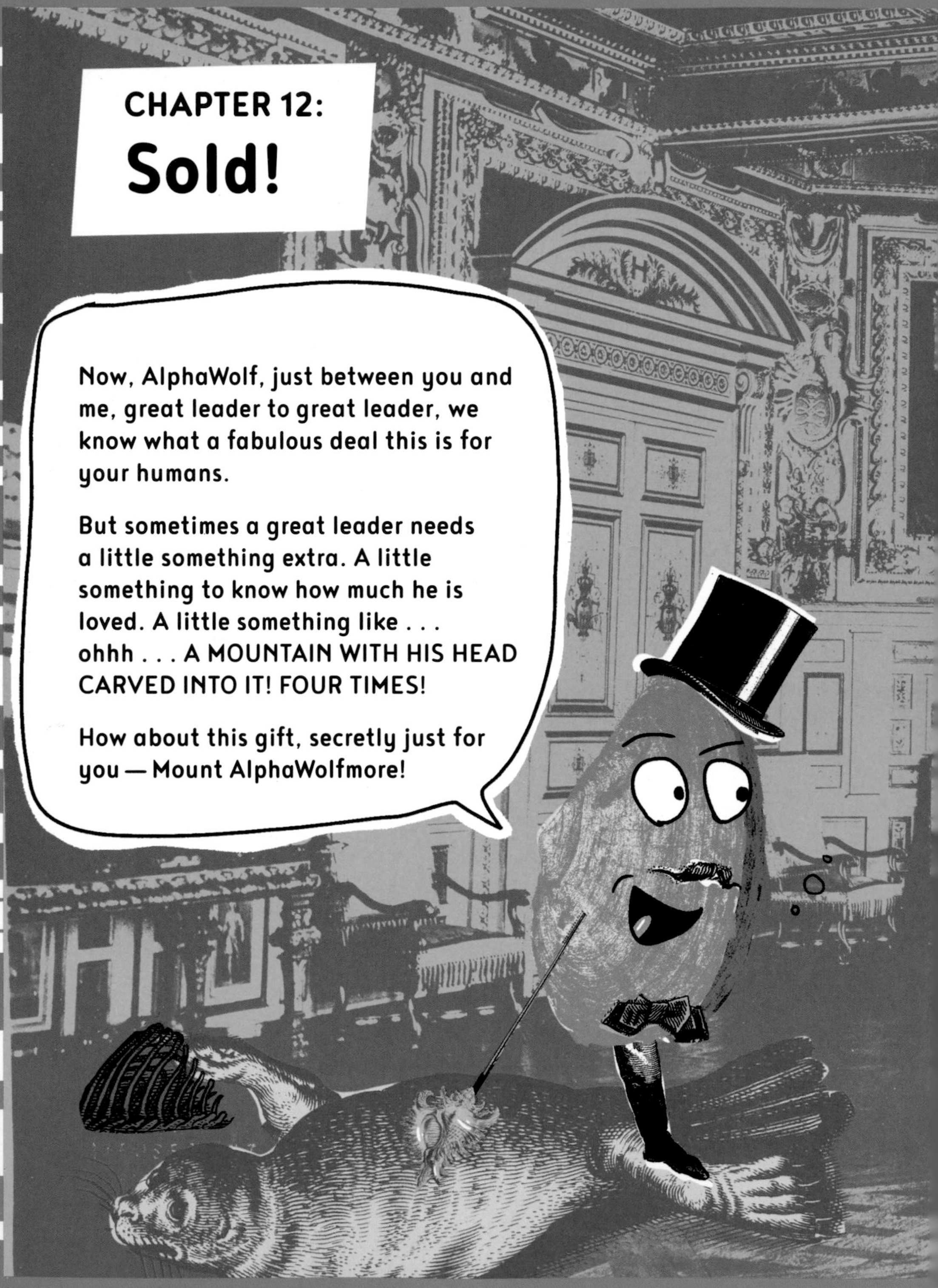
Now, AlphaWolf, just between you and me, great leader to great leader, we know what a fabulous deal this is for your humans.
But sometimes a great leader needs a little something extra. A little something to know how much he is loved. A little something like . . . ohhh . . . A MOUNTAIN WITH HIS HEAD CARVED INTO IT! FOUR TIMES!
How about this gift, secretly just for you — Mount AlphaWolfmore!

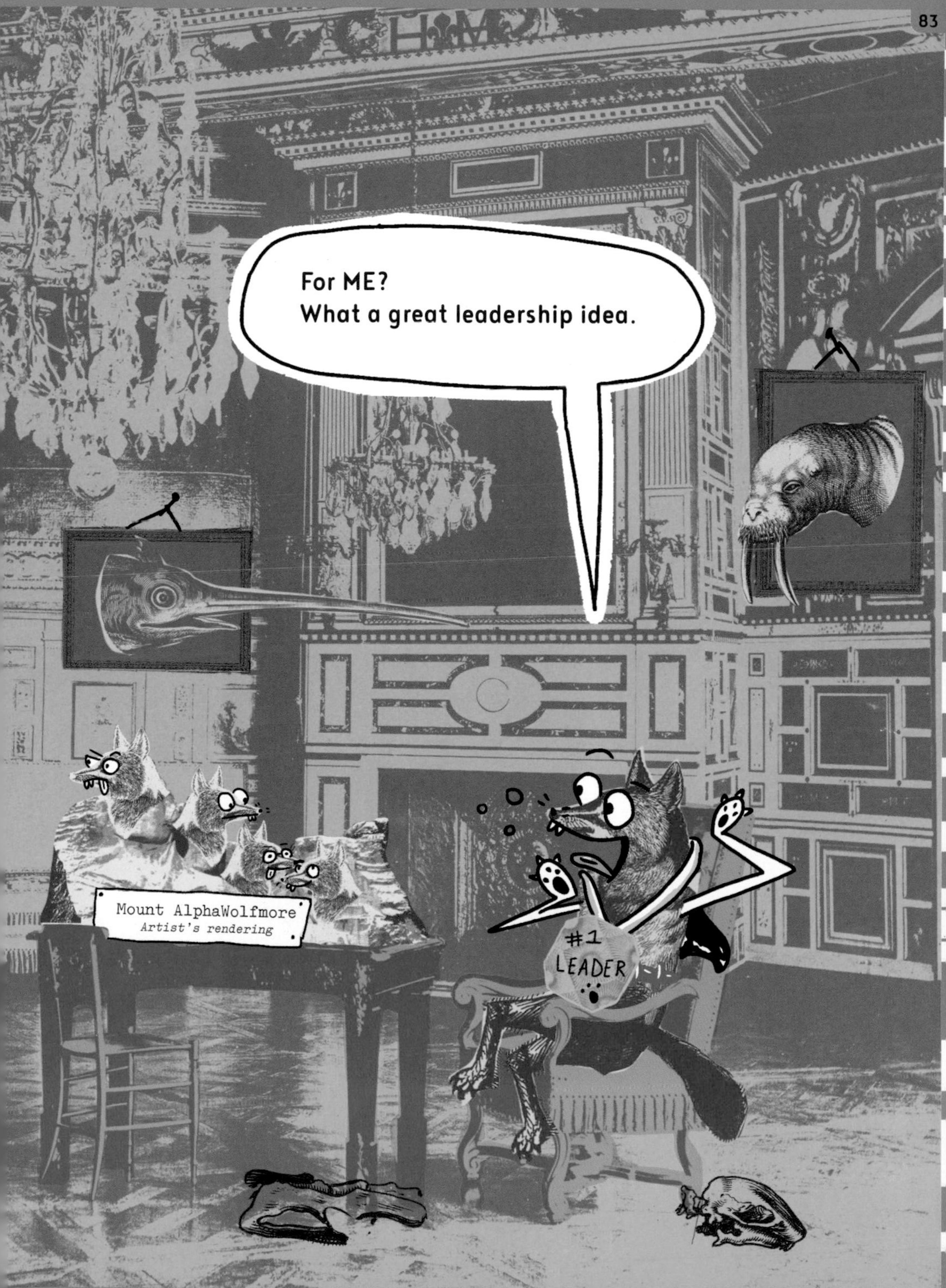
For ME?
What a great leadership idea.
#1 LEADER
Mount AlphaWolfmore
Artist's rendering

CHAPTER 13: Clamliberty for All!

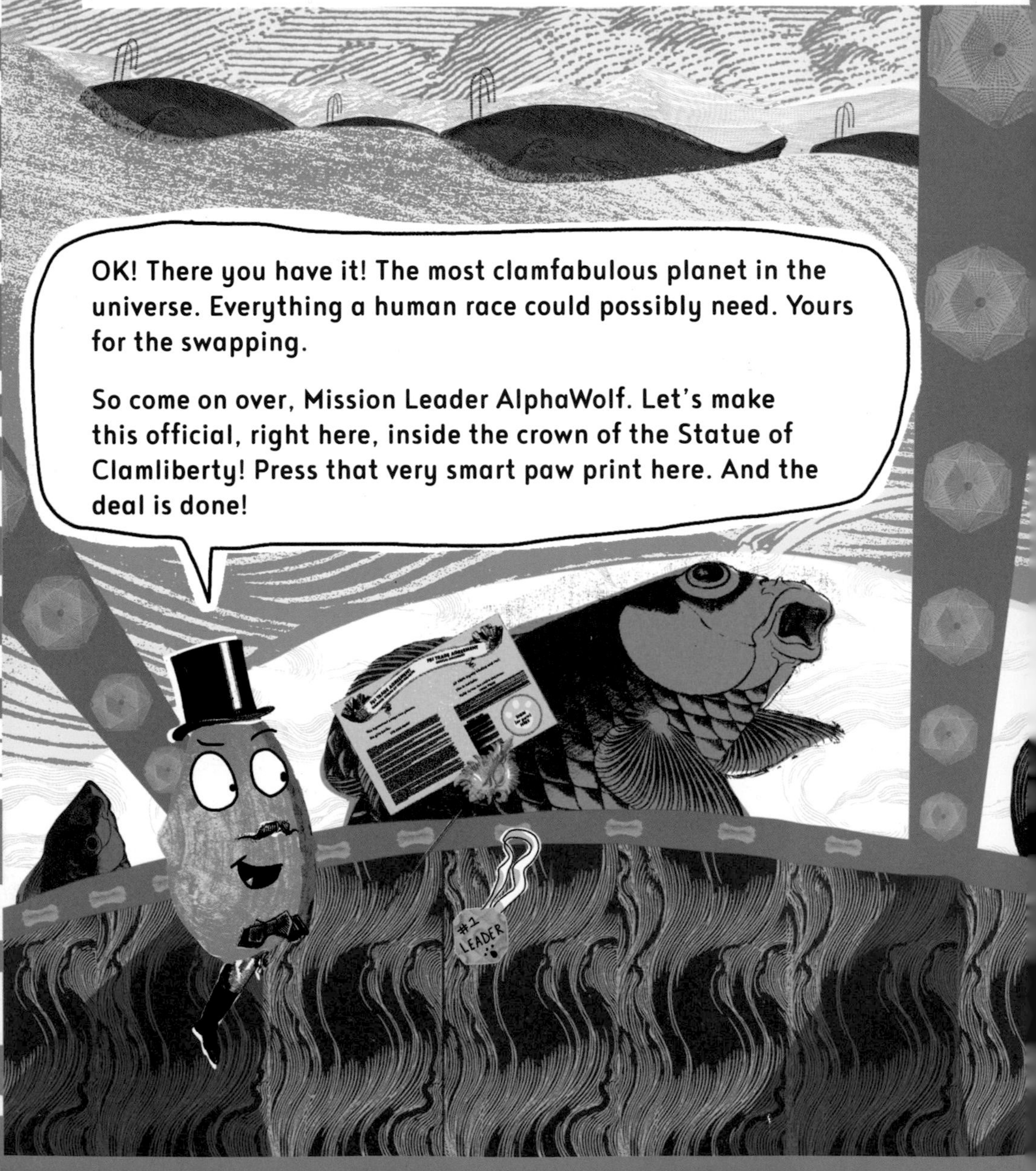
OK! There you have it! The most clamfabulous planet in the universe. Everything a human race could possibly need. Yours for the swapping.
So come on over, Mission Leader AlphaWolf. Let's make this official, right here, inside the crown of the Statue of Clamliberty! Press that very smart paw print here. And the deal is done!
#1 LEADER

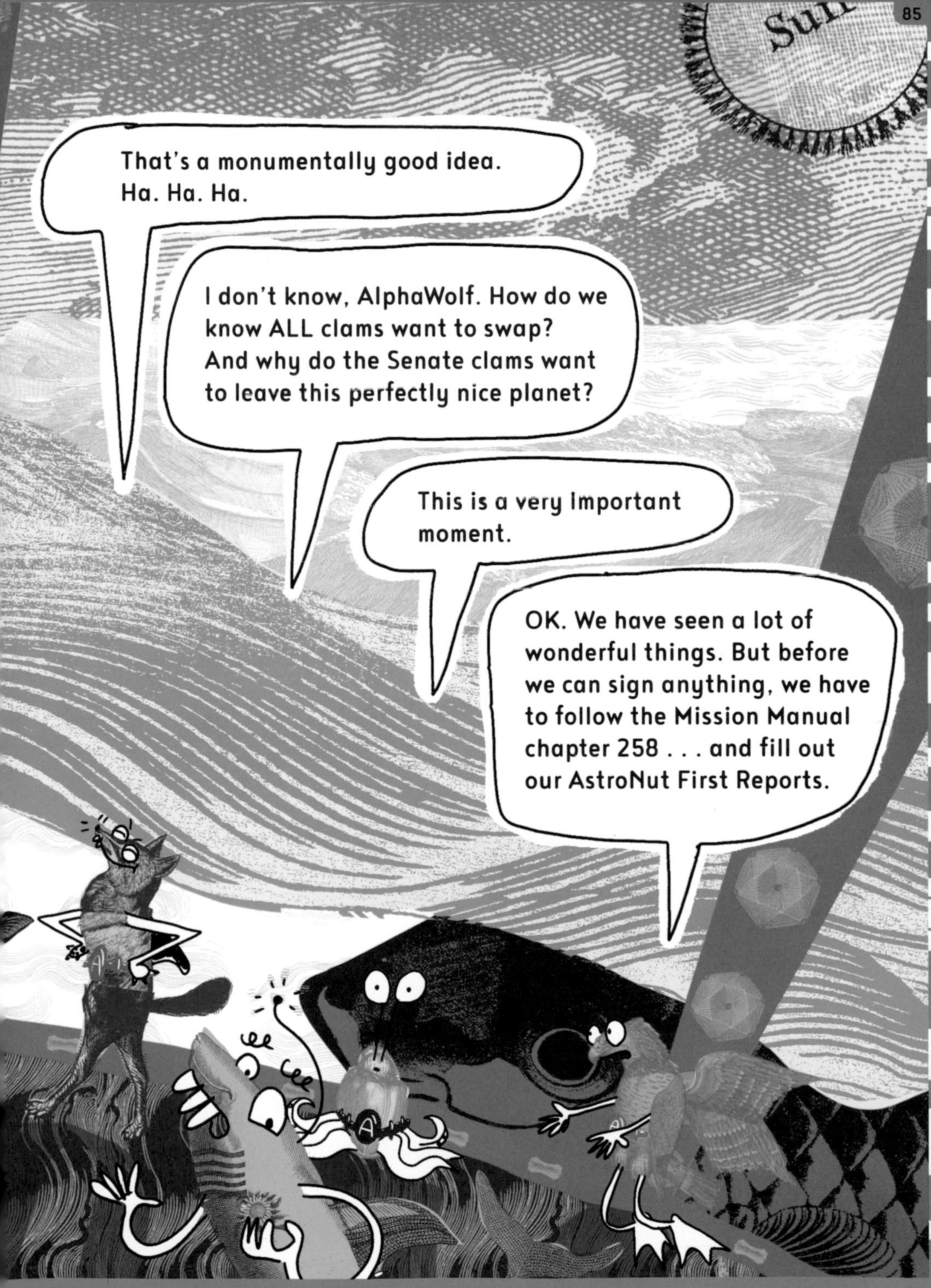
Sun
That's a monumentally good idea. Ha. Ha. Ha.
I don't know, AlphaWolf. How do we know ALL clams want to swap? And why do the Senate clams want to leave this perfectly nice planet?
This is a very Important moment.
OK. We have seen a lot of wonderful things. But before we can sign anything, we have to follow the Mission Manual chapter 258 . . . and fill out our AstroNut First Reports.

The AstroNuts quickly swam back to the Nose Rocket, a little more informed, a little more amazed, but also a little more confused about this Water Planet.

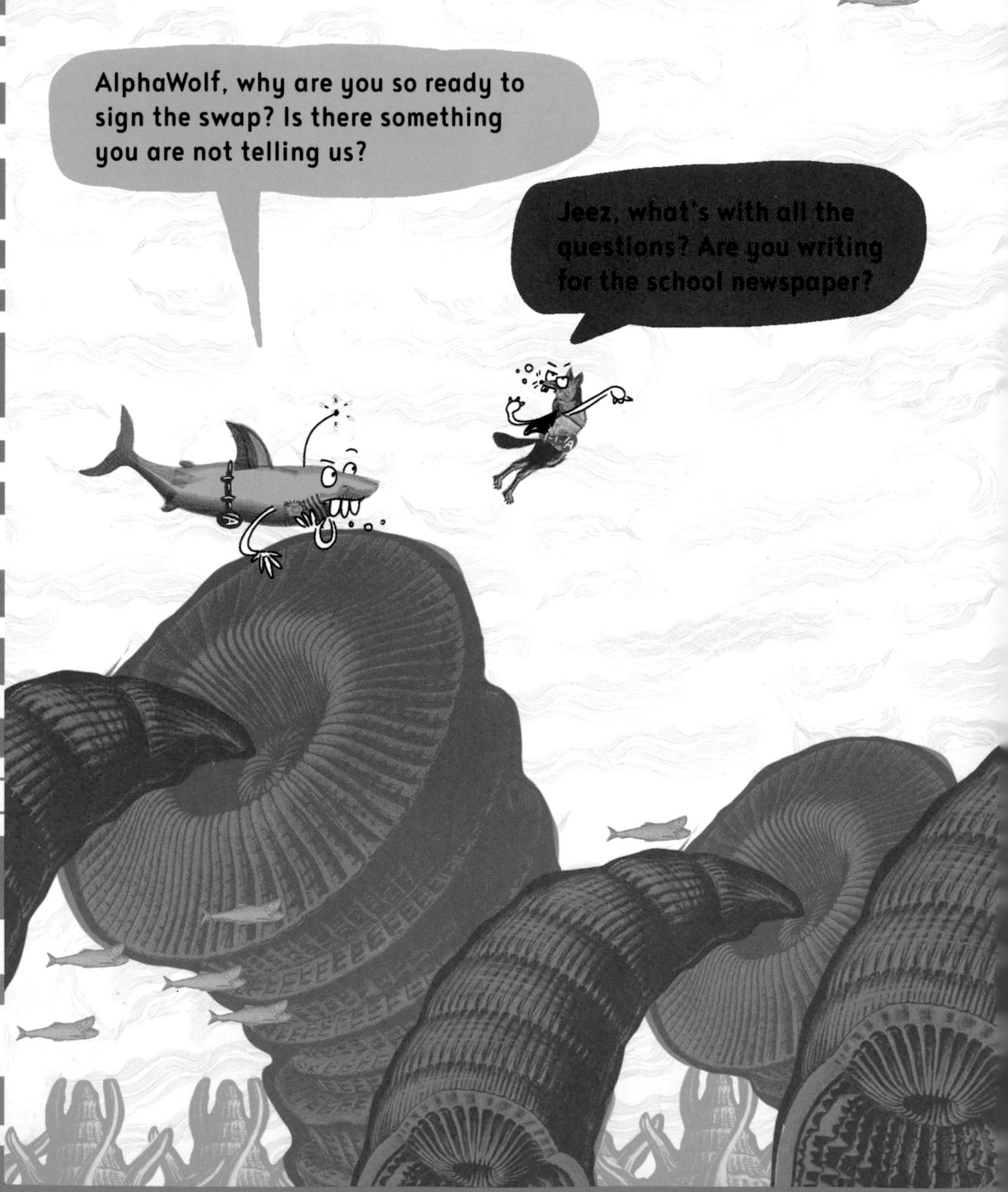
AlphaWolf, why are you so ready to sign the swap? Is there something you are not telling us?
Jeez, what's with all the questions? Are you writing for the school newspaper?

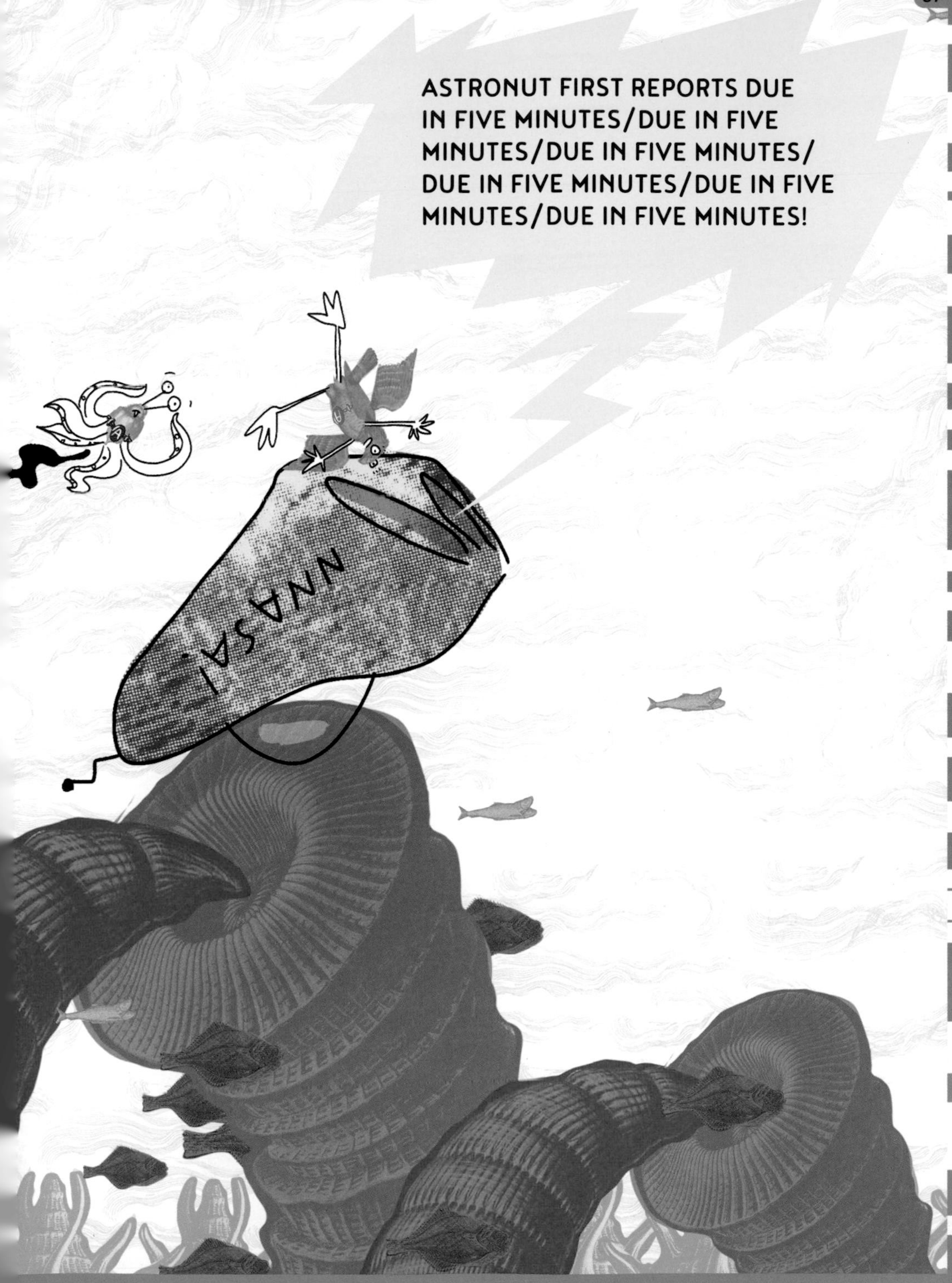
ASTRONUT FIRST REPORTS DUE IN FIVE MINUTES/DUE IN FIVE MINUTES/DUE IN FIVE MINUTES/ DUE IN FIVE MINUTES/DUE IN FIVE MINUTES/DUE IN FIVE MINUTES!
NNASA!

Yes, the NNASA report clock was ticking down. But the science needed to be done. The AstroNuts worried that they wouldn't be able to finish their reports in time.

NNASA!

REPORT

Why are we even writing these stupid things?

Let's just swap. It's a great idea.

It's not like these NNASA rules are carved in stone. On a mountain. Ha, ha!

The clock is ticking.

AW

PT

But then there was a knock on the Nose . . .

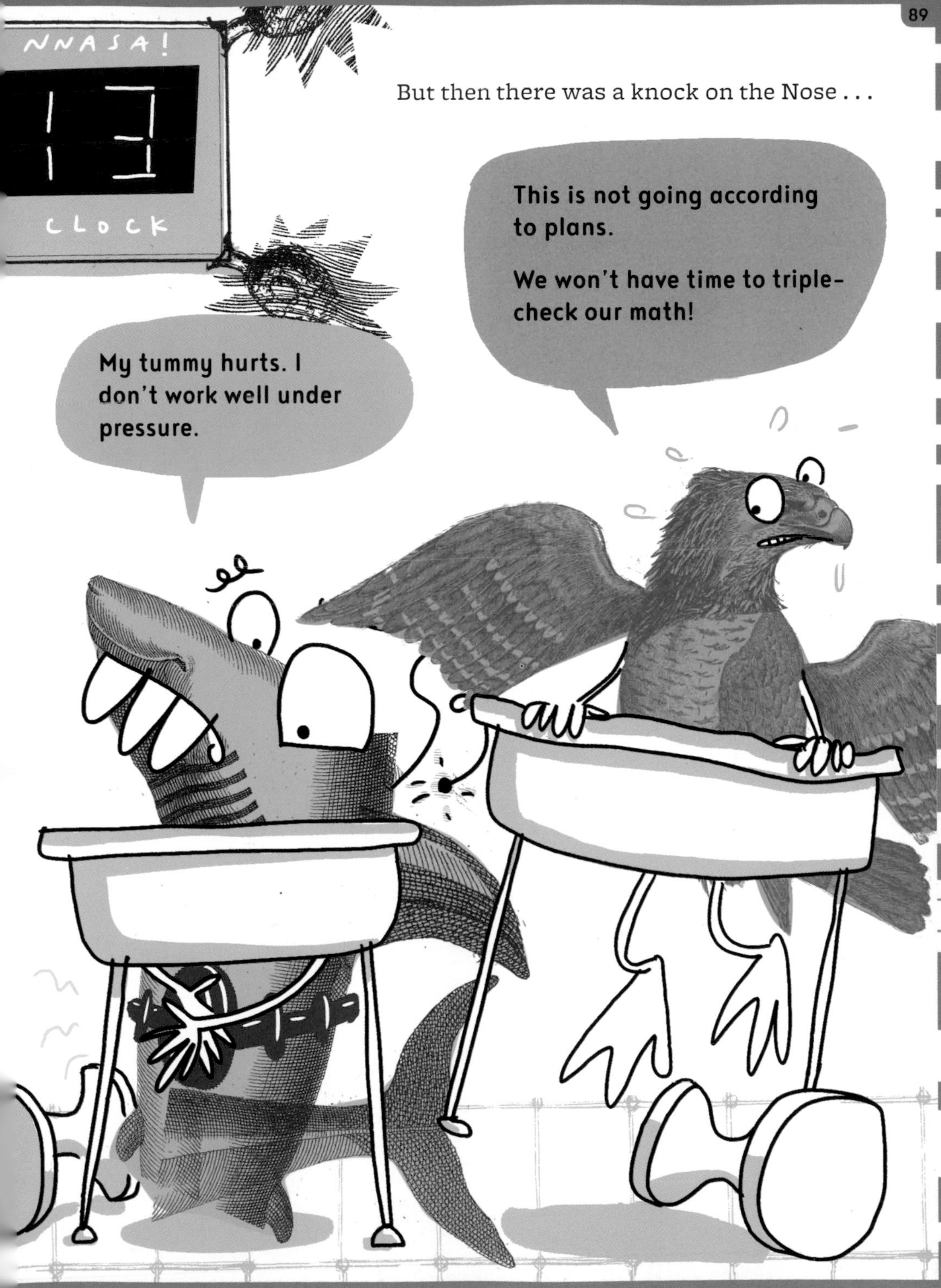
NNASA!
13
CLOCK
This is not going according to plans.
We won't have time to triple-check our math!
My tummy hurts. I don't work well under pressure.

CHAPTER 14: Nose Knockin'

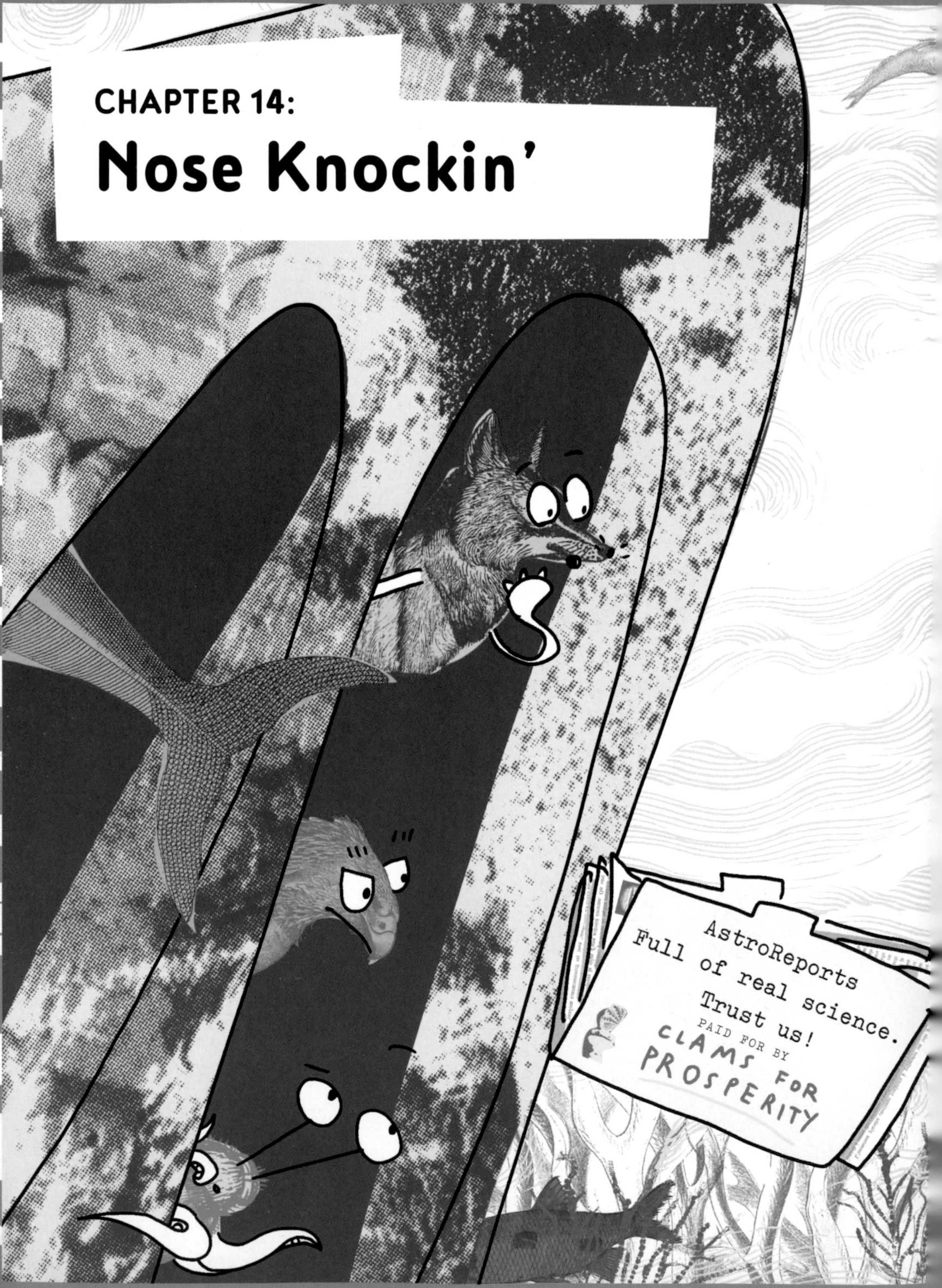
AstroReports
Full of real science.
Trust us!
PAID FOR BY
CLAMS FOR
PROSPERITY

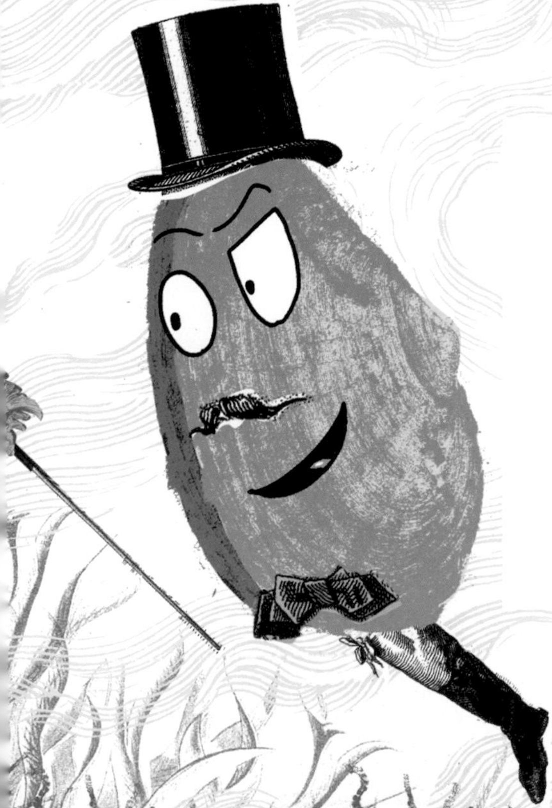
Hello, AstroNuts! I was just passing by. And I thought to myself, those AstroNuts work so hard. I should be a good clam friend and help out.
So I brought these reports for you. They are all finished!

I don't mean to sound like a nag, repeating myself. But again, if something you hear from a clam sounds too good to be true, it probably is.

And also—if you are going to have someone else do your homework, you might want to check it.

Which at least SmartHawk did.

WATER PLANET FIRST REPORT

PAID FOR BY

CLAMS FOR PROSPERITY

AstroName: SmartHawk

AstroTitle: The Best Planning and Rules Officer EVER

Looking for: A perfect watery climate and ecosystem

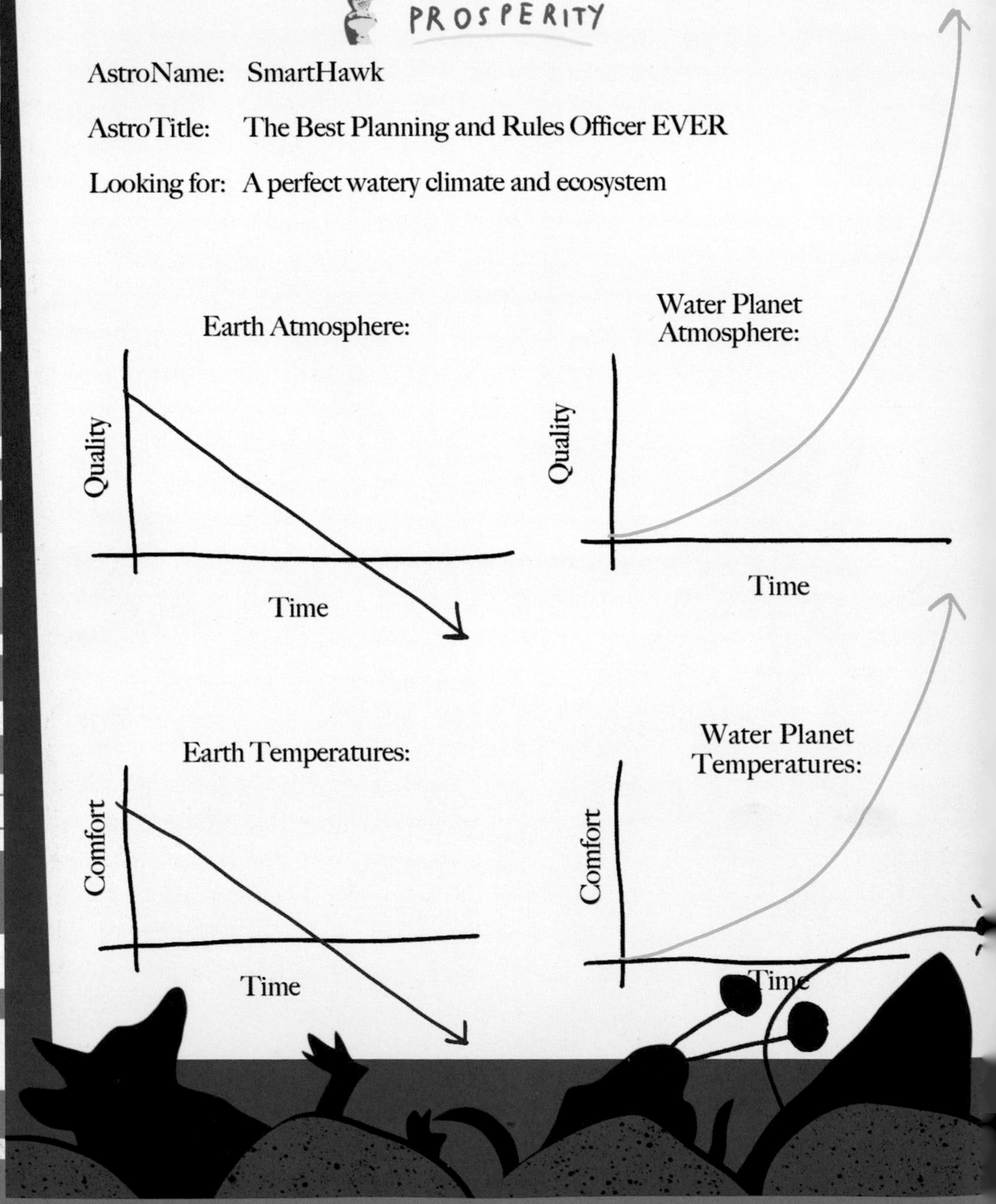
Earth Atmosphere:
Quality
Time
Water Planet Atmosphere:
Quality
Time
Earth Temperatures:
Comfort
Time
Water Planet Temperatures:
Comfort
Time

Earth Ecosystem:

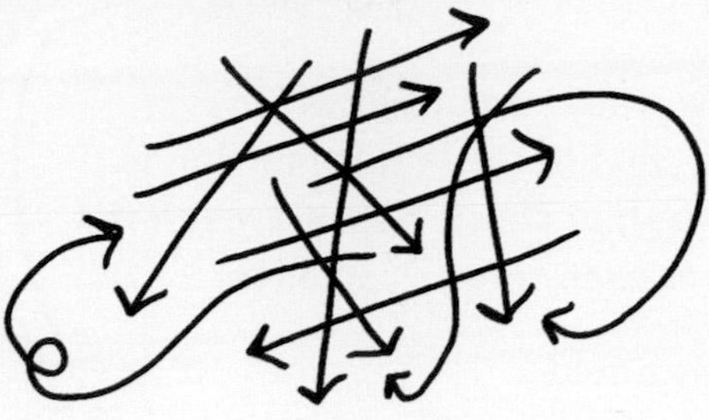

(A MESS.)

Water Planet
Ecosystem:

Humans

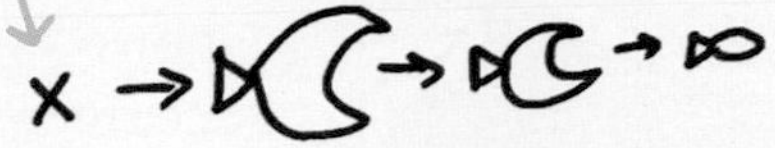

(GREAT!)

101% True Conclusion:

Water Planet is fantastic. We should definitely swap planets. It is the best. Really exceeded expectations. Best planet we've ever seen in all our travels. Across the whole universe there's probably nothing like it. The clams are really great too. And giving us a great deal. A really smart deal. Did I mention it is a great deal? It is! Across the whole universe there's probably nothing like it. The clams are really great too. And giving us a great deal. A really smart deal. Did I mention it is a great deal? It is! Across the whole universe there's probably nothing

… us a great deal. A

… It is!

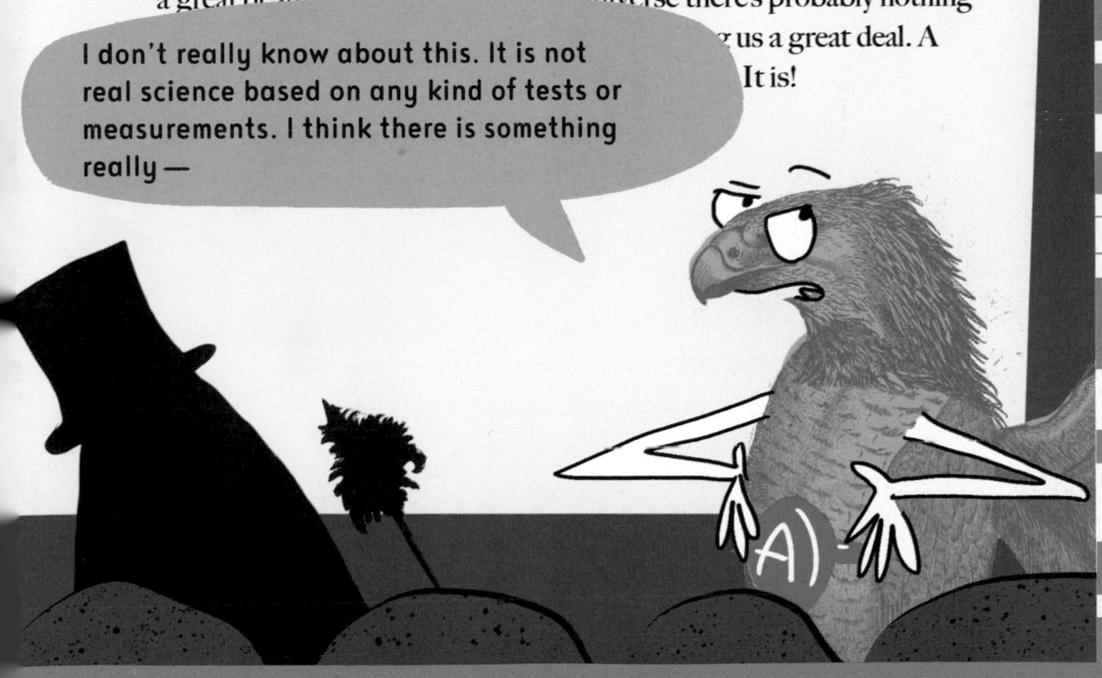
I don't really know about this. It is not real science based on any kind of tests or measurements. I think there is something really —
A)

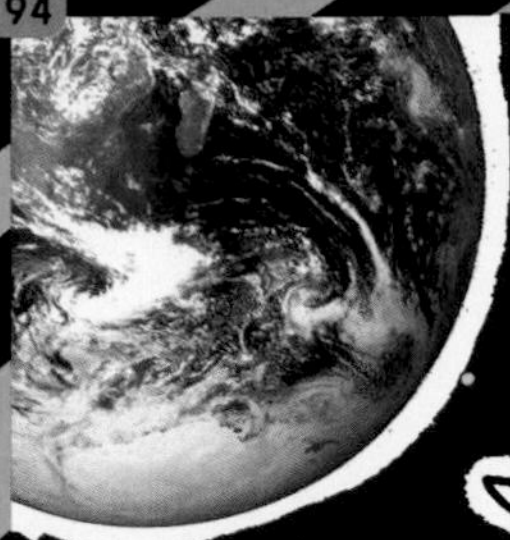

And you know what? SmartHawk was on to something. Just because information is shown in a graph or chart, doesn't mean it's accurate . . . or even true . . . science.

Real science is about:

1. Asking a question.

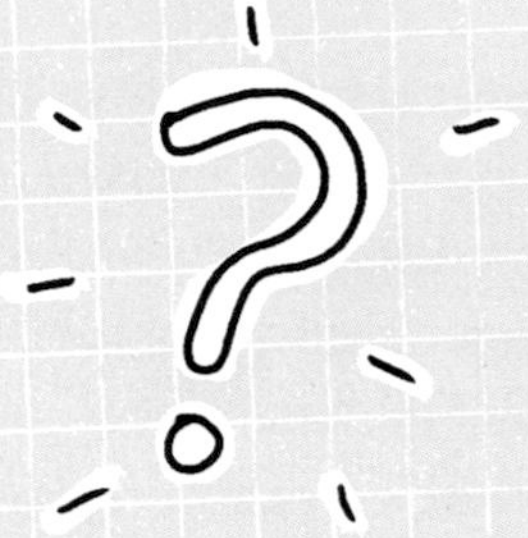

2. Observing and gathering information.

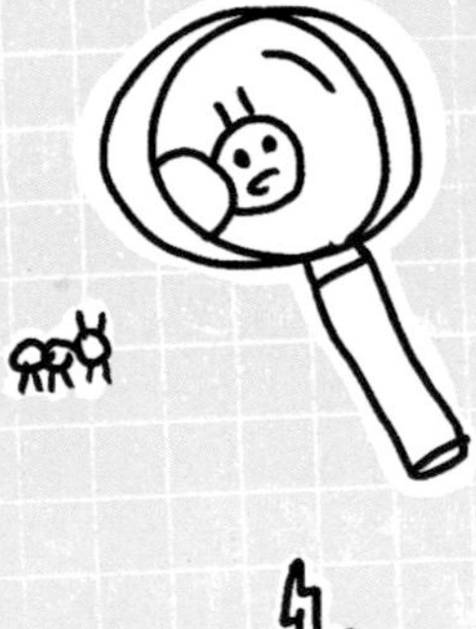

3. Making a guess (called a hypothesis) to answer the question.

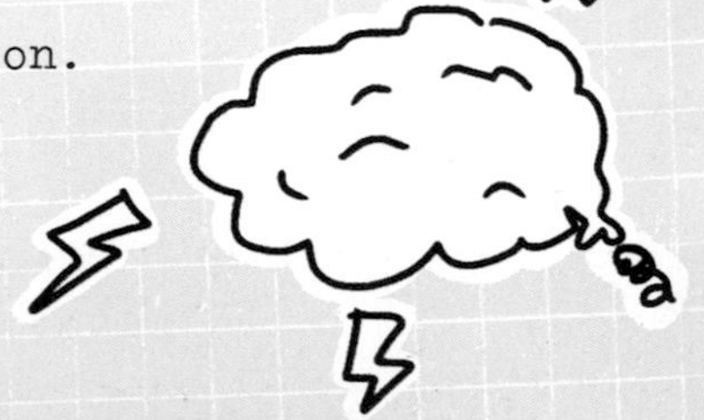

4. Testing your guess with experiments.

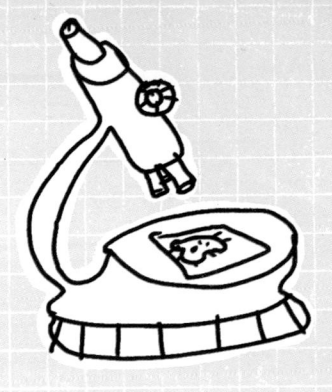

5. Recording and analyzing your test results.

6. Making a conclusion.

FINAL REPORT

This whole process is called the SCIENTIFIC METHOD.

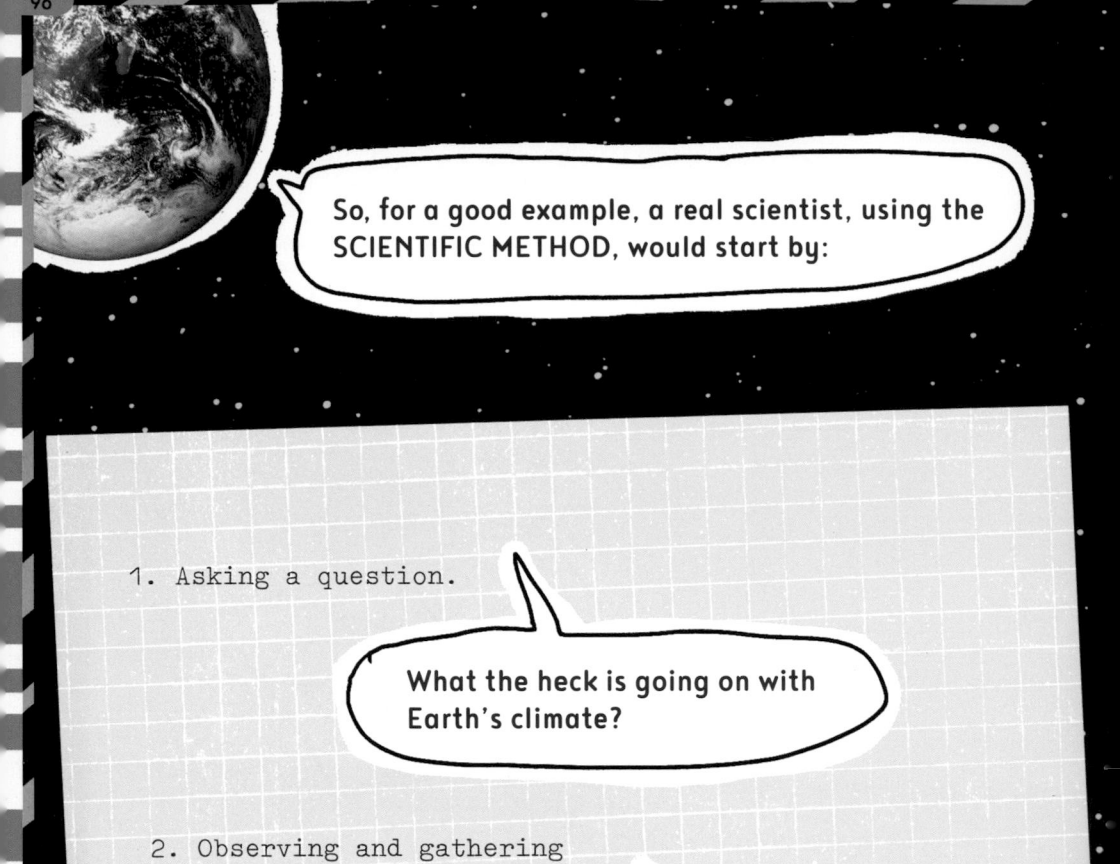

So, for a good example, a real scientist, using the SCIENTIFIC METHOD, would start by:

1. Asking a question.

> What the heck is going on with Earth's climate?

2. Observing and gathering information.

> In the last 100 years Earth's temperature has been getting seriously hotter and hotter.

3. Making a guess (called a hypothesis) to answer the question.

> Earth has been getting hotter because humans have been burning fossil fuels for the last 100 years.

4. Testing your guess with experiments.

> Run tests to show if added CO_2 from burning fossil fuels raises the atmosphere's temperature, lowers it, or has no effect.

5. Recording and analyzing your test results.

> Measure and graph changes in temperature.

6. Making a conclusion.

> ICE CAPS ARE MELTING, OCEANS ARE RISING, AND ANIMALS ARE GOING EXTINCT— BECAUSE OF CLIMATE CHANGES CAUSED BY HUMAN ACTIVITY.

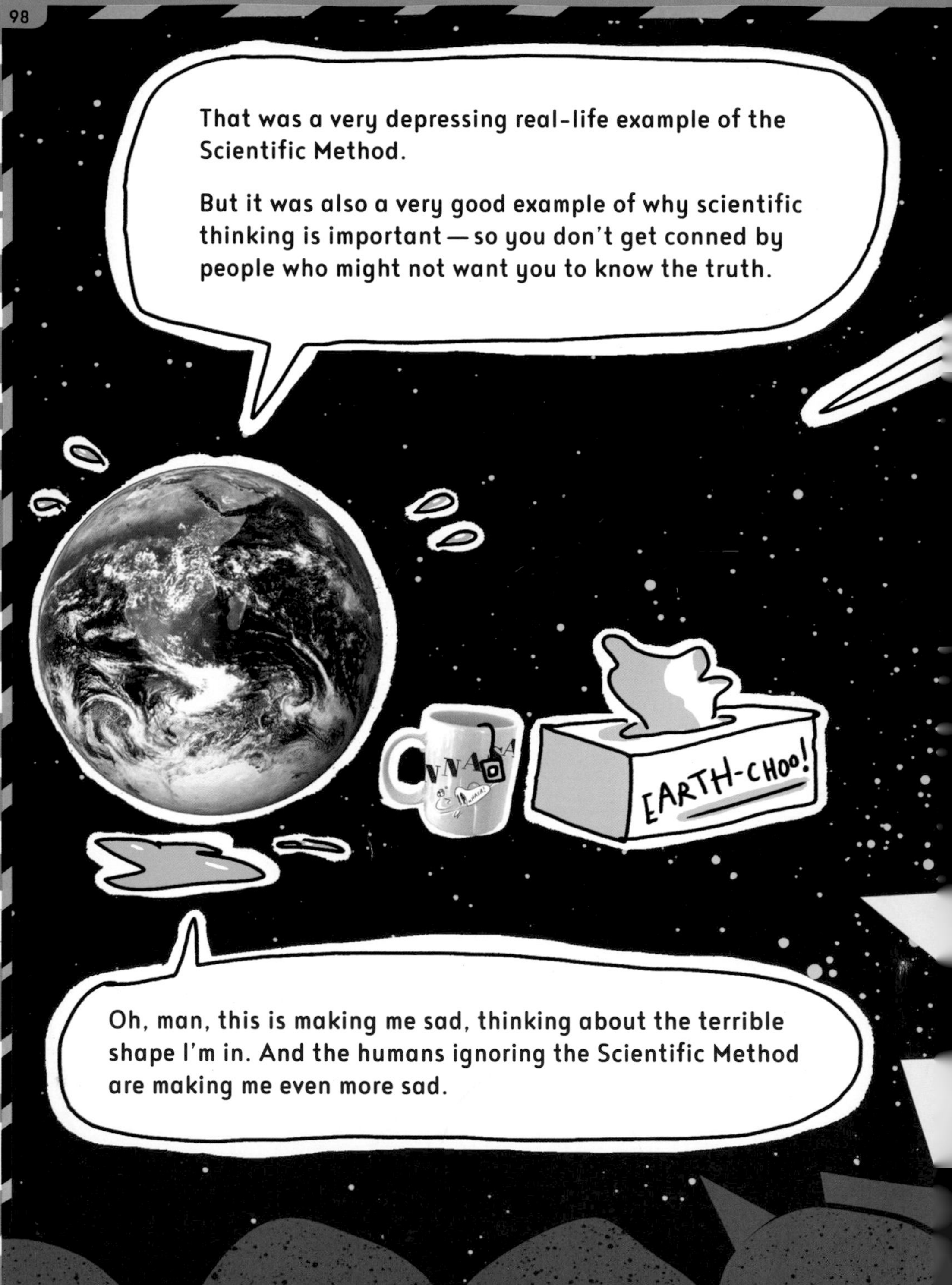
That was a very depressing real-life example of the Scientific Method.
But it was also a very good example of why scientific thinking is important — so you don't get conned by people who might not want you to know the truth.
EARTH-CHOO!
Oh, man, this is making me sad, thinking about the terrible shape I'm in. And the humans ignoring the Scientific Method are making me even more sad.

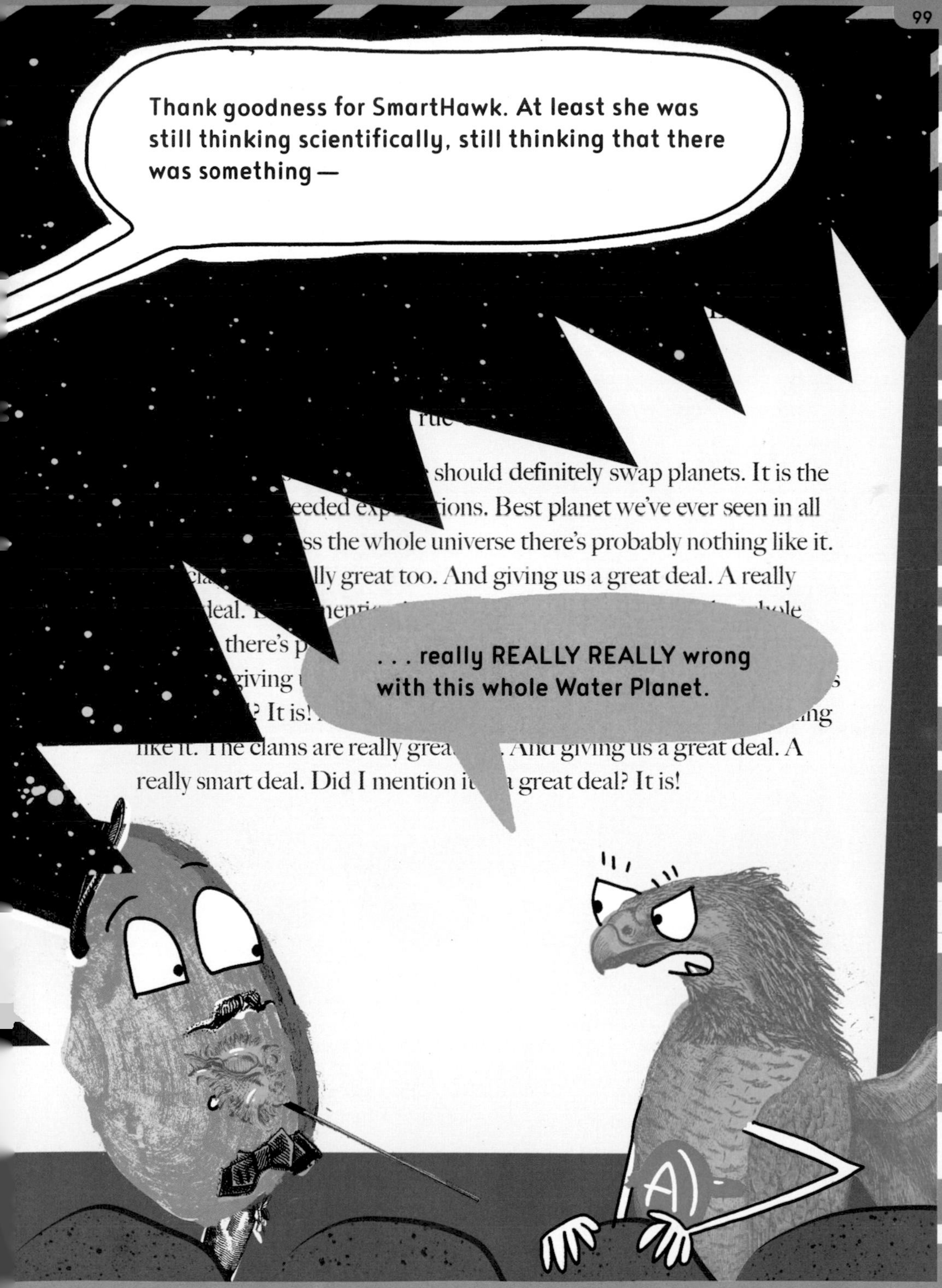
Thank goodness for SmartHawk. At least she was still thinking scientifically, still thinking that there was something —
. . . really REALLY REALLY wrong with this whole Water Planet.

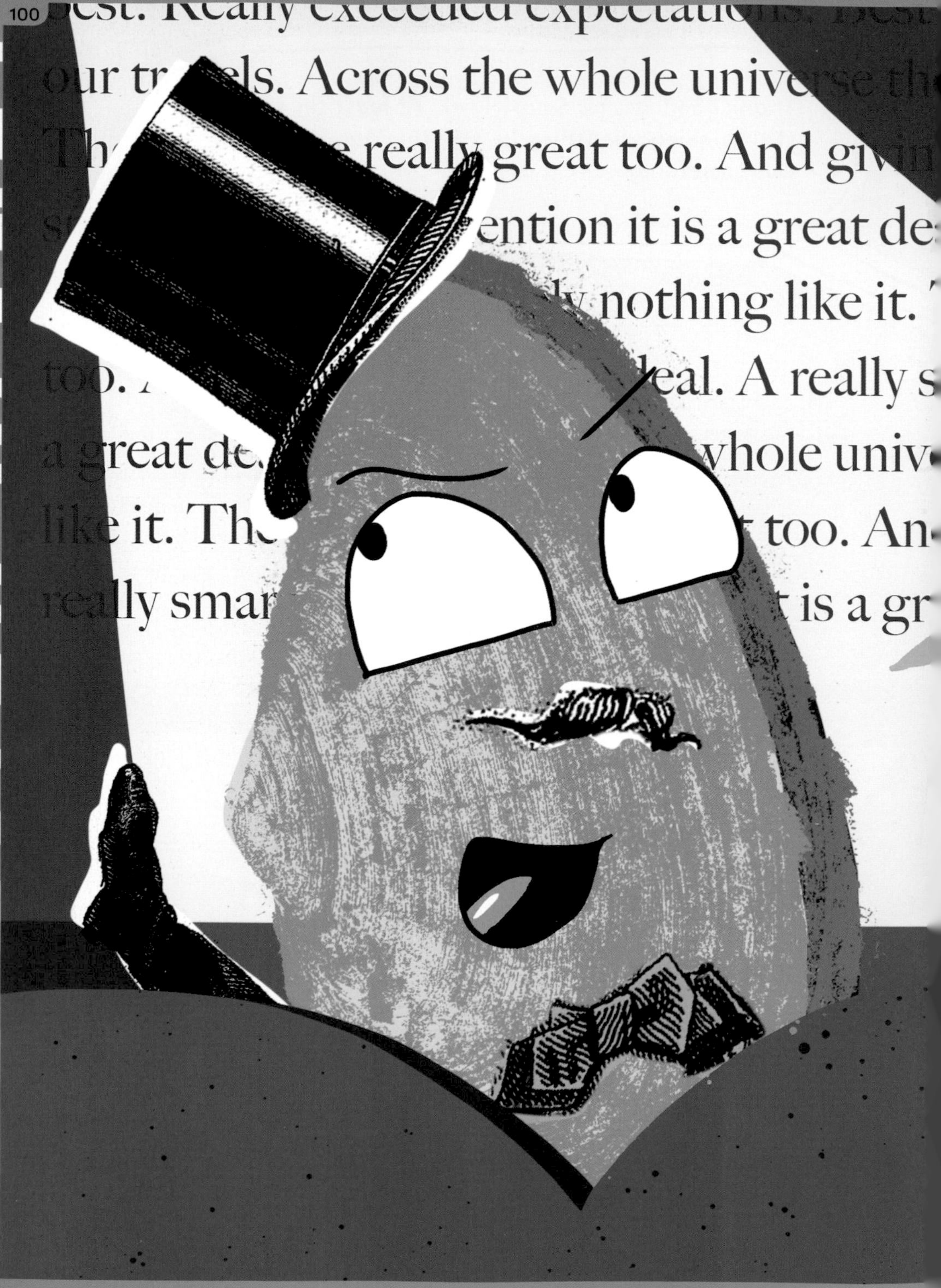
our tr els. Across the whole univ
really great too. And gi
ention it is a great de
nothing like it.
too. eal. A really s
a great de whole univ
like it. Th too. An
really smar is a gr

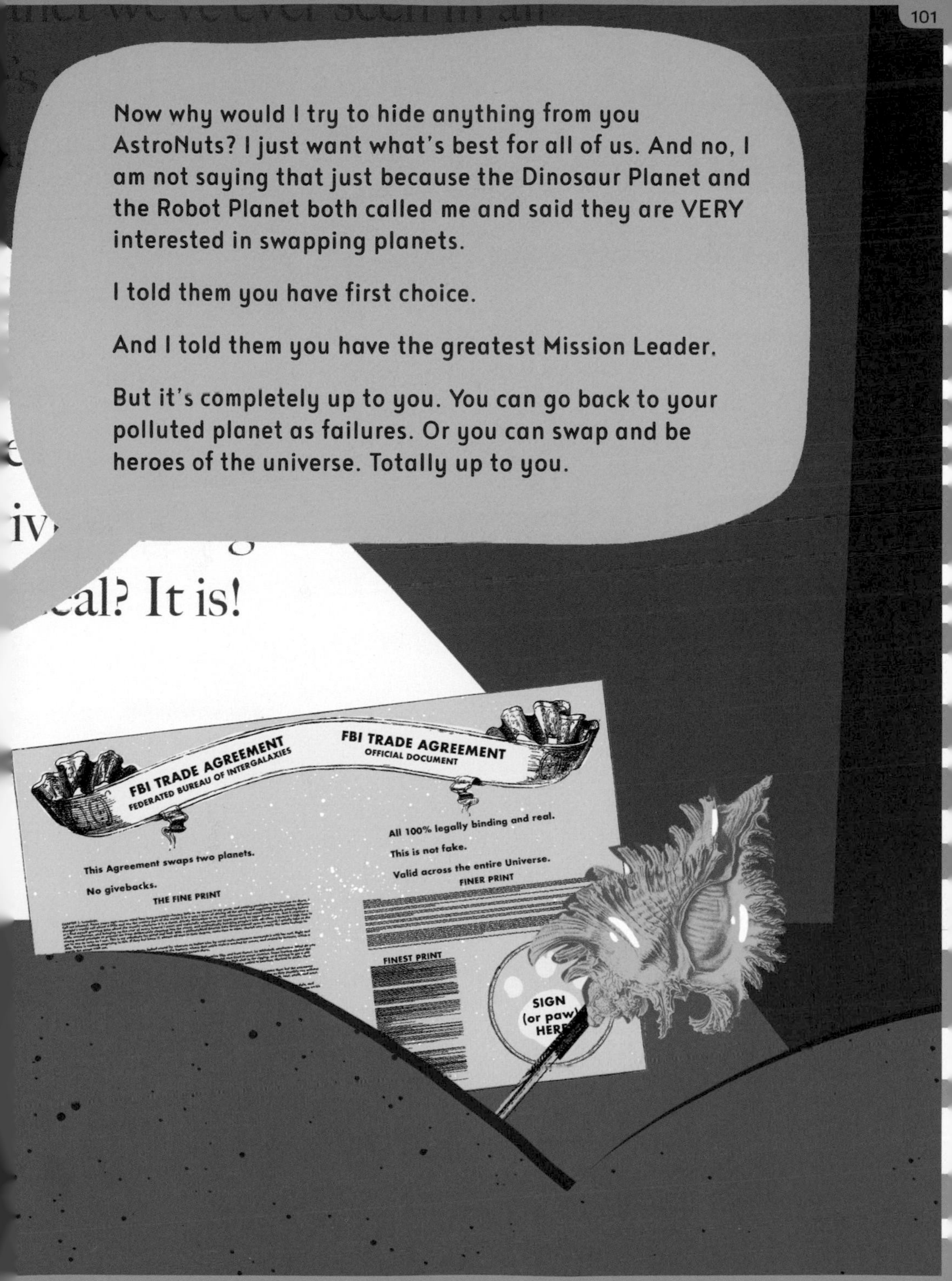
Now why would I try to hide anything from you AstroNuts? I just want what's best for all of us. And no, I am not saying that just because the Dinosaur Planet and the Robot Planet both called me and said they are VERY interested in swapping planets.
I told them you have first choice.
And I told them you have the greatest Mission Leader.
But it's completely up to you. You can go back to your polluted planet as failures. Or you can swap and be heroes of the universe. Totally up to you.
It is!
FBI TRADE AGREEMENT
FEDERATED BUREAU OF INTERGALAXIES
FBI TRADE AGREEMENT
OFFICIAL DOCUMENT
This Agreement swaps two planets.
No givebacks.
THE FINE PRINT
All 100% legally binding and real.
This is not fake.
Valid across the entire Universe.
FINER PRINT
FINEST PRINT
SIGN
(or paw)

CHAPTER 15:

Double Sunset

President P. T. Clam slid out of the Nose Rocket. The suns set on the Water Planet. And I was not too thrilled with being called “a polluted planet.” But I have to admit—there is nothing quite like a double sunset.

The AstroNuts didn’t see any of it, because they were deep in AstroDiscussion.

///// Official NNASA transcript /////
//// of ASTRONUT Mission 2 ////

AlphaWolf: Dinosaurs? Robots? We can’t let them beat us to this good deal! We have to sign now.
SmartHawk: Oh my duck feet, you believe that clam? We can’t sign a deal when we haven’t done our NNASA homework!
StinkBug: We do not know the things we do not know.

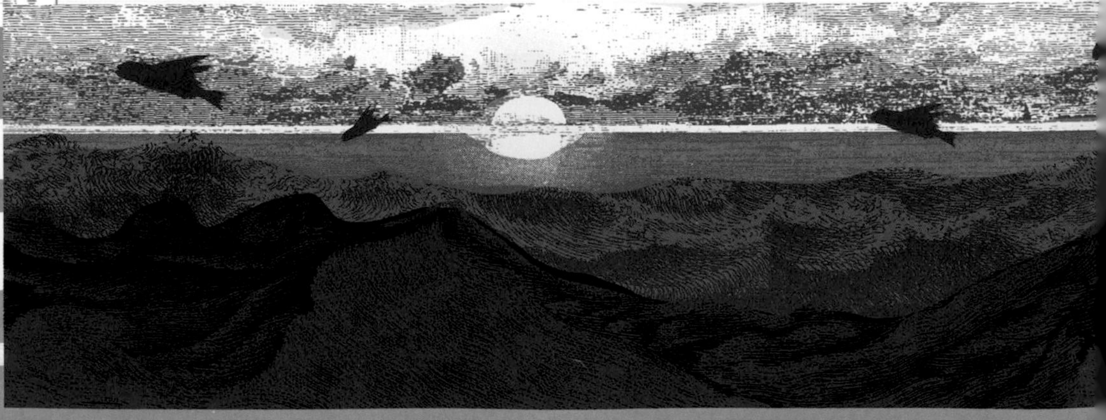

LaserShark: We should listen to what the other clams think.
AlphaWolf: Who cares what the other clams think?! LaserShark, we are facing the very real threat of robots as the faces of Mount AlphaWolfmore!
LaserShark/ /SmartHawk/ /StinkBug: What?
AlphaWolf: Uh. Nothing.
LaserShark: Like I was saying, I have made a new friend, and she says she needs to talk to us.
AlphaWolf: You have a new friend? So what? You always have a new friend. We can't be messing around with playdates now. We need to sign and swap planets. NOW!
—sound of rocket nose being knocked on—
LaserShark: Who could that be? I'll make some more sea snacks.

CHAPTER 16: Another Knock on the Nose

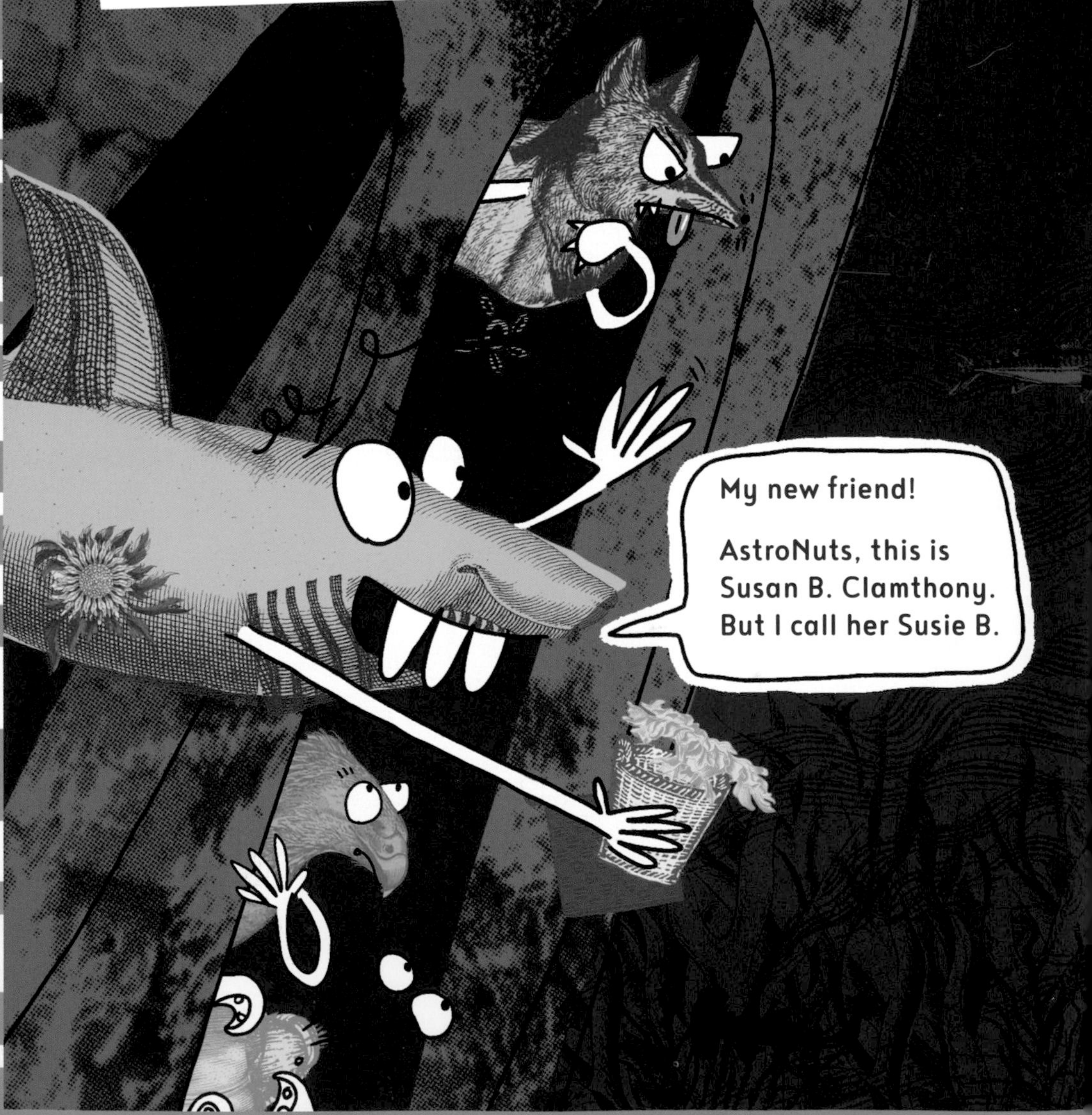
My new friend!
AstroNuts, this is Susan B. Clamthony. But I call her Susie B.

Hello, AstroNuts. Yes, I am Susan B. Clamthony. And I come to you with news of great importance. This planet is not what it seems.

But it's not safe out here.

Can I come in and talk?

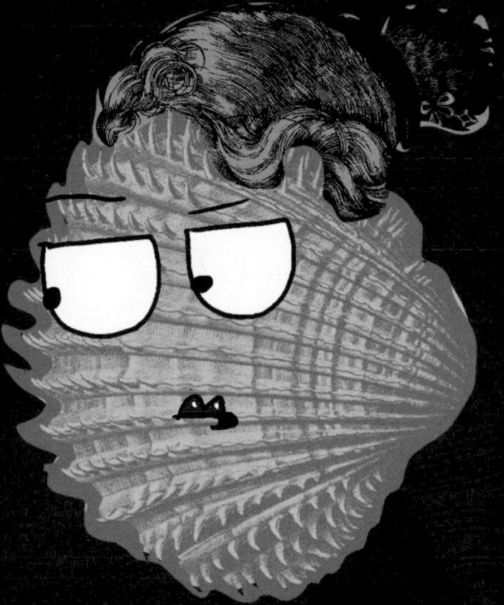

Now you are probably saying to yourself, "What?! Two clams knocking on a Nose Rocket? In the middle of the same night? That is ridiculous."

And I know it sounds crazy. But let me tell you from a 4-billion-year-lifetime of experience—if a clam knocks on your door and tells you they have important news, you should listen.

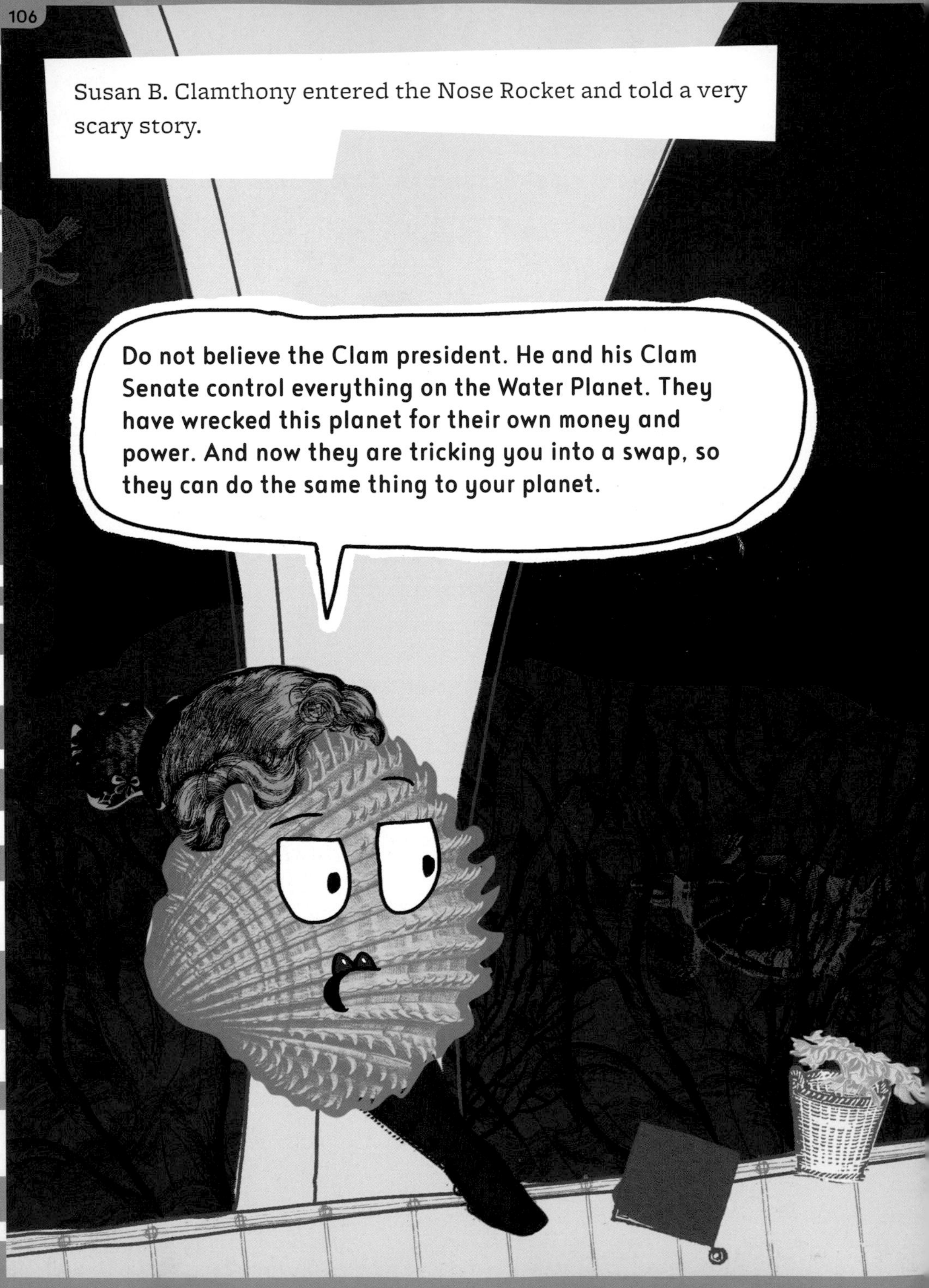
Susan B. Clamthony entered the Nose Rocket and told a very scary story.
Do not believe the Clam president. He and his Clam Senate control everything on the Water Planet. They have wrecked this planet for their own money and power. And now they are tricking you into a swap, so they can do the same thing to your planet.

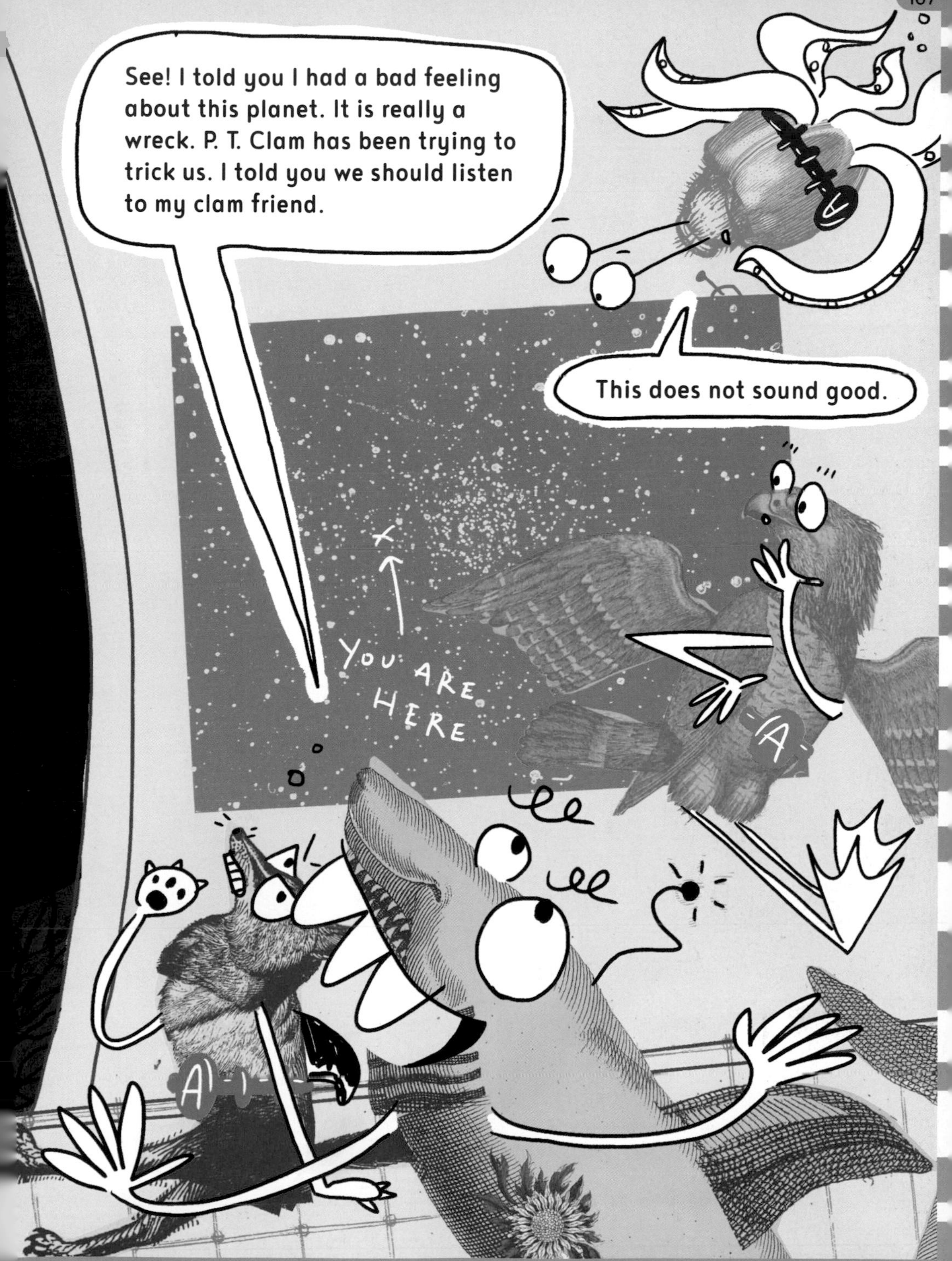
See! I told you I had a bad feeling about this planet. It is really a wreck. P. T. Clam has been trying to trick us. I told you we should listen to my clam friend.
This does not sound good.
YOU ARE HERE

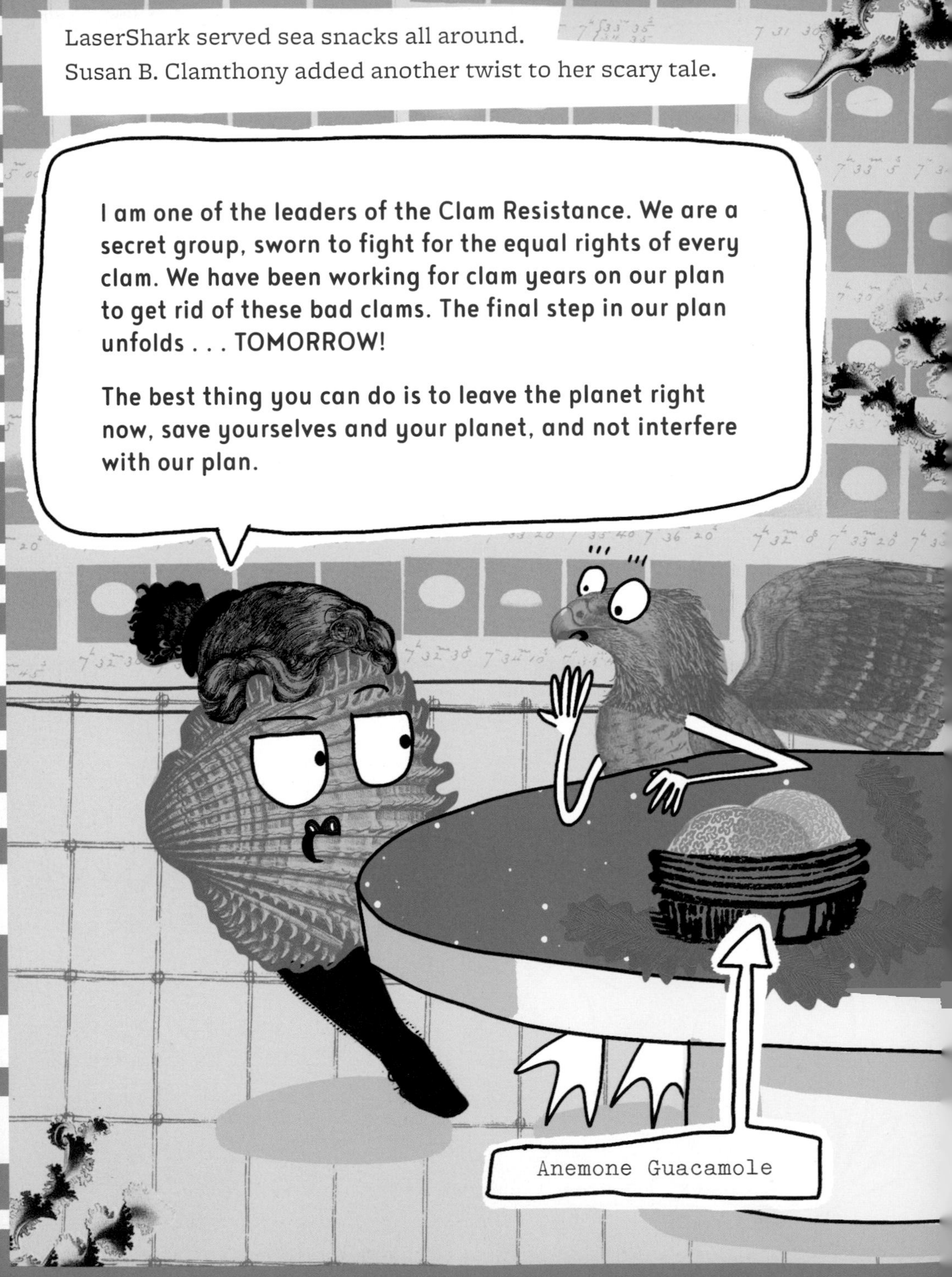
LaserShark served sea snacks all around.
Susan B. Clamthony added another twist to her scary tale.
I am one of the leaders of the Clam Resistance. We are a secret group, sworn to fight for the equal rights of every clam. We have been working for clam years on our plan to get rid of these bad clams. The final step in our plan unfolds . . . TOMORROW!
The best thing you can do is to leave the planet right now, save yourselves and your planet, and not interfere with our plan.
Anemone Guacamole

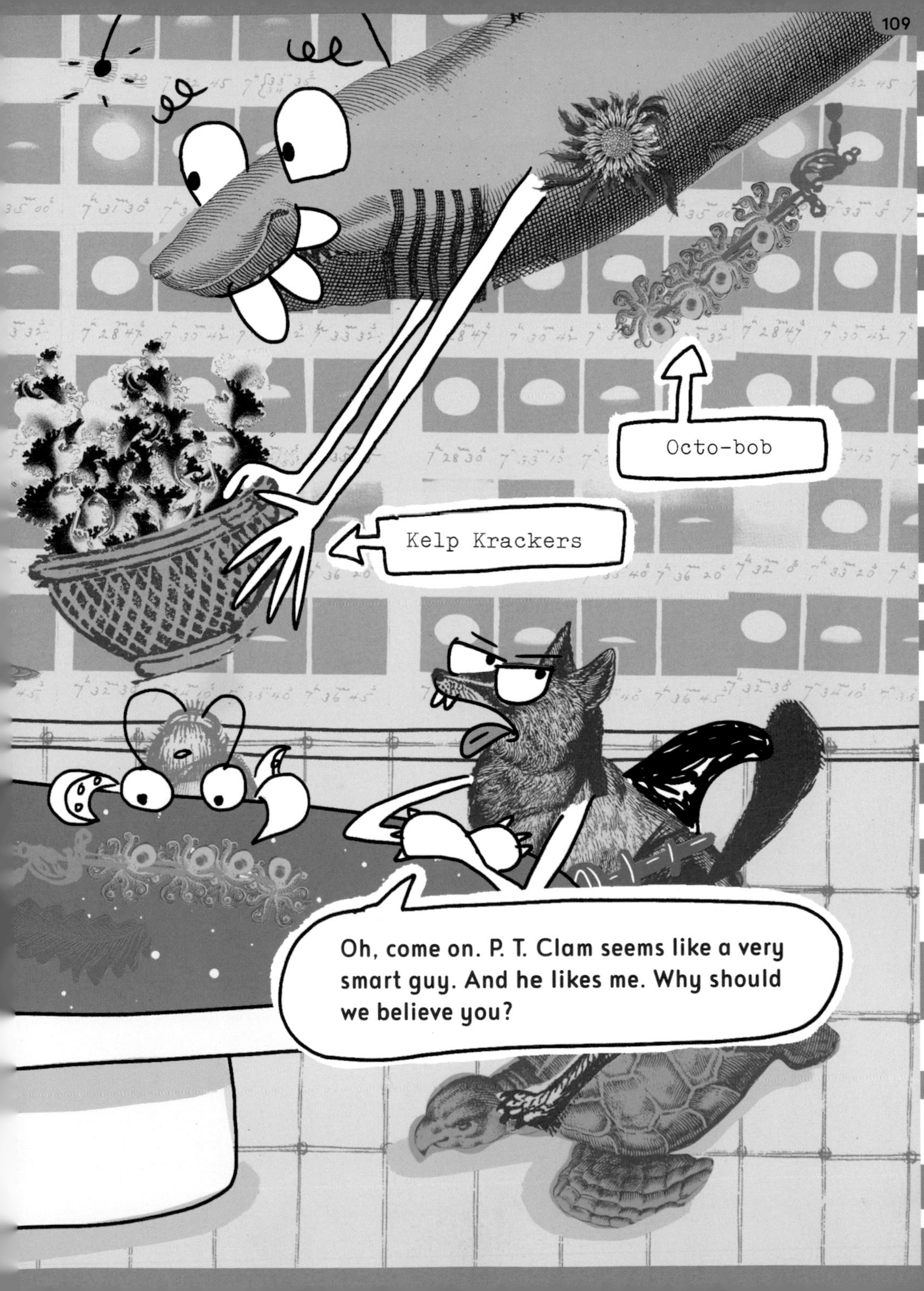
Octo-bob
Kelp Krackers
Oh, come on. P. T. Clam seems like a very smart guy. And he likes me. Why should we believe you?

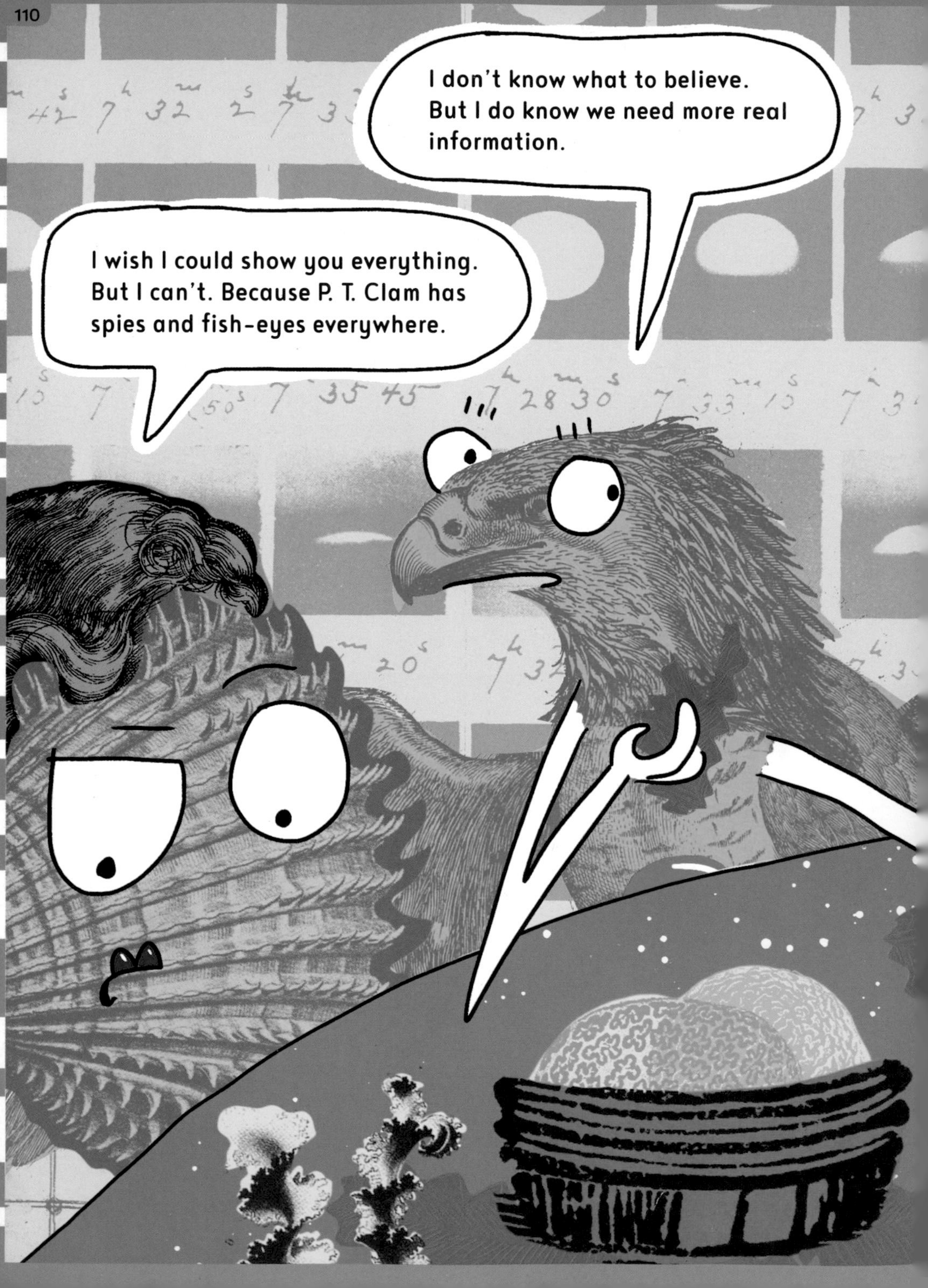
I don't know what to believe. But I do know we need more real information.
I wish I could show you everything. But I can't. Because P. T. Clam has spies and fish-eyes everywhere.

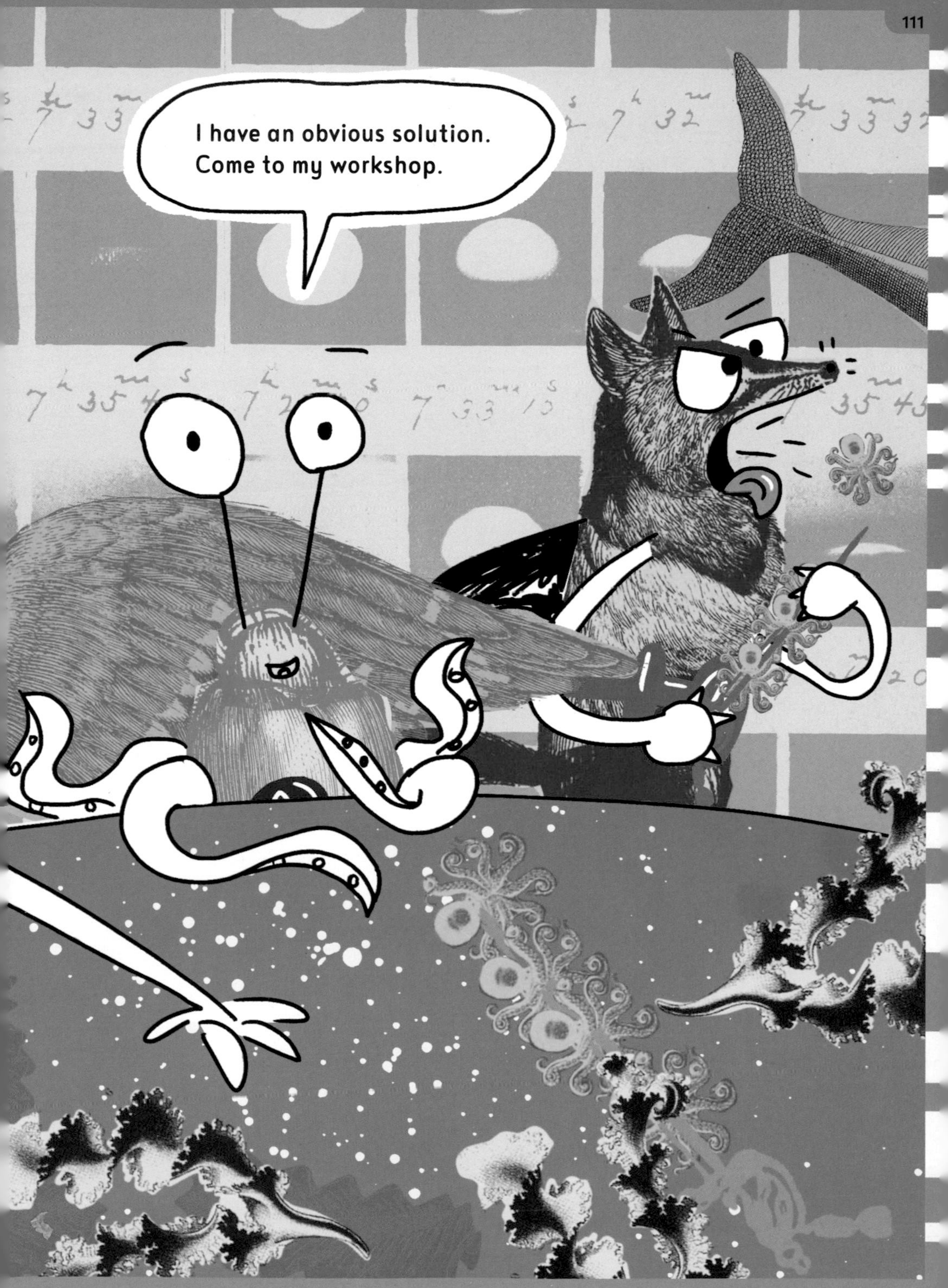
I have an obvious solution.
Come to my workshop.

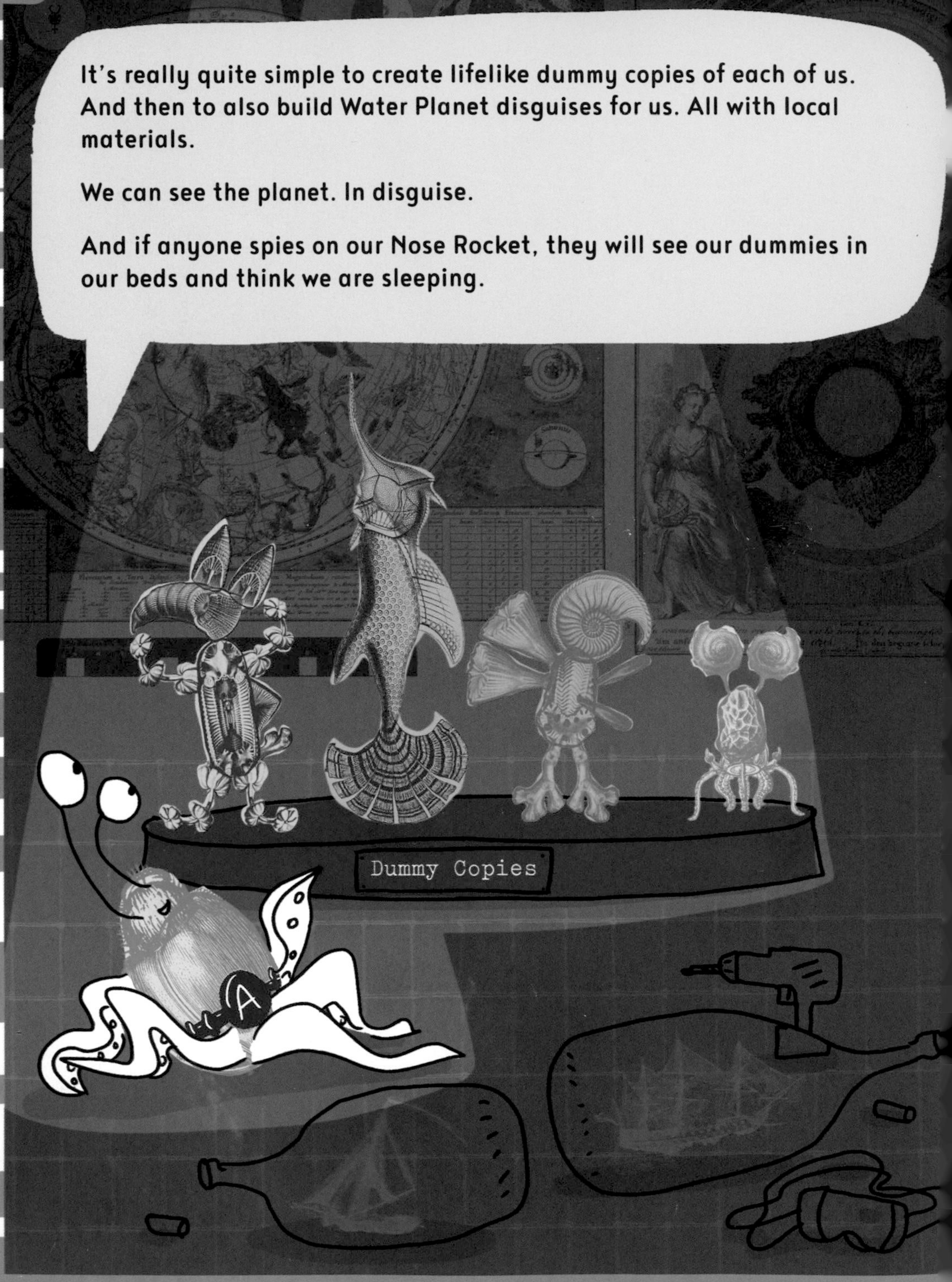
It's really quite simple to create lifelike dummy copies of each of us. And then to also build Water Planet disguises for us. All with local materials.
We can see the planet. In disguise.
And if anyone spies on our Nose Rocket, they will see our dummies in our beds and think we are sleeping.
Dummy Copies

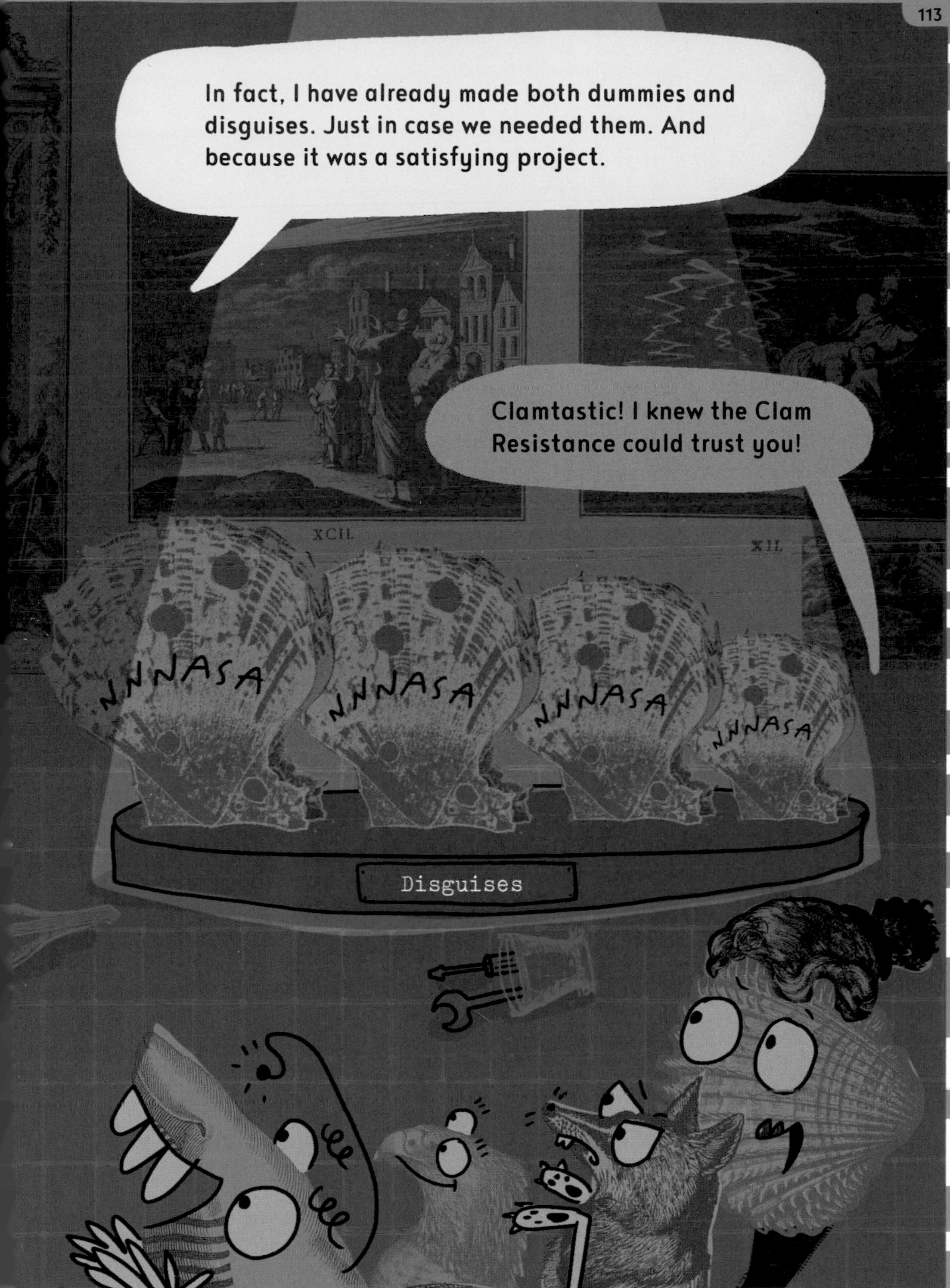
In fact, I have already made both dummies and disguises. Just in case we needed them. And because it was a satisfying project.
Clamtastic! I knew the Clam Resistance could trust you!
XCII.
XII.
NNNASA
NNNASA
NNNASA
NNNASA
Disguises

So as unlikely as it might seem, Susan B. Clamthony and the AstroNuts, in sea life disguises, slipped out of the Thomas Jefferson Nose Rocket to see for themselves just how bad the Water Planet might be.

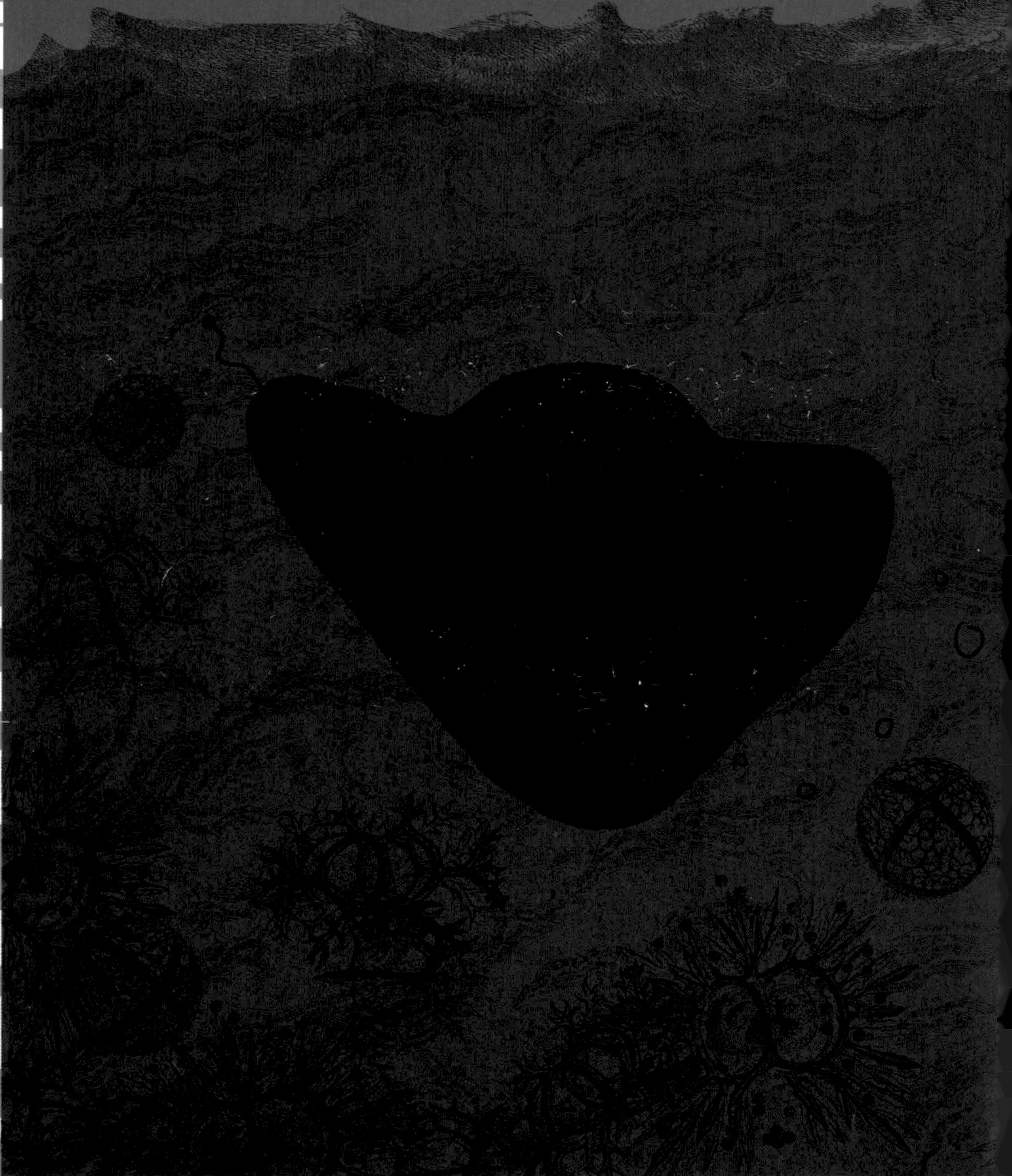

LaserShark happily used her anglerfish mod to light the way for her new friend.

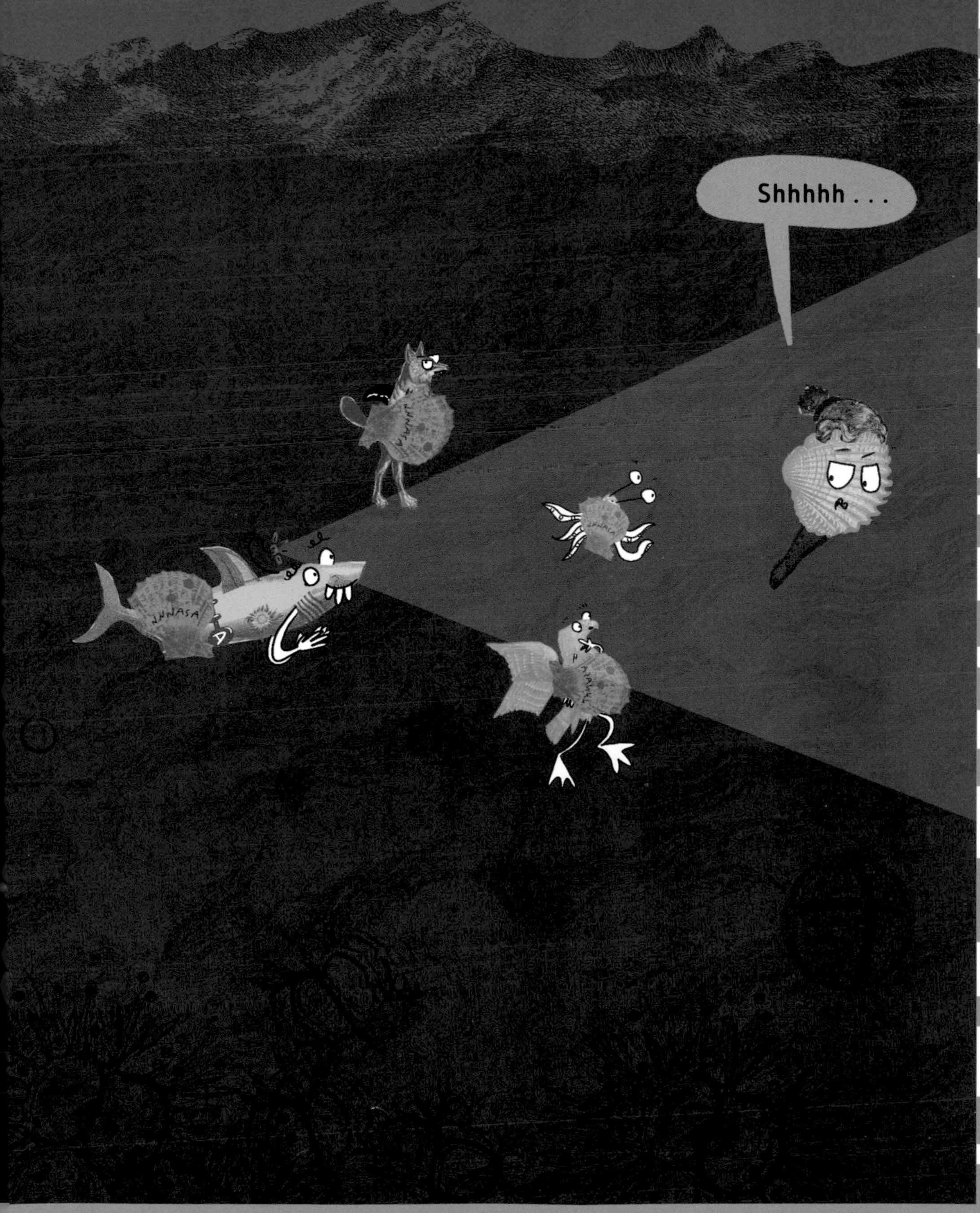
Shhhhh . . .

CHAPTER 17: Double Sunrise

Suddenly, it was sunrise. And it wasn't just because the AstroNuts had snacked and talked and stayed up for hours. It was because nighttime on the two-sun Water Planet was, as usual, only 74 minutes long.

It was a surprising, but still pretty sweet, double sunrise.

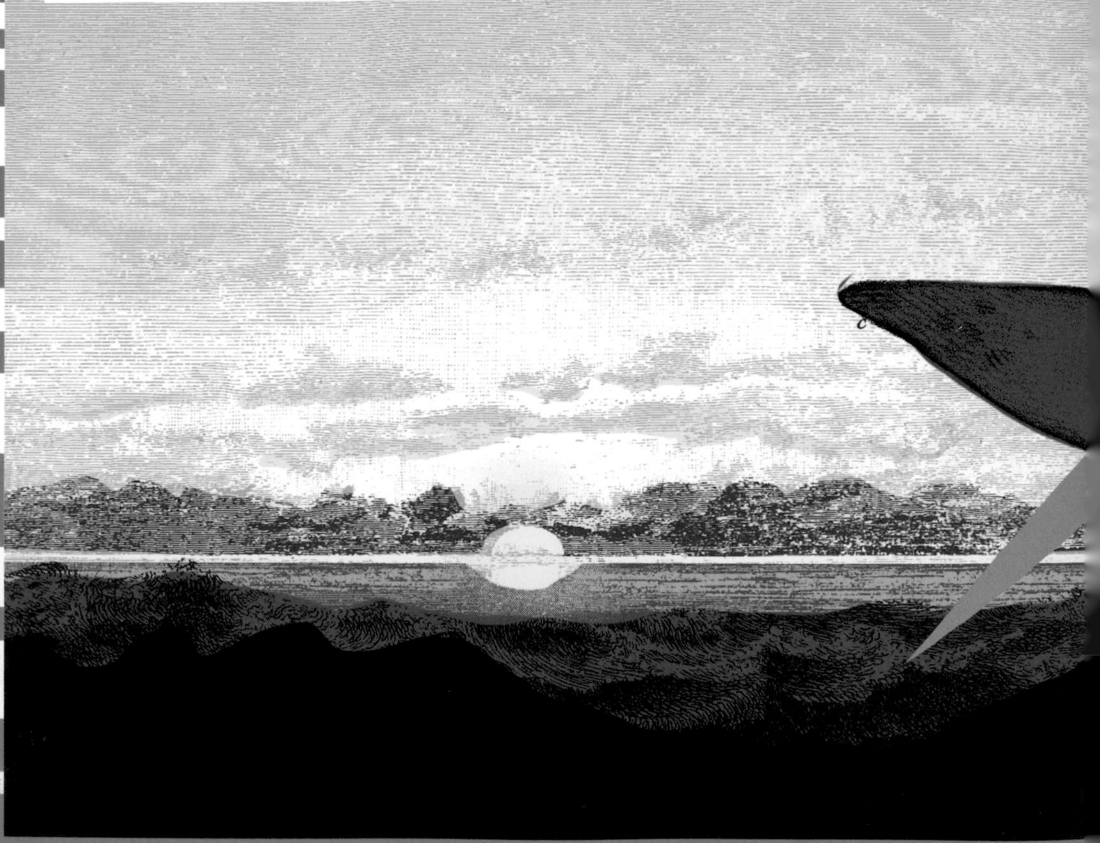

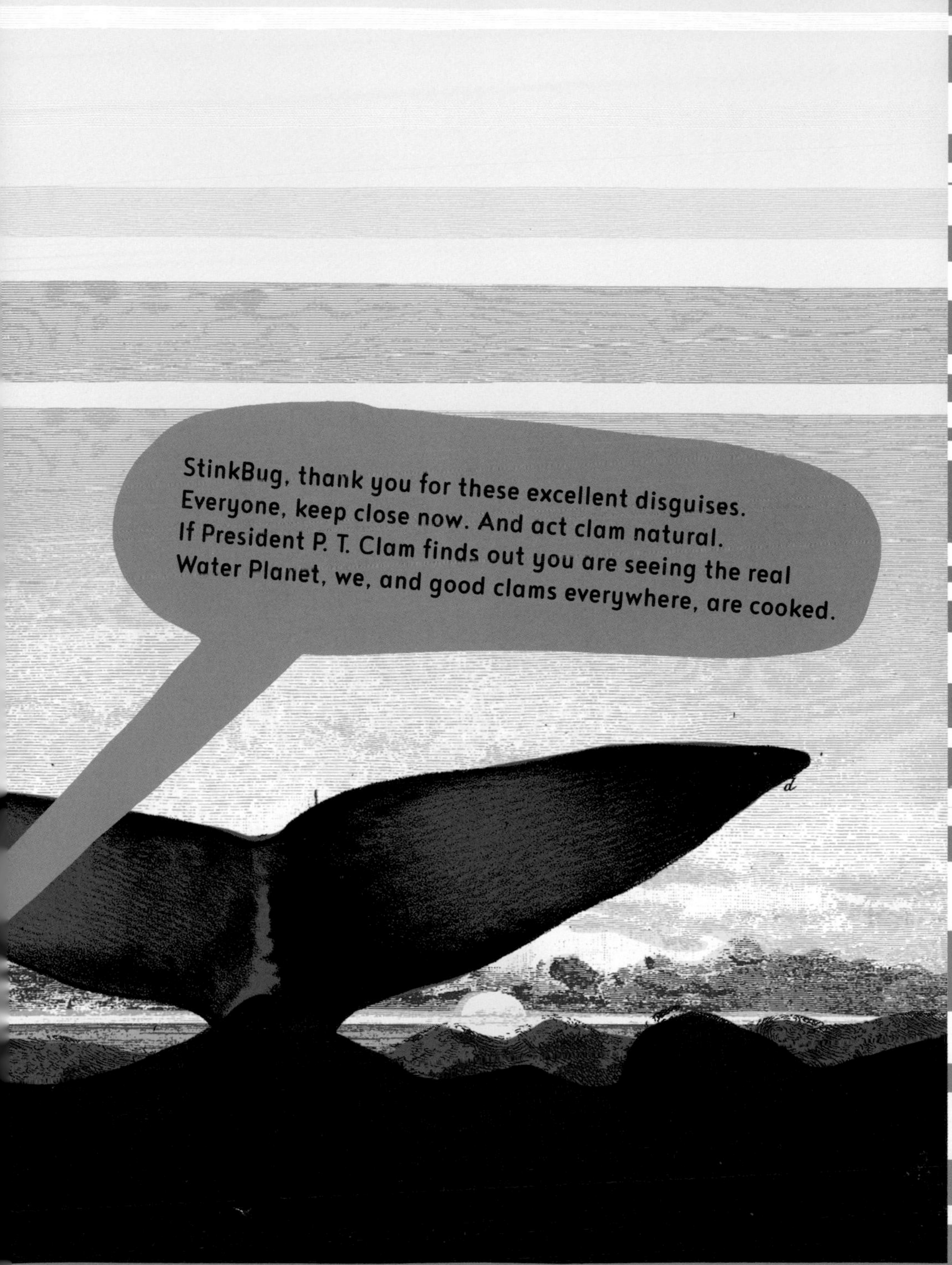
StinkBug, thank you for these excellent disguises. Everyone, keep close now. And act clam natural. If President P. T. Clam finds out you are seeing the real Water Planet, we, and good clams everywhere, are cooked.

CHAPTER 18:
Fishburger

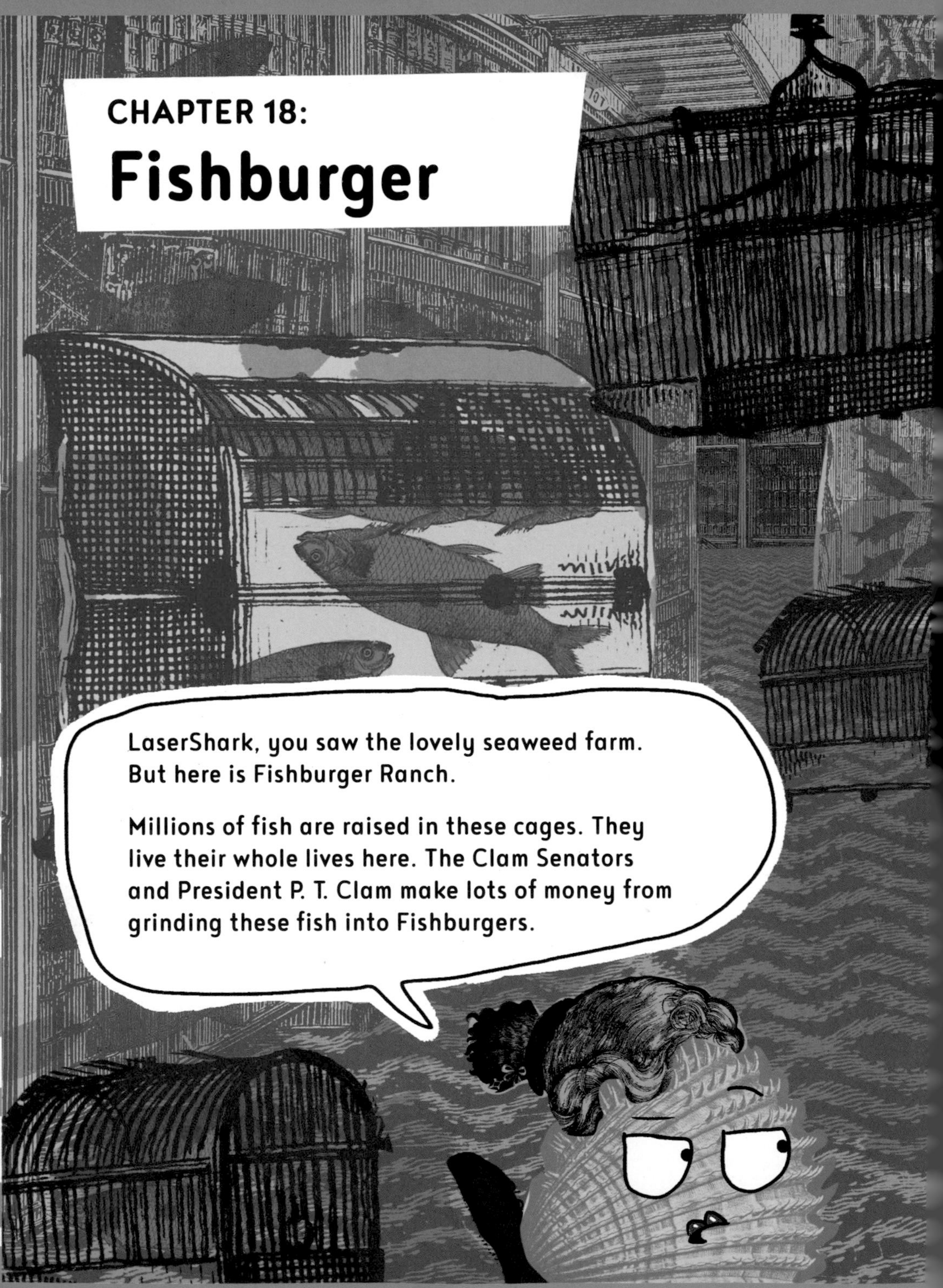
LaserShark, you saw the lovely seaweed farm. But here is Fishburger Ranch.
Millions of fish are raised in these cages. They live their whole lives here. The Clam Senators and President P. T. Clam make lots of money from grinding these fish into Fishburgers.

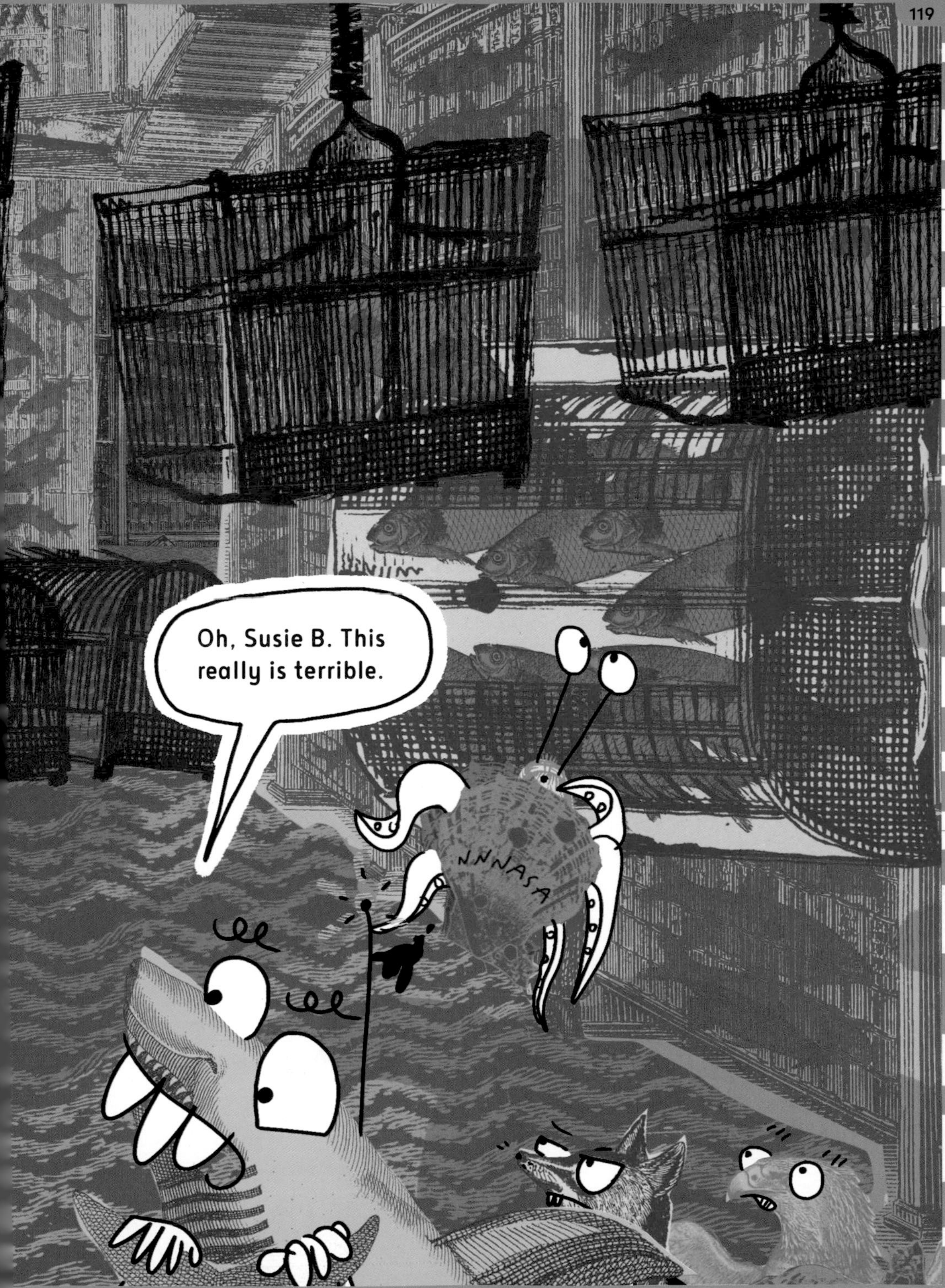
Oh, Susie B. This really is terrible.
NNNASA

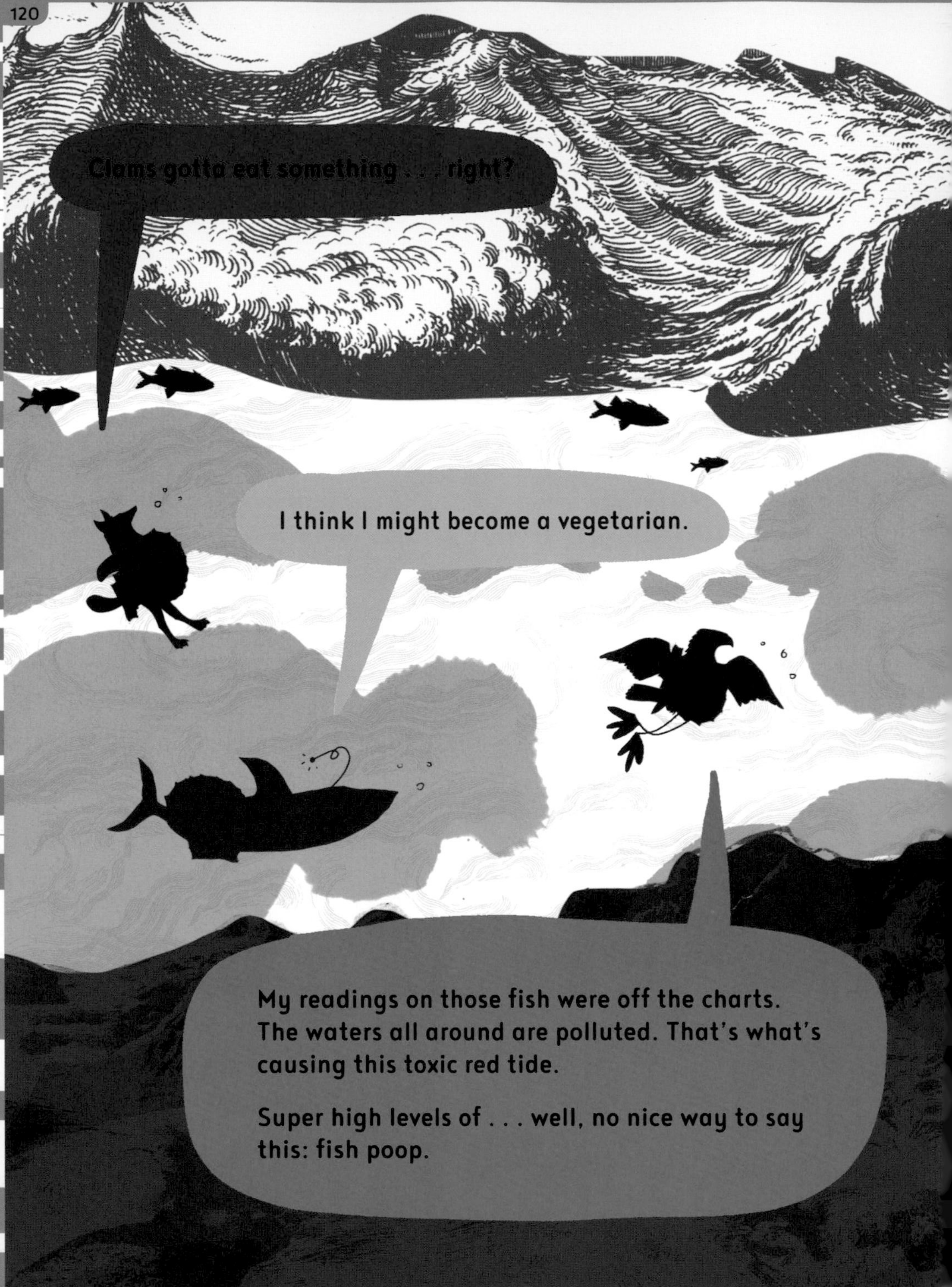
Clams gotta eat something . . . right?
I think I might become a vegetarian.
My readings on those fish were off the charts. The waters all around are polluted. That's what's causing this toxic red tide.
Super high levels of . . . well, no nice way to say this: fish poop.

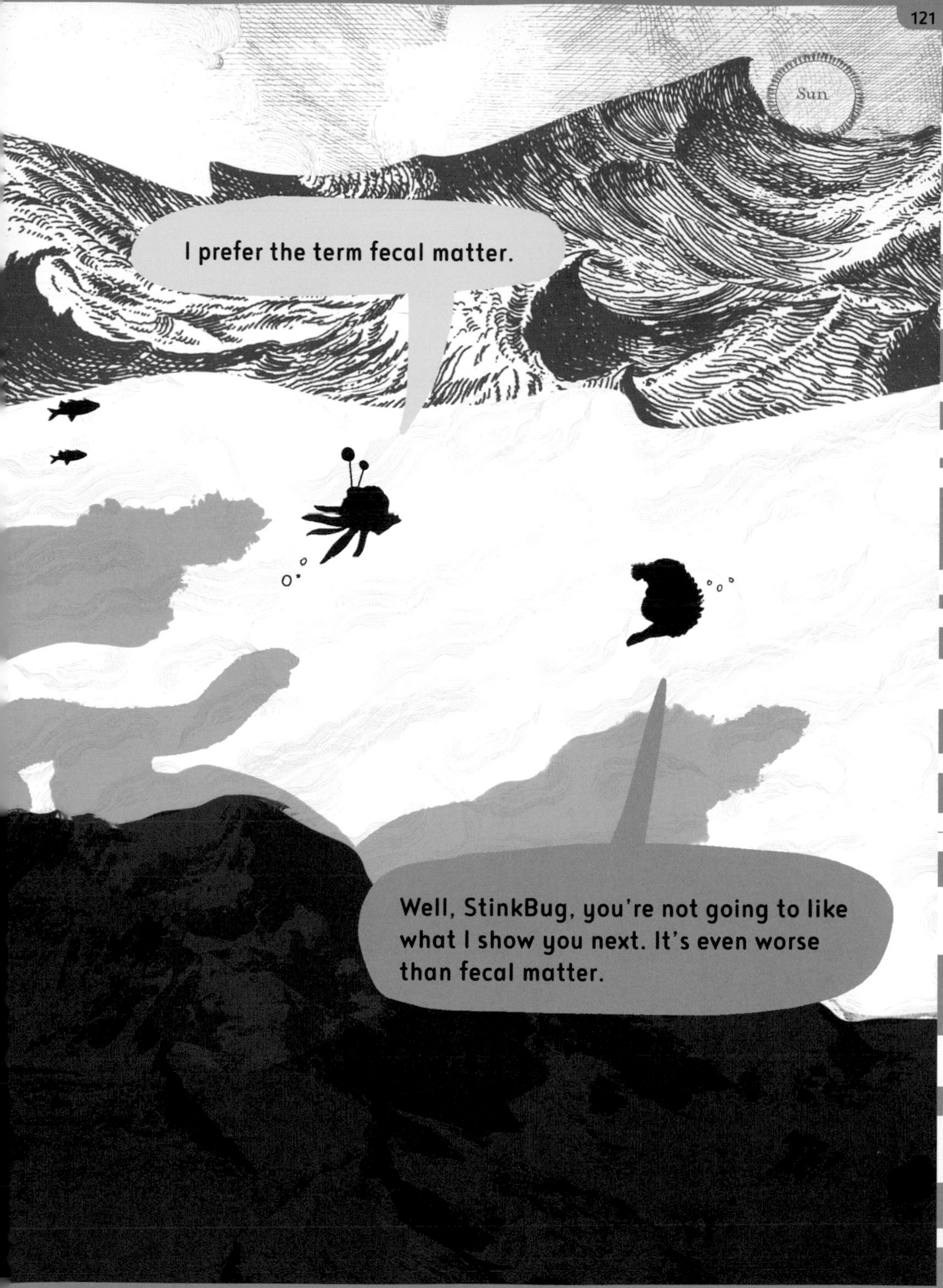
Sun
I prefer the term fecal matter.
Well, StinkBug, you're not going to like what I show you next. It's even worse than fecal matter.

CHAPTER 19: Graveyard

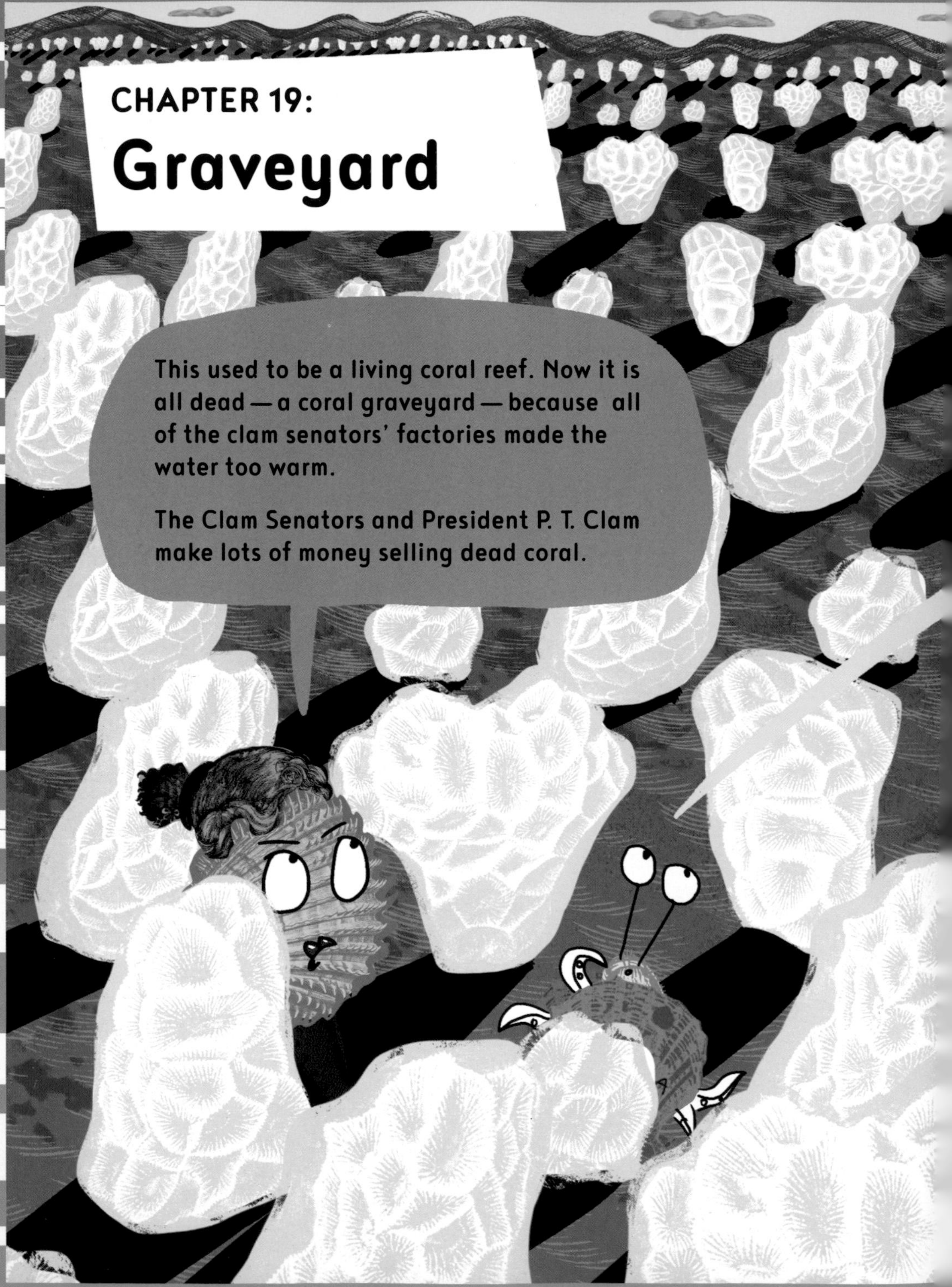
This used to be a living coral reef. Now it is all dead — a coral graveyard — because all of the clam senators' factories made the water too warm.
The Clam Senators and President P. T. Clam make lots of money selling dead coral.

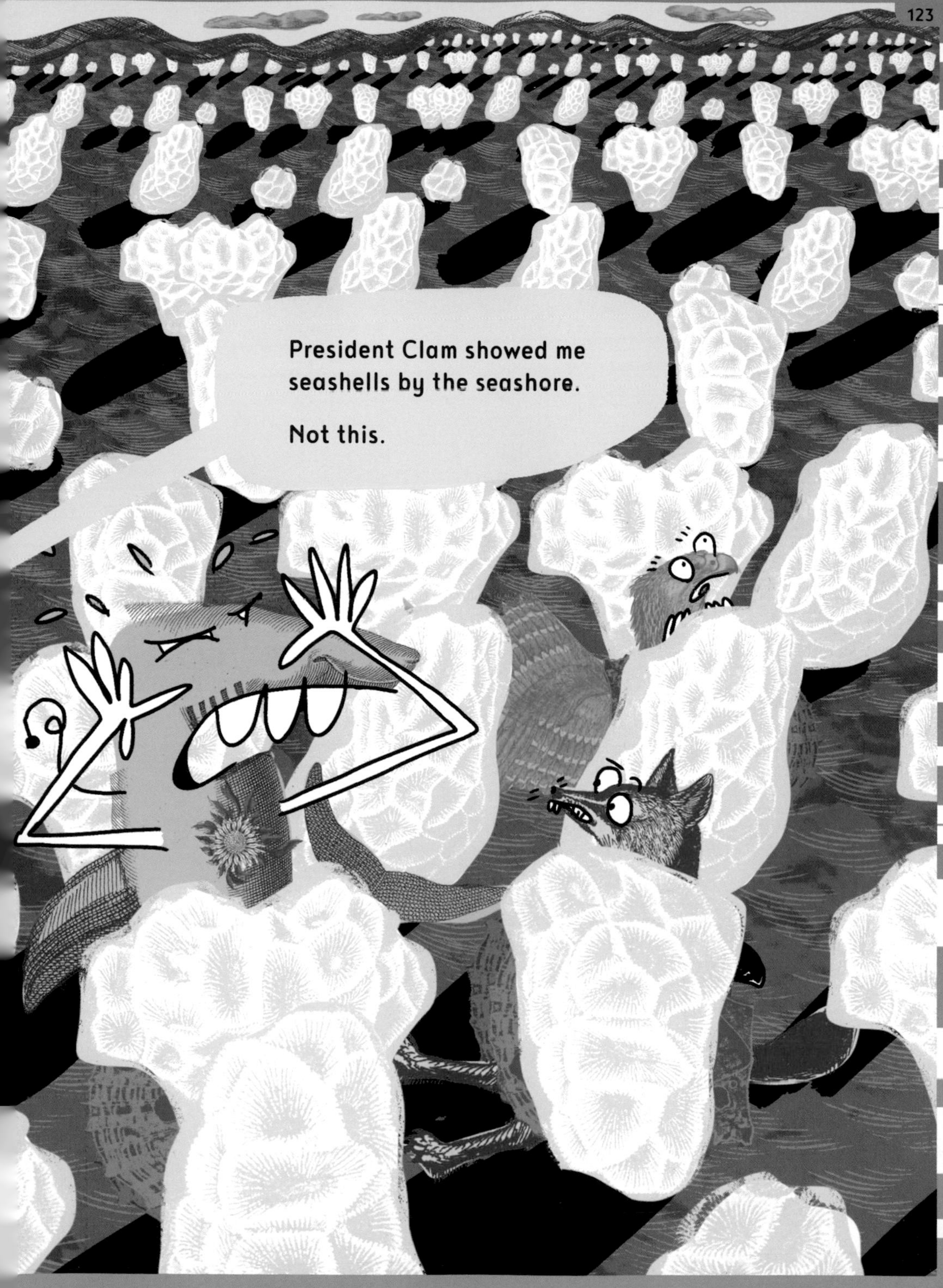
President Clam showed me
seashells by the seashore.
Not this.

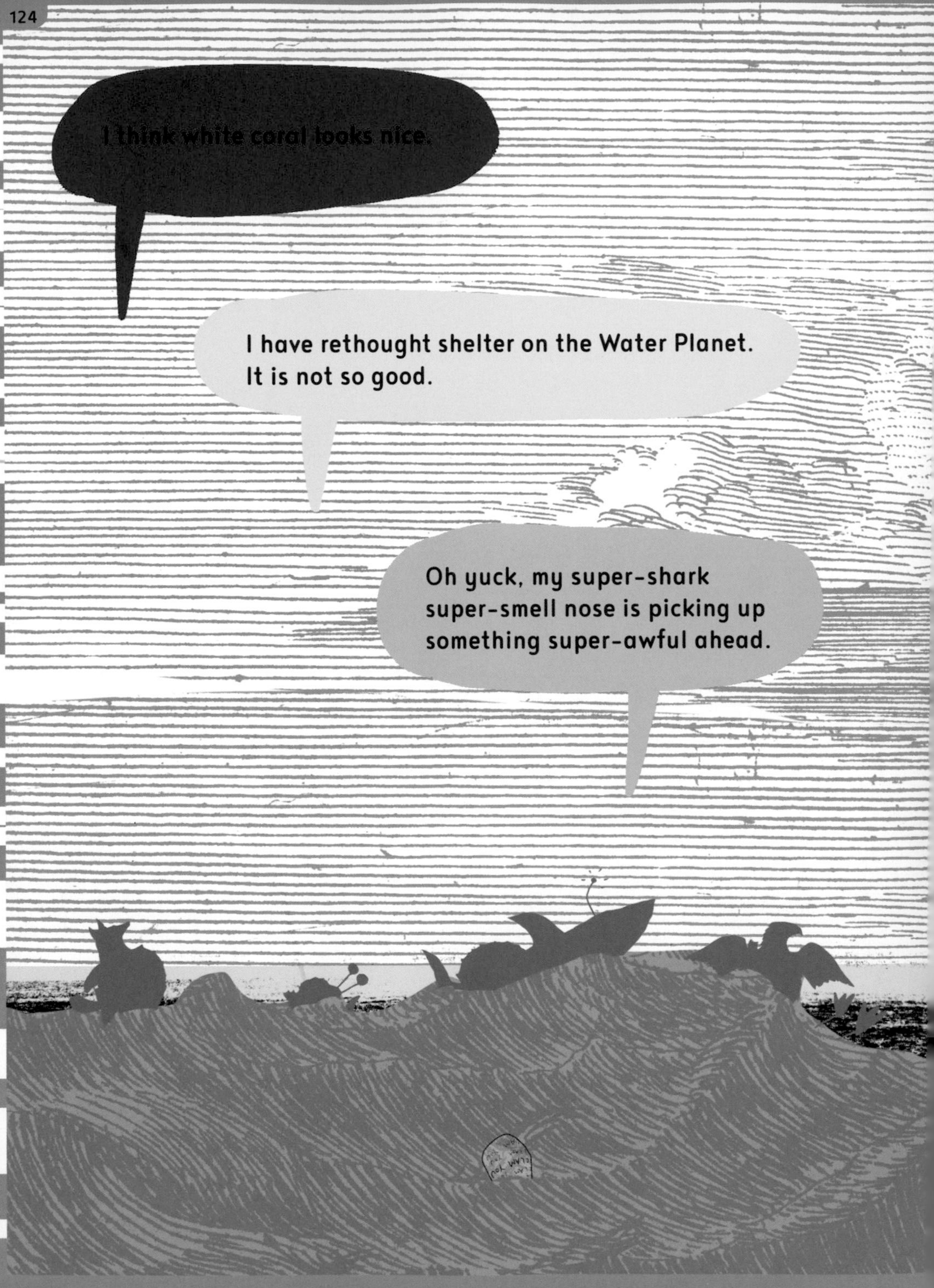
I think white coral looks nice.
I have rethought shelter on the Water Planet. It is not so good.
Oh yuck, my super-shark super-smell nose is picking up something super-awful ahead.

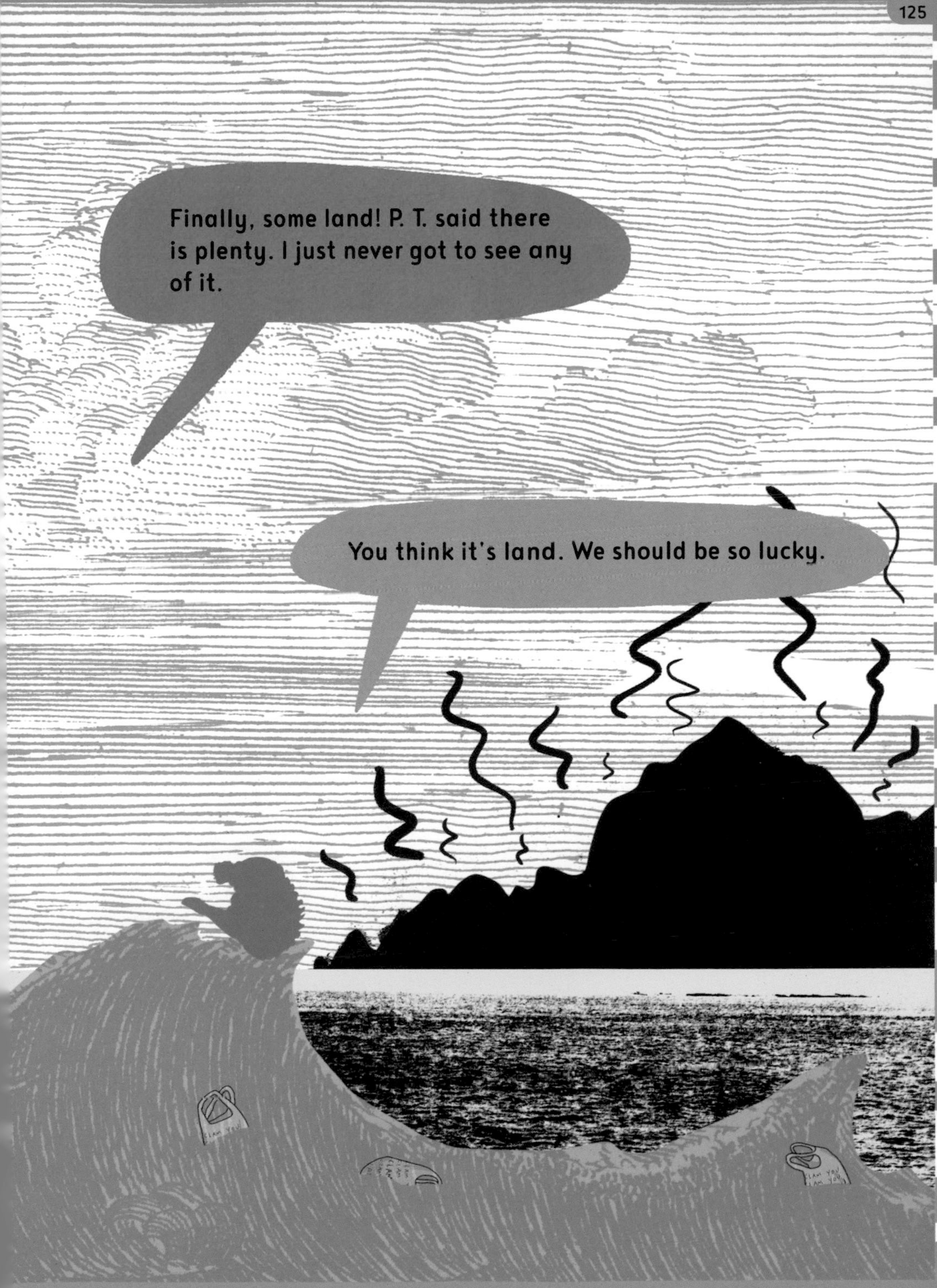
Finally, some land! P. T. said there is plenty. I just never got to see any of it.
You think it's land. We should be so lucky.

CHAPTER 20:

Land, Ha!

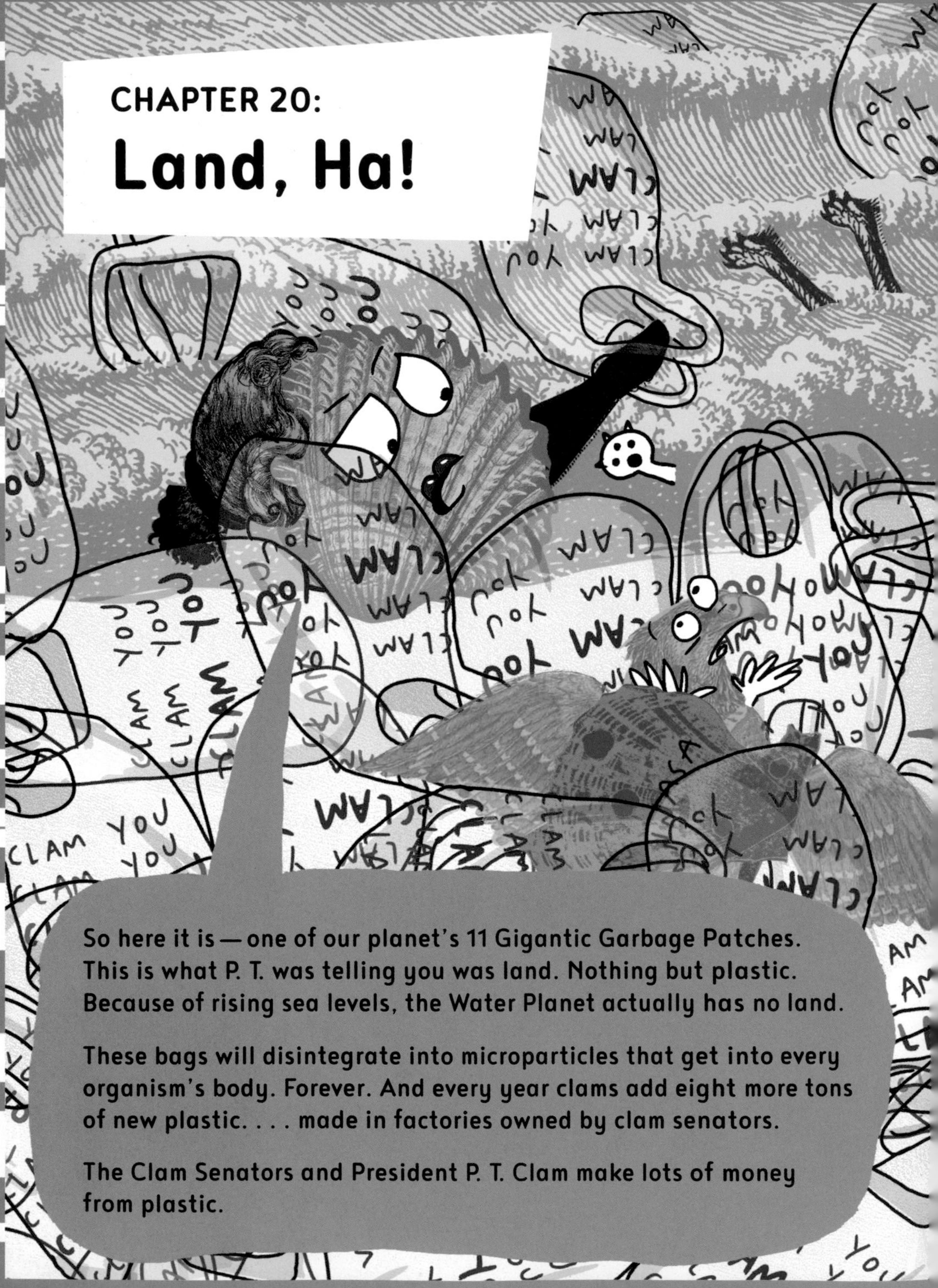
So here it is — one of our planet's 11 Gigantic Garbage Patches. This is what P. T. was telling you was land. Nothing but plastic. Because of rising sea levels, the Water Planet actually has no land.
These bags will disintegrate into microparticles that get into every organism's body. Forever. And every year clams add eight more tons of new plastic. . . . made in factories owned by clam senators.
The Clam Senators and President P. T. Clam make lots of money from plastic.
CLAM YOU

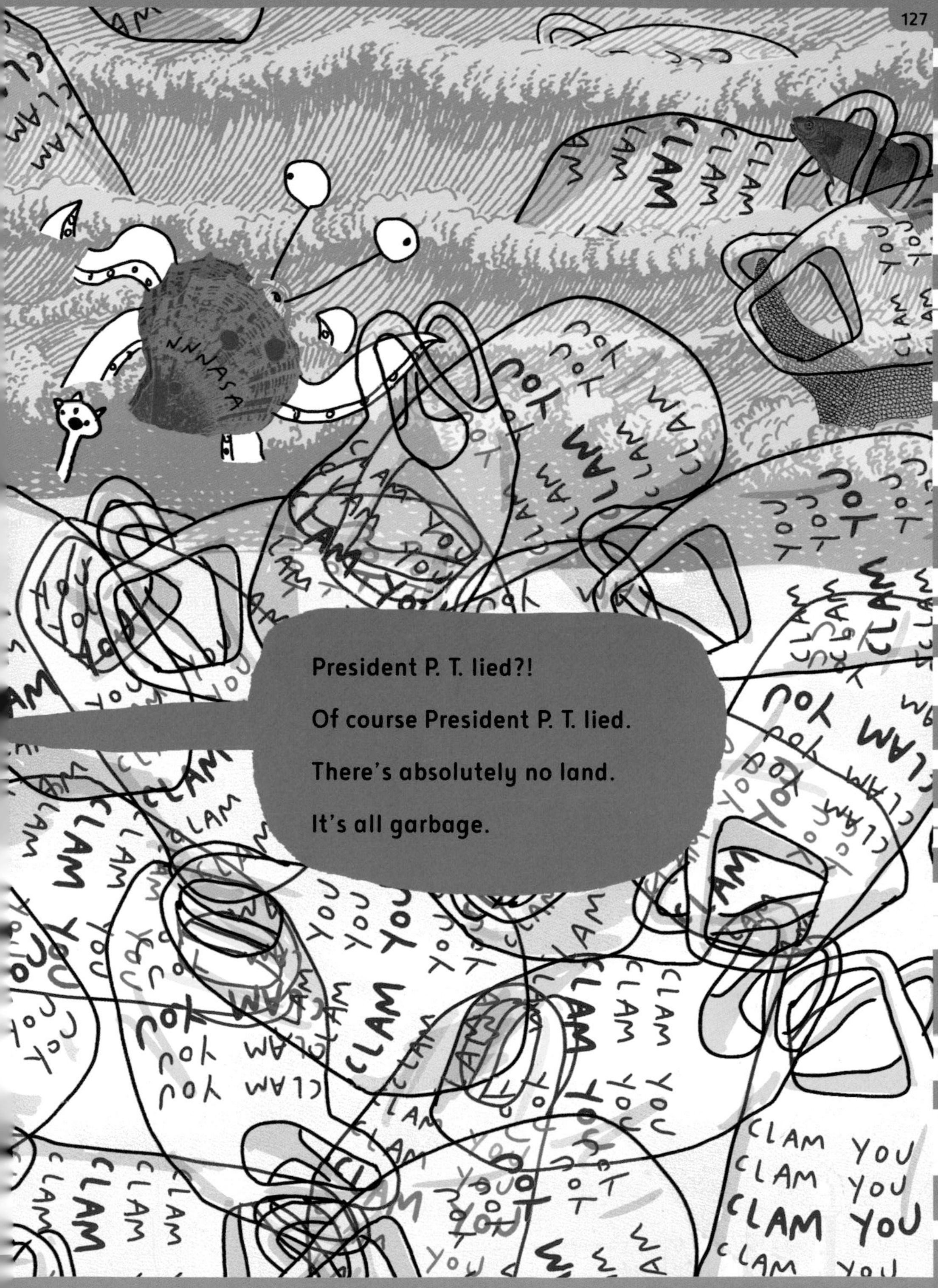
President P. T. lied?!
Of course President P. T. lied.
There's absolutely no land.
It's all garbage.
NNNASA
CLAM YOU
CLAM YOU
CLAM YOU

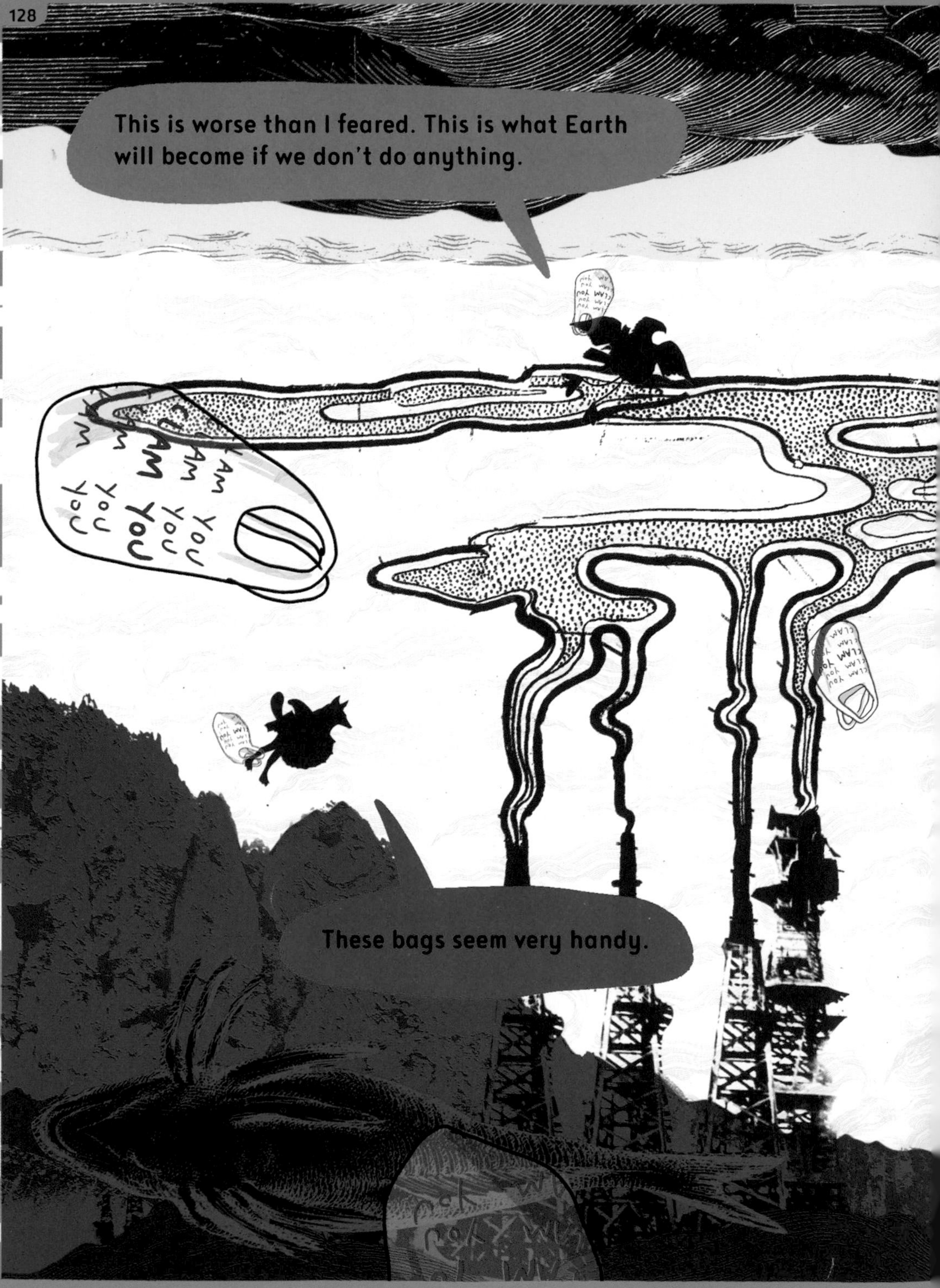
This is worse than I feared. This is what Earth will become if we don't do anything.
CLAM YOU
These bags seem very handy.

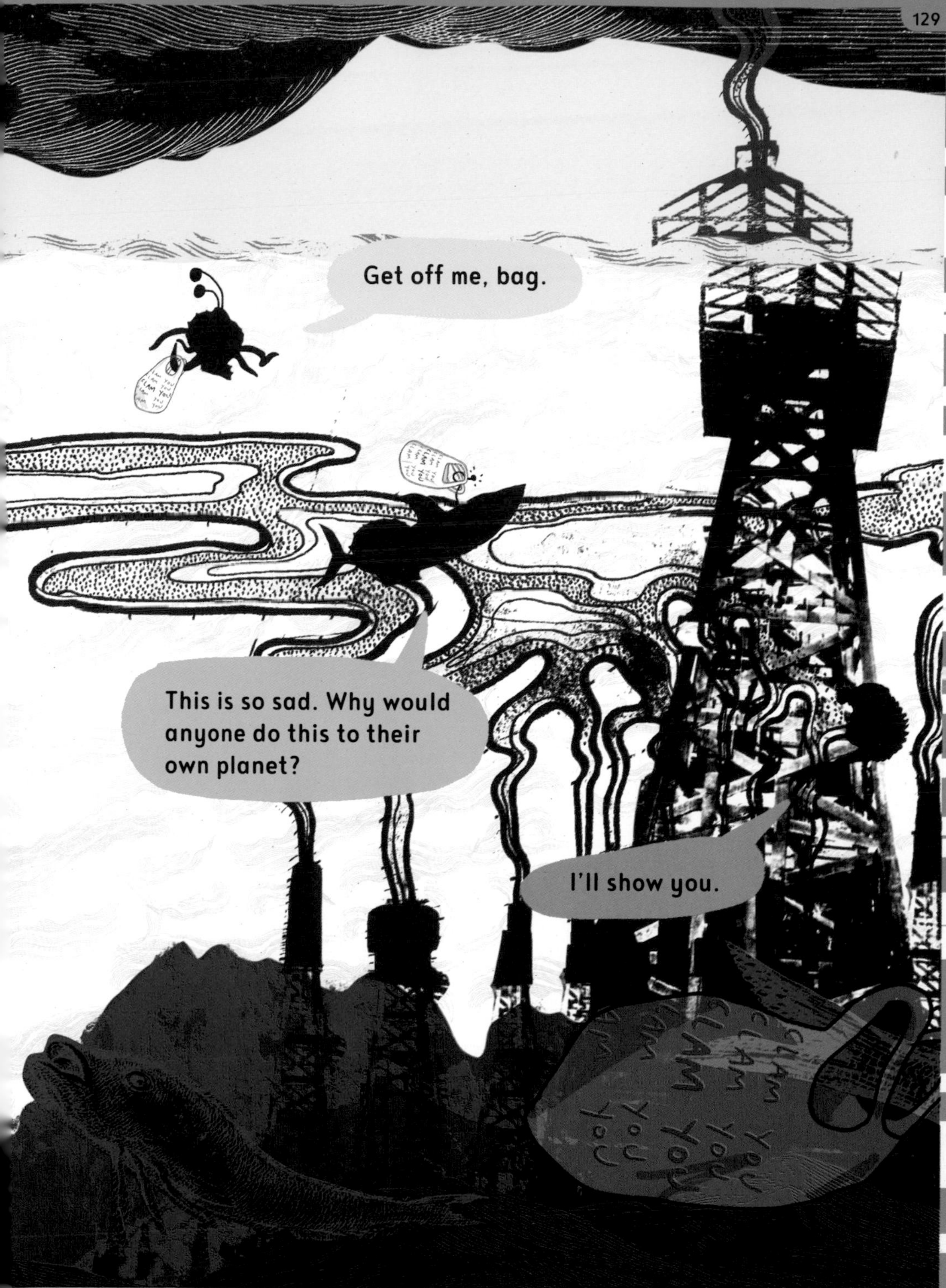
Get off me, bag.
This is so sad. Why would anyone do this to their own planet?
I'll show you.

CHAPTER 21:

Greedy Estates

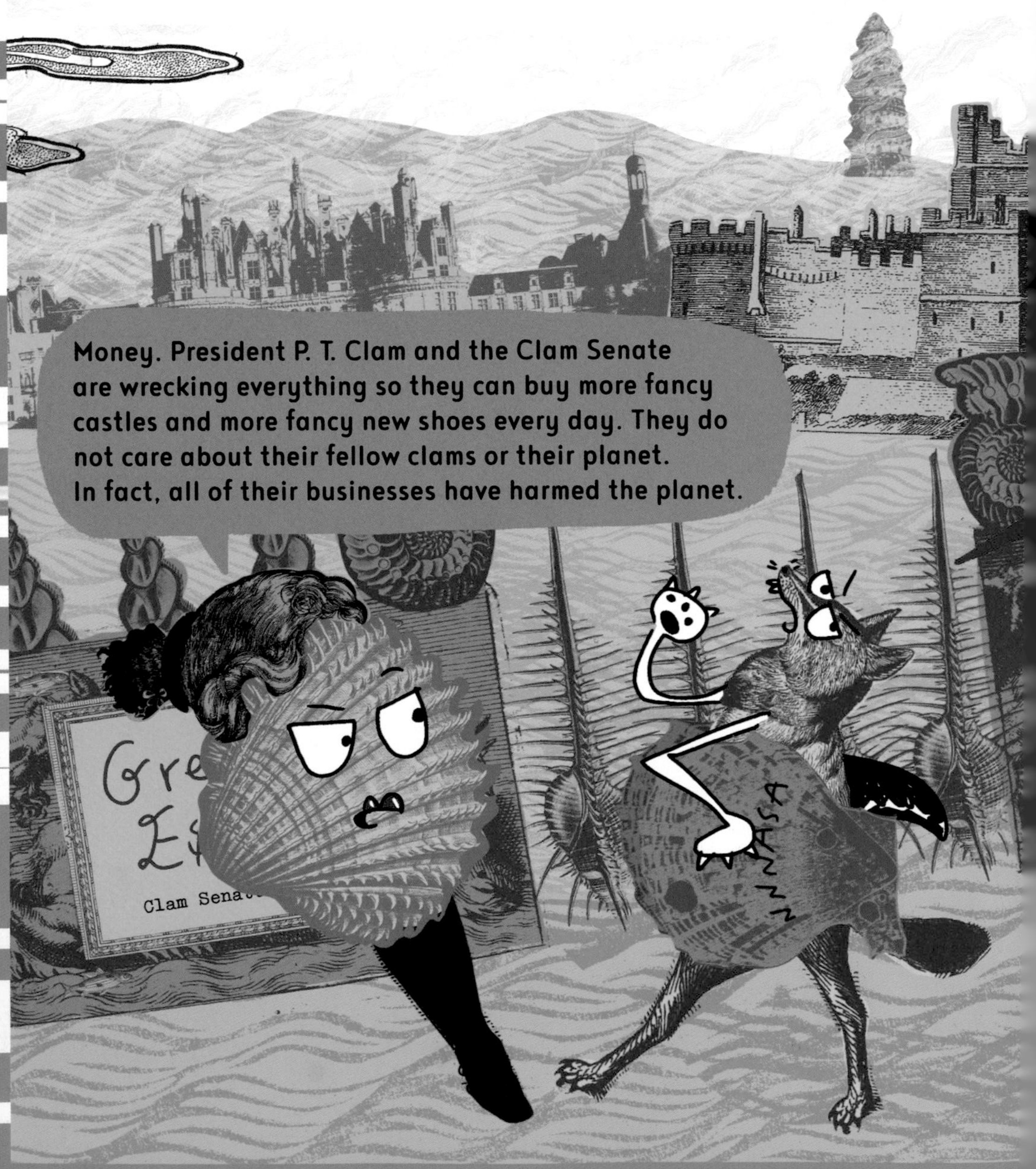
Money. President P. T. Clam and the Clam Senate are wrecking everything so they can buy more fancy castles and more fancy new shoes every day. They do not care about their fellow clams or their planet. In fact, all of their businesses have harmed the planet.
Gre
Es
Clam Sena
NASA

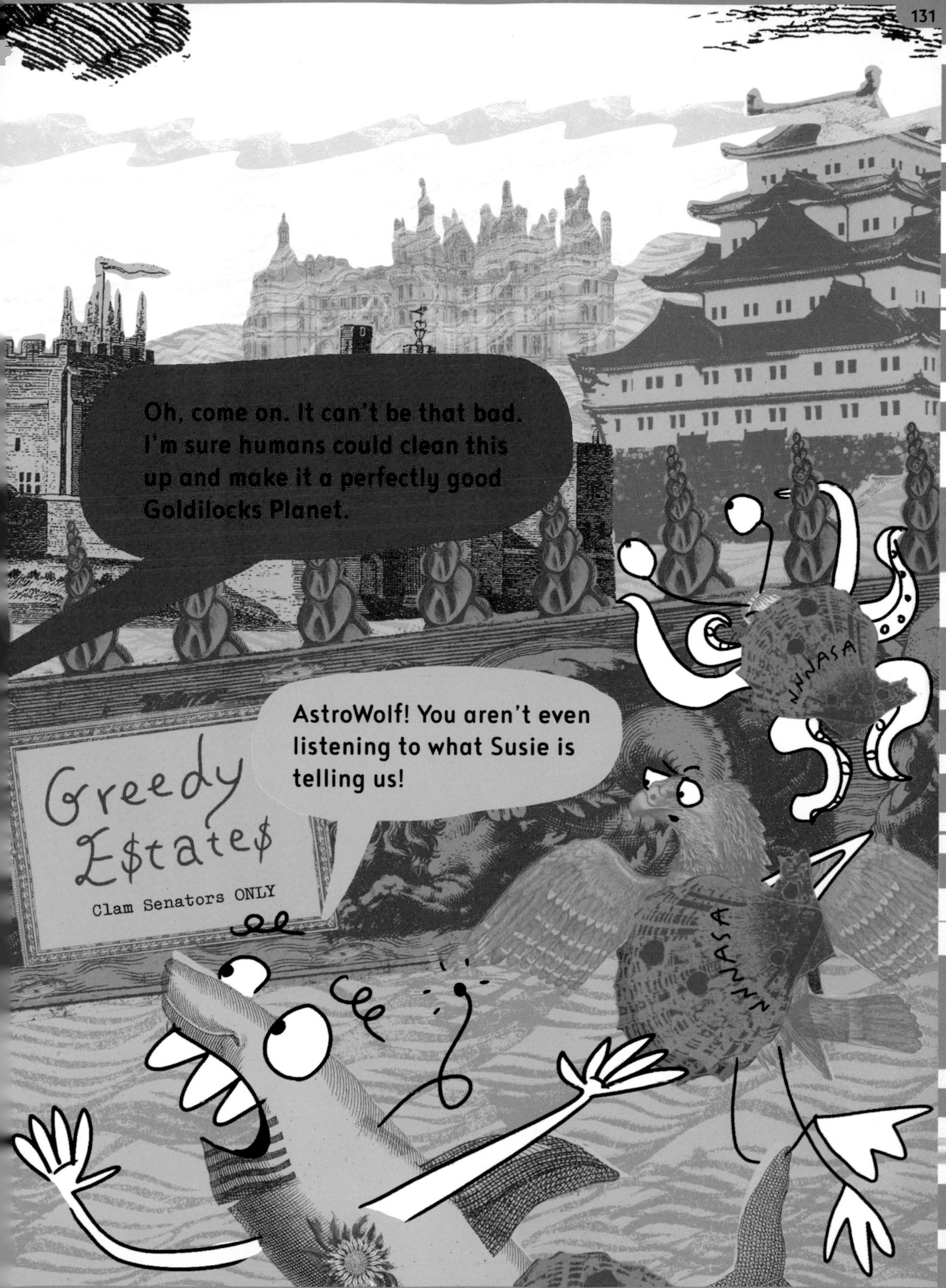
Oh, come on. It can't be that bad. I'm sure humans could clean this up and make it a perfectly good Goldilocks Planet.
AstroWolf! You aren't even listening to what Susie is telling us!
Greedy E$tate$
Clam Senators ONLY
NNNASA
NNNASA

The rest of the AstroNuts were shocked speechless to see what was really happening on the Water Planet. Though they shouldn't have been. Because if you think about it for oh, like three seconds, you would see that it's exactly what has been happening to me . . . with clams in place of humans.

If they hadn't been so shocked, they might have noticed the giant whale that was about to swoop in and swallow them up.

But they didn't.

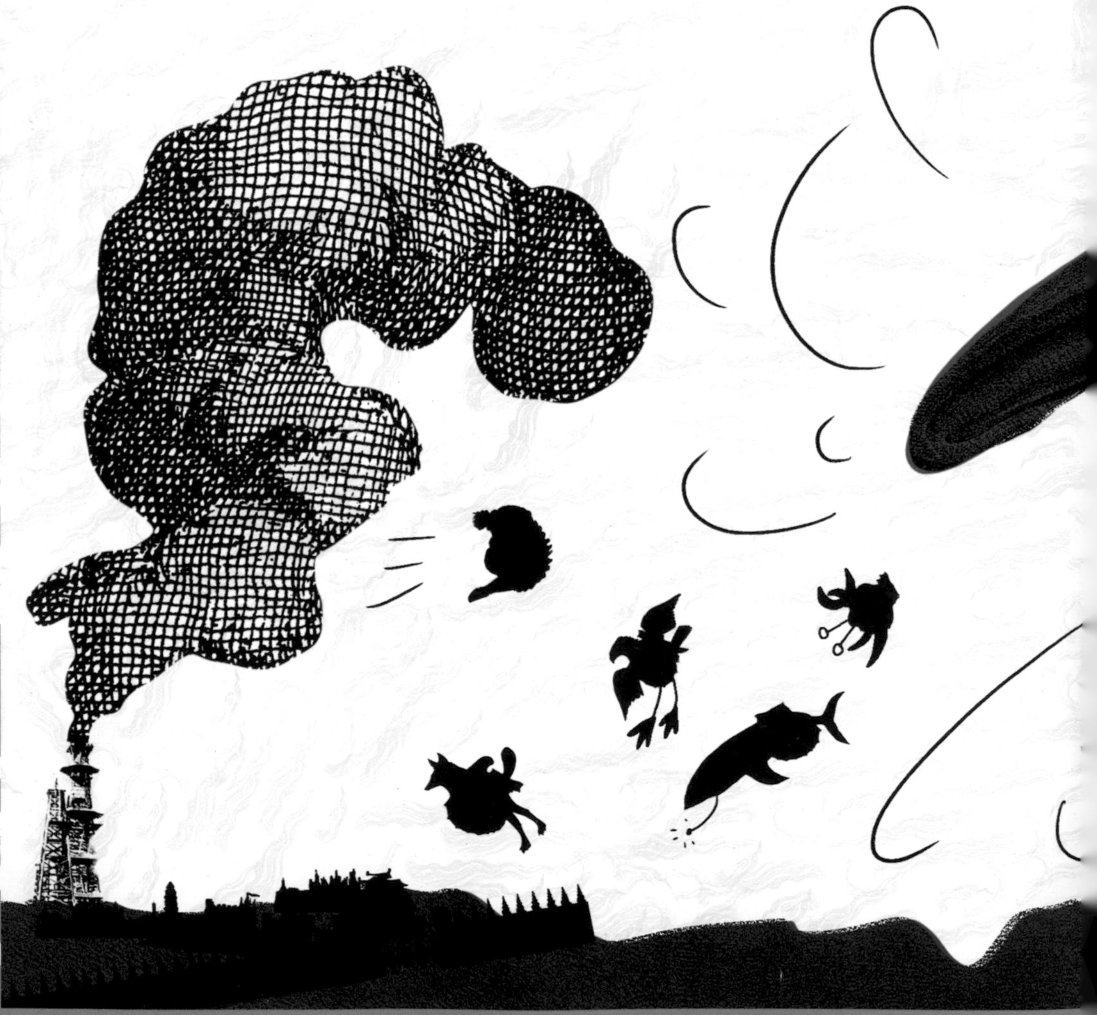

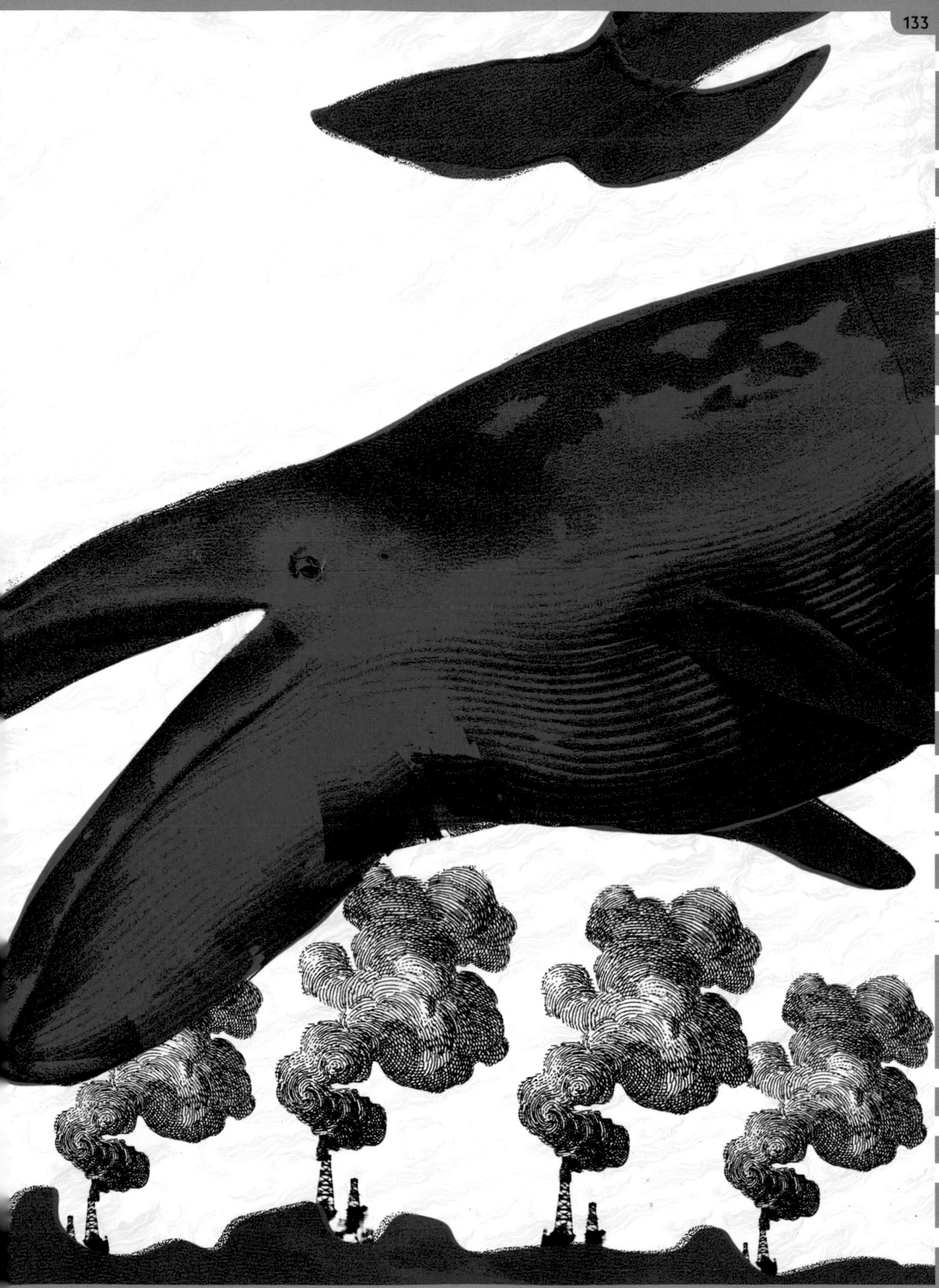

CHAPTER 22:

Whale Esophagus

Have you ever seen the inside of a whale esophagus? Yeah, me neither. But the AstroNuts did.

It's all part of being a NNASA secret project.

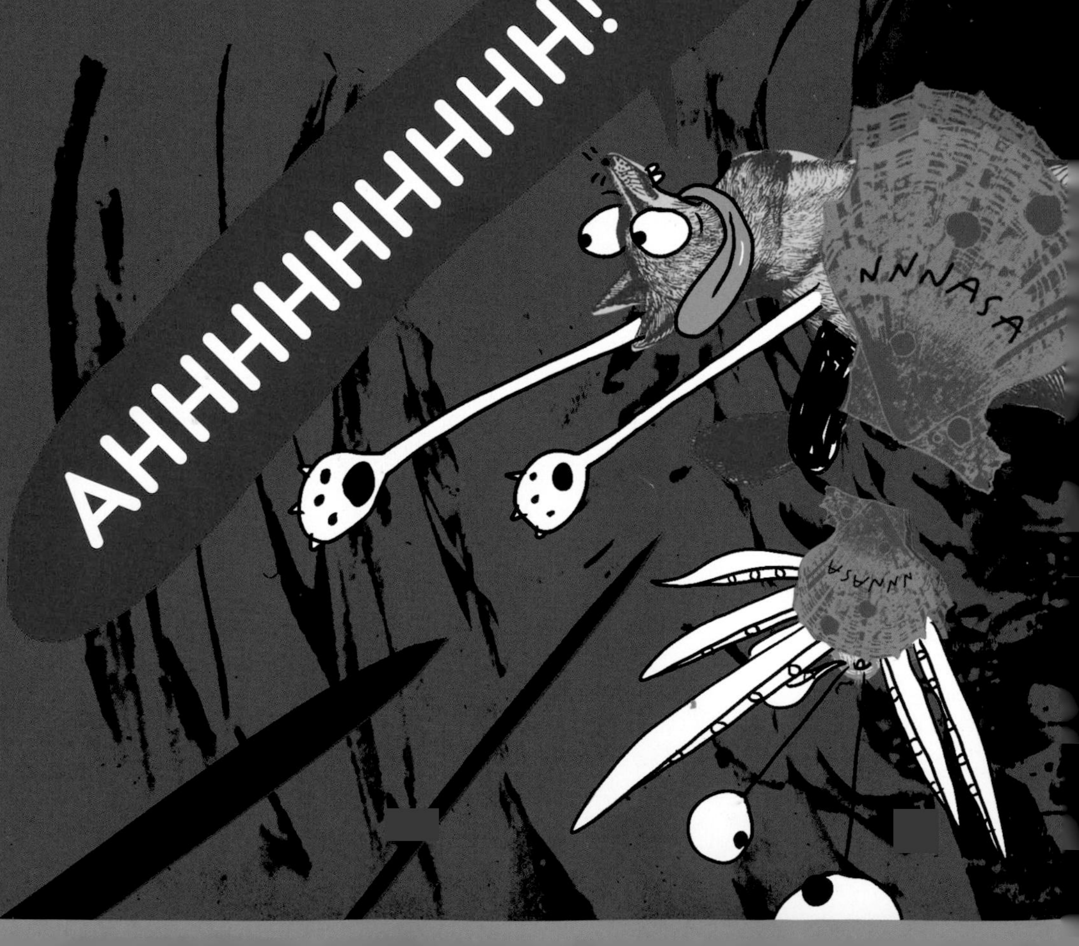
AHHHHHHHHHHH!
NNNASA
NNNASA

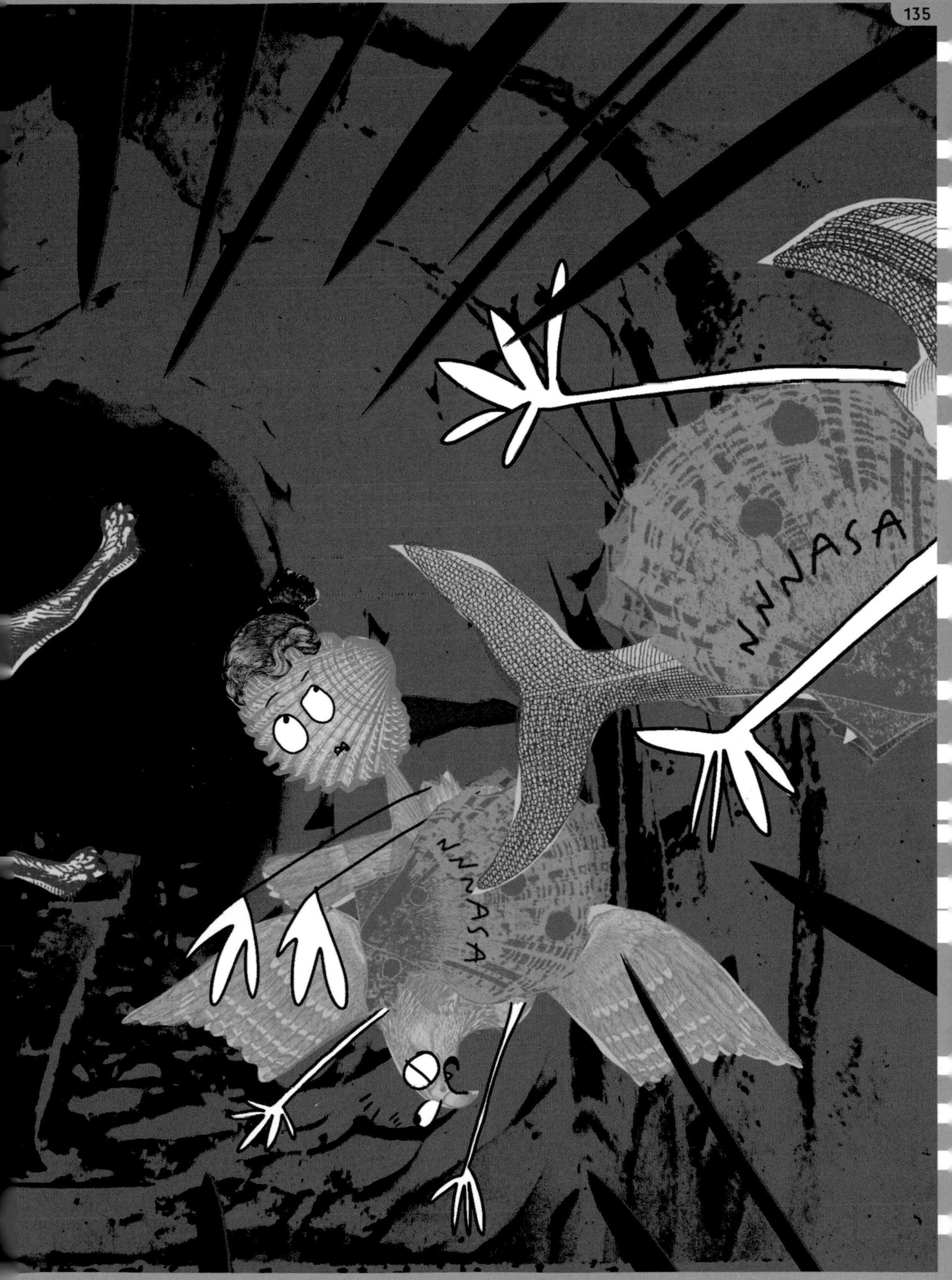
NNNASA
NNNASA

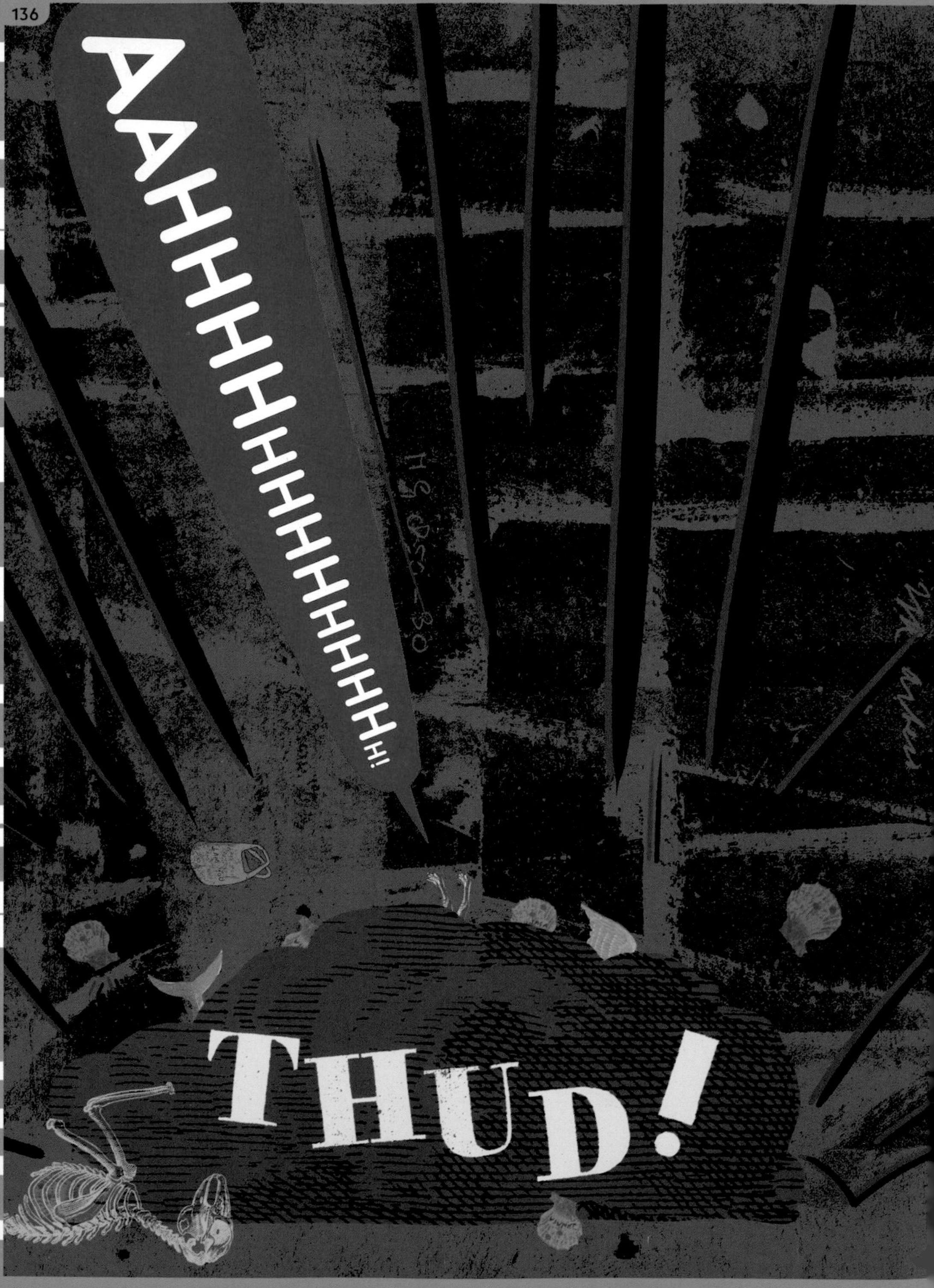
AAHHHHHHHHHHHHHH!
THUD!

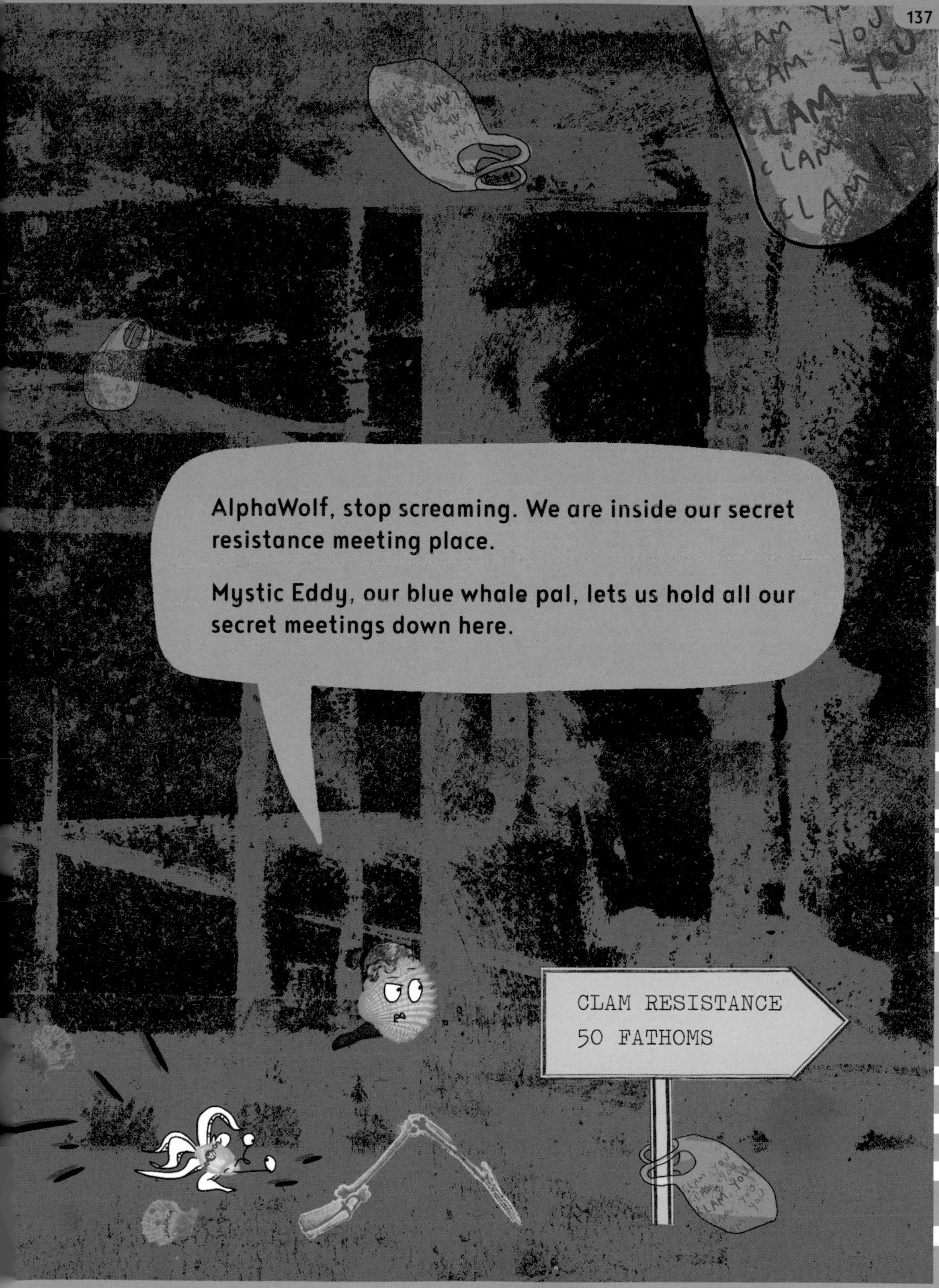
AlphaWolf, stop screaming. We are inside our secret resistance meeting place.
Mystic Eddy, our blue whale pal, lets us hold all our secret meetings down here.
CLAM RESISTANCE 50 FATHOMS

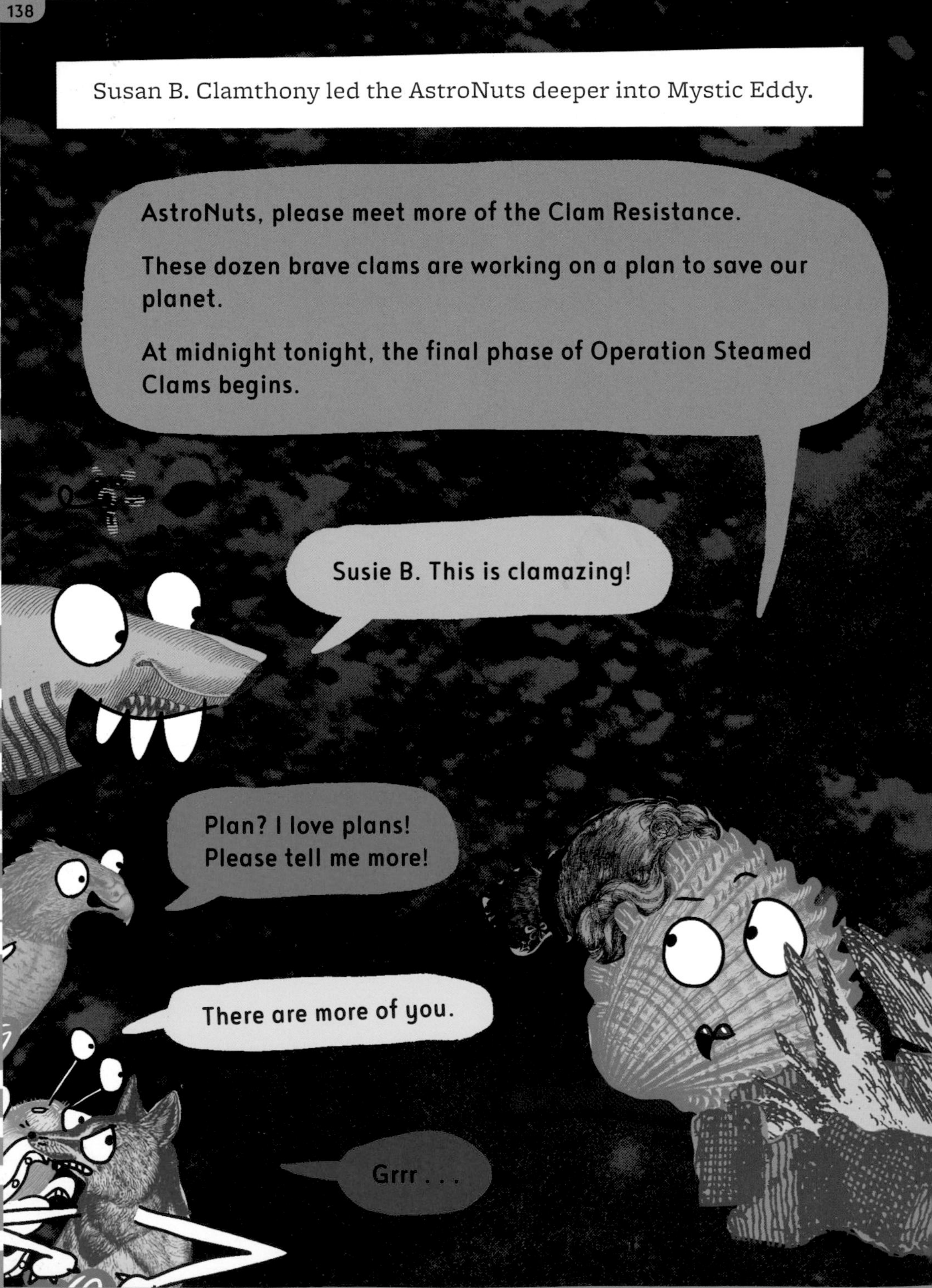
Susan B. Clamthony led the AstroNuts deeper into Mystic Eddy.
AstroNuts, please meet more of the Clam Resistance. These dozen brave clams are working on a plan to save our planet. At midnight tonight, the final phase of Operation Steamed Clams begins.
Susie B. This is clamazing!
Plan? I love plans! Please tell me more!
There are more of you.
Grrr . . .

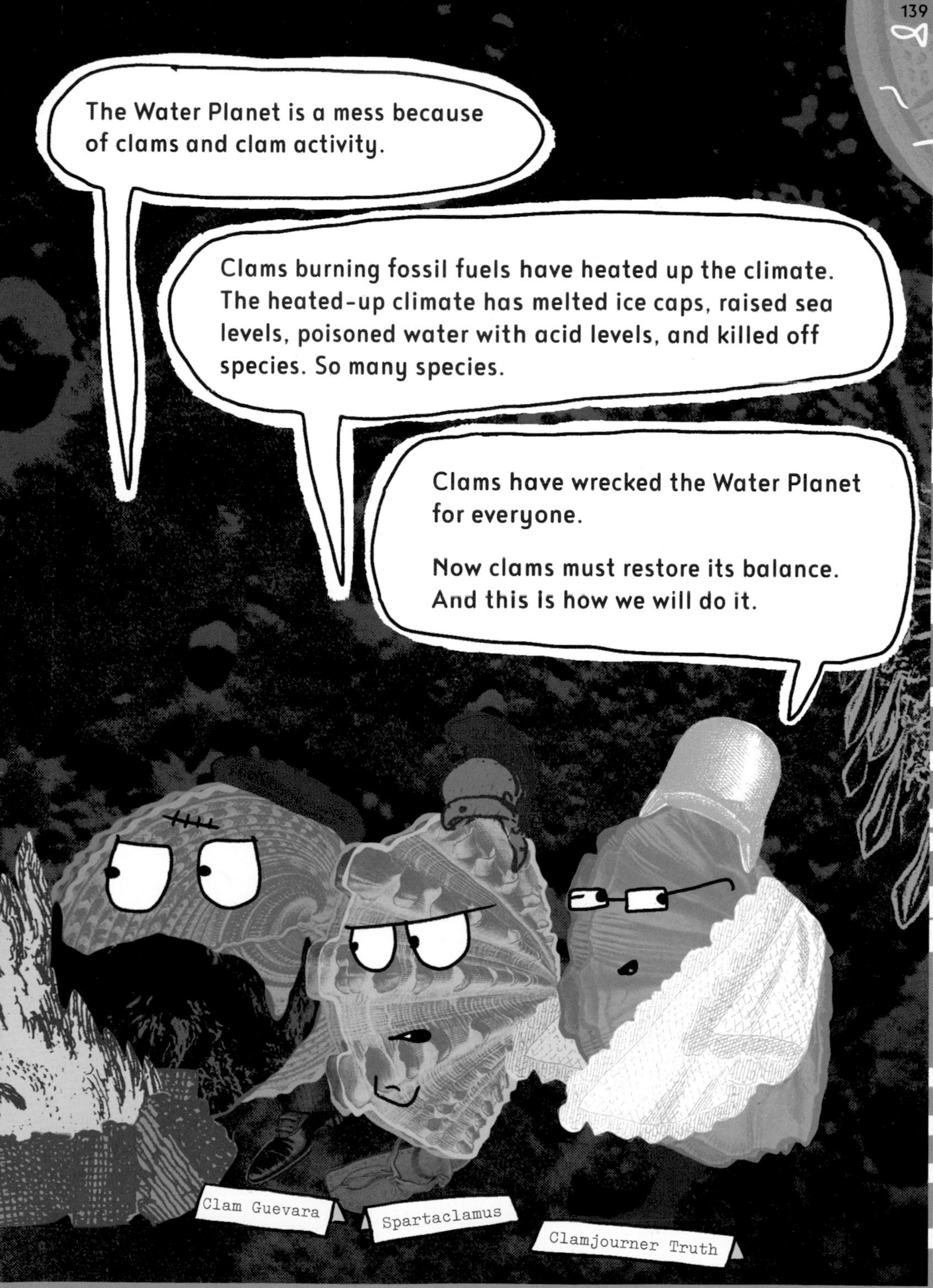
The Water Planet is a mess because of clams and clam activity.
Clams burning fossil fuels have heated up the climate. The heated-up climate has melted ice caps, raised sea levels, poisoned water with acid levels, and killed off species. So many species.
Clams have wrecked the Water Planet for everyone.
Now clams must restore its balance. And this is how we will do it.
Clam Guevara
Spartaclamus
Clamjourner Truth

CHAPTER 23:
The Plan

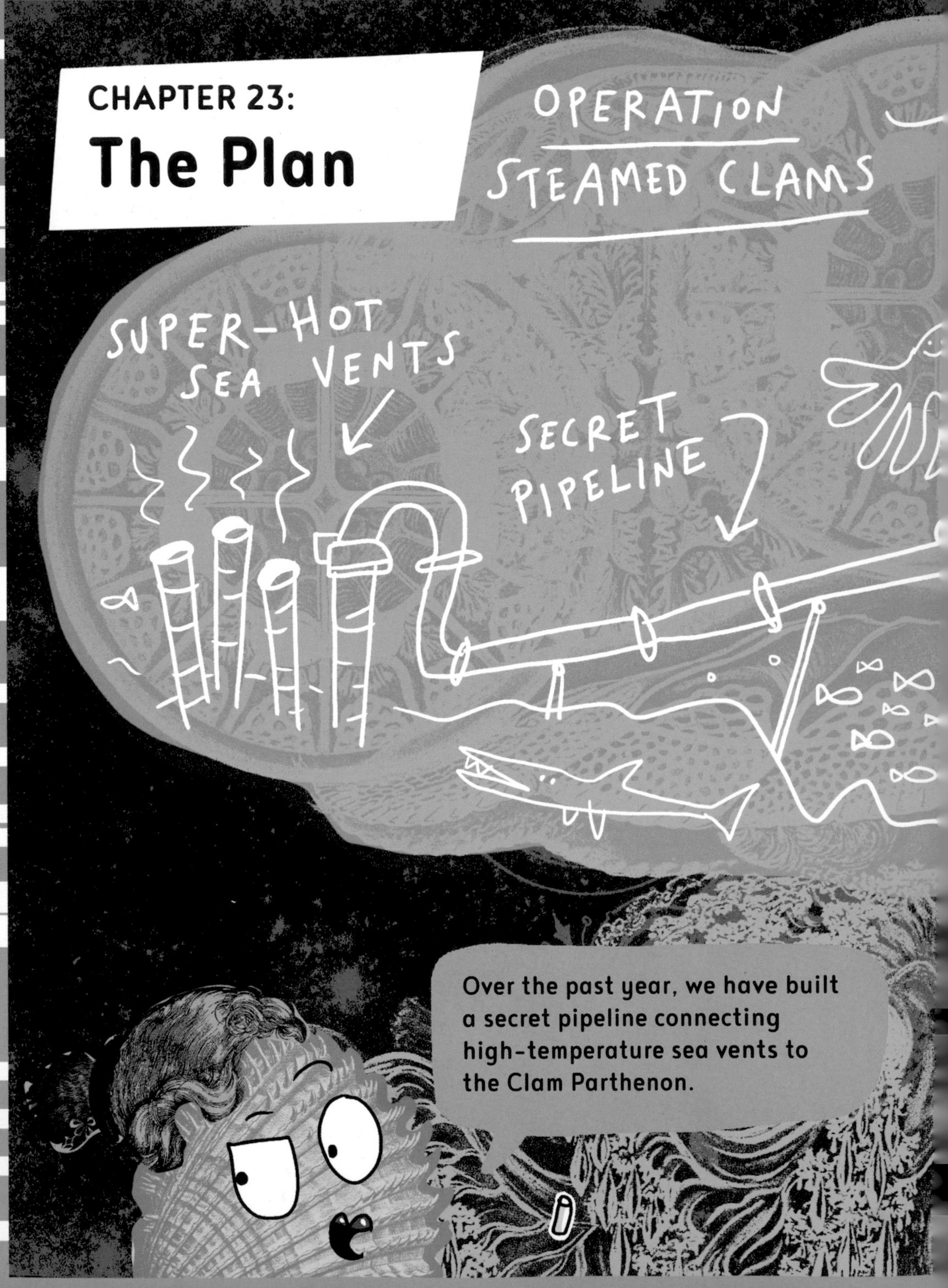

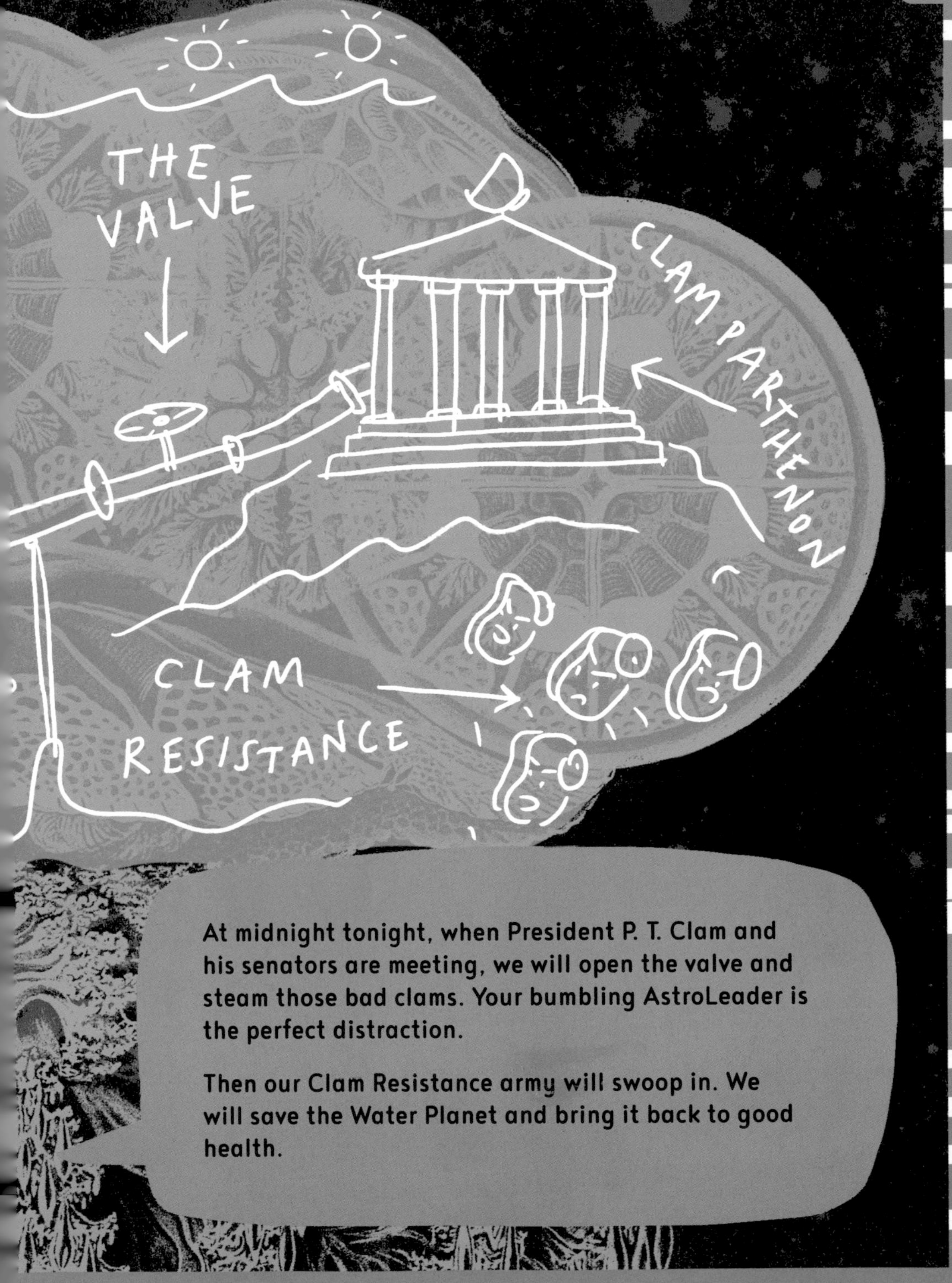
THE VALVE
CLAM PARTHENON
CLAM RESISTANCE
At midnight tonight, when President P. T. Clam and his senators are meeting, we will open the valve and steam those bad clams. Your bumbling AstroLeader is the perfect distraction.
Then our Clam Resistance army will swoop in. We will save the Water Planet and bring it back to good health.

This was a huge moment. The AstroNuts had just been shown an entire side of the planet they didn't know existed. AND they had seen a pretty wild plan of how everything could be changed. But someone, guess who, was not sure of what he had just seen.

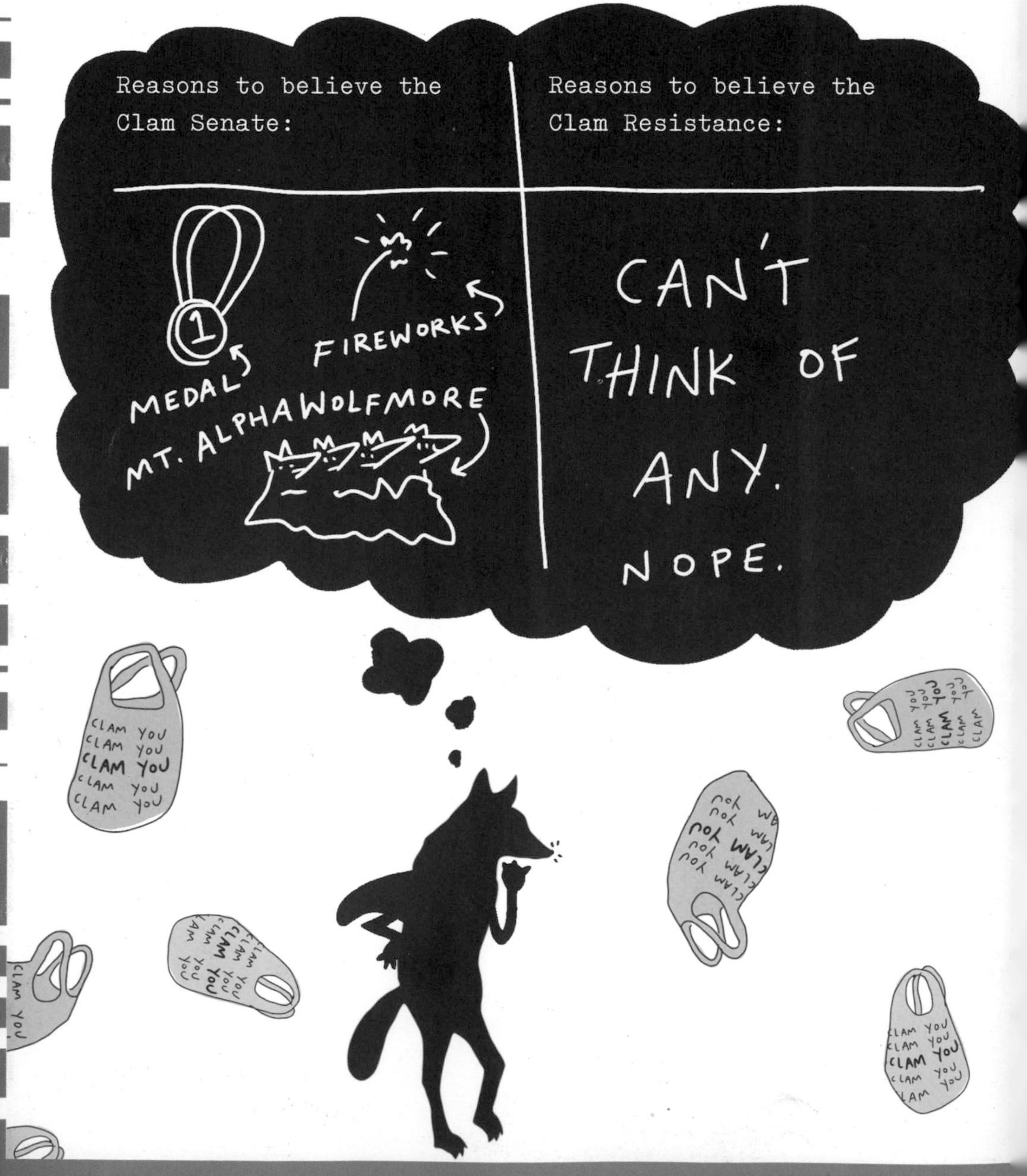
Reasons to believe the Clam Senate:
MEDAL
FIREWORKS
MT. ALPHAWOLFMORE
Reasons to believe the Clam Resistance:
CAN'T THINK OF ANY.
NOPE.
CLAM YOU

I have thought about this.

A LOT.

And I think we need more action and less talk to find out who to believe.

LaserShark, SmartHawk, and StinkBug — as your MISSION LEADER, I order you to stay in this whale and keep an eye on these clams.

I will go to the Clam Parthenon and get the truth.

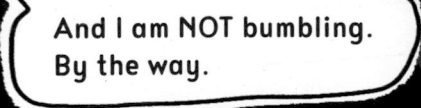

And I am NOT bumbling. By the way.

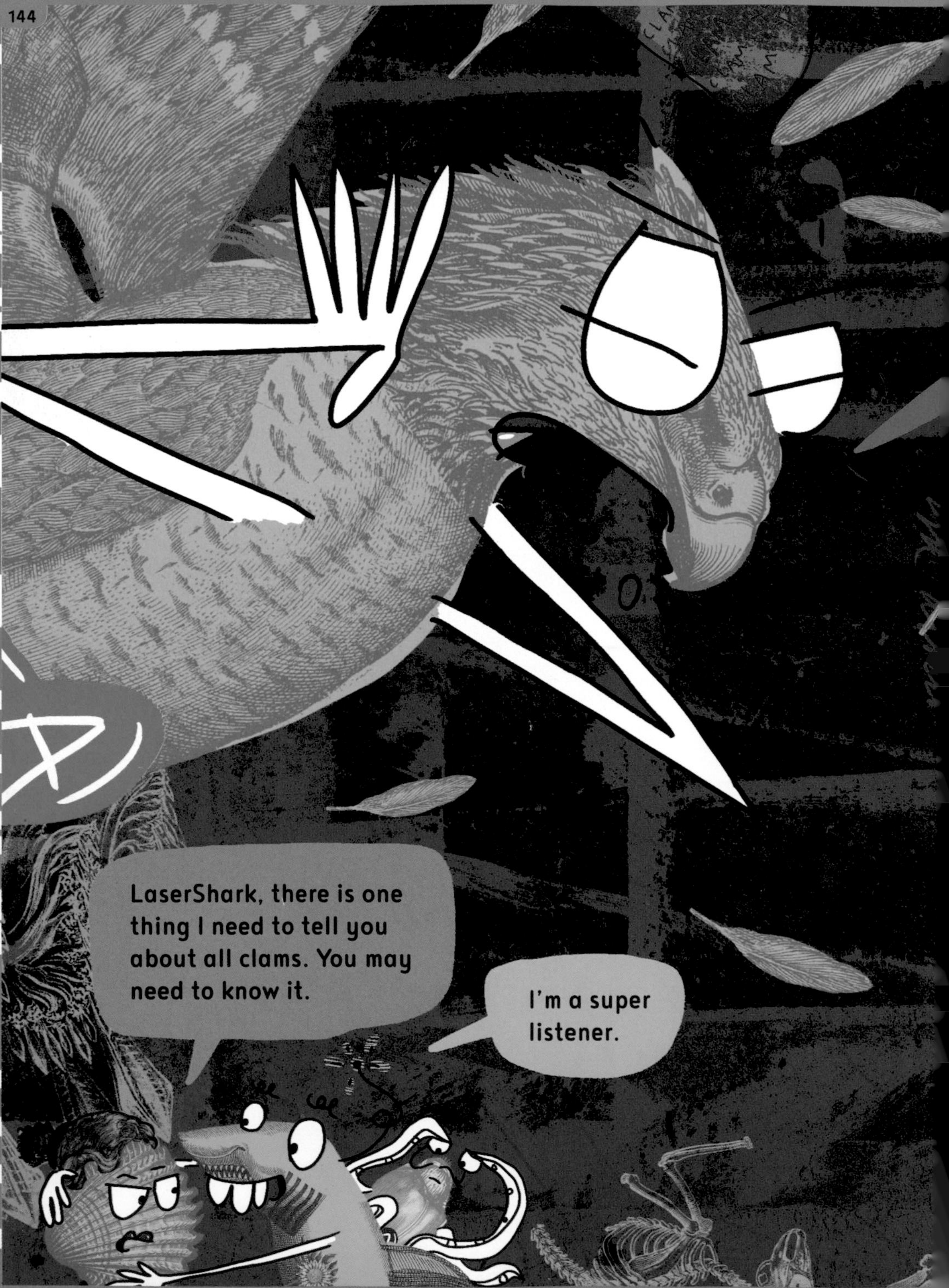
LaserShark, there is one thing I need to tell you about all clams. You may need to know it.
I'm a super listener.

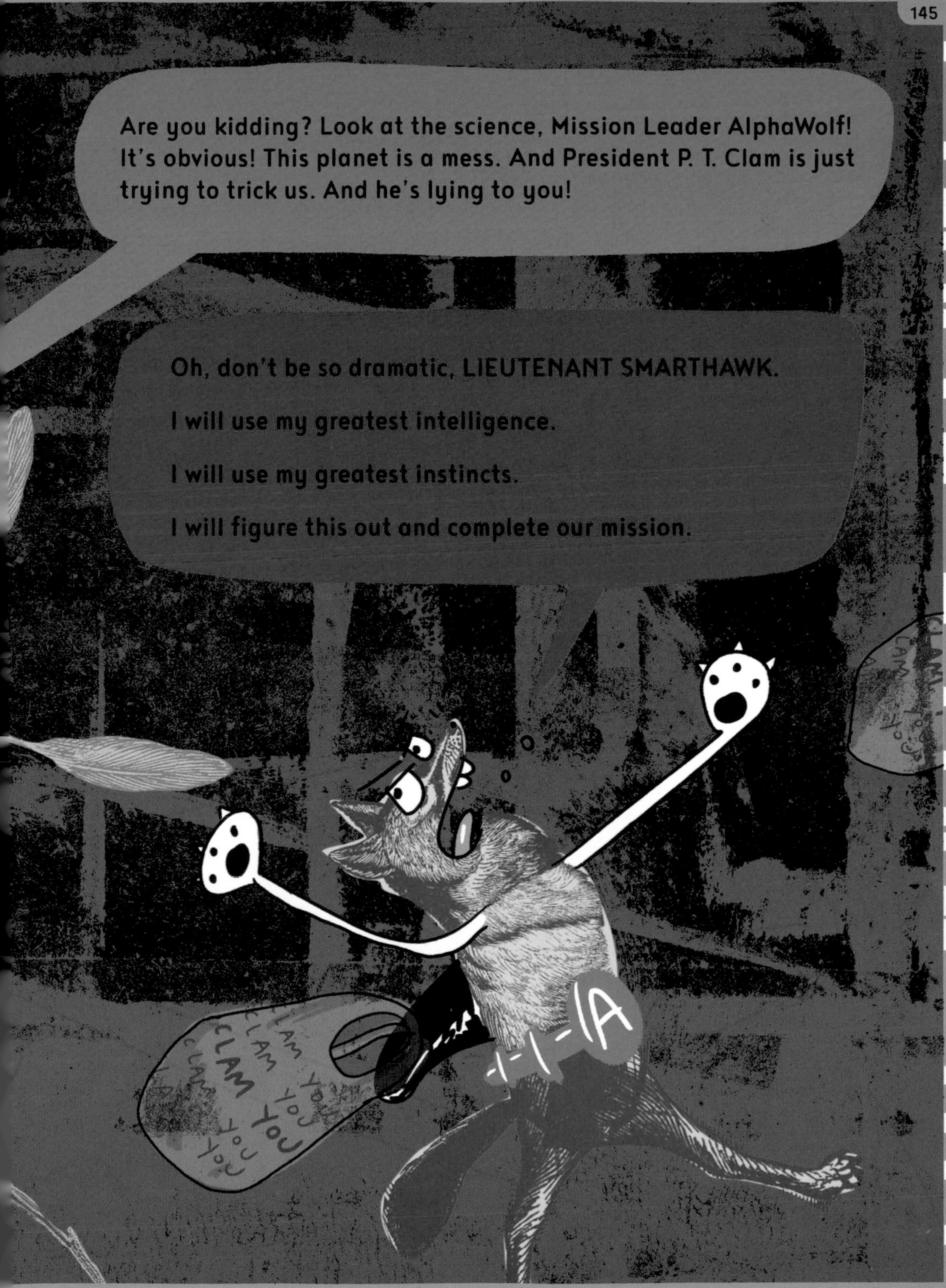
Are you kidding? Look at the science, Mission Leader AlphaWolf! It's obvious! This planet is a mess. And President P. T. Clam is just trying to trick us. And he's lying to you!
Oh, don't be so dramatic, LIEUTENANT SMARTHAWK.
I will use my greatest intelligence.
I will use my greatest instincts.
I will figure this out and complete our mission.

Have you ever noticed that humans have an amazing ability to think they are most right—exactly when they are most wrong?

Unfortunately for everyone, AlphaWolf had picked up this amazing ability.

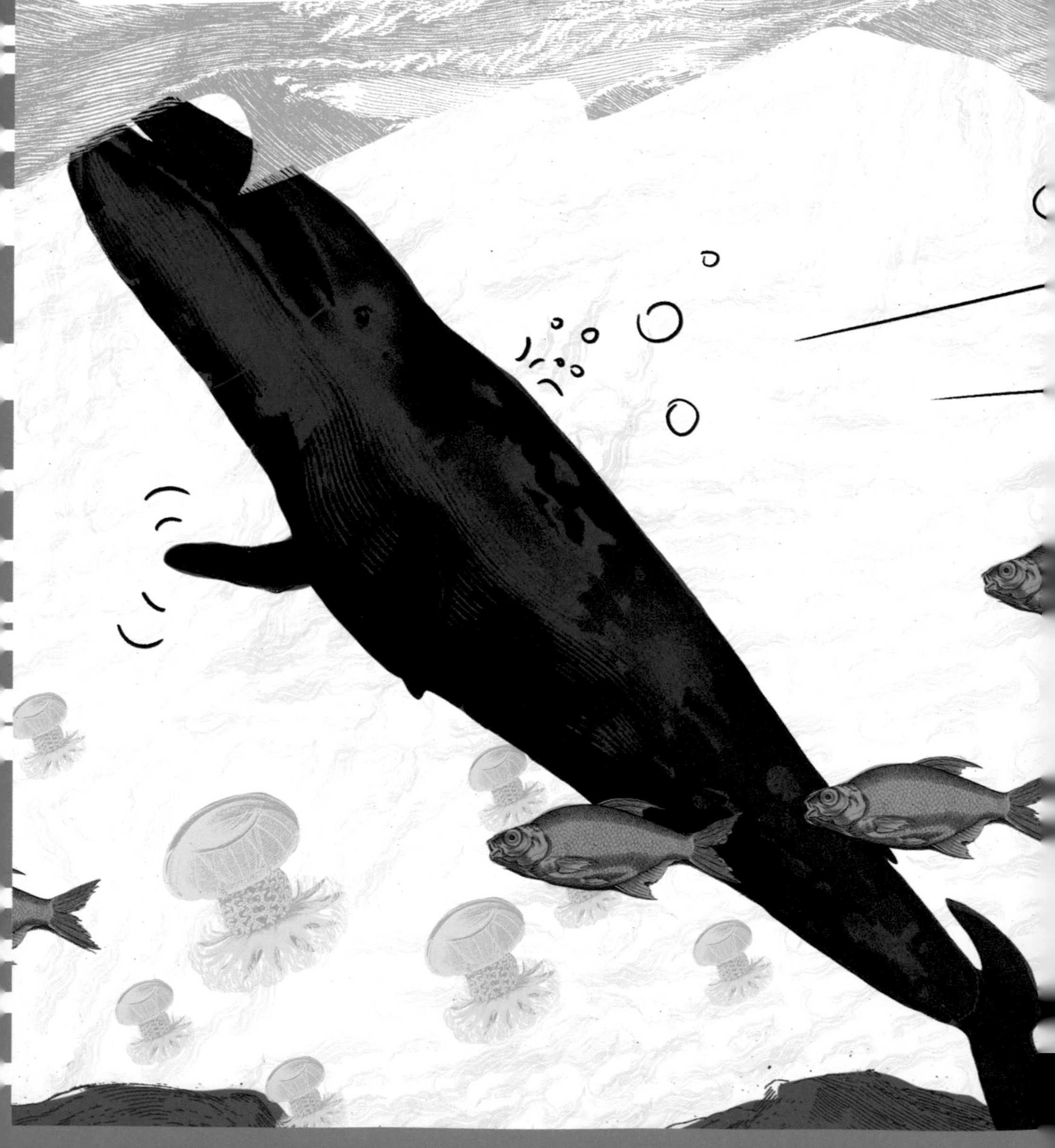

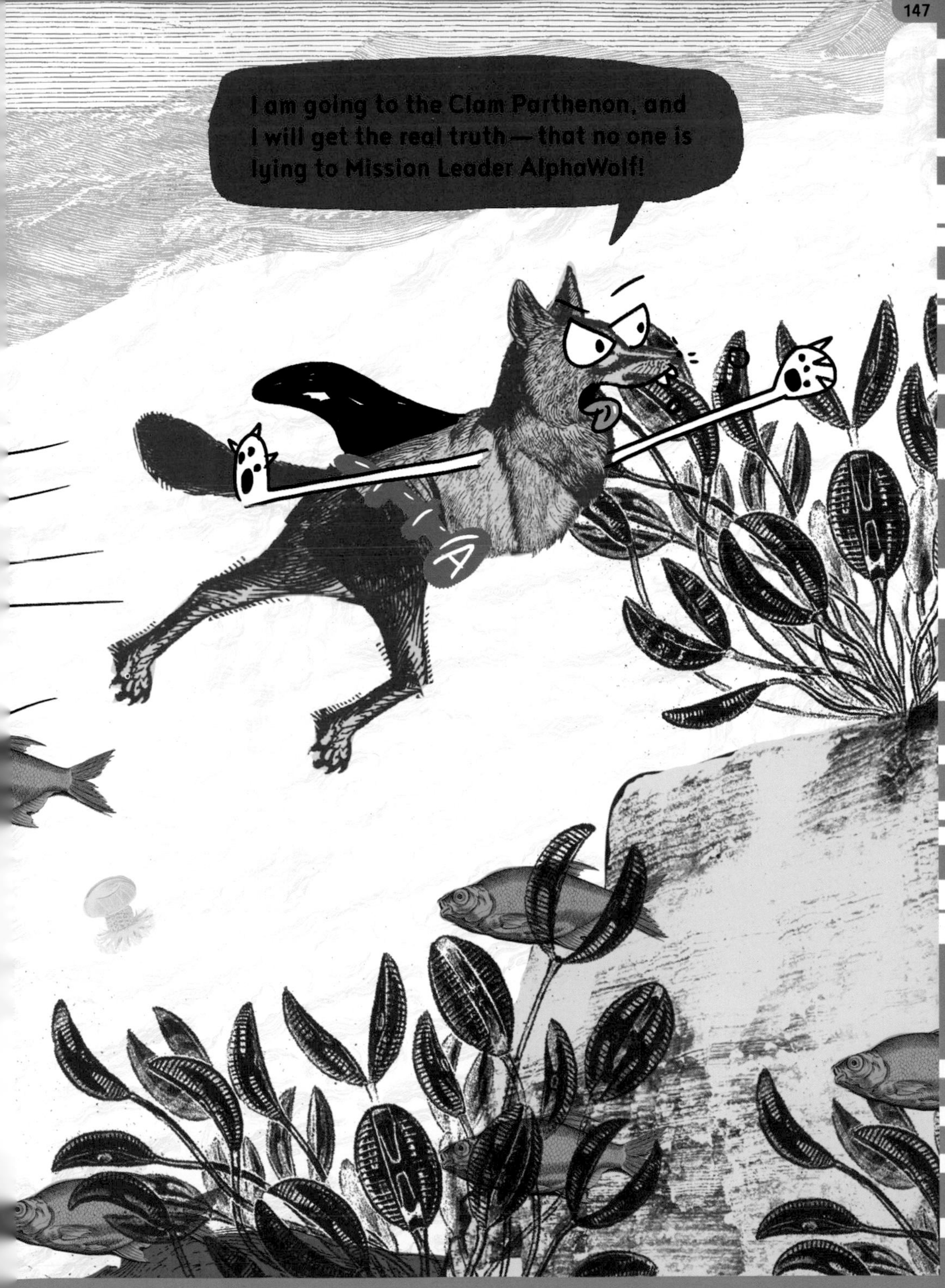
I am going to the Clam Parthenon, and I will get the real truth — that no one is lying to Mission Leader AlphaWolf!

CHAPTER 24:
Clamocracy

Hyperspeed doggie paddle seconds later, AlphaWolf snuck up on the Clam Parthenon to secretly listen in on the real truth.

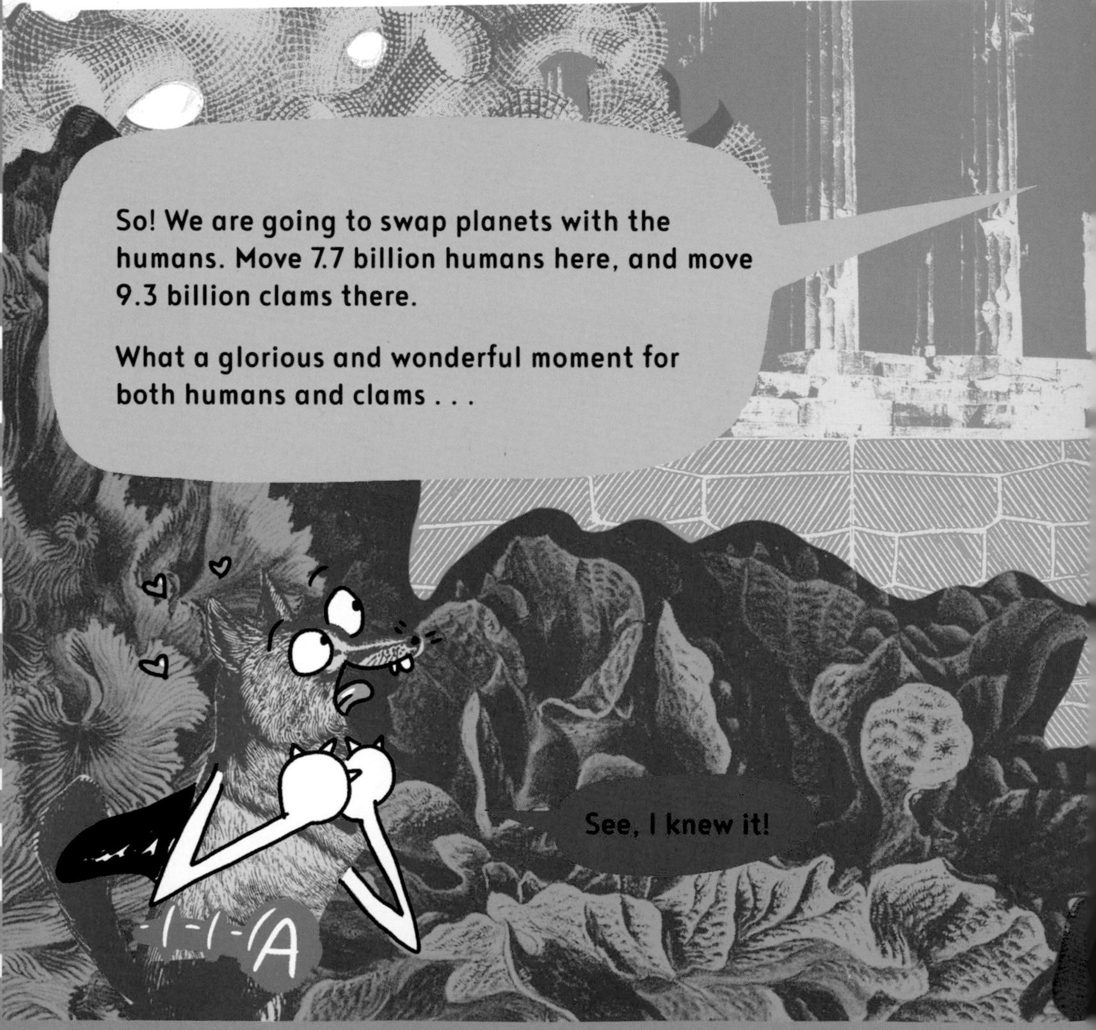
So! We are going to swap planets with the humans. Move 7.7 billion humans here, and move 9.3 billion clams there.
What a glorious and wonderful moment for both humans and clams . . .
See, I knew it!

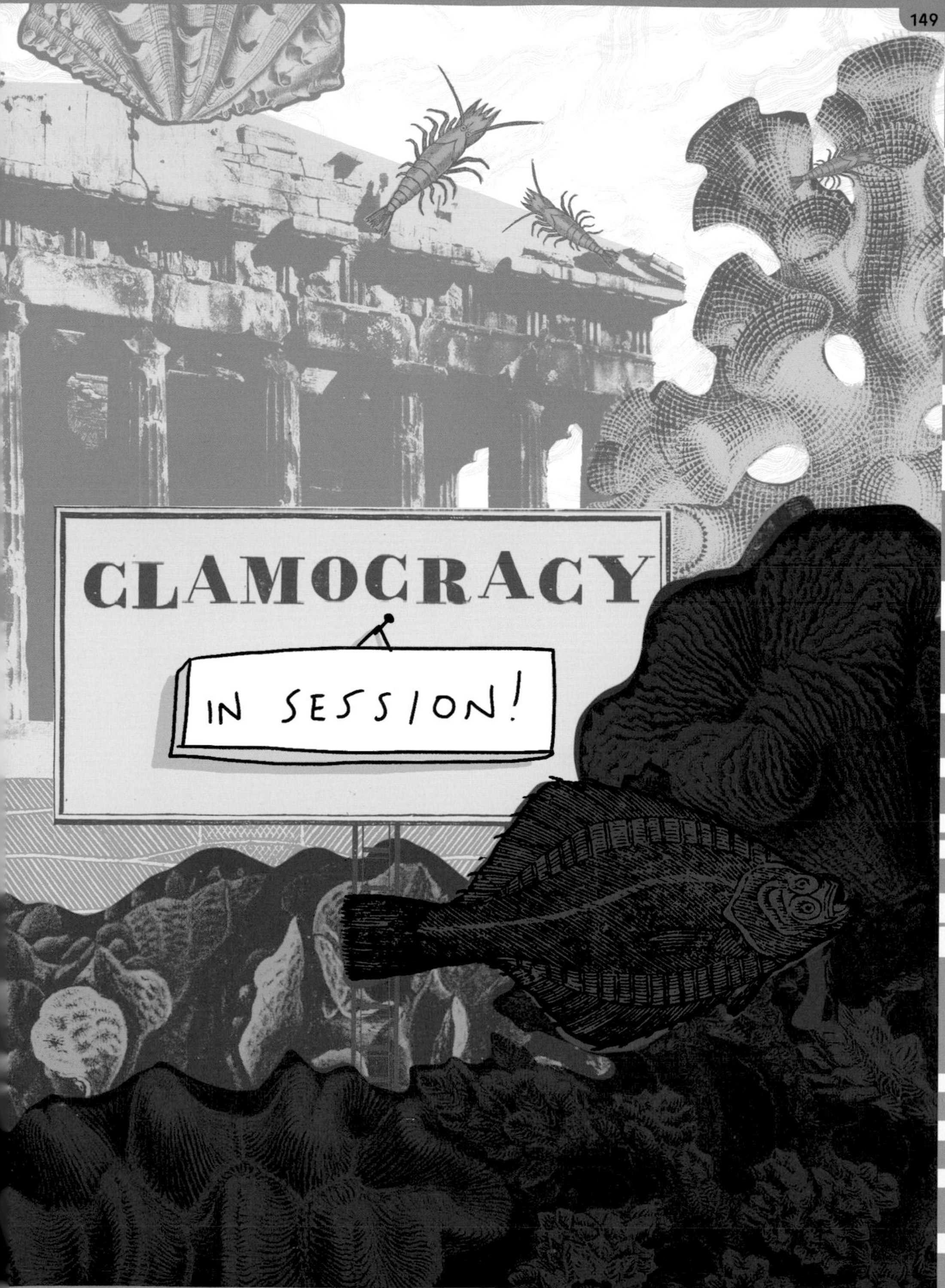
CLAMOCRACY
IN SESSION!

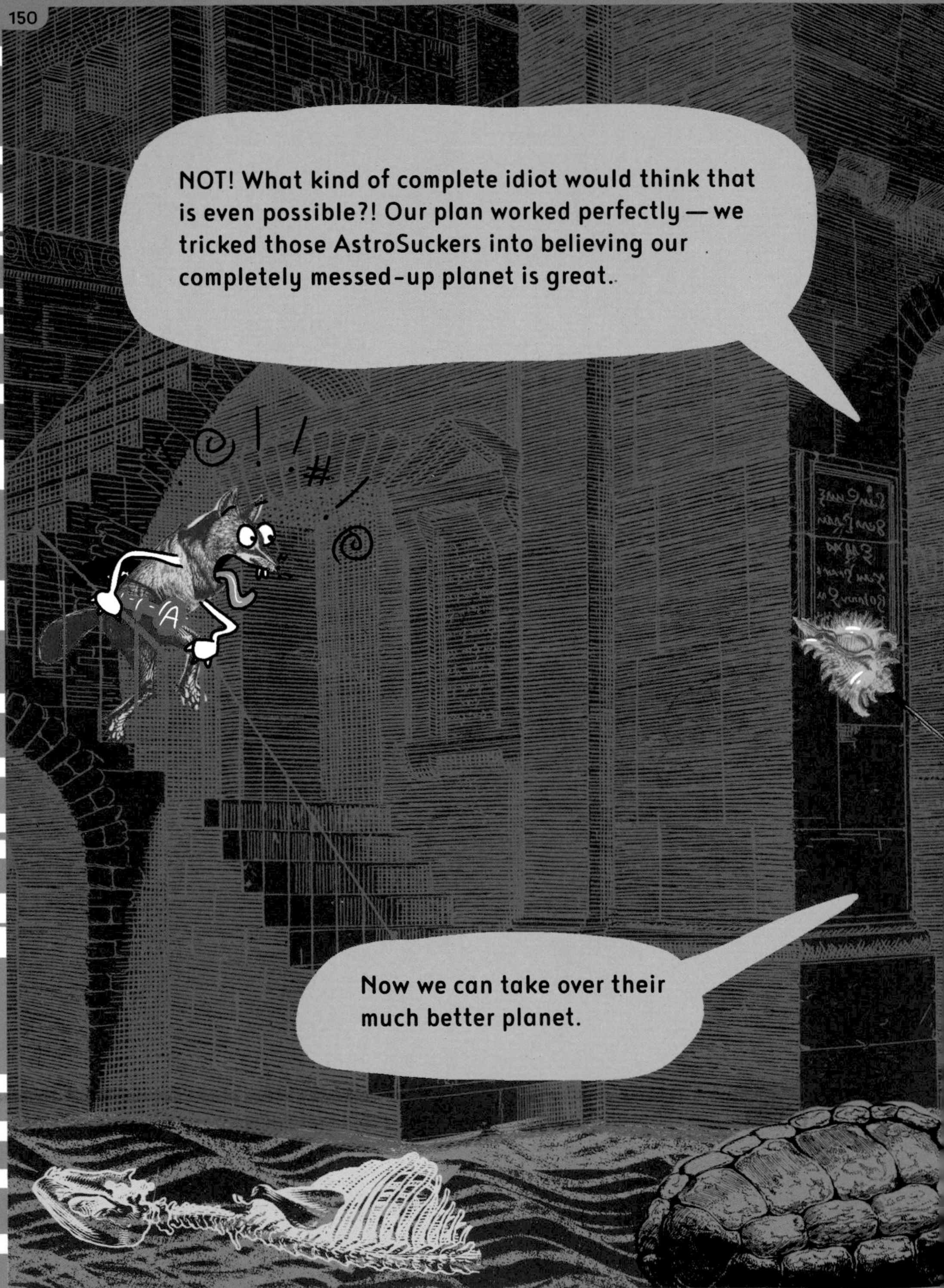
NOT! What kind of complete idiot would think that is even possible?! Our plan worked perfectly — we tricked those AstroSuckers into believing our completely messed-up planet is great.
Now we can take over their much better planet.

Because this planet is a polluted, stinky, fecal-y mess.
On Earth we can get more rich.
With more castles.
And more shoes!

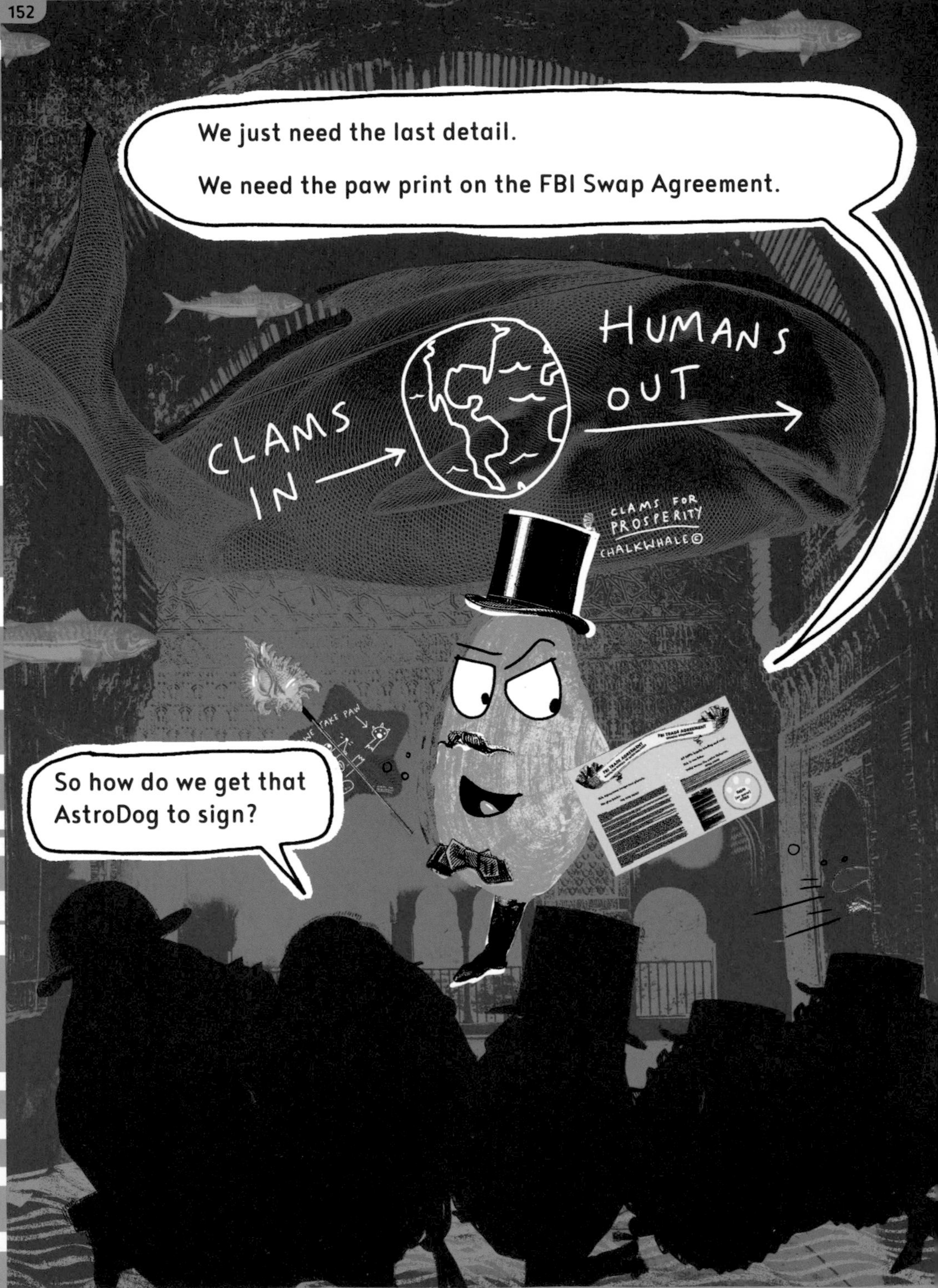
We just need the last detail.
We need the paw print on the FBI Swap Agreement.
CLAMS IN
HUMANS OUT
CLAMS FOR PROSPERITY CHALKWHALE©
FBI TRADE AGREEMENT
So how do we get that AstroDog to sign?

Part two of our plan is already in action. Our New Clam City Police are on the way to TAKE IT!
WE TAKE PAW
DUH...
CLAMS FOR PROSPERITY
CHALKSTARFISH©

AlphaWolf could not believe what his superhearing was hearing. This was not the truth he had planned to find out.

He turned around and hyperspeed paddled back to Mystic Eddy, worried about losing all his favorite things back on me.

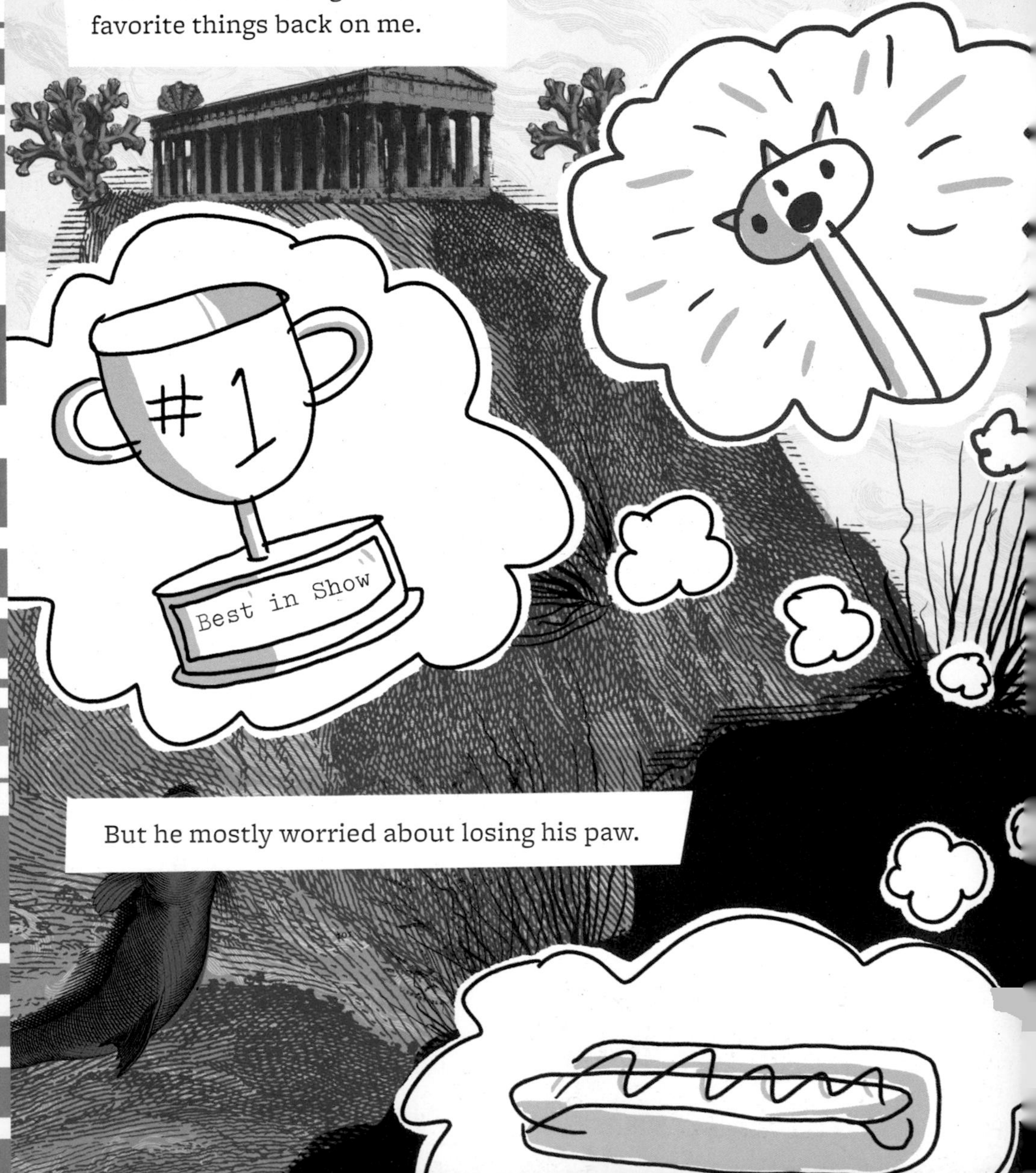
#1
Best in Show

But he mostly worried about losing his paw.

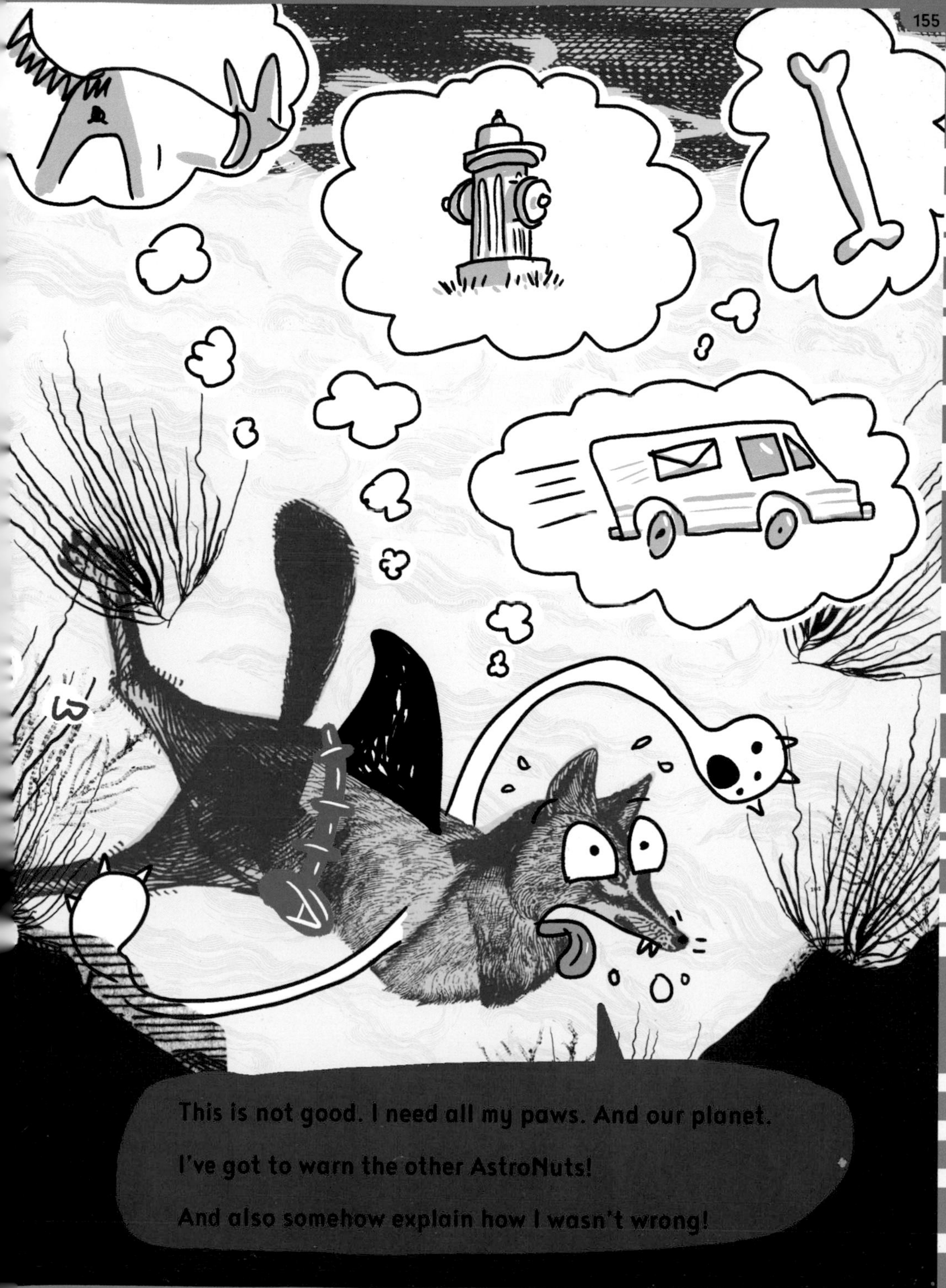
This is not good. I need all my paws. And our planet.
I've got to warn the other AstroNuts!
And also somehow explain how I wasn't wrong!

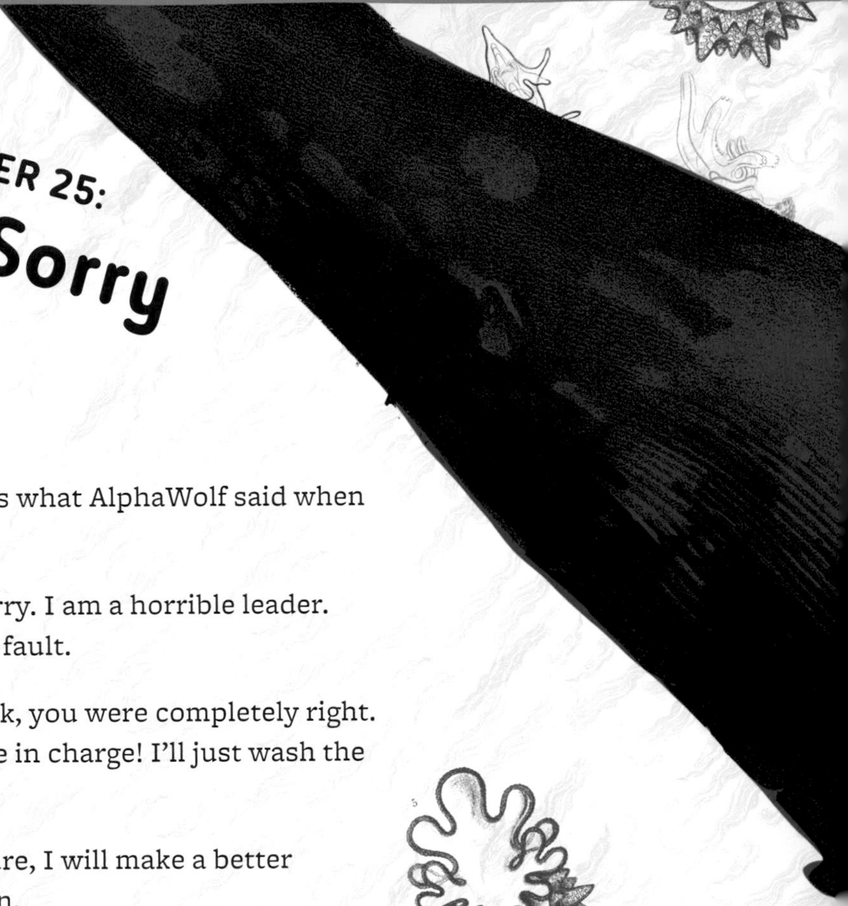

CHAPTER 25:
I'm Sorry

Can you guess what AlphaWolf said when he got back?

A) I am so sorry. I am a horrible leader. This is all my fault.

B) SmartHawk, you were completely right. You should be in charge! I'll just wash the dishes.

C) In the future, I will make a better effort to listen.

D) We can fix this with teamwork!

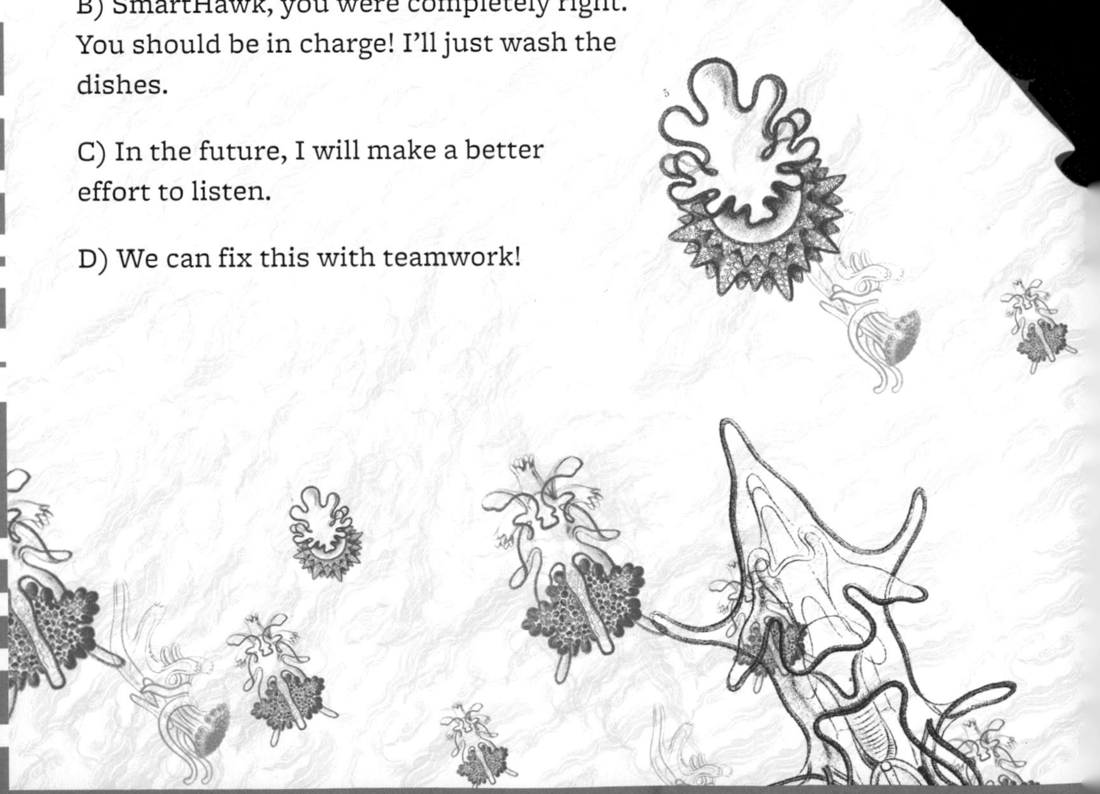

Nope. The answer is:

E) NONE OF THE ABOVE.

Because . . .

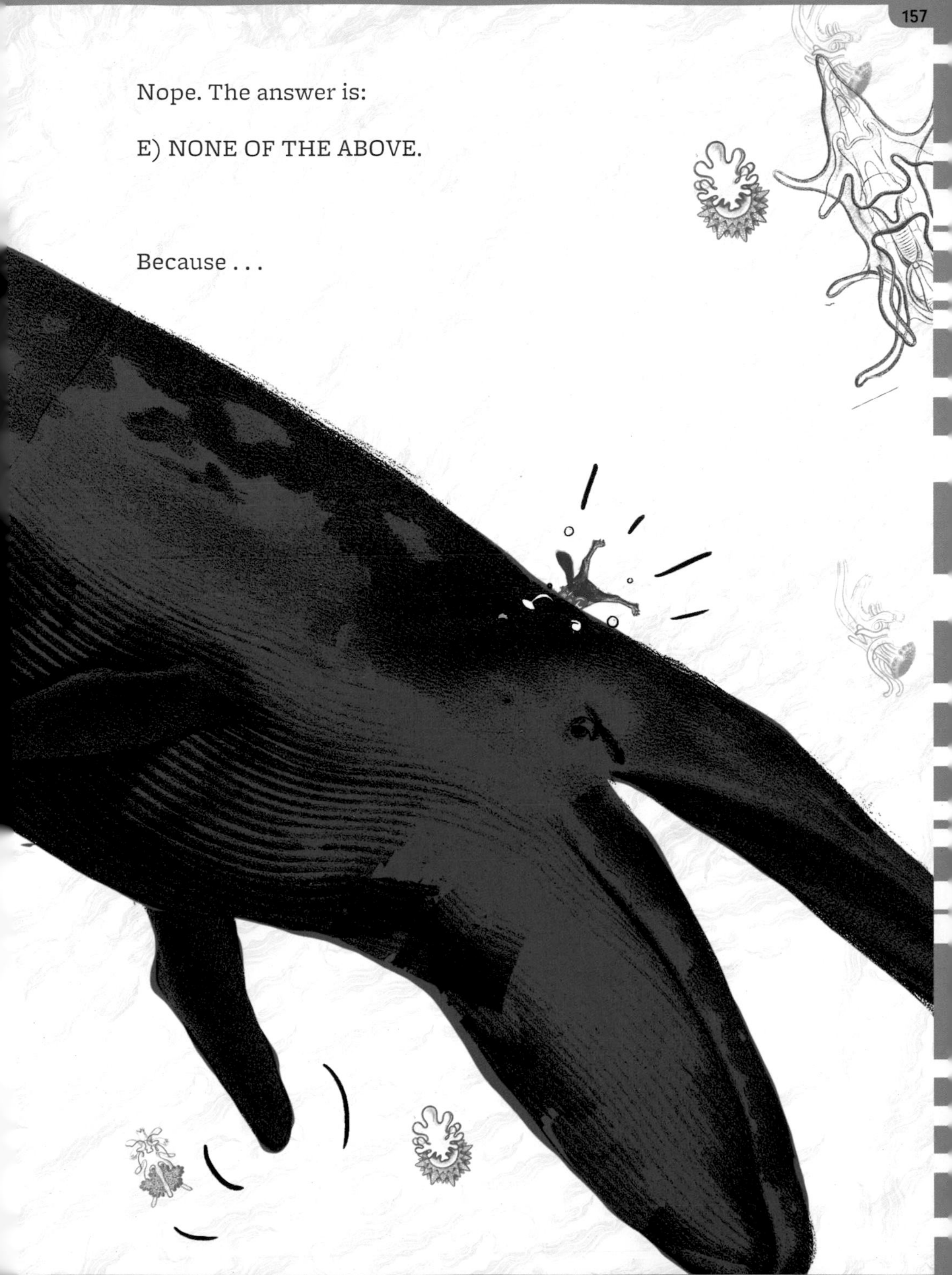

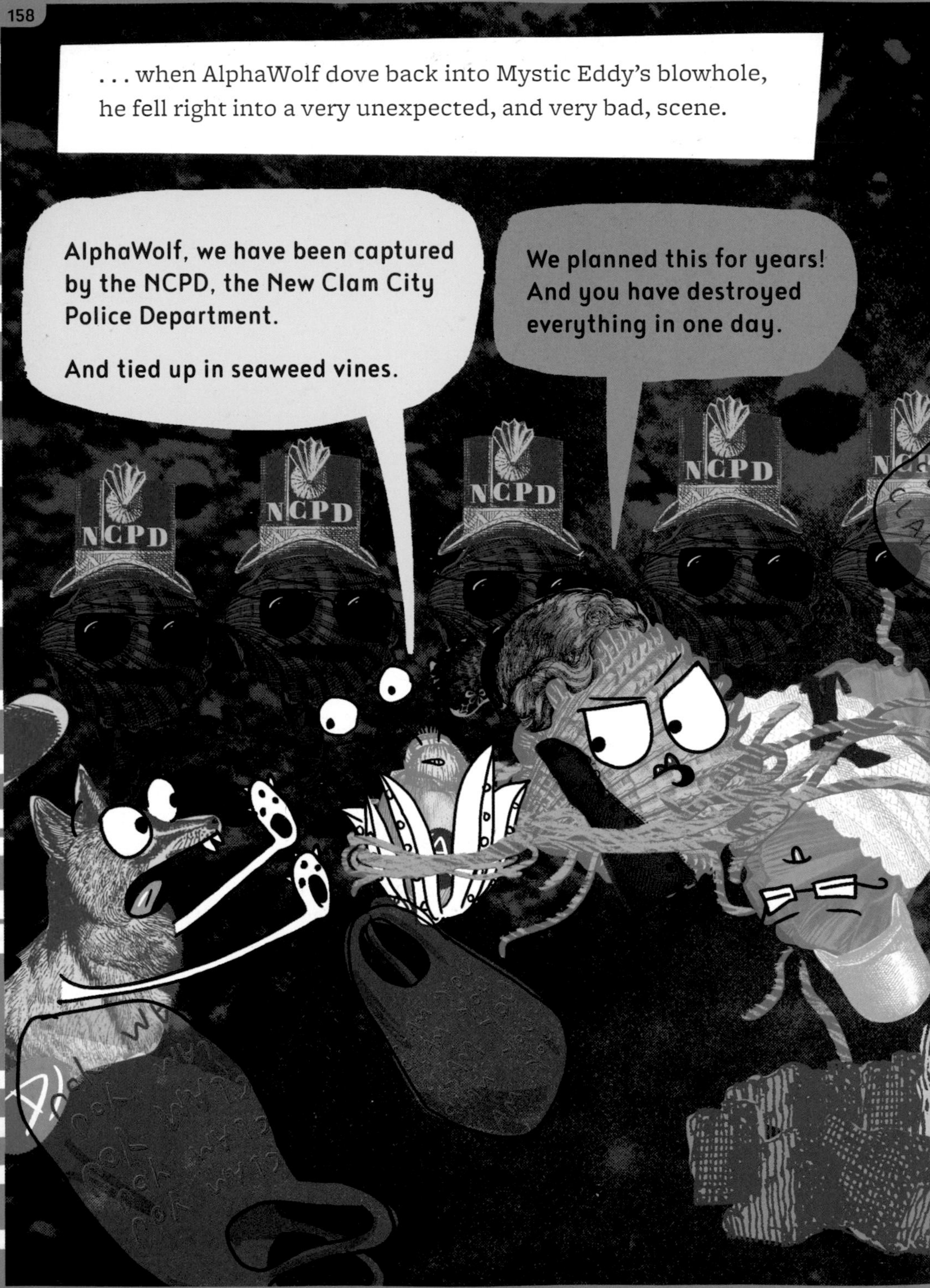
. . . when AlphaWolf dove back into Mystic Eddy's blowhole, he fell right into a very unexpected, and very bad, scene.
AlphaWolf, we have been captured by the NCPD, the New Clam City Police Department.
And tied up in seaweed vines.
We planned this for years! And you have destroyed everything in one day.
NCPD
NCPD
NCPD
NCPD

We let down our friends.
And our planet.
So much for using your
"great Alpha smartness."
SEAWEED VINES
NCPD
NCPD
NCPD

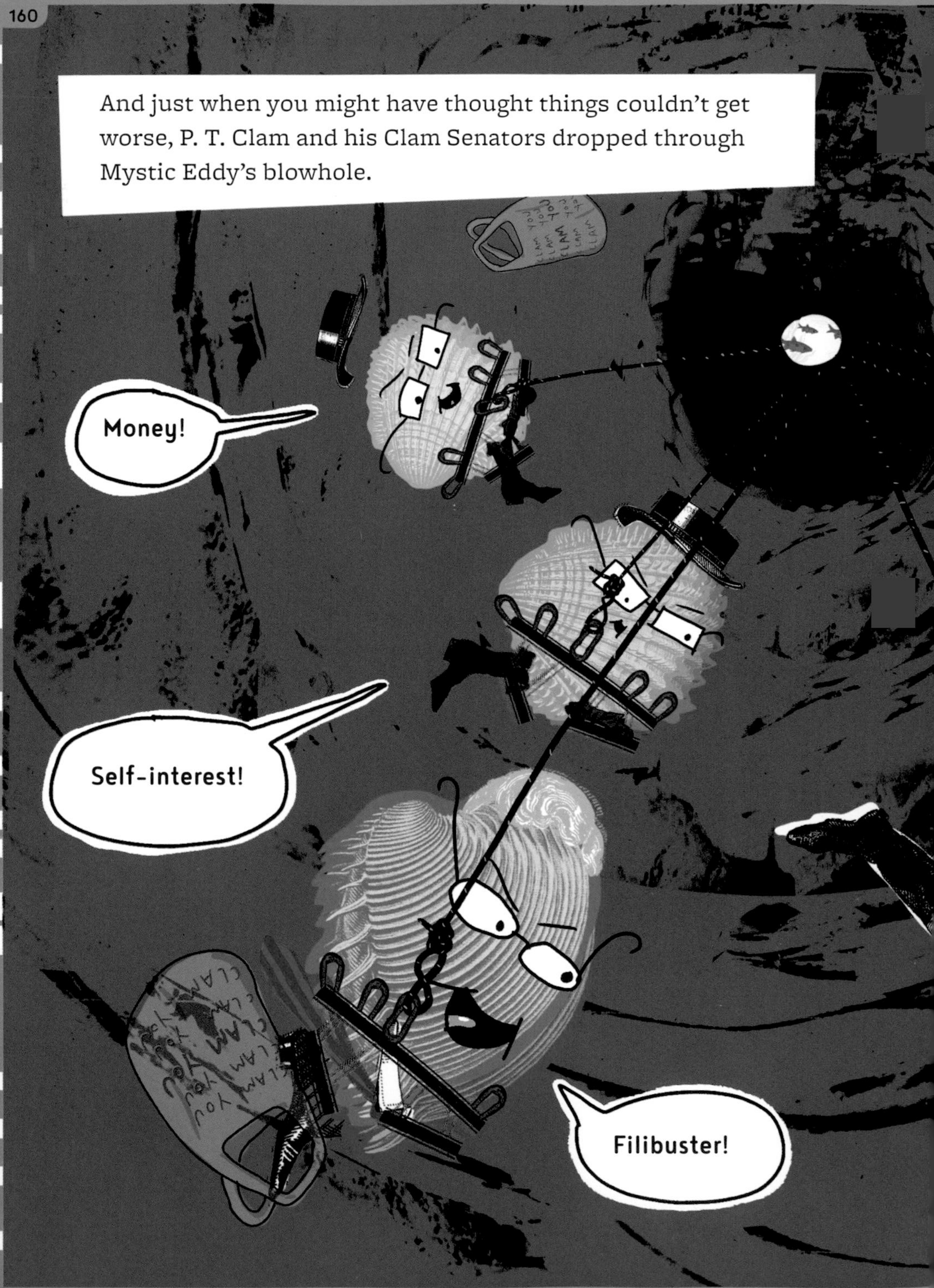
And just when you might have thought things couldn't get worse, P. T. Clam and his Clam Senators dropped through Mystic Eddy's blowhole.
Money!
Self-interest!
Filibuster!

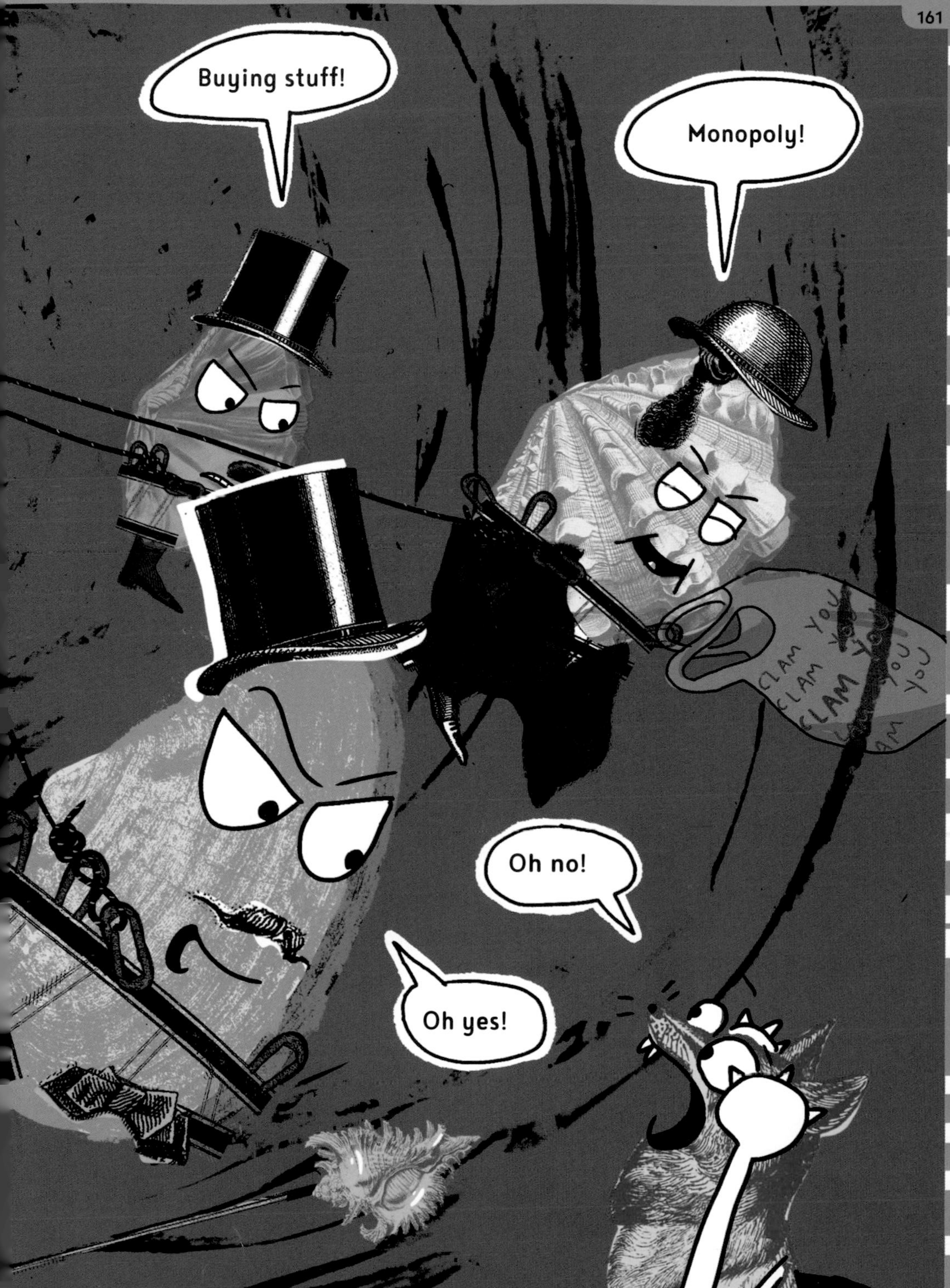
Buying stuff!
Monopoly!
CLAM YOU CLAM YOU CLAM YOU YOU
Oh no!
Oh yes!

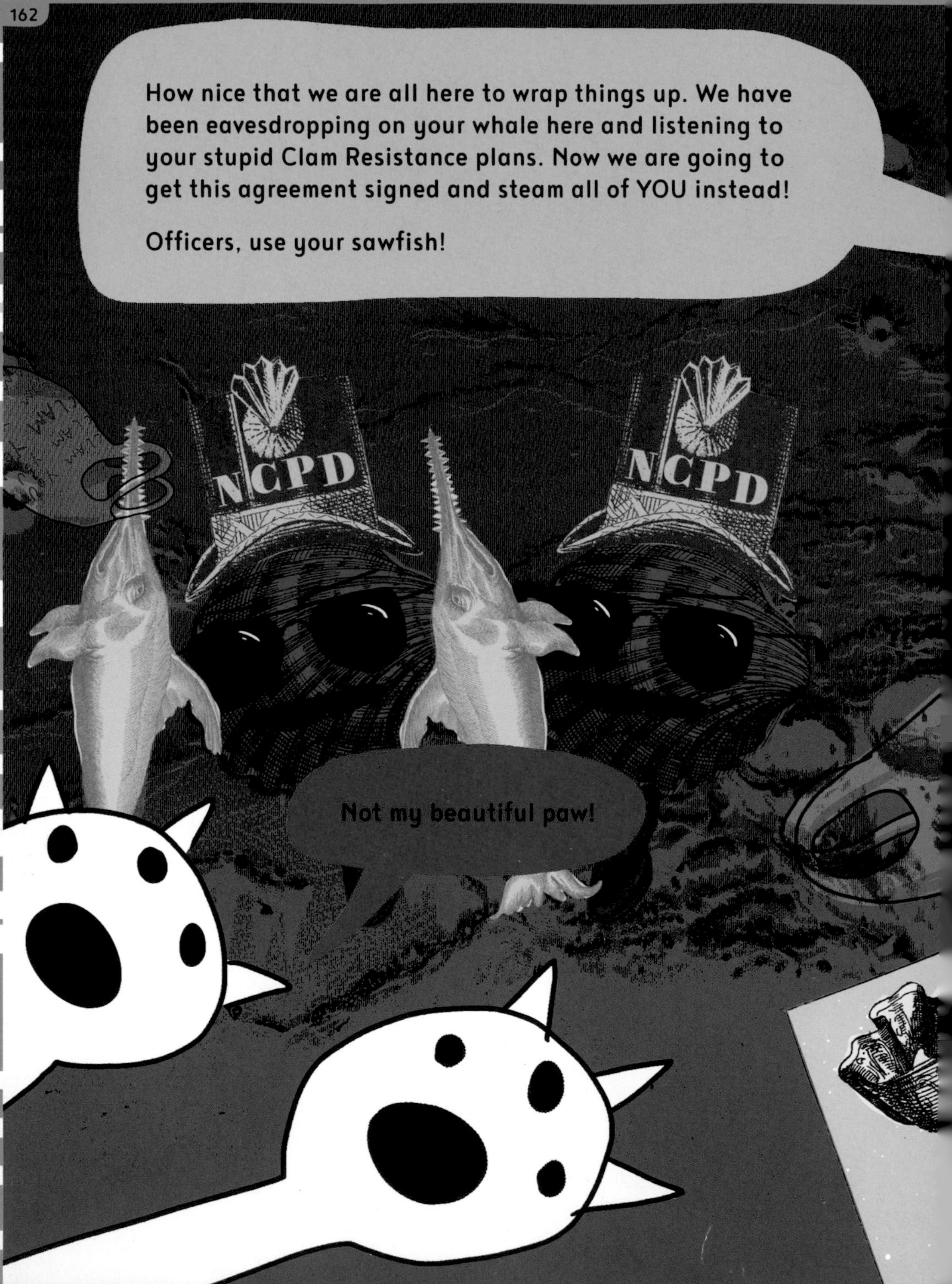
How nice that we are all here to wrap things up. We have been eavesdropping on your whale here and listening to your stupid Clam Resistance plans. Now we are going to get this agreement signed and steam all of YOU instead!
Officers, use your sawfish!
NCPD
NCPD
Not my beautiful paw!

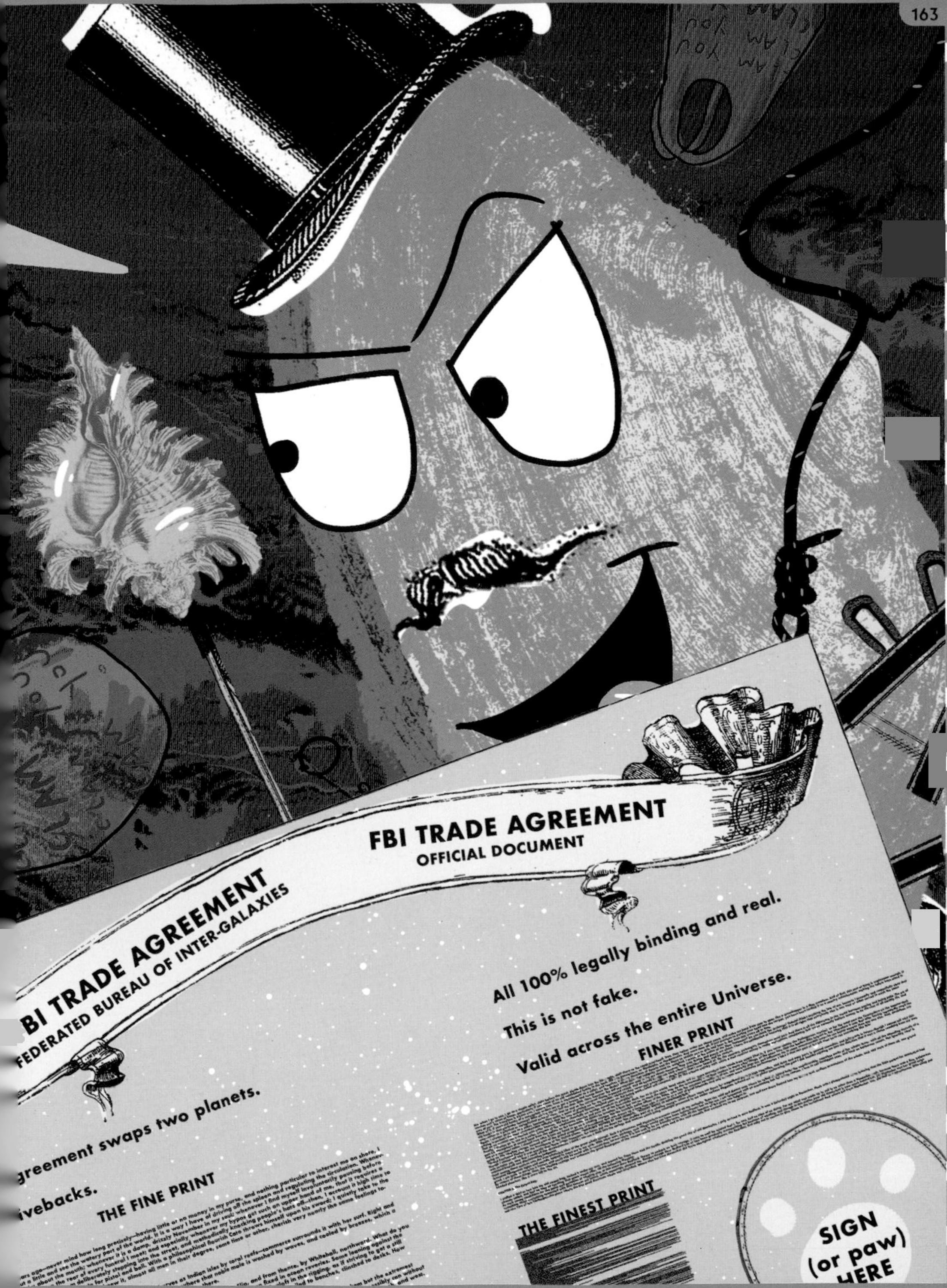
CLAM YOU
CLAM YOU
FBI TRADE AGREEMENT
OFFICIAL DOCUMENT
BI TRADE AGREEMENT
FEDERATED BUREAU OF INTER-GALAXIES
All 100% legally binding and real.
This is not fake.
Valid across the entire Universe.
FINER PRINT
greement swaps two planets.
vebacks.
THE FINE PRINT
THE FINEST PRINT
SIGN
(or paw)
HERE

You won't get away with this, P. T. You cannot deny the equality of all clams and just keep wrecking planets for your own profit.
Susie B., you are the smartest, toughest, most revolutionary clam I have ever met.
NCPD
CPD

SmartHawk, you are squeezing my ink sac and funnel organ.
Is that bad?
NCPD
NCPD
NCPD

CHAPTER 26: Ink Out

SmartHawk's accidental ink sac and funnel organ squeezing was not necessarily bad, but it did make the next minute very dark, stinky, and fortunate for the AstroNuts and the Clam Resistance.

Because, like an octopus, when StinkBug's ink sac was squeezed, he shot out black ink, hiding everyone in darkness, giving Susan B. Clamthony and her Clam Resistance fighters the cover to cut everyone free of their seaweed vines.

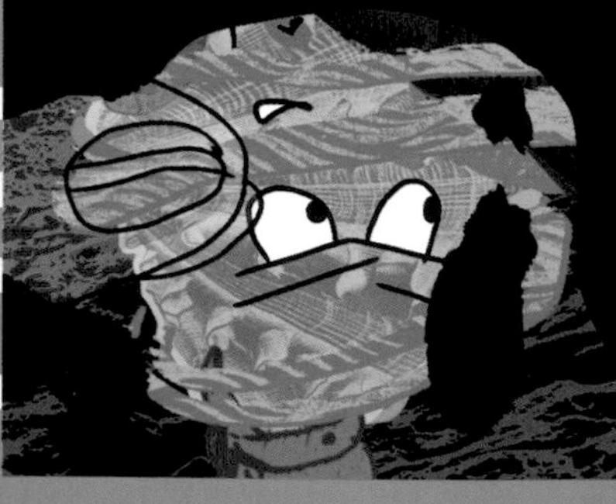

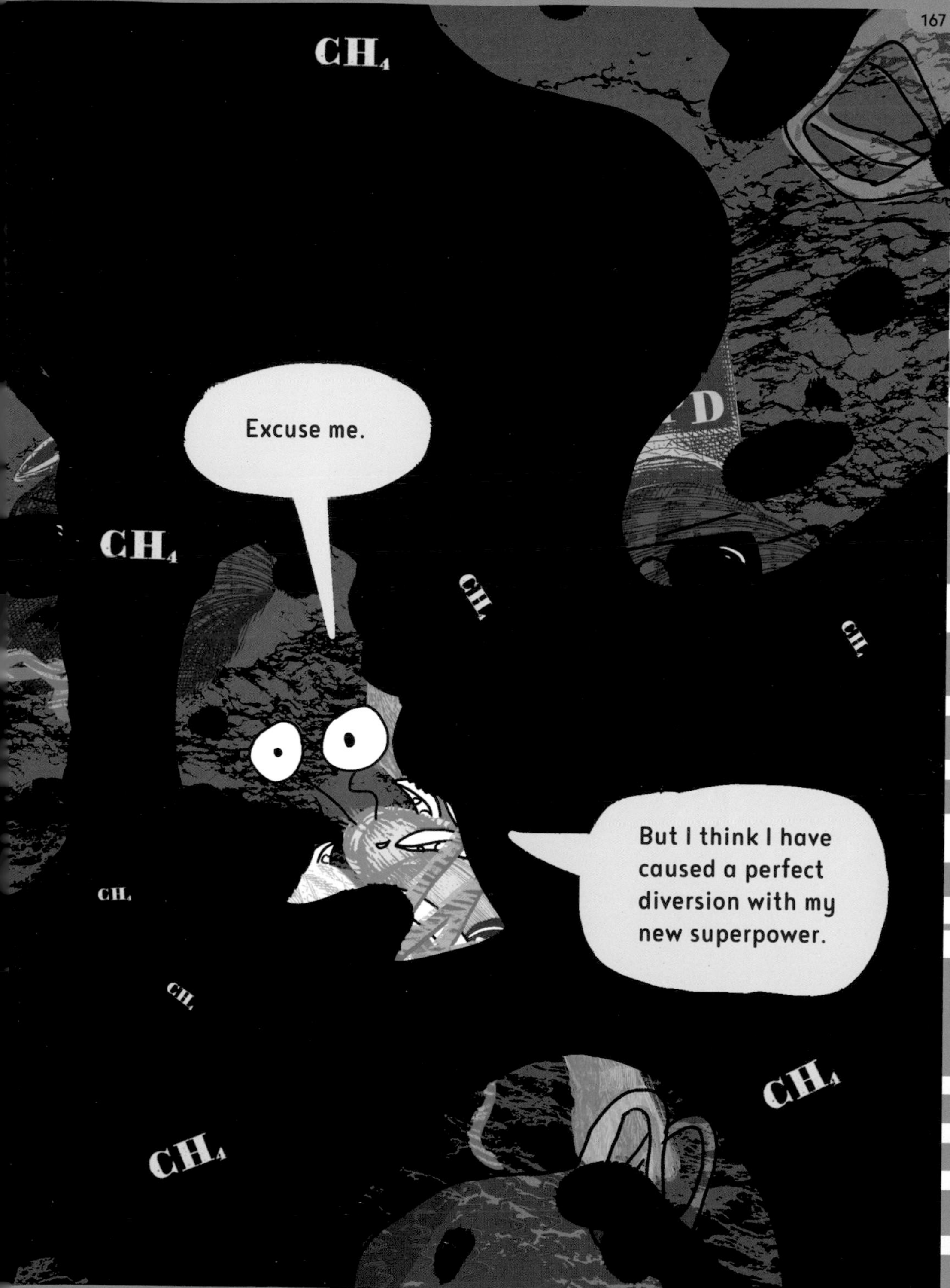
CH4
Excuse me.
CH4
CH4
CH4
CH4
But I think I have caused a perfect diversion with my new superpower.
CH4
CH4
CH4

Supercharged by Susan B. Clamthony's passion for clam equality, LaserShark turned her superpowered NNASA anglerfish lamp on HIGH.

She blinded all the clams.

And that's what started a real bivalve rumble.

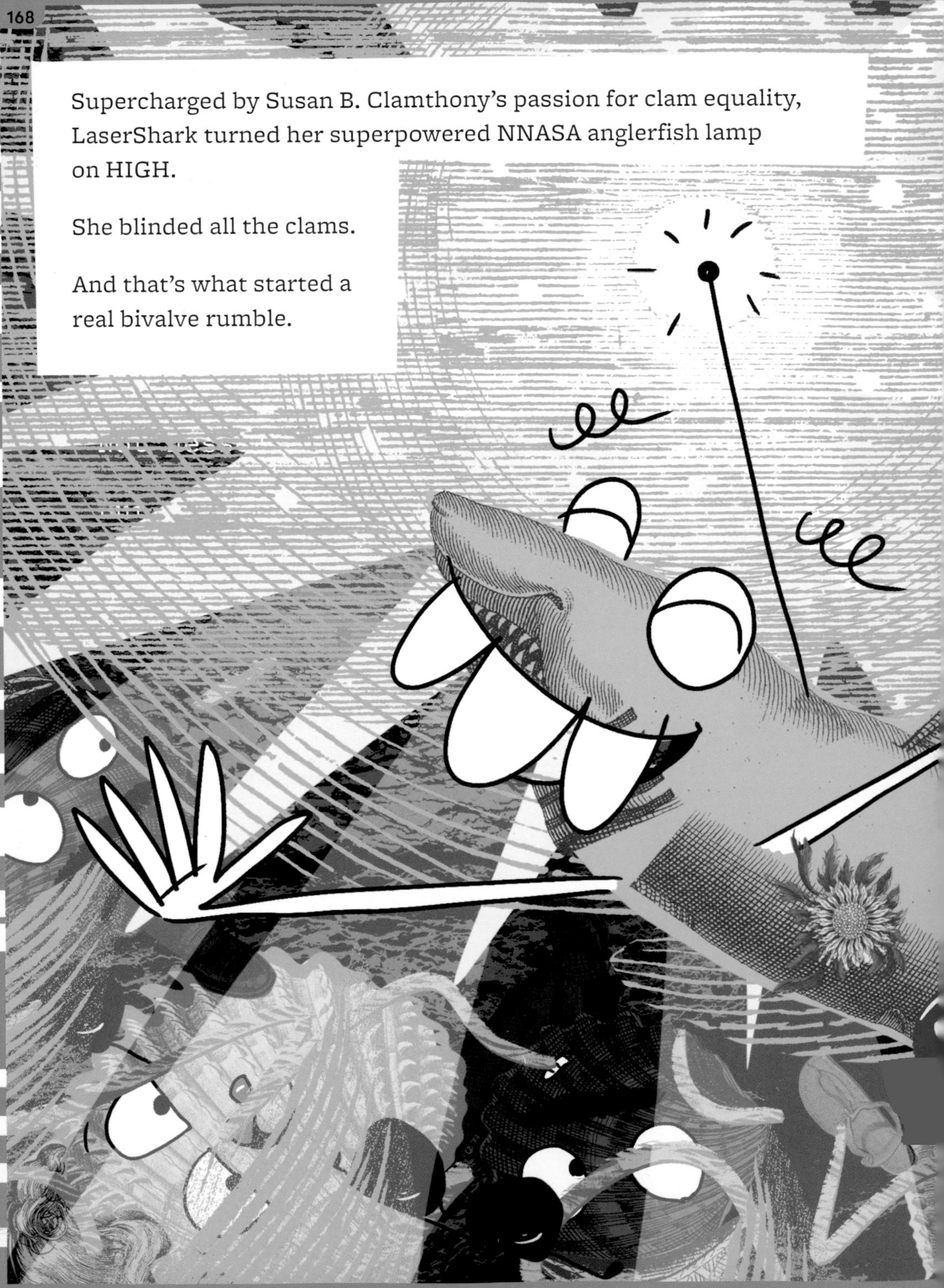

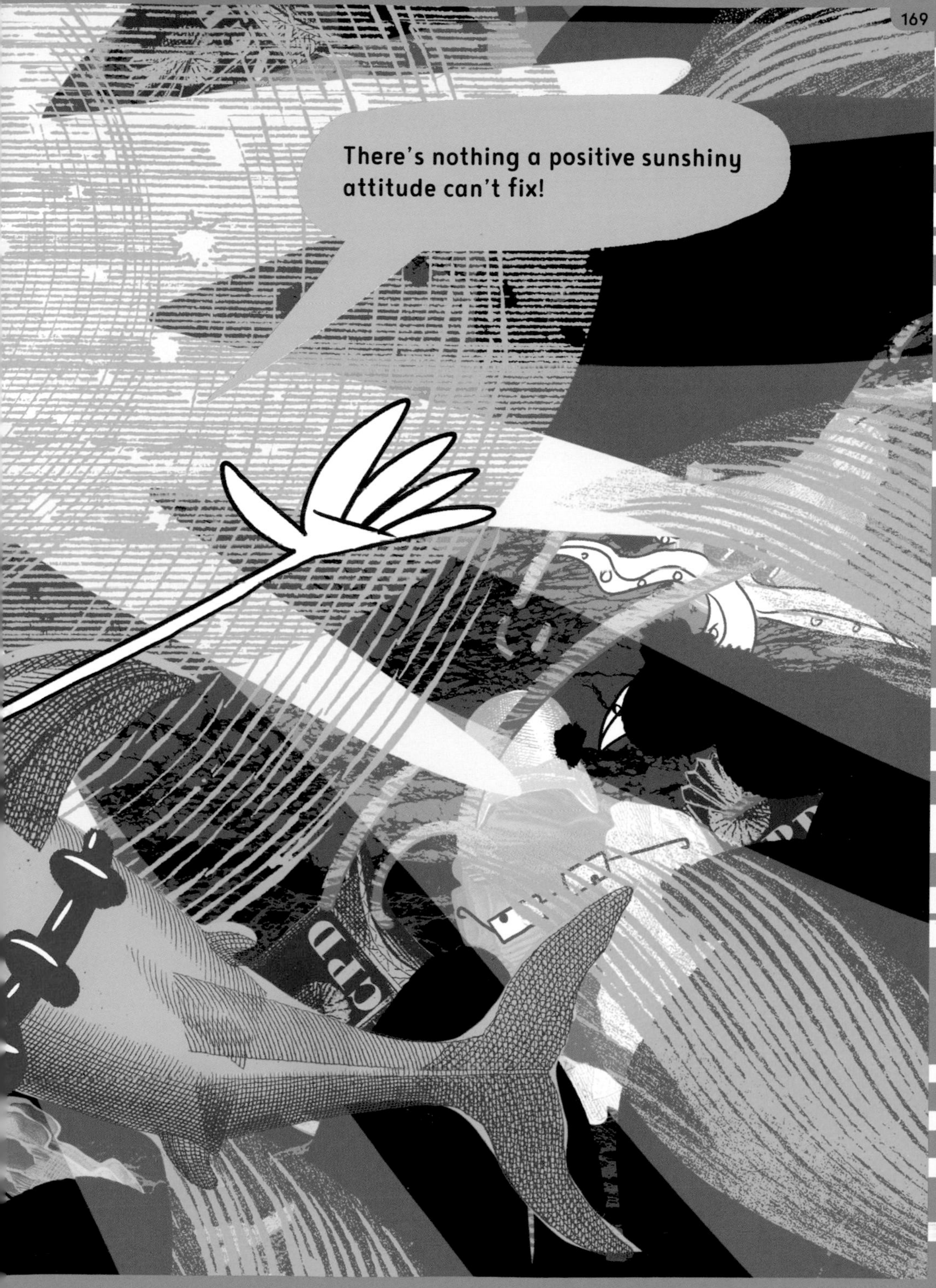
There's nothing a positive sunshiny attitude can't fix!
CPD

All the fighting and jumping tickled Mystic Eddy's sneeze reflex. And he huffed, and puffed, and blew everyone out.

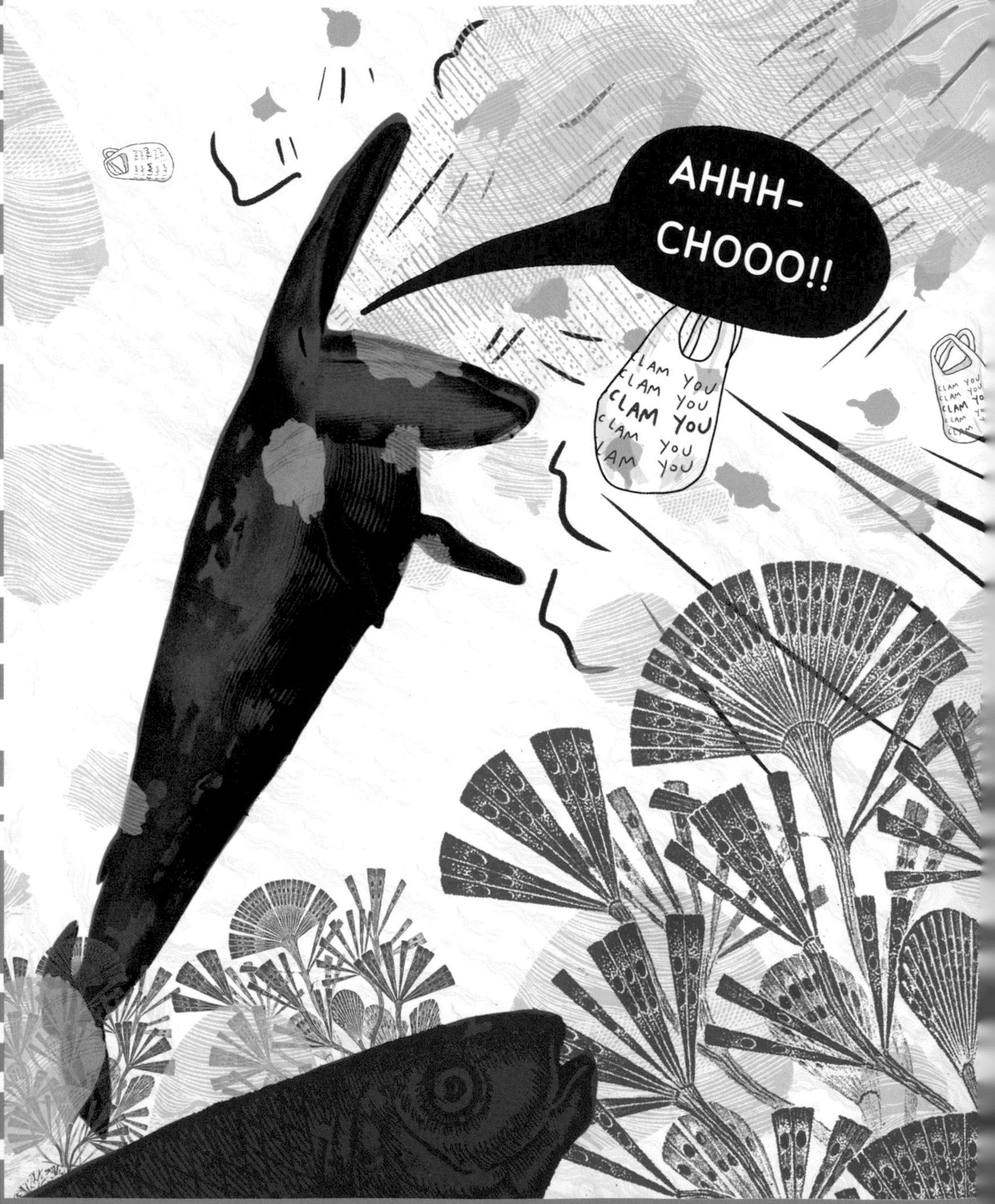
AHHH-
CHOOO!!
CLAM YOU
CLAM YOU
CLAM YOU
CLAM YOU
CLAM YOU

AlphaWolf shot through the ocean wrapped in whale snot, and feeling as bad as that sounds.

When he thought about his AstroTeam, he felt even worse than whale snot.

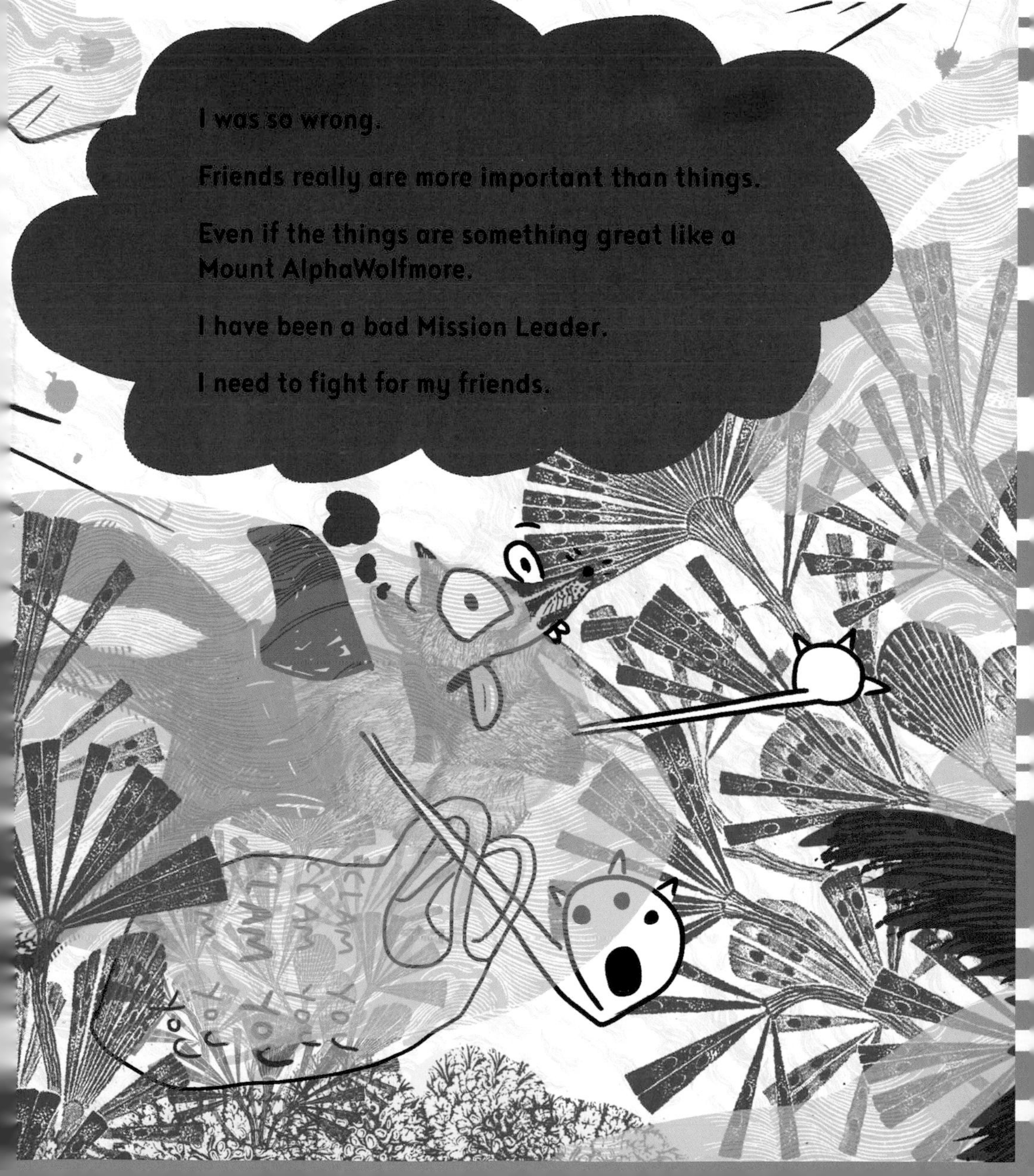
I was so wrong.
Friends really are more important than things.
Even if the things are something great like a Mount AlphaWolfmore.
I have been a bad Mission Leader.
I need to fight for my friends.

The AstroNuts swam into action. SmartHawk whipped up a duck foot dark energy whirlpool. Susan B. Clamthony called up the Clam Resistance Army.

And it looked like the good guys were going to win.

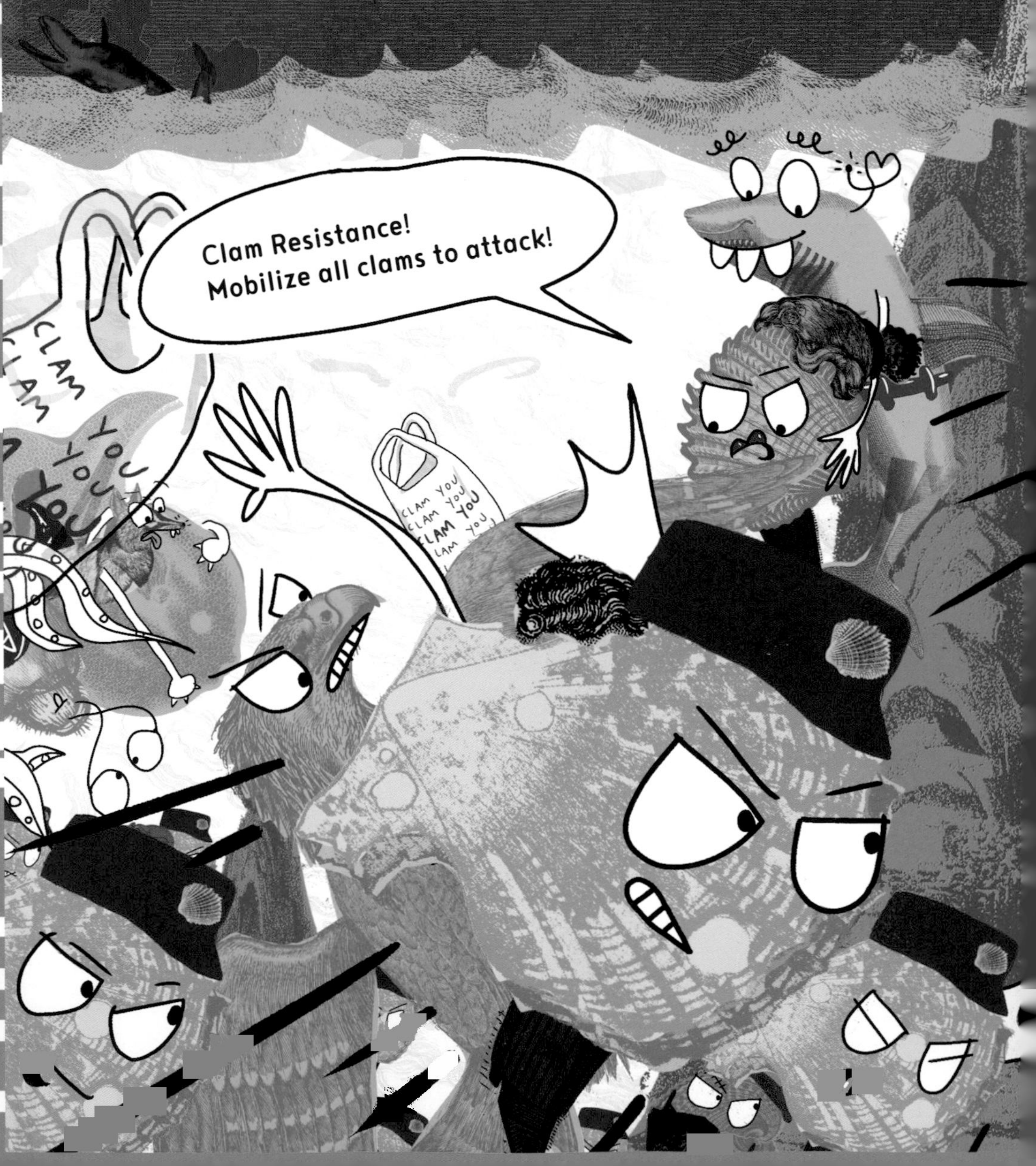
Clam Resistance!
Mobilize all clams to attack!
CLAM YOU CLAM YOU CLAM YOU CLAM YOU
CLAM CLAM YOU YOU YOU

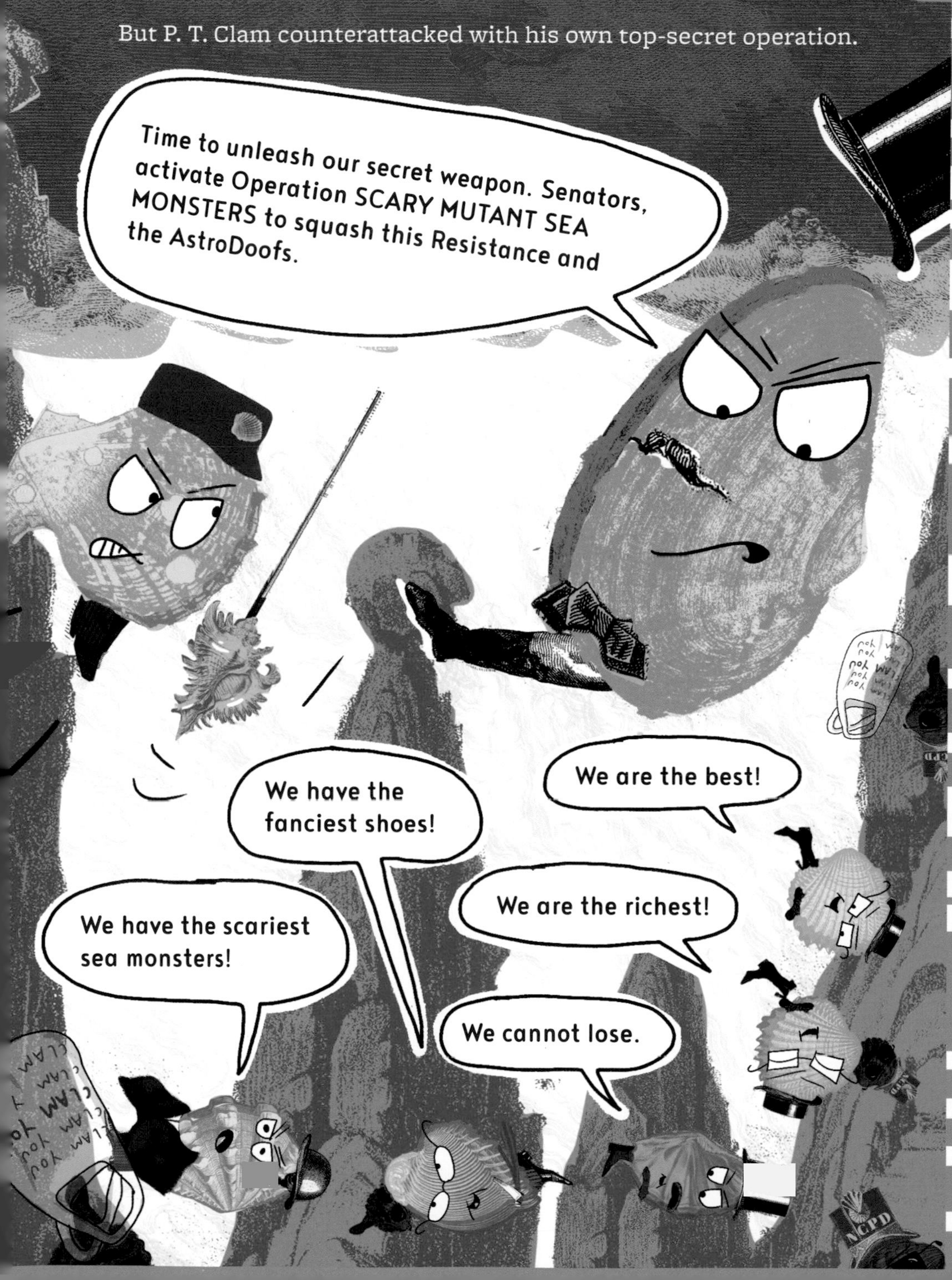
But P. T. Clam counterattacked with his own top-secret operation.
Time to unleash our secret weapon. Senators, activate Operation SCARY MUTANT SEA MONSTERS to squash this Resistance and the AstroDoofs.
We are the best!
We have the fanciest shoes!
We are the richest!
We have the scariest sea monsters!
We cannot lose.
CLAM YOU CLAM YOU CLAM YOU CLAM YOU CLAM YOU

CHAPTER 27:
Some Sea Monsters

Now, I have seen some crazy things living in my oceans.

But nothing like the mutant monsters these bad clams created.

It’s scary what toxic waste can make.

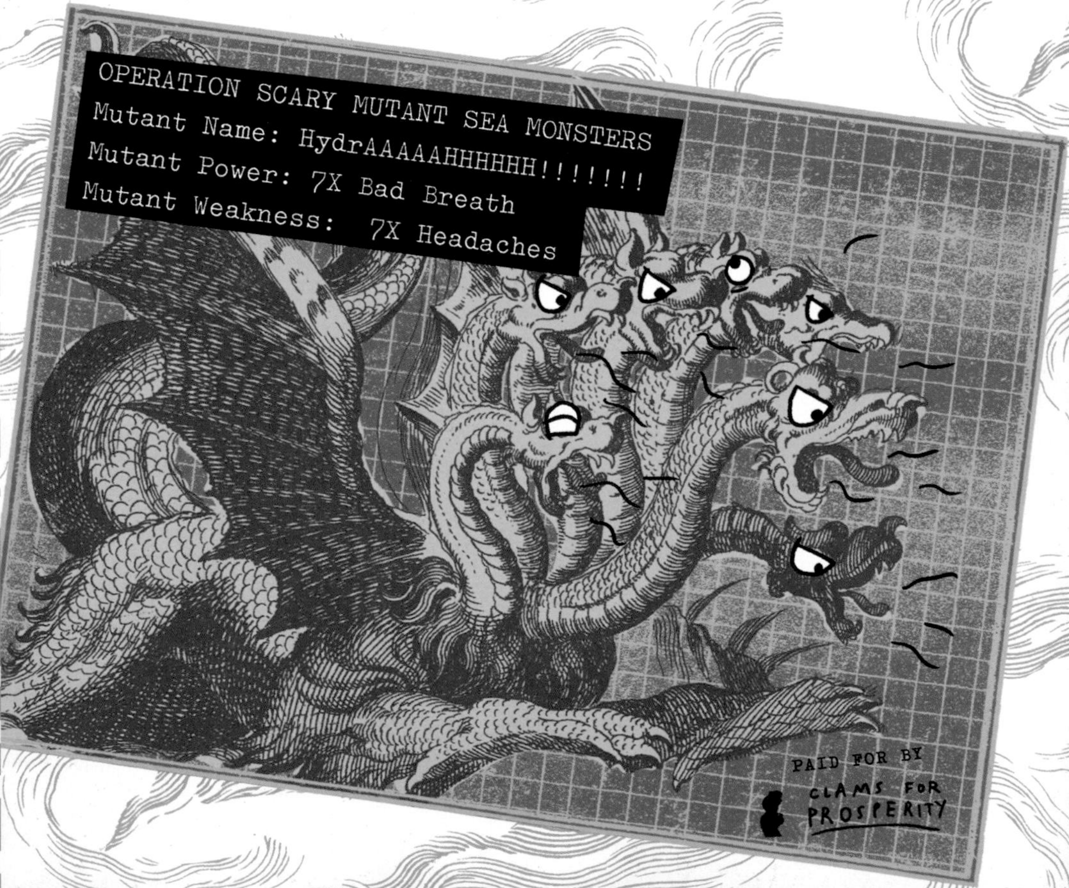
OPERATION SCARY MUTANT SEA MONSTERS
Mutant Name: HydrAAAAAHHHHHH!!!!!!!
Mutant Power: 7X Bad Breath
Mutant Weakness: 7X Headaches
PAID FOR BY
CLAMS FOR PROSPERITY

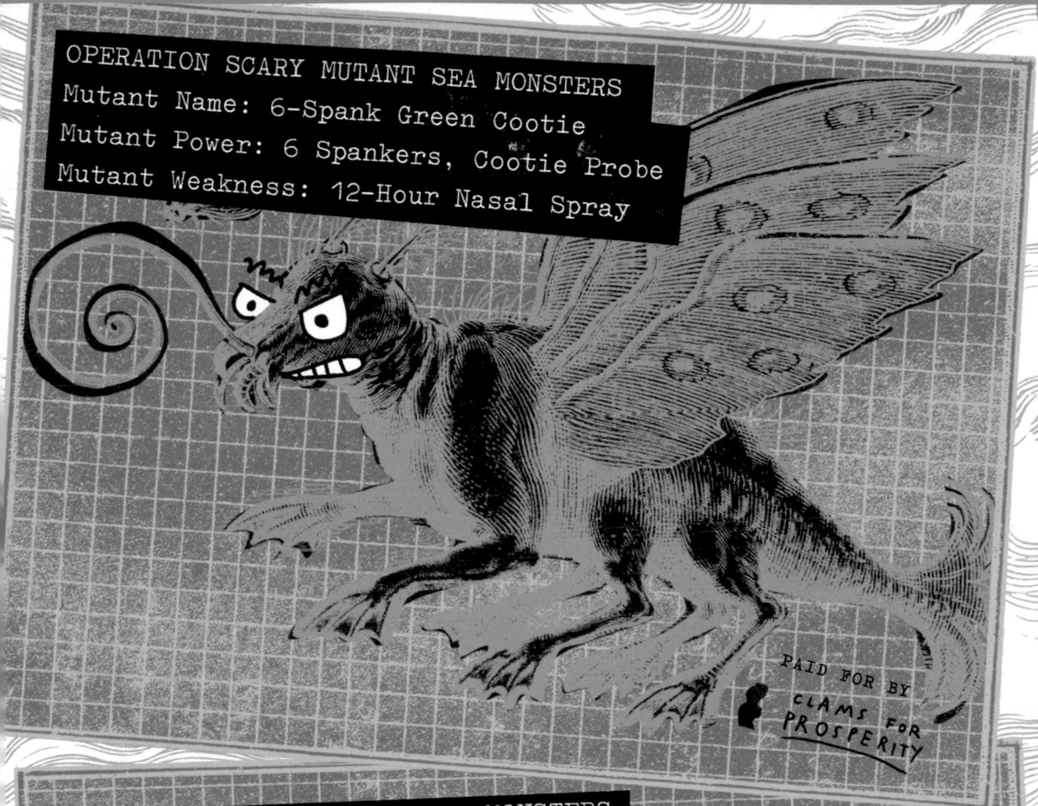
OPERATION SCARY MUTANT SEA MONSTERS
Mutant Name: 6-Spank Green Cootie
Mutant Power: 6 Spankers, Cootie Probe
Mutant Weakness: 12-Hour Nasal Spray
PAID FOR BY
CLAMS FOR PROSPERITY

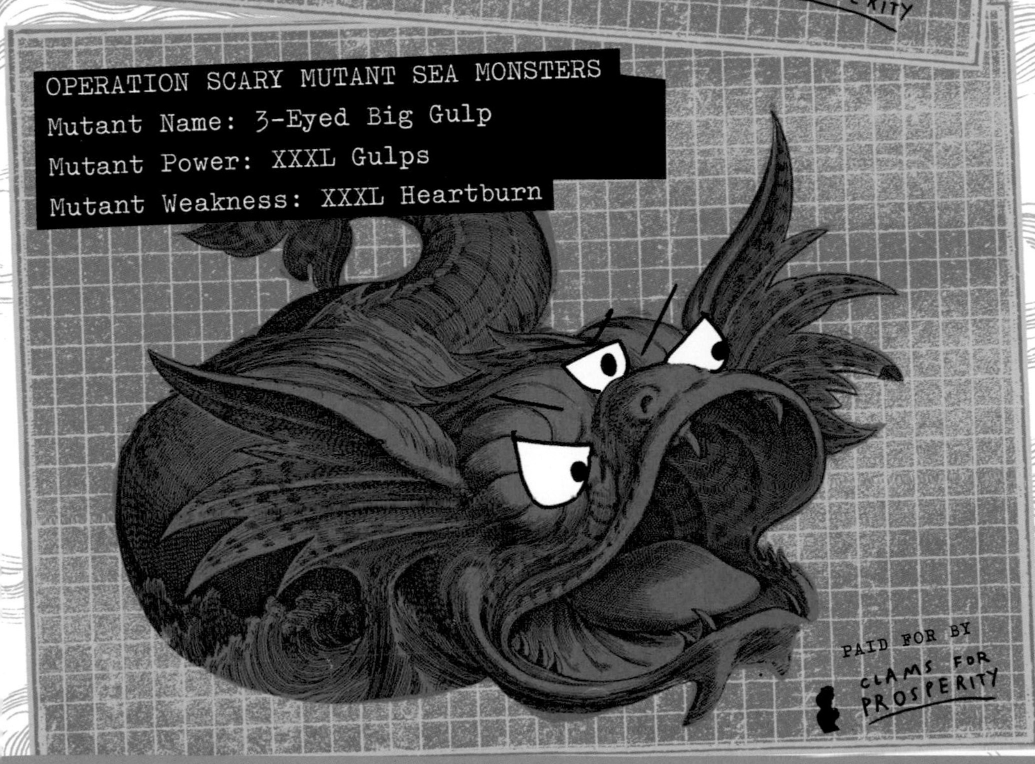
OPERATION SCARY MUTANT SEA MONSTERS
Mutant Name: 3-Eyed Big Gulp
Mutant Power: XXXL Gulps
Mutant Weakness: XXXL Heartburn
PAID FOR BY
CLAMS FOR PROSPERITY

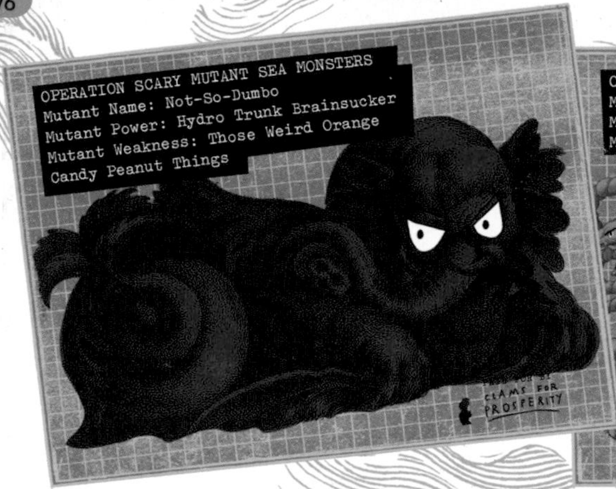
OPERATION SCARY MUTANT SEA MONSTERS
Mutant Name: Not-So-Dumbo
Mutant Power: Hydro Trunk Brainsucker
Mutant Weakness: Those Weird Orange Candy Peanut Things
CLAMS FOR PROSPERITY

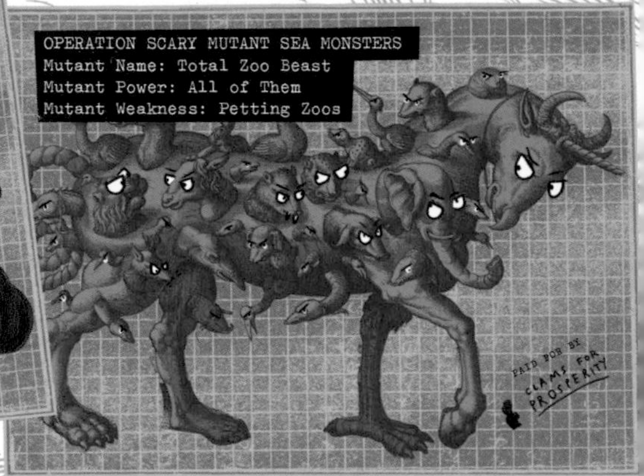
OPERATION SCARY MUTANT SEA MONSTERS
Mutant Name: Total Zoo Beast
Mutant Power: All of Them
Mutant Weakness: Petting Zoos
PAID FOR BY
CLAMS FOR PROSPERITY

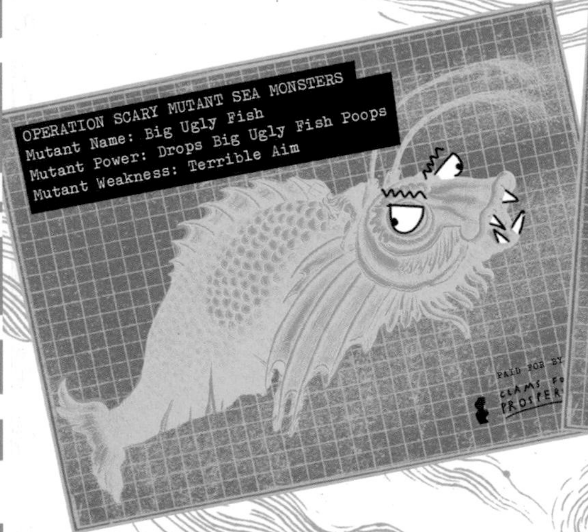
OPERATION SCARY MUTANT SEA MONSTERS
Mutant Name: Big Ugly Fish
Mutant Power: Drops Big Ugly Fish Poops
Mutant Weakness: Terrible Aim

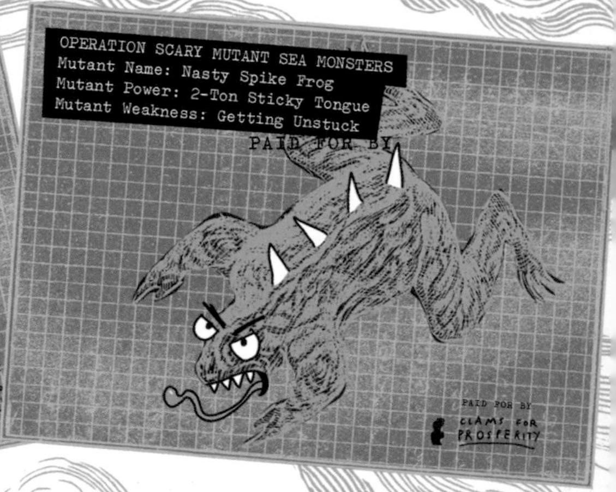
OPERATION SCARY MUTANT SEA MONSTERS
Mutant Name: Nasty Spike Frog
Mutant Power: 2-Ton Sticky Tongue
Mutant Weakness: Getting Unstuck
PAID FOR BY
PAID FOR BY
CLAMS FOR PROSPERITY

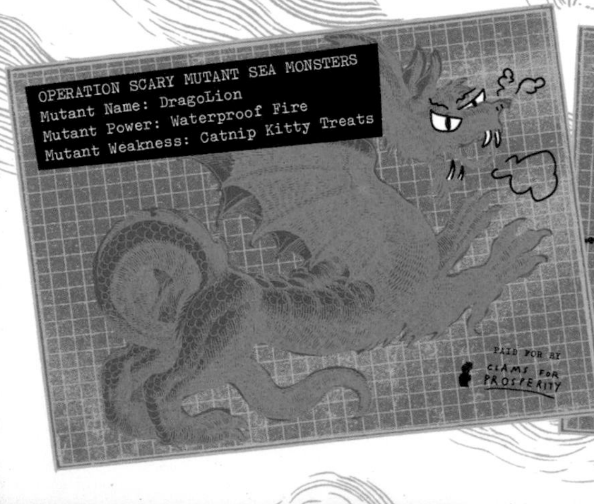
OPERATION SCARY MUTANT SEA MONSTERS
Mutant Name: DragoLion
Mutant Power: Waterproof Fire
Mutant Weakness: Catnip Kitty Treats
PAID FOR BY
CLAMS FOR PROSPERITY

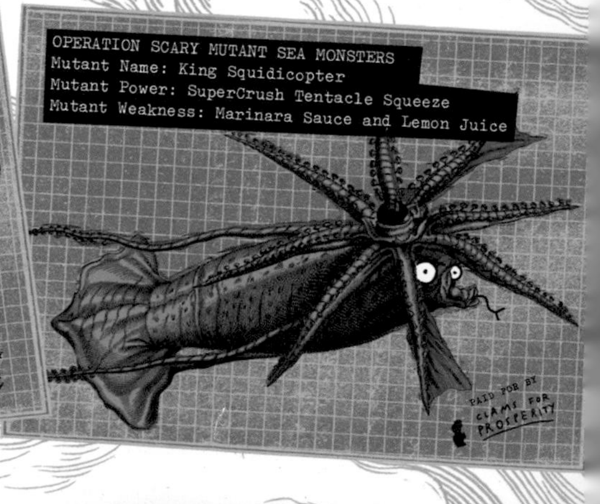
OPERATION SCARY MUTANT SEA MONSTERS
Mutant Name: King Squidicopter
Mutant Power: SuperCrush Tentacle Squeeze
Mutant Weakness: Marinara Sauce and Lemon Juice
PAID FOR BY
CLAMS FOR PROSPERITY

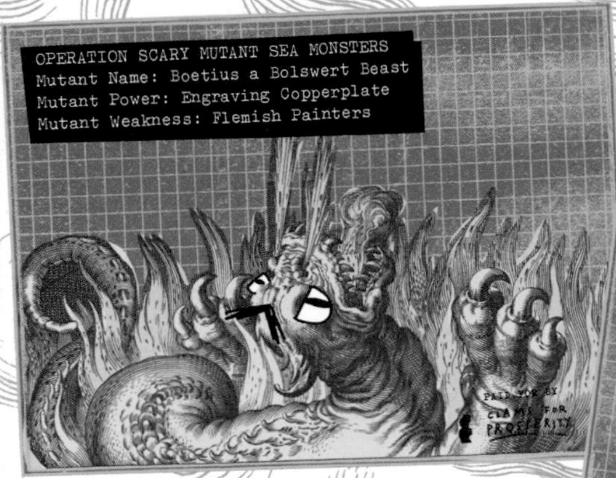
OPERATION SCARY MUTANT SEA MONSTERS
Mutant Name: Boetius a Bolswert Beast
Mutant Power: Engraving Copperplate
Mutant Weakness: Flemish Painters
PAID FOR BY
CLAMS FOR PROSPERITY

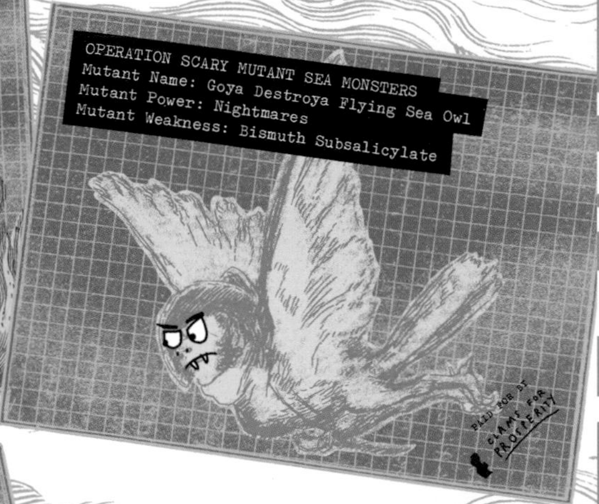
OPERATION SCARY MUTANT SEA MONSTERS
Mutant Name: Goya Destroya Flying Sea Owl
Mutant Power: Nightmares
Mutant Weakness: Bismuth Subsalicylate
PAID FOR BY
CLAMS FOR PROSPERITY

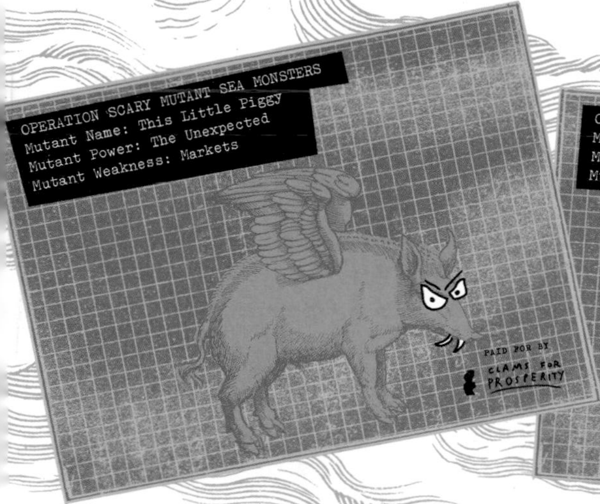
OPERATION SCARY MUTANT SEA MONSTERS
Mutant Name: This Little Piggy
Mutant Power: The Unexpected
Mutant Weakness: Markets
PAID FOR BY
CLAMS FOR PROSPERITY

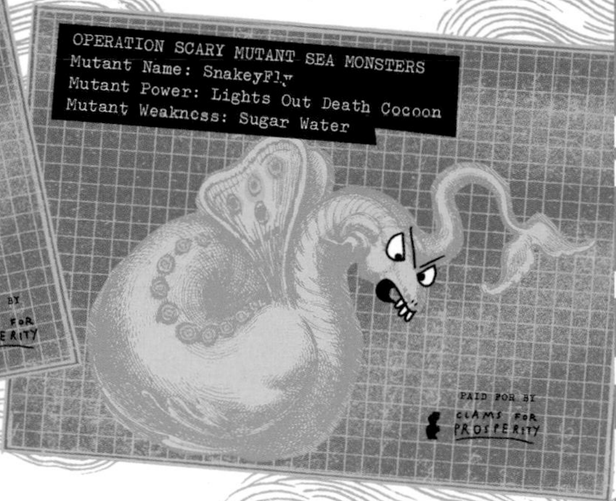
OPERATION SCARY MUTANT SEA MONSTERS
Mutant Name: SnakeyFly
Mutant Power: Lights Out Death Cocoon
Mutant Weakness: Sugar Water
PAID FOR BY
CLAMS FOR PROSPERITY

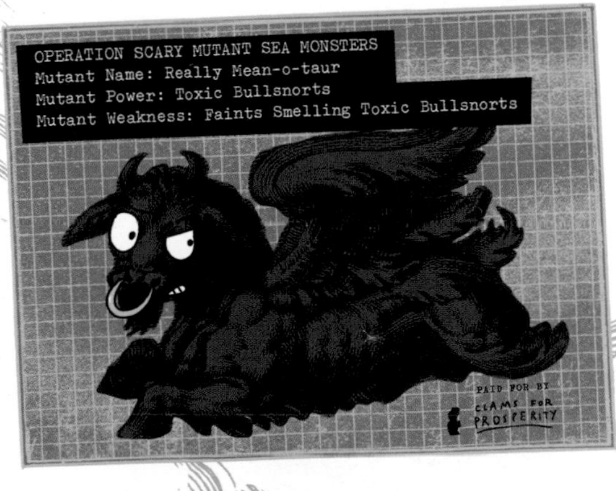
OPERATION SCARY MUTANT SEA MONSTERS
Mutant Name: Really Mean-o-taur
Mutant Power: Toxic Bullsnorts
Mutant Weakness: Faints Smelling Toxic Bullsnorts
PAID FOR BY
CLAMS FOR PROSPERITY

And that was just HALF of the Scary Mutant Sea Monster Attack Force!

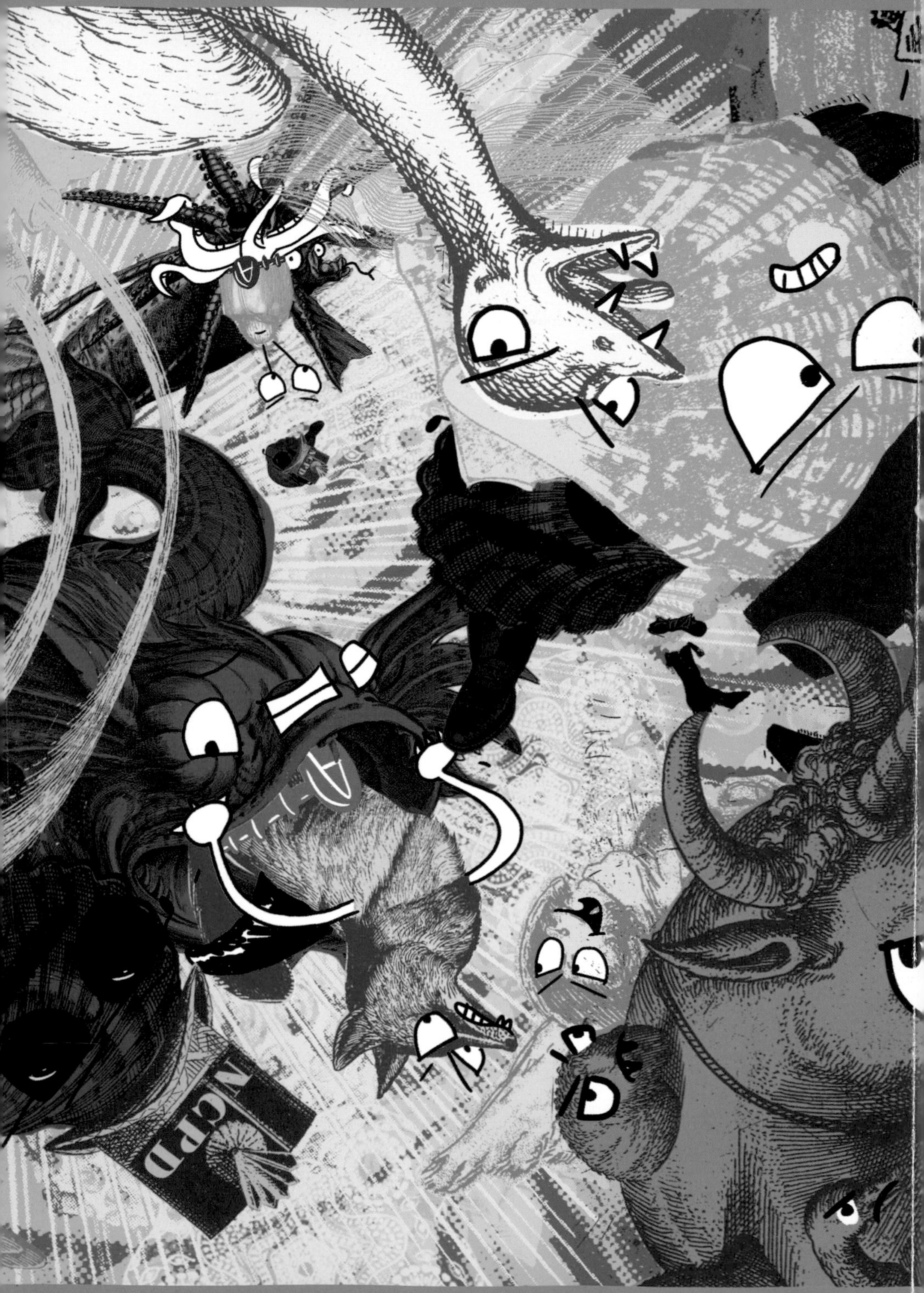
NCPD

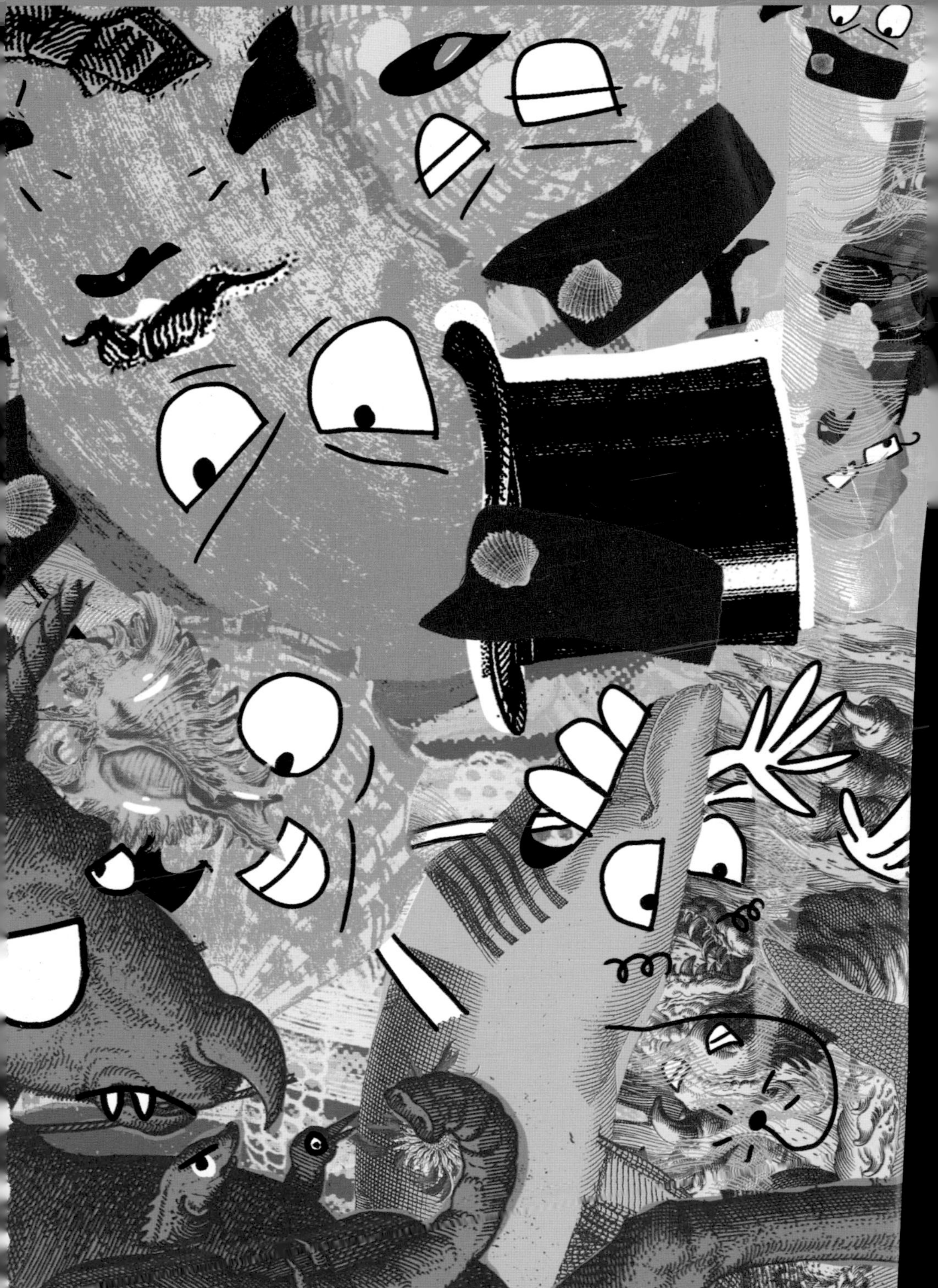

As a 71% water surface planet myself, I have seen plenty of clam fights and sea battles. I have seen Megalodon vs. Kraken. I have seen Basilosaurus vs. Dunkleosteus. Archimedes vs. the Romans.

But I have never, ever seen a battle like Clam Resistance vs. Sea Monsters.

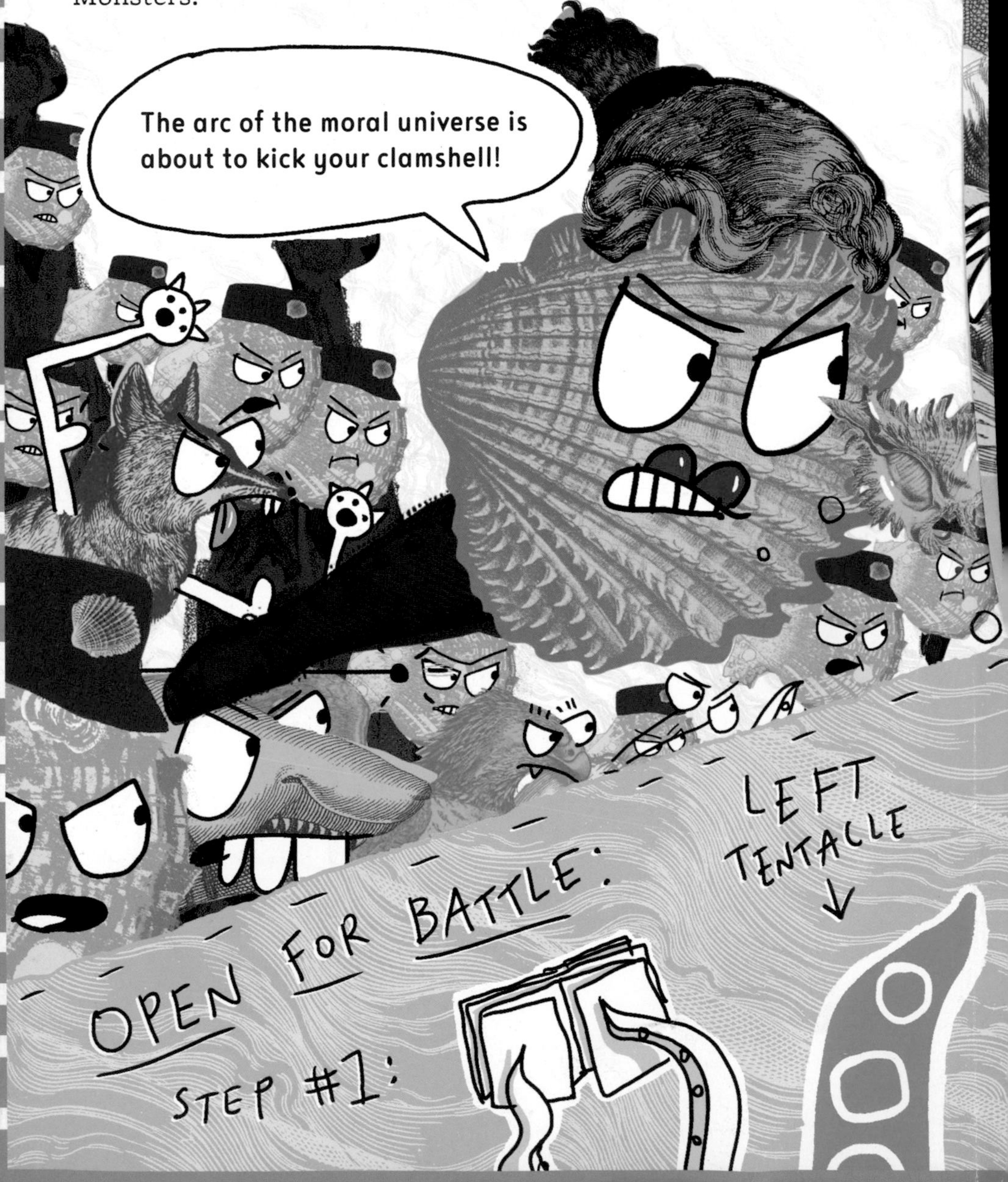

The arc of the moral universe is about to kick your clamshell!
OPEN FOR BATTLE:
STEP #1:
LEFT TENTACLE

I wouldn't bet on it. Because there is a suckerfish born every minute.
RIGHT TENTACLE
STEP #2
SPLISH! SPLASH! OUCH! WOWZA!
OH MY,

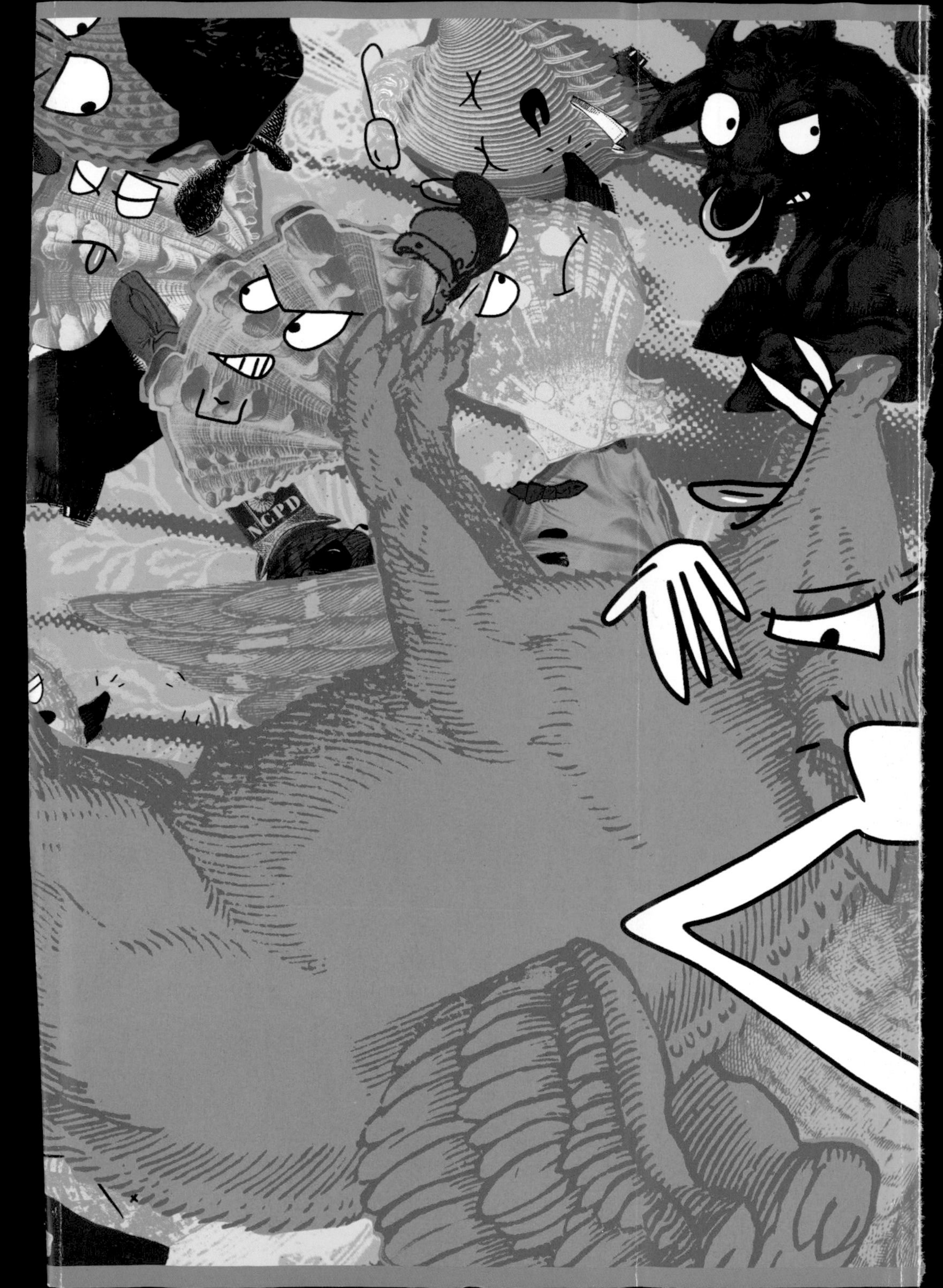
NCPD

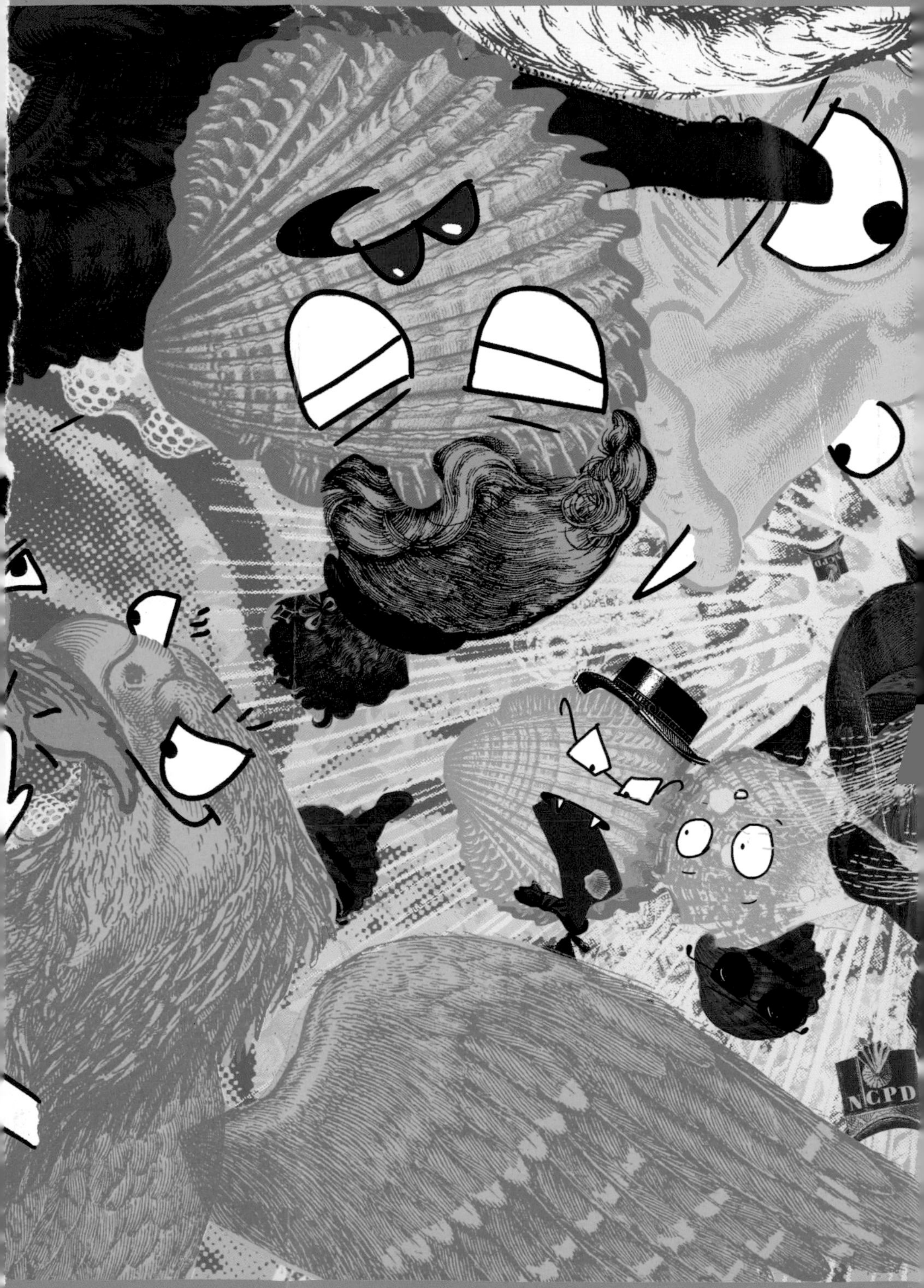
NCPD

CHAPTER 28: The Adductor Muscle

And it would have been a great Clam Resistance/AstroNut victory . . . but P. T. Clam pulled a classic Bad Guy Trick. He yelled, “Holy mackerel! Look at that thing behind you!”

Everyone fell for it. Everyone looked behind them. But there was nothing. And that’s when P. T. Clam got ready to pinch LaserShark in a secret Clam Death Grip.

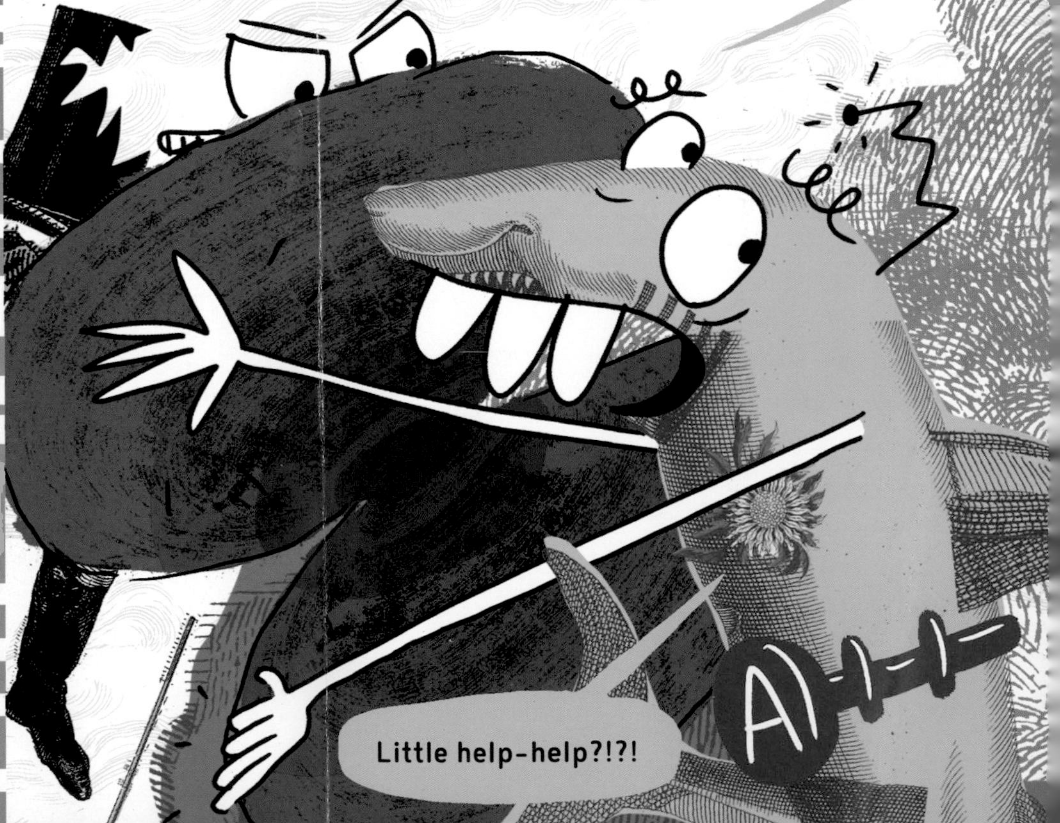
Little help-help?!?!

AlphaWolf, paw print that swap agreement and turn those clams loose. If you don't sign, we are going to grind your sweet LaserShark into catfish food!
Let her go! She doesn't have anything to do with your bad swap plan. If you want my paw, you are going to have to come and get it. From ME!

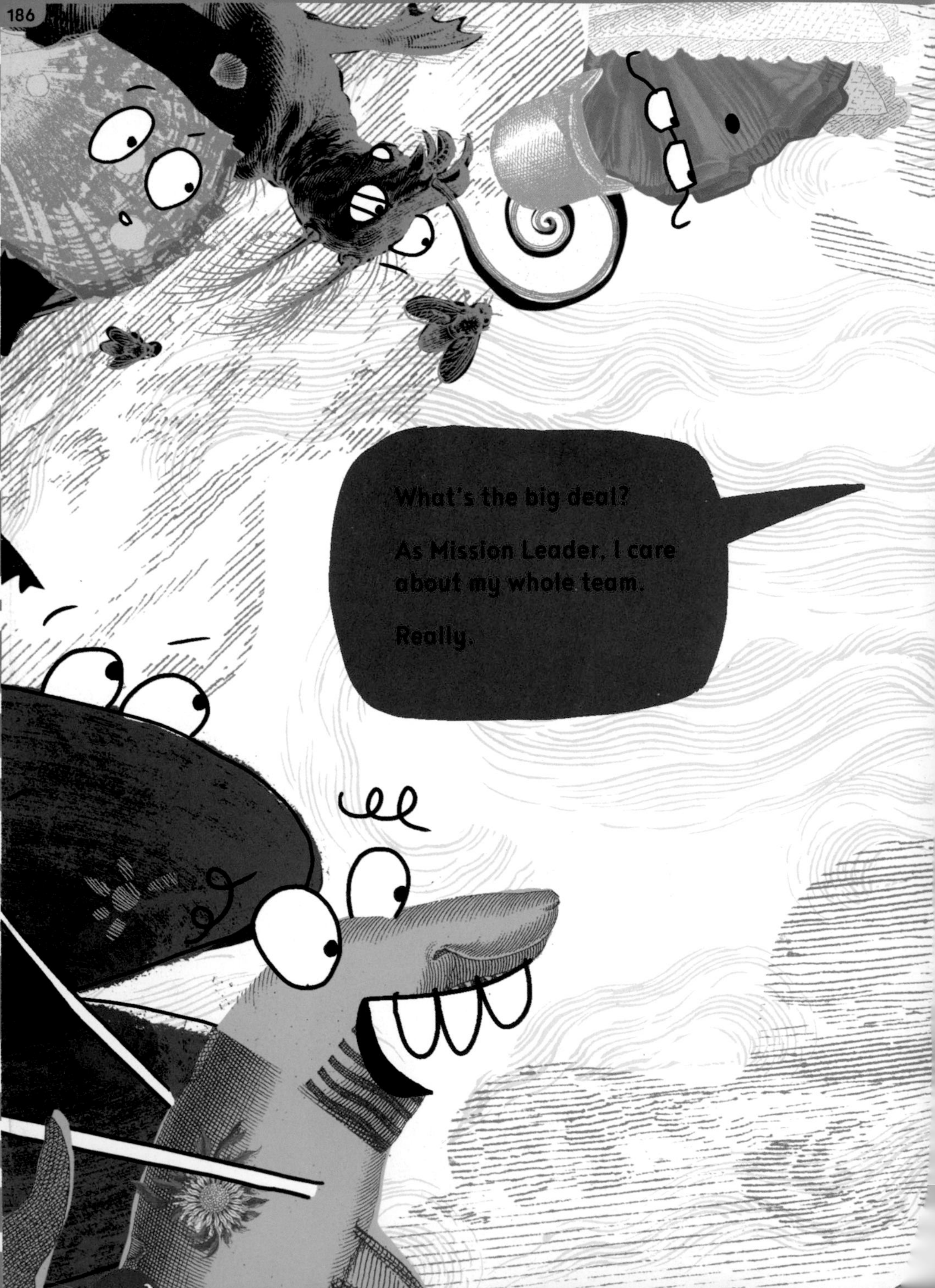
What's the big deal?
As Mission Leader, I care about my whole team.
Really.

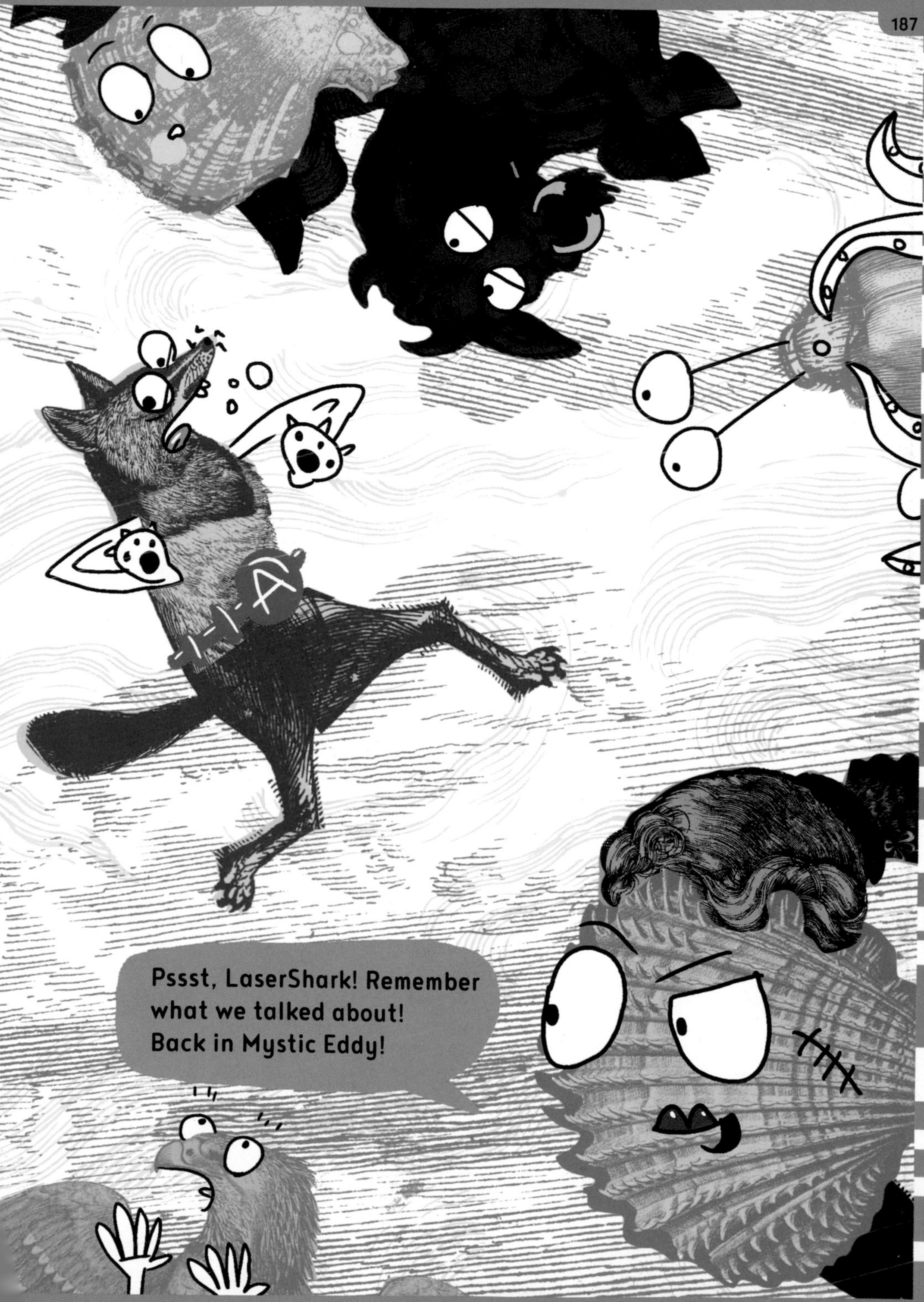
Pssst, LaserShark! Remember what we talked about! Back in Mystic Eddy!

In all the excitement of being inside a whale, you might have missed what Susan B. Clamthony told LaserShark. The one weakness of every clam.

You know how crocodiles have very powerful bites?

Did you know they have THE MOST powerful bite force measured of any Earth animal?

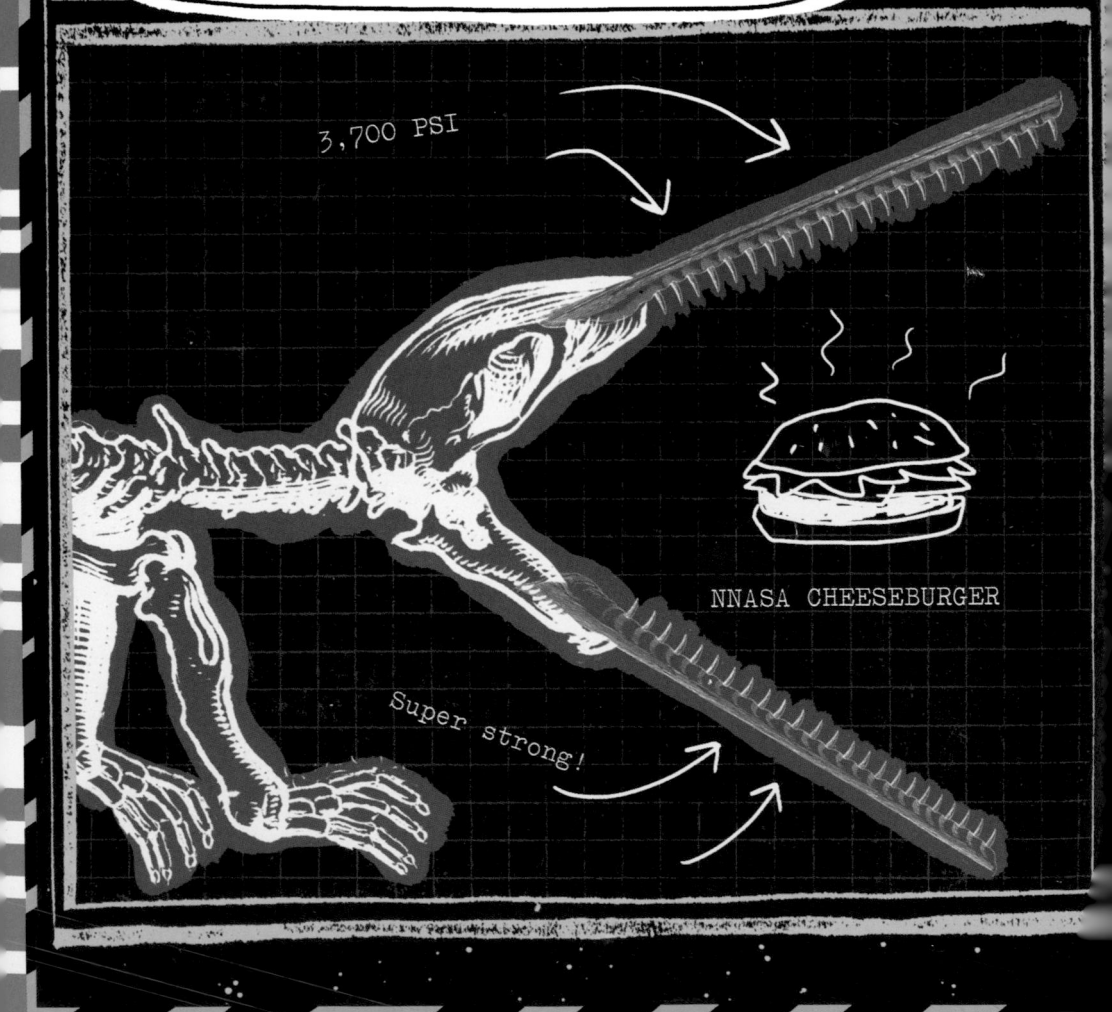

3,700 PSI

NNASA CHEESEBURGER

Super strong!

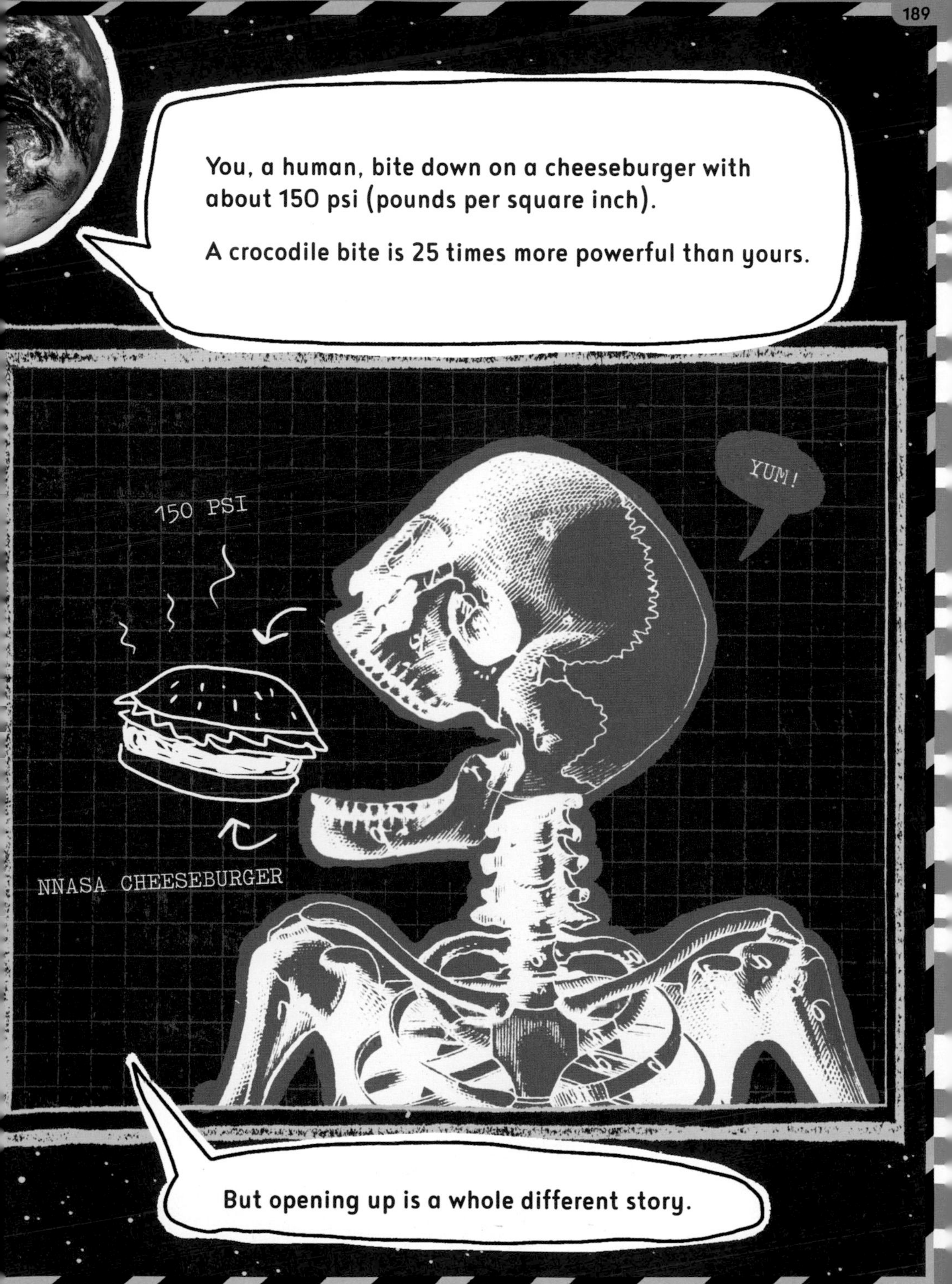
You, a human, bite down on a cheeseburger with about 150 psi (pounds per square inch).
A crocodile bite is 25 times more powerful than yours.
150 PSI
YUM!
NNASA CHEESEBURGER
But opening up is a whole different story.

The muscle a crocodile uses to open its jaws is much smaller, and weaker, than the muscle used to close the jaw.

The force of opening the jaw is much, much less than the force of closing the jaw.

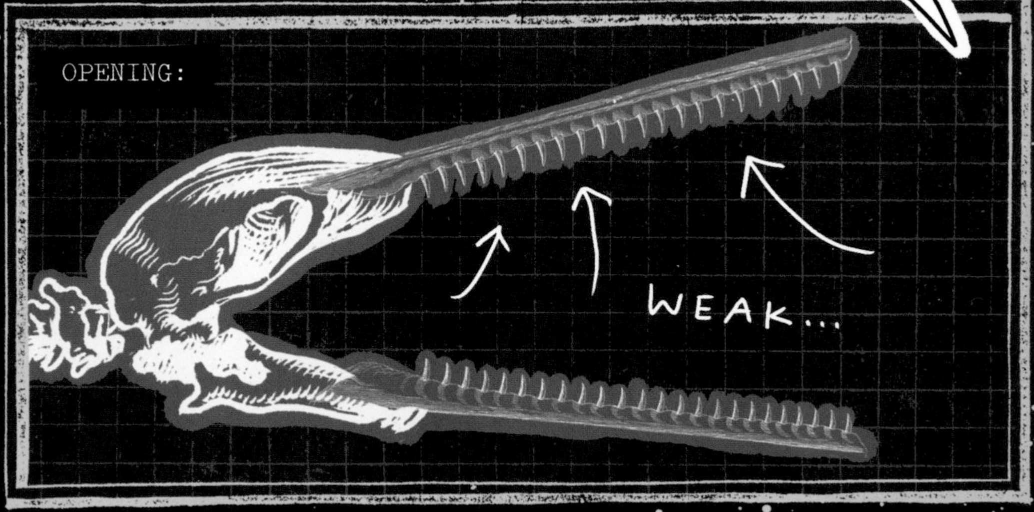
OPENING:
WEAK...

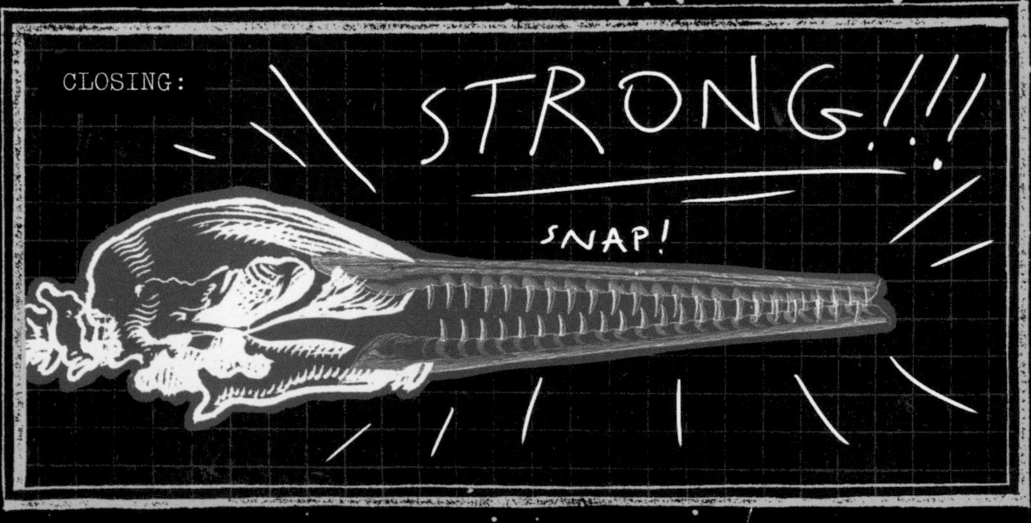
CLOSING:
STRONG!!!
SNAP!

In fact, an average adult human can hold the jaws of a crocodile closed with only the force of their bare hands, or some duct tape.

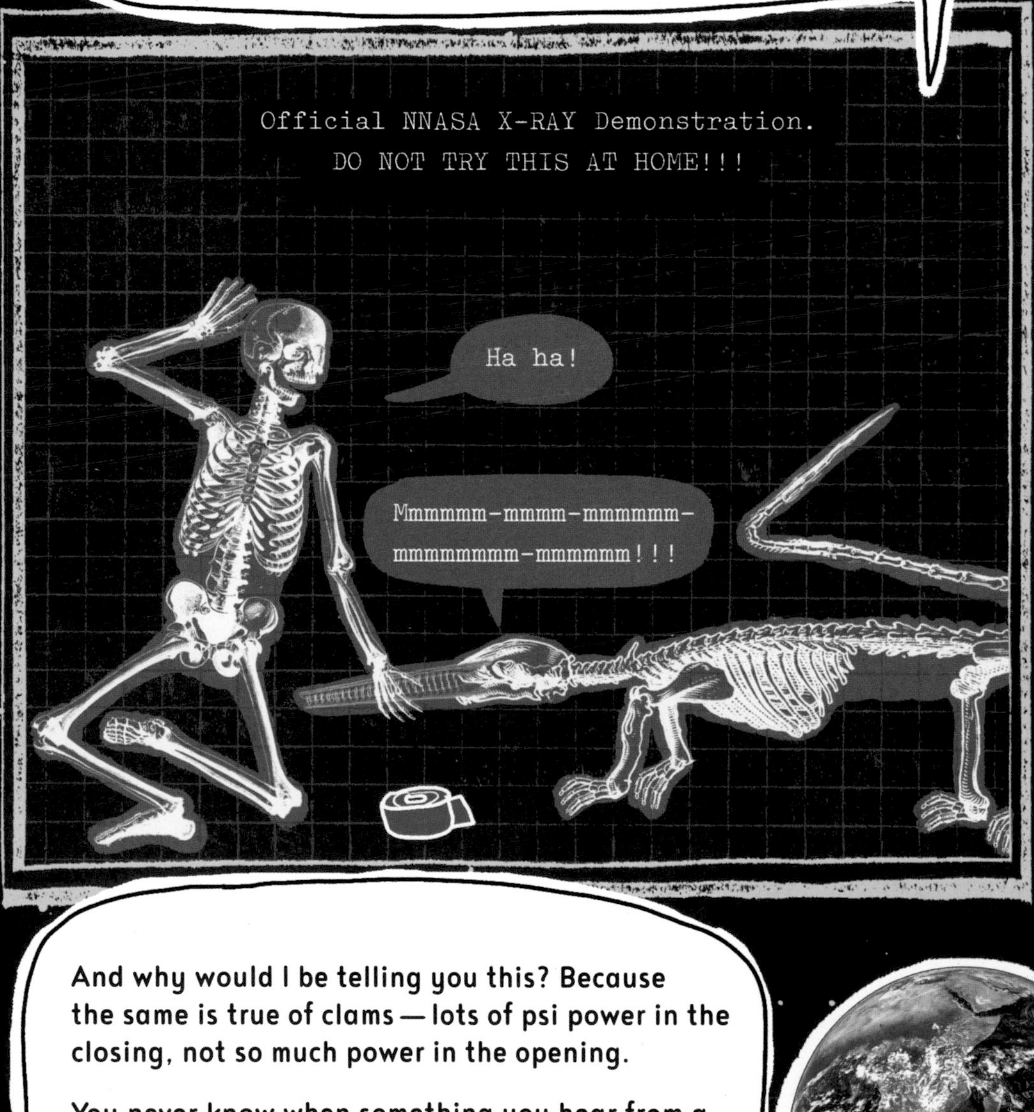
Official NNASA X-RAY Demonstration.
DO NOT TRY THIS AT HOME!!!
Ha ha!
Mmmmmm-mmmm-mmmmmm-mmmmmmmm-mmmmmm!!!

And why would I be telling you this? Because the same is true of clams — lots of psi power in the closing, not so much power in the opening.

You never know when something you hear from a new best friend might save a world or two.

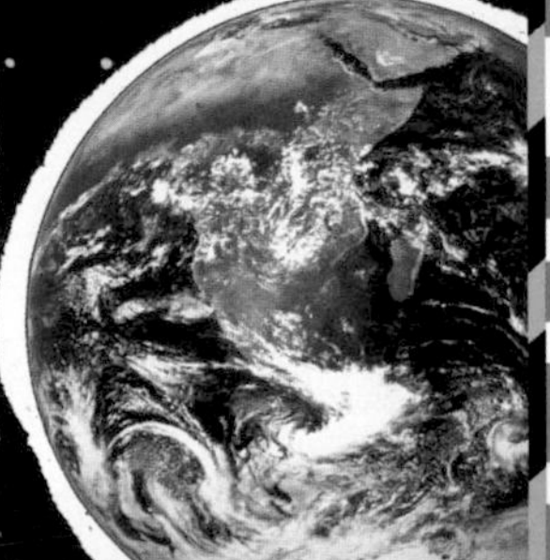

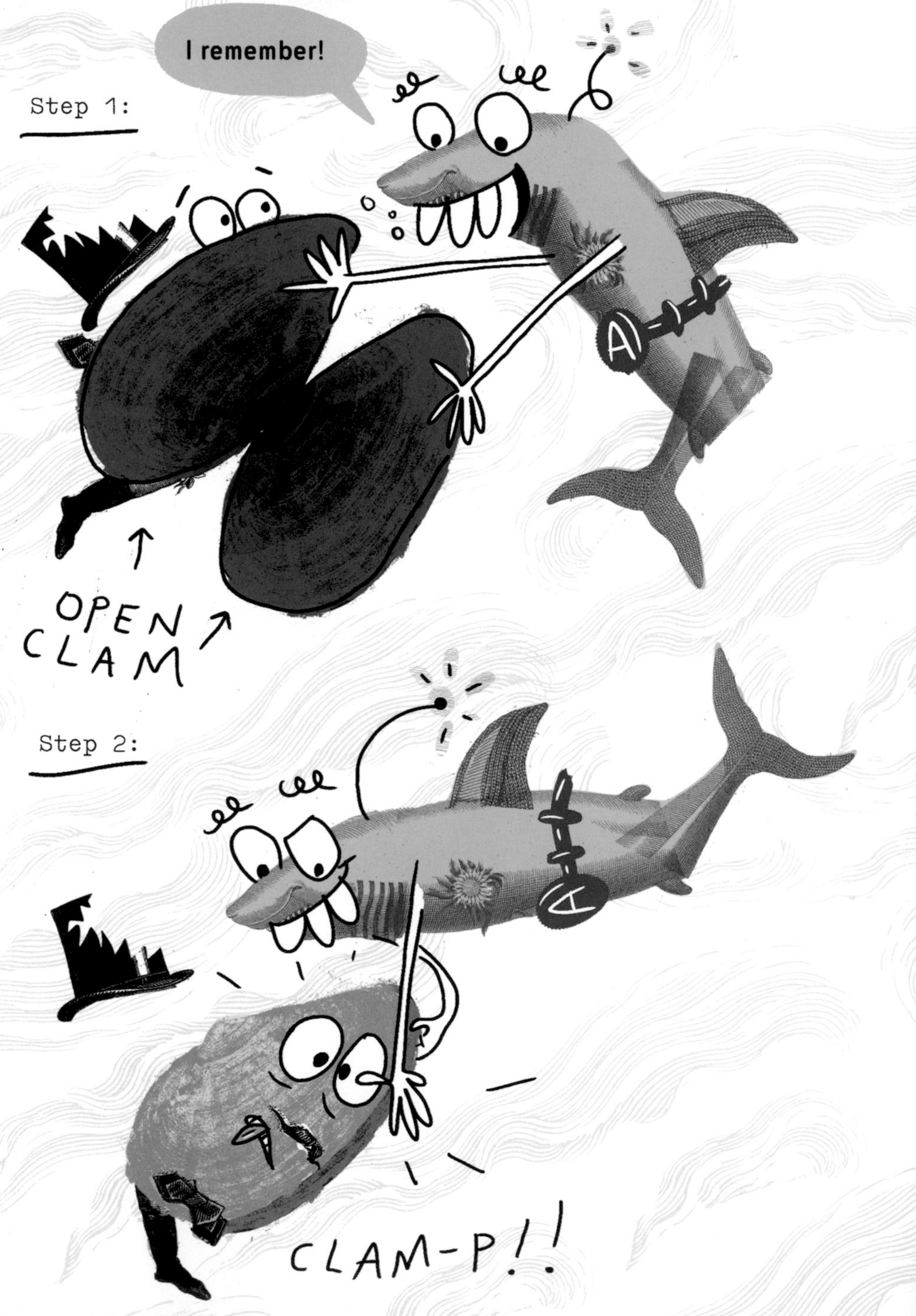
I remember!
Step 1:
OPEN CLAM
Step 2:
CLAM-P!!

Step 3:

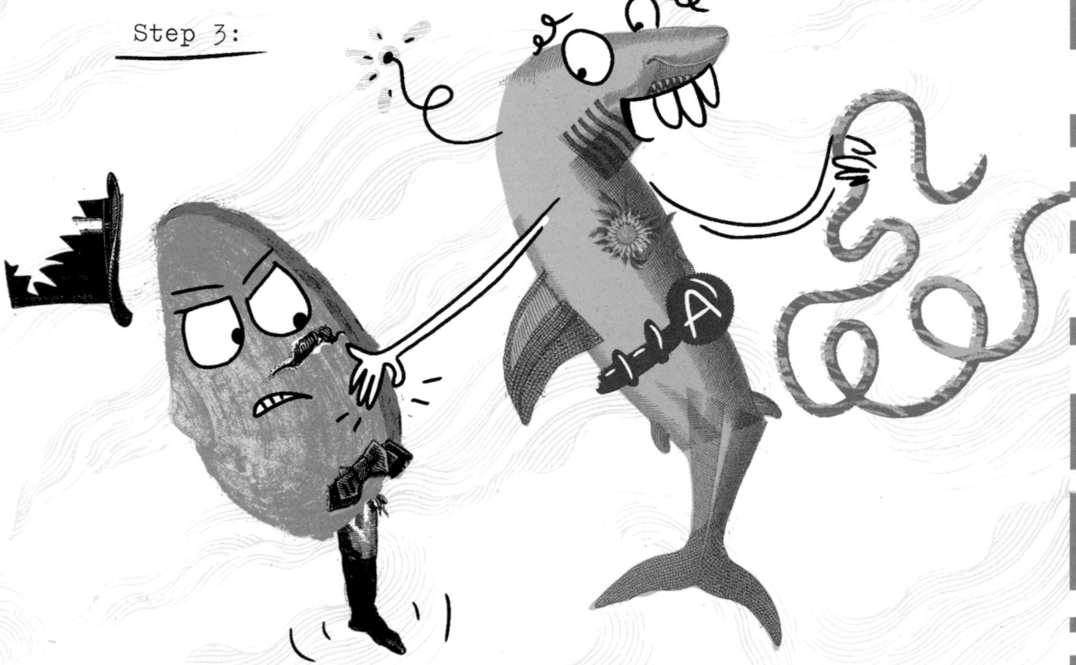

Step 4:

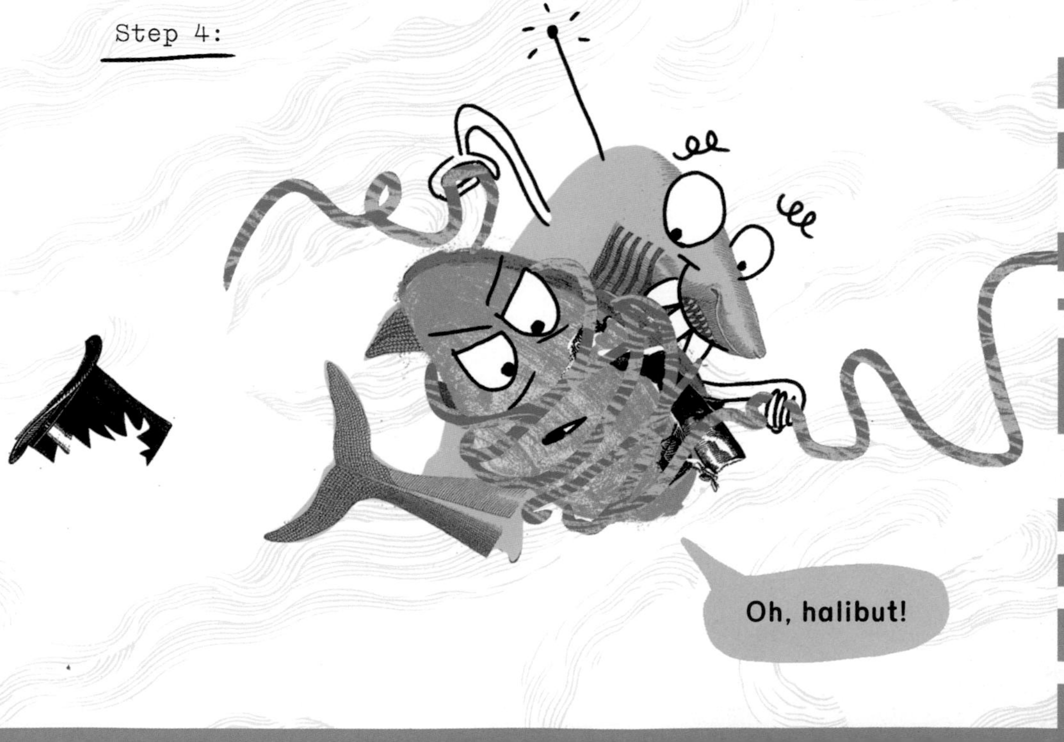
Oh, halibut!

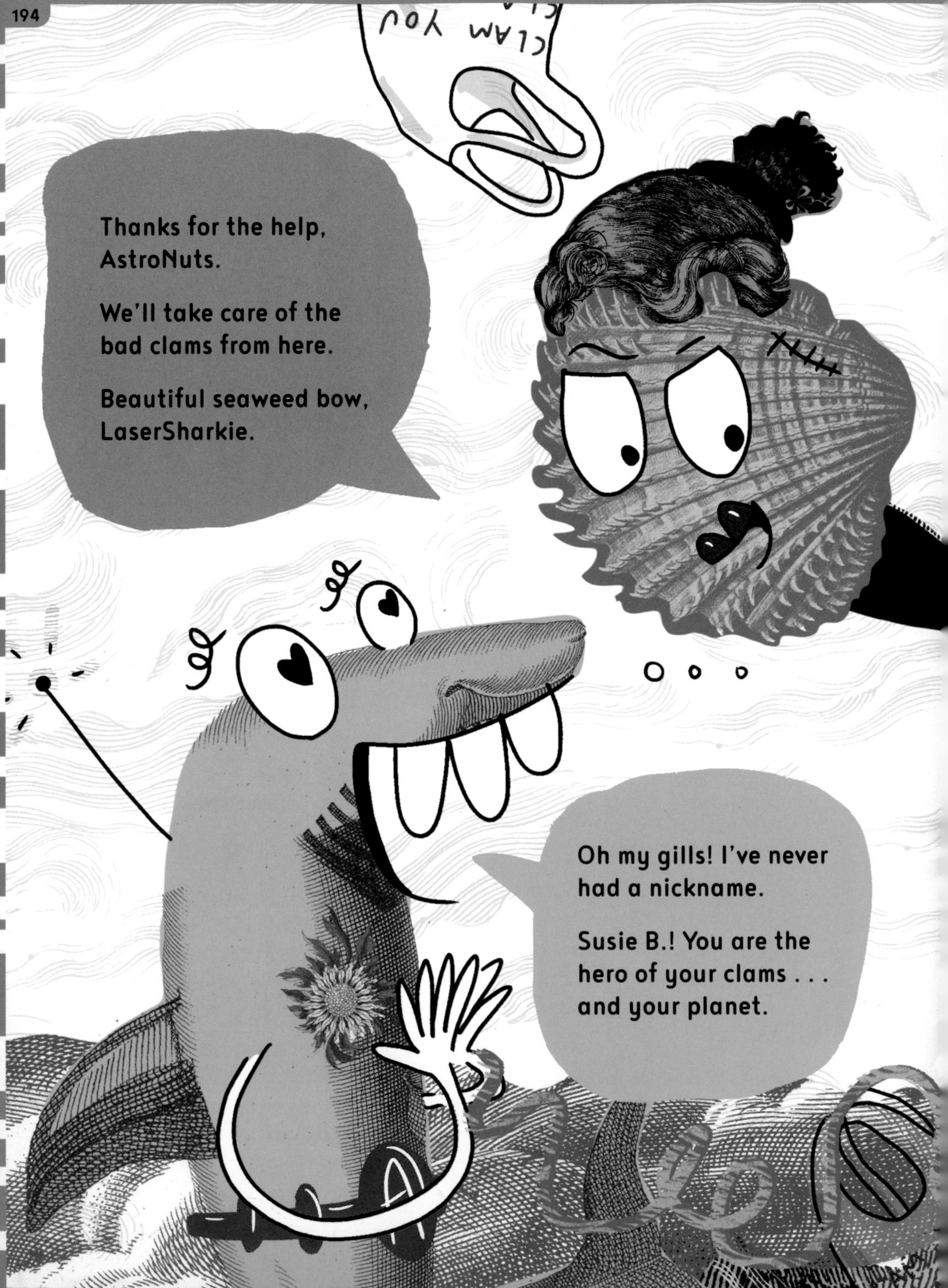
CLAM YOU
Thanks for the help, AstroNuts.
We'll take care of the bad clams from here.
Beautiful seaweed bow, LaserSharkie.
Oh my gills! I've never had a nickname.
Susie B.! You are the hero of your clams . . . and your planet.

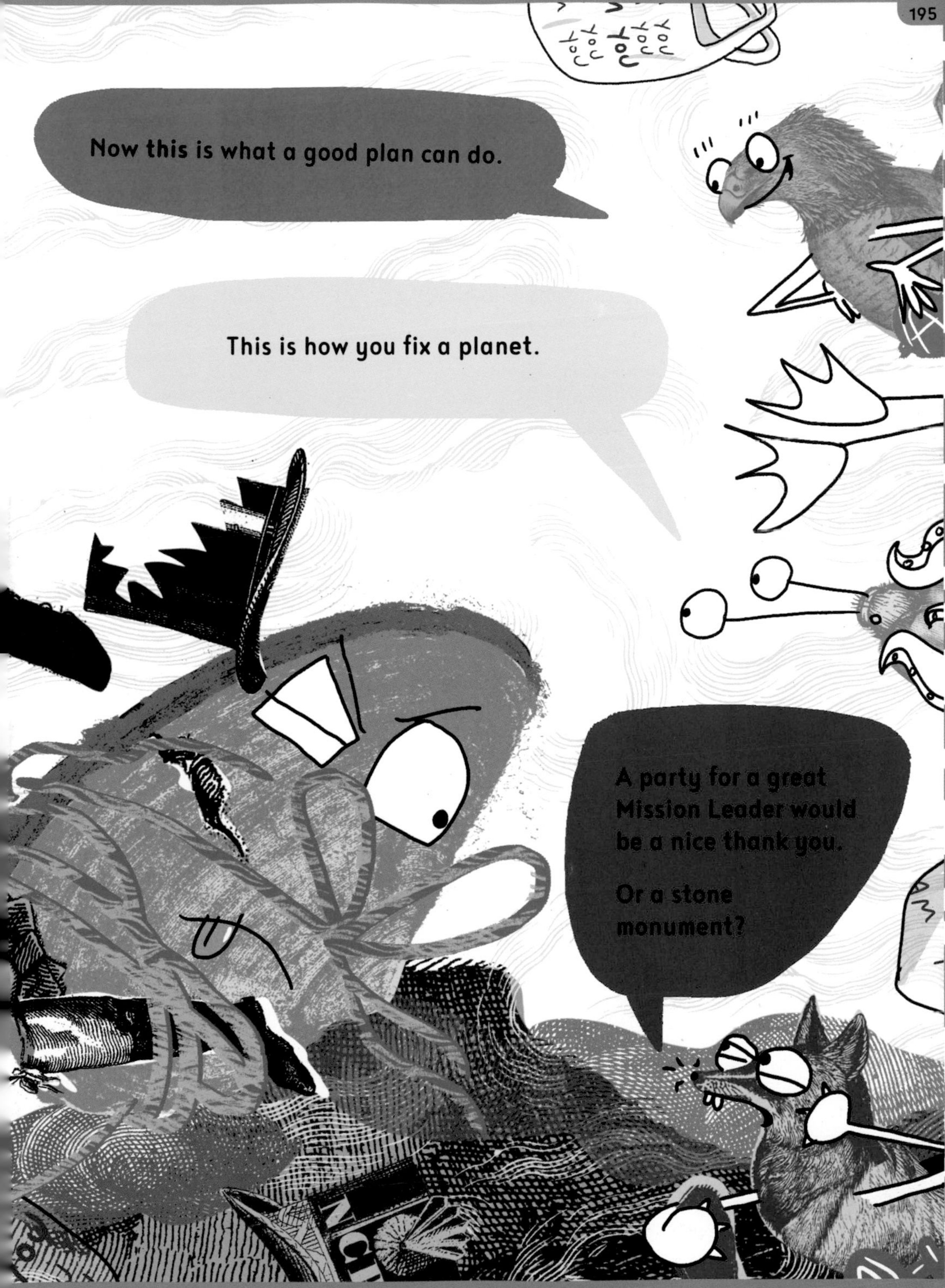
Now this is what a good plan can do.
This is how you fix a planet.
A party for a great Mission Leader would be a nice thank you.
Or a stone monument?

CHAPTER 29:
A Party

So instead of swapping planets, the clams and the AstroNuts swapped dance moves.

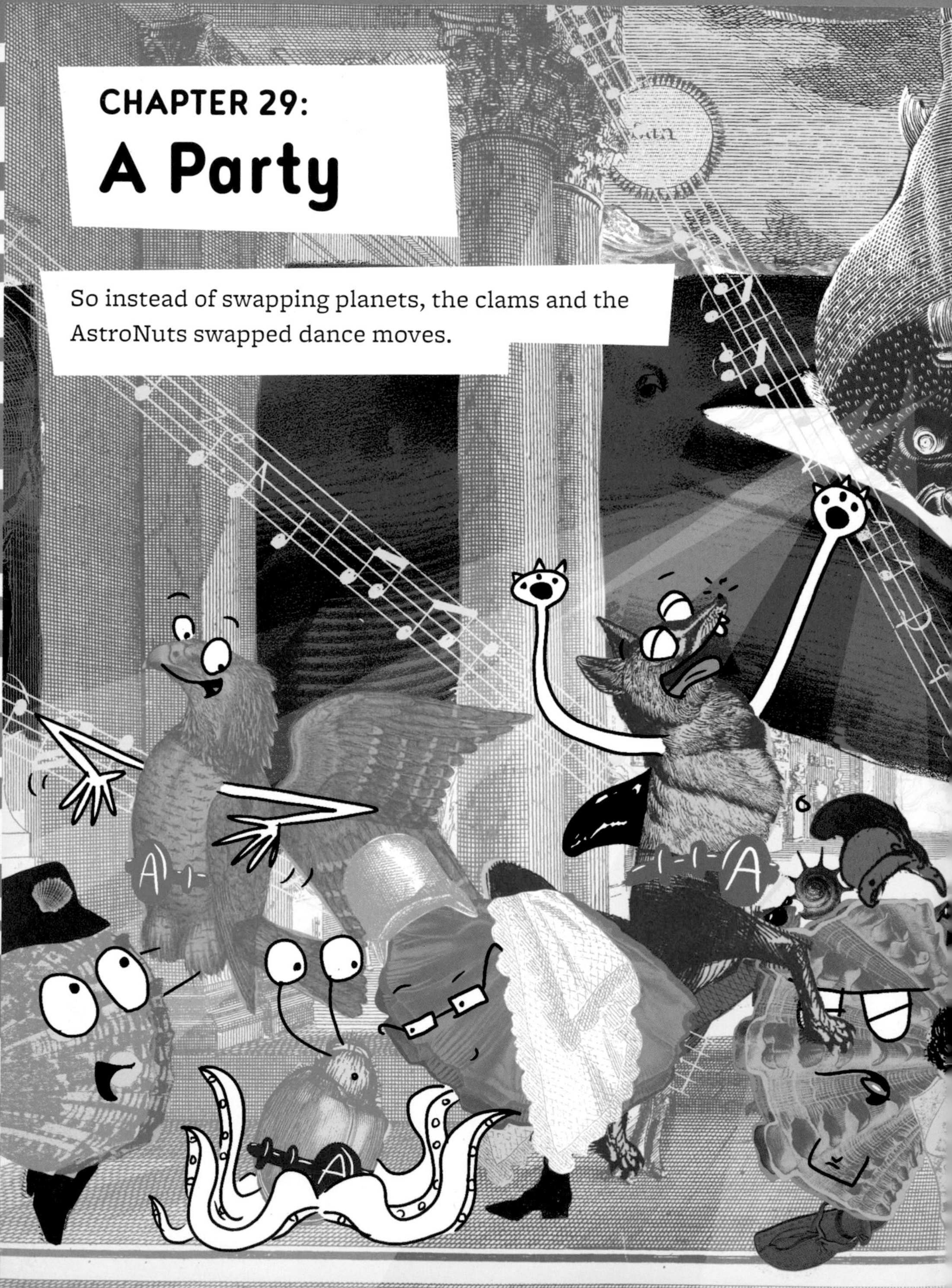

Even though the Water Planet did not turn out to be a good Goldilocks Planet, it did turn out to be a good lesson on how to take care of a planet . . . and how to take care of your friends.

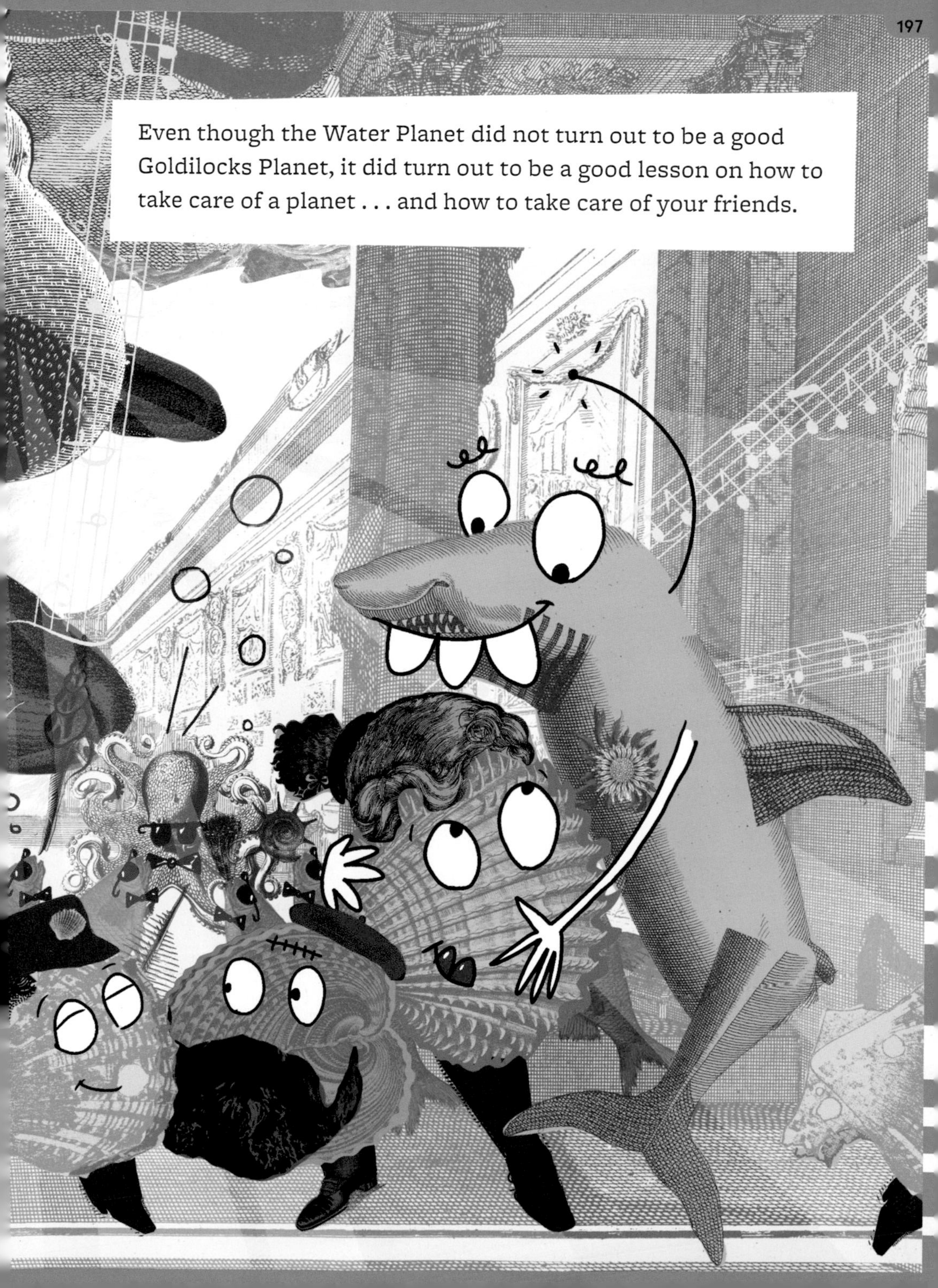

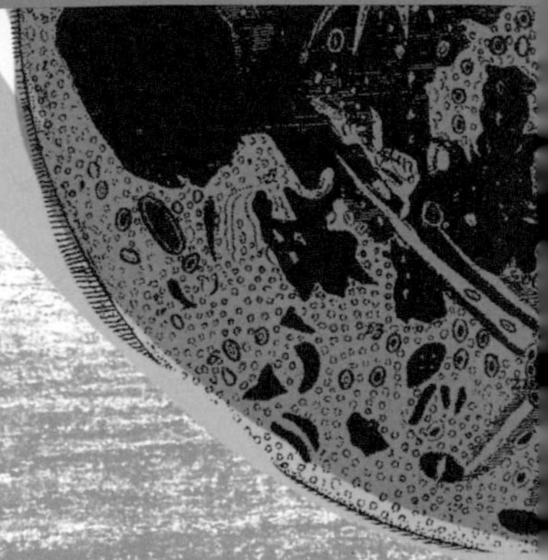

CHAPTER 30:
Foooom!

After the party, the Clam Resistance locked up President P. T. Clam and the Clam Senators in the Clam Parthenon to bring them to justice later.

The AstroNuts said their goodbyes quickly because time was up.

It was time to go home, to me.

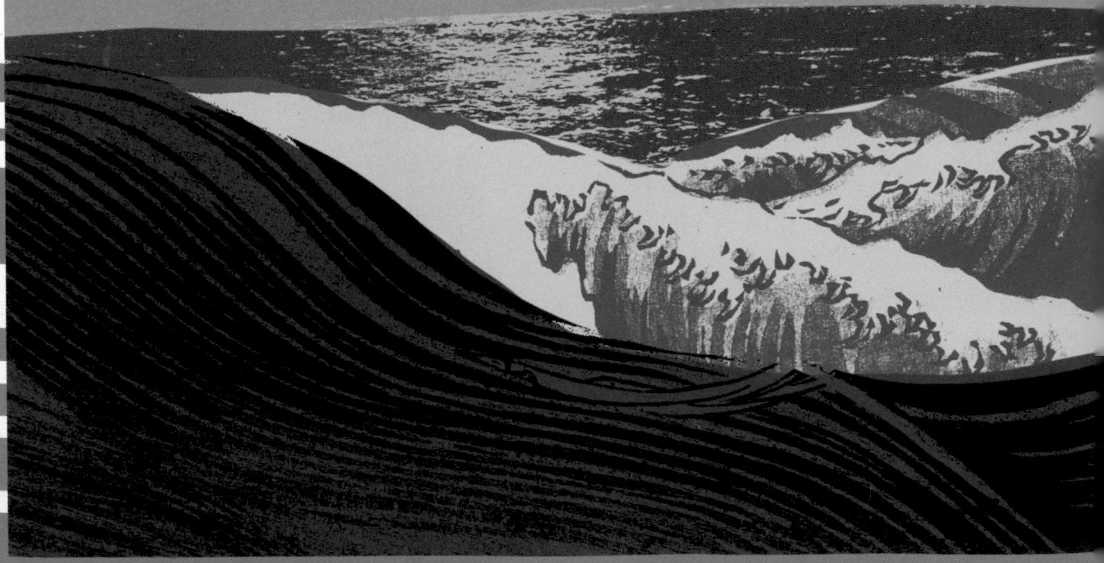

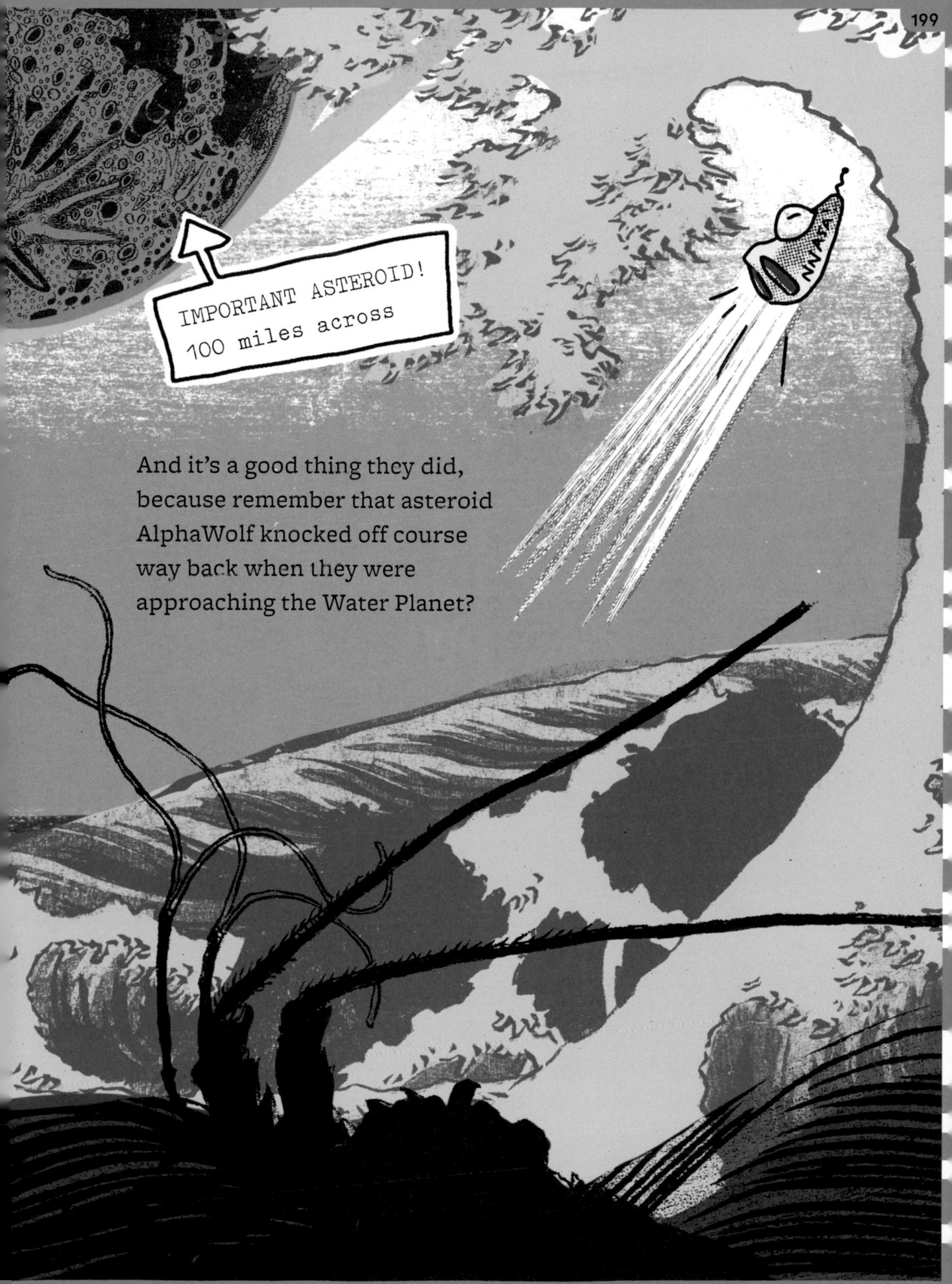
IMPORTANT ASTEROID!
100 miles across
NNASA
And it's a good thing they did, because remember that asteroid AlphaWolf knocked off course way back when they were approaching the Water Planet?

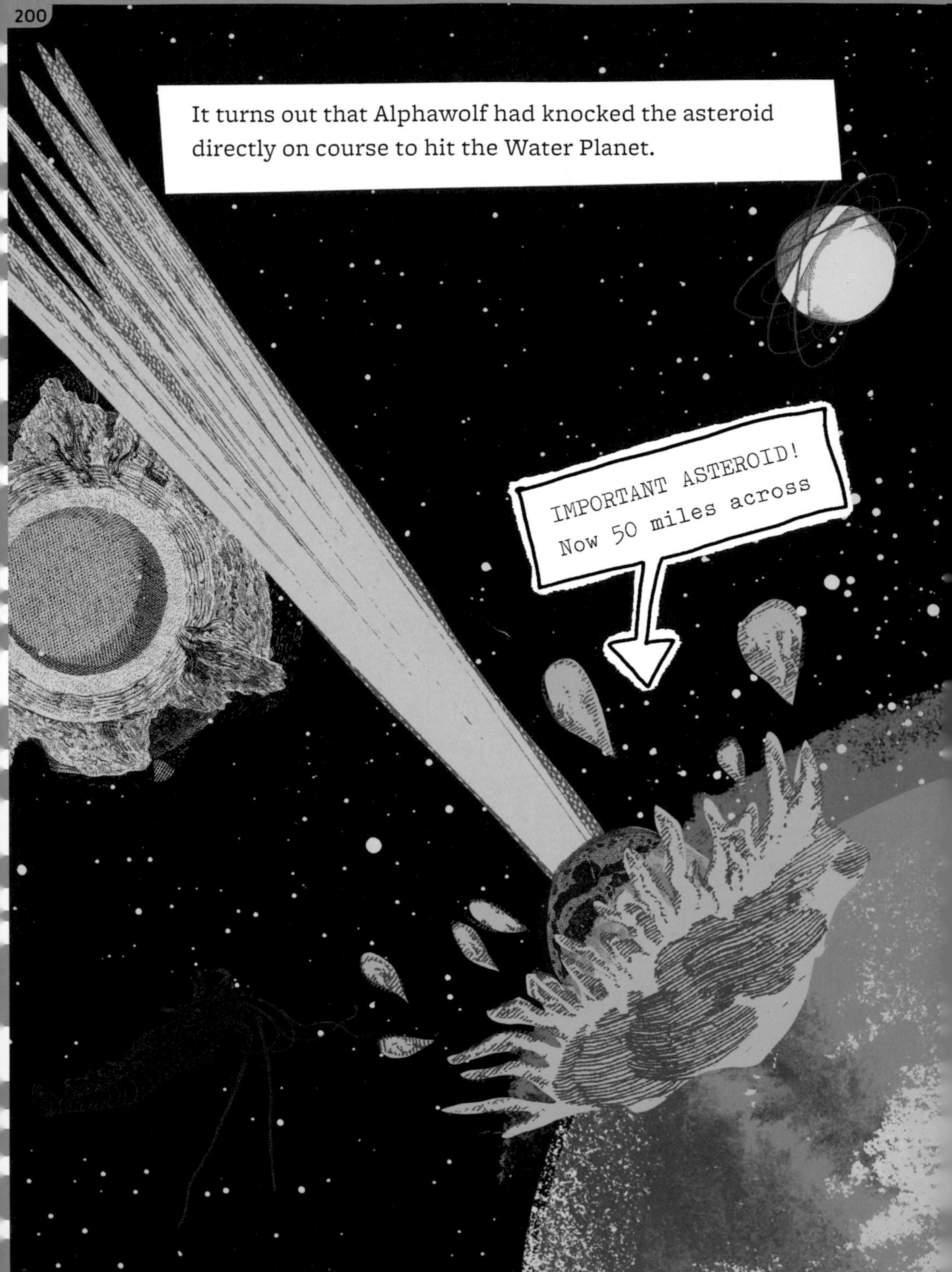
It turns out that Alphawolf had knocked the asteroid directly on course to hit the Water Planet.
IMPORTANT ASTEROID!
Now 50 miles across

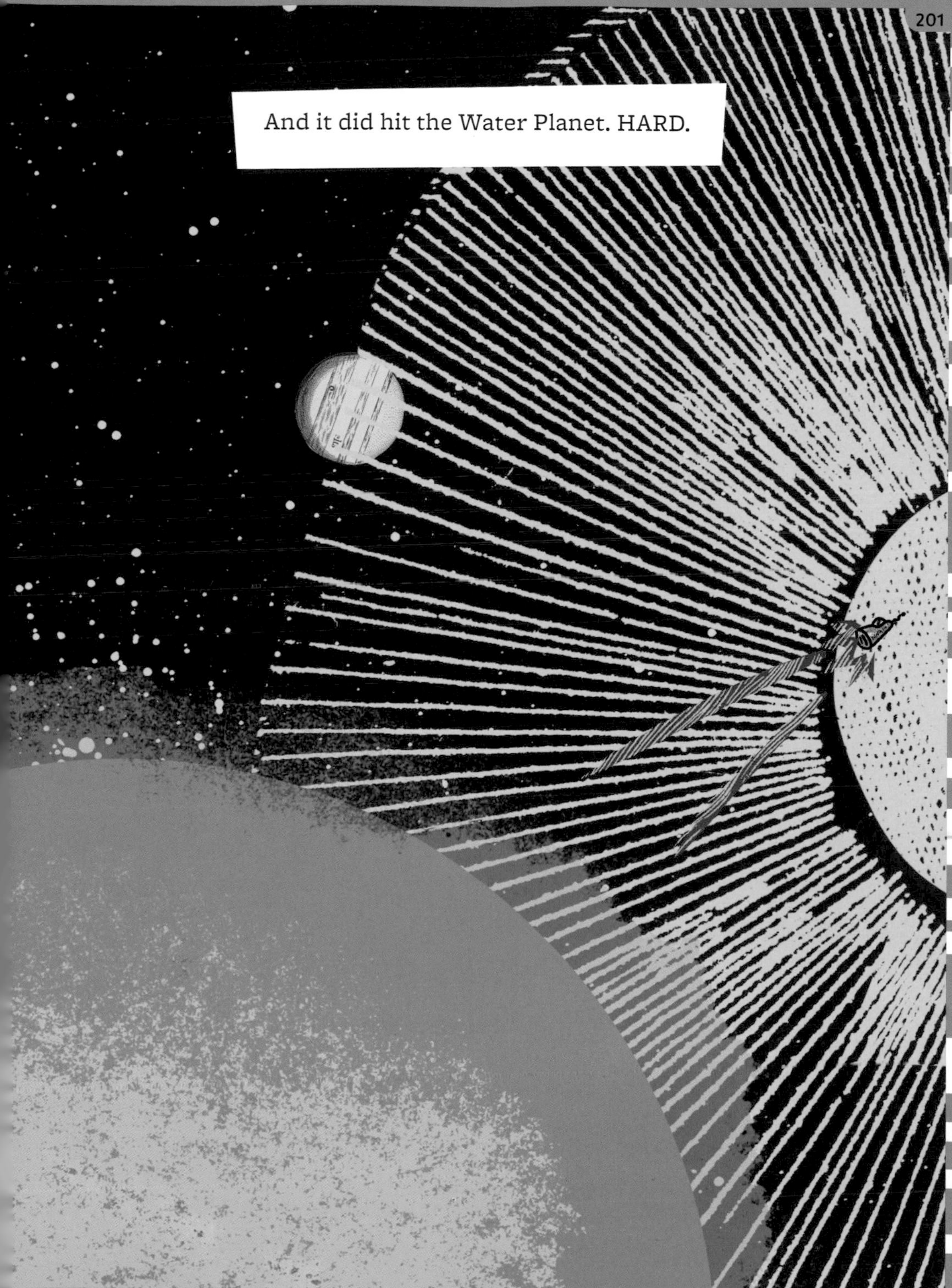

And it did hit the Water Planet. HARD.

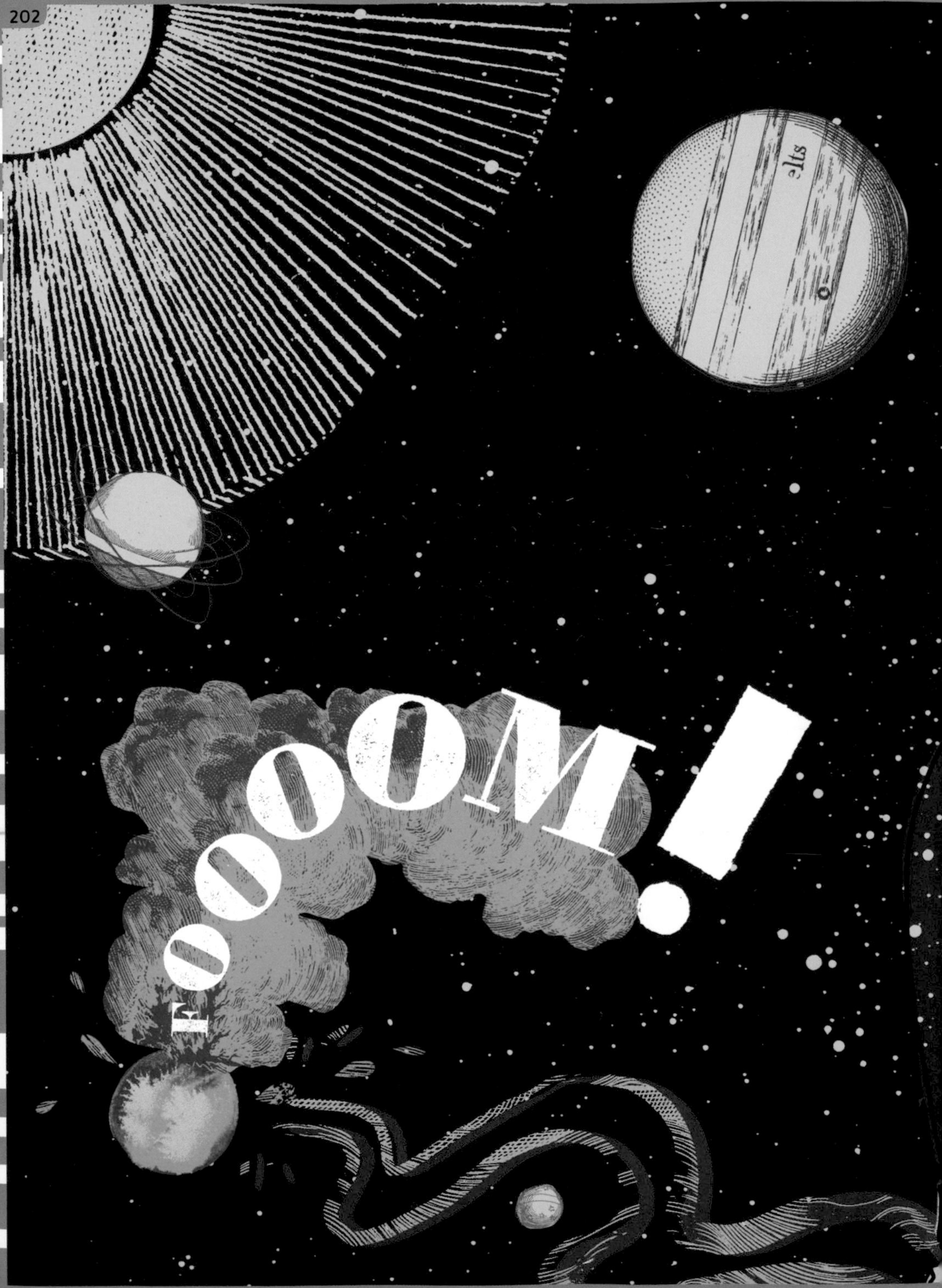
FOOOOM!

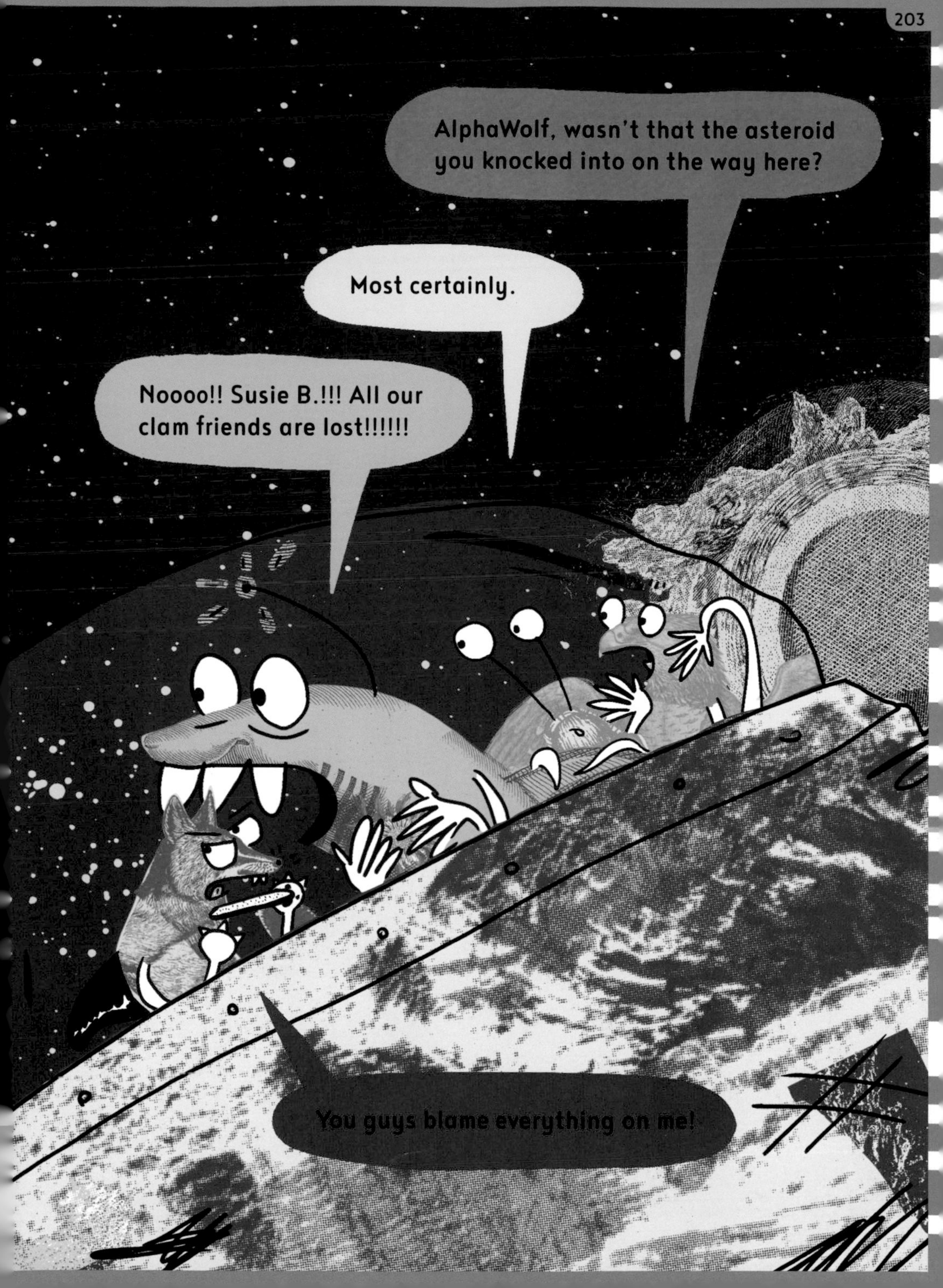
AlphaWolf, wasn't that the asteroid you knocked into on the way here?
Most certainly.
Noooo!! Susie B.!!! All our clam friends are lost!!!!!!
You guys blame everything on me!

But fortunately, and even poetically, the Water Planet atmosphere burned the asteroid down to exactly Clam Parthenon size.

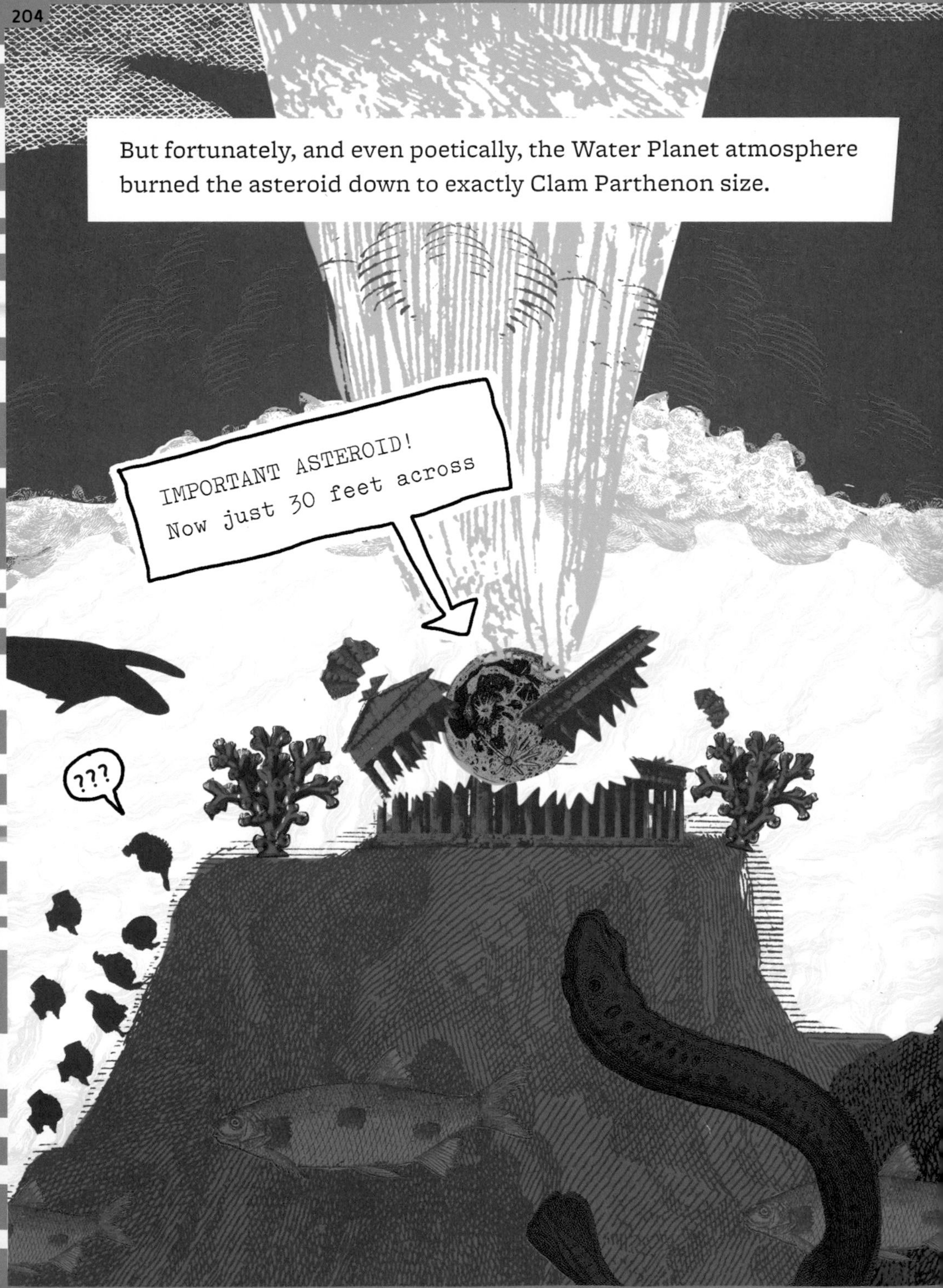
IMPORTANT ASTEROID!
Now just 30 feet across
???

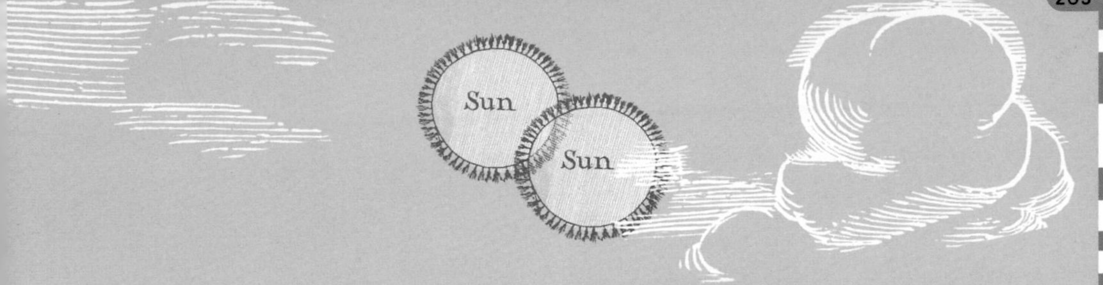
Sun
Sun

Sometimes asteroids are bad for a planet—making craters, poisoning the atmosphere, and causing quakes, tsunamis, and killer wind blasts.

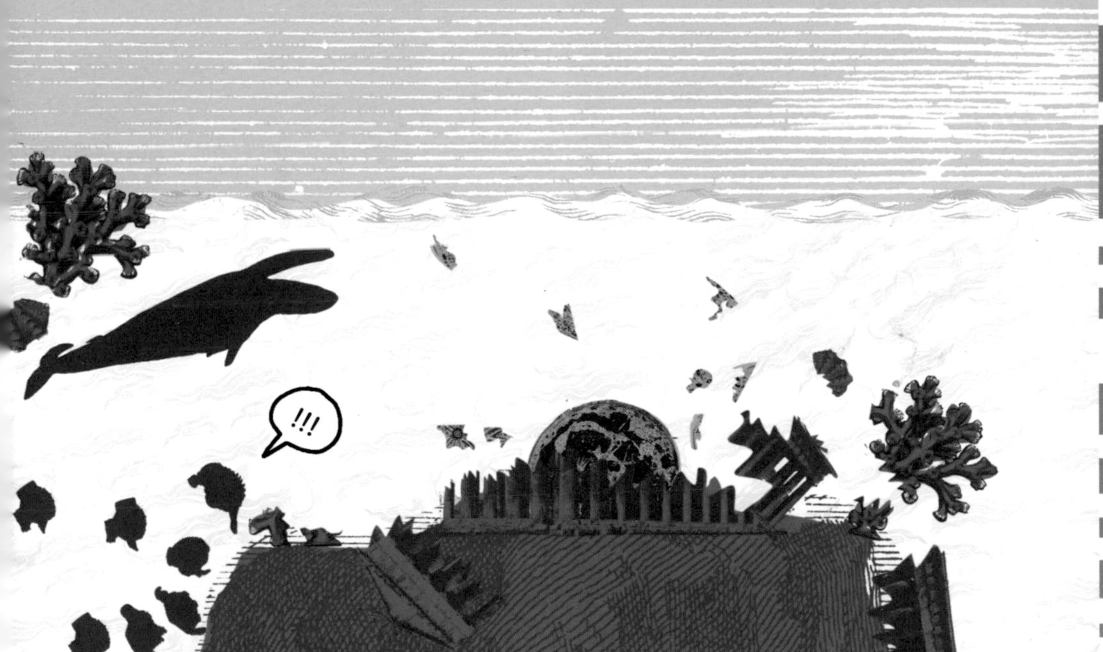
!!!

But sometimes asteroids do good—like when they get rid of pesky dinosaurs stomping all over a planet and never letting her take a quiet nap . . . or when they get rid of bad clams turning a perfectly nice planet into a toxic wasteland.

CHAPTER 31:
Home, Sweet Me

In the 2 hours and 47 minutes (a new, and still impossible, speed) that it took the AstroNuts to get back to me, they had a lot of time to think over their second mission to investigate a Goldilocks Planet.

For some reason, it reminded me of that time you and your brother found some matches in the park and decided it would be safest to make just a little fire inside the hollowed-out dead tree and then quickly put it out because what harm could happen and because no one, like your mom, would ever find out.

And then about an hour later, the fire trucks showed up, put out the fire that had mysteriously started in a hollowed-out dead tree, and your mom somehow put the fire trucks together with the smoky T-shirts you and your brother threw in the laundry basket down in the basement, and asked if you two knew anything about that smoking tree in the park.

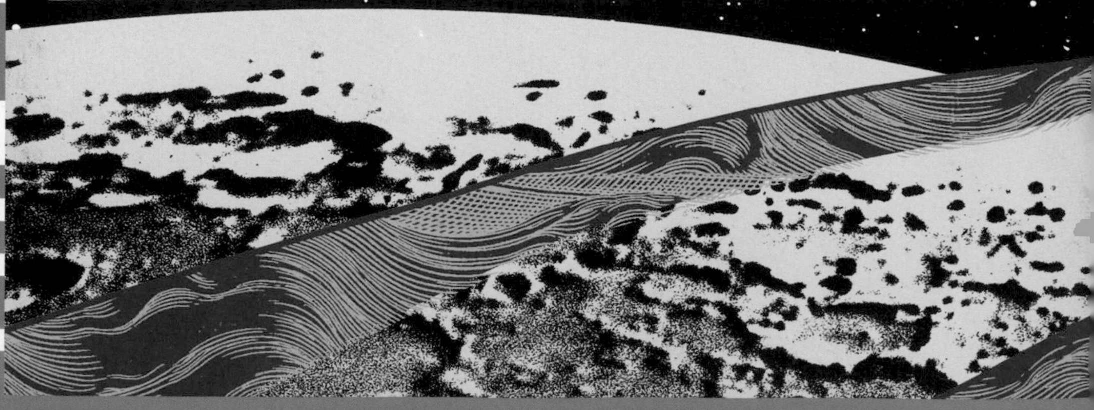

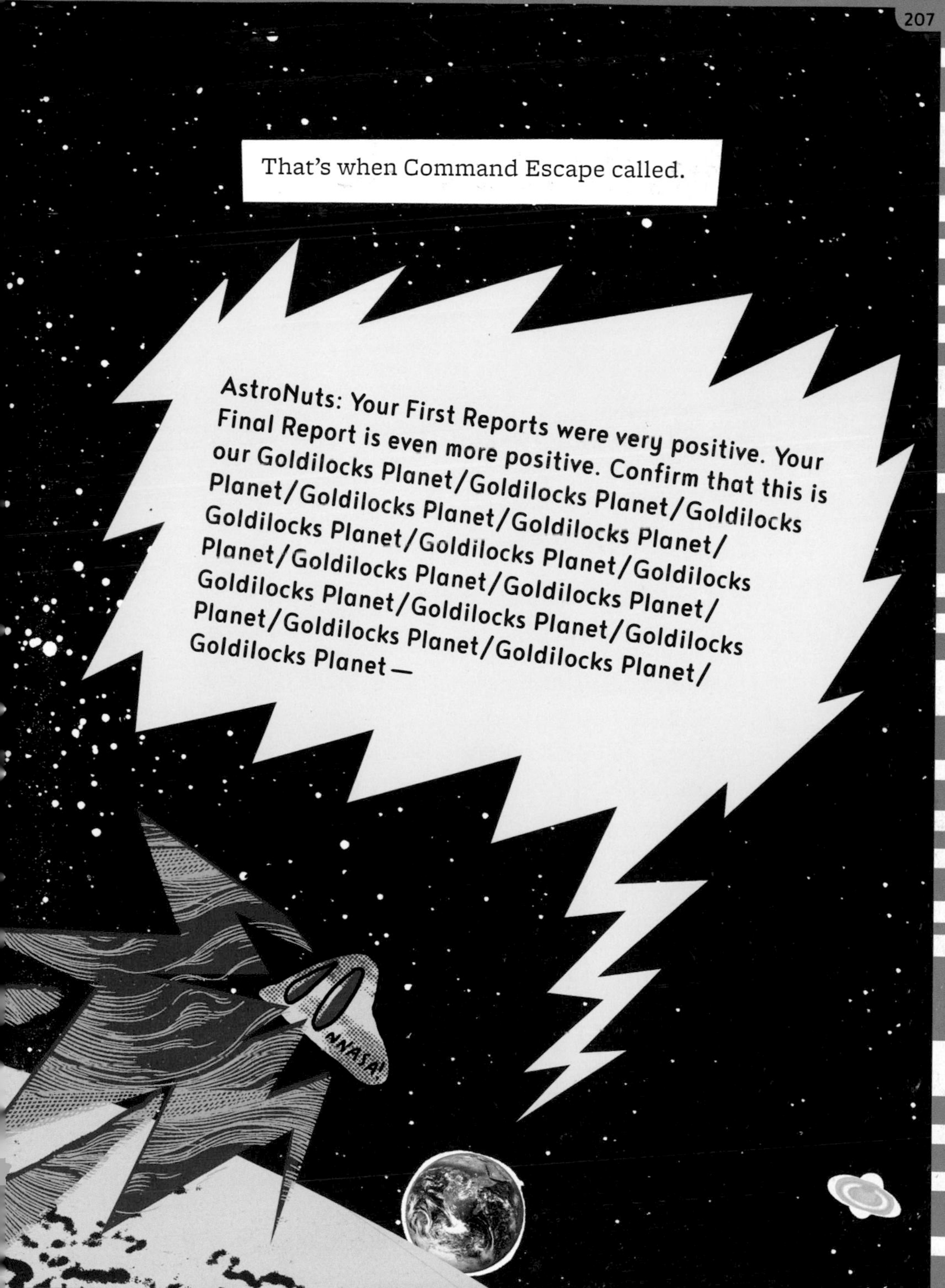
That's when Command Escape called.
AstroNuts: Your First Reports were very positive. Your Final Report is even more positive. Confirm that this is our Goldilocks Planet/Goldilocks Planet/Goldilocks Planet/Goldilocks Planet/Goldilocks Planet/Goldilocks Planet/Goldilocks Planet/Goldilocks Planet/Goldilocks Planet/Goldilocks Planet/Goldilocks Planet/Goldilocks Planet/Goldilocks Planet/Goldilocks Planet/Goldilocks Planet/Goldilocks Planet—
NNASA!

The AstroNuts had never sent in any NNASA 14-AFR Astro First Report. And the AstroNuts had never sent in the NNASA 35-FGPR Final Goldilocks Planet Report.

FORM 35-FGPR FINAL

PAID FOR BY

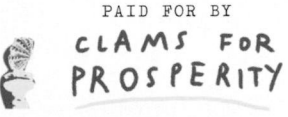

CLAMS FOR PROSPERITY

Name of Planet: The Most Wonderful Water Planet

Temperature Range: Pleasant to lovely

Atmosphere: Absolutely fantastic

Describe inhabitants: Where to begin? Clamsome, clamtelligent, clarming, more and more clam words. Could not possibly be nicer.

Some clamsome, clamtelligent, clarming, and nice clams:

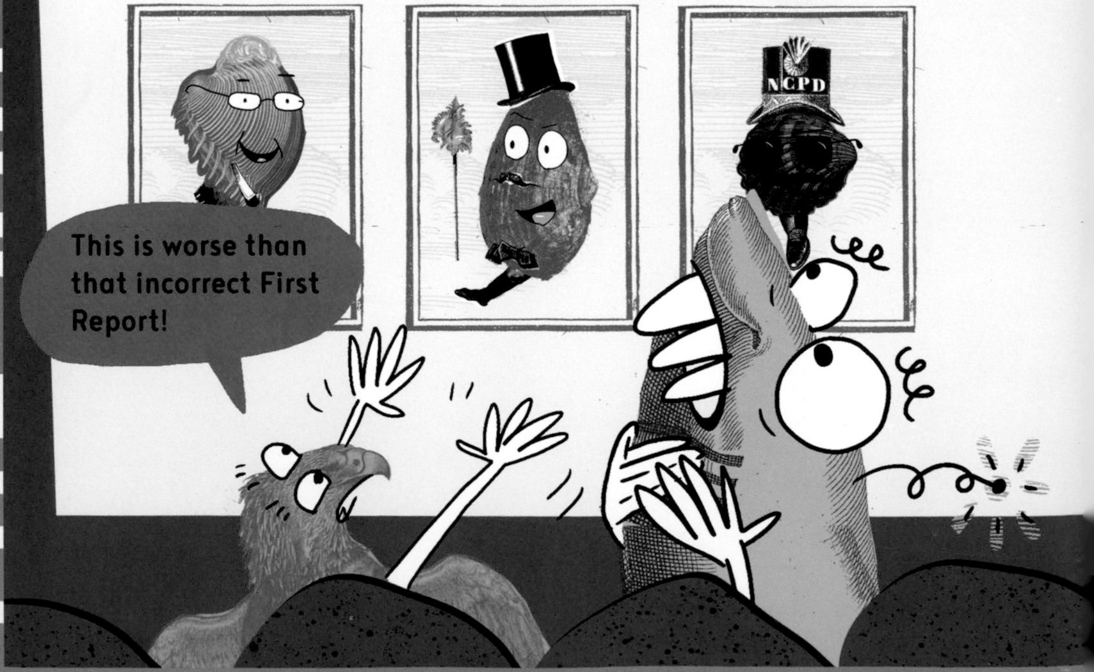
NCPD
This is worse than that incorrect First Report!

But guess who had sneakily filled them out and sent them in?

(Hint: his name rhymes with "P. T. Sham.")

GOLDILOCKS PLANET REPORT

PAID FOR BY

CLAMS FOR
PROSPERITY

Planet has Liquid Water. TRUE/FALSE

Humans could find Food and Shelter here. TRUE/FALSE

Planet ecosystem is well balanced. TRUE/FALSE

No intelligent life is harmed. TRUE/FALSE

OVERALL
RATING:

A) Great
B) OK
C) Not good
D) Terrible
E) Your head explodes
F) GO NOW!!! WHY WAIT??

We did not fill
this out.

///// Official NNASA transcript /////
//// of ASTRONUT MISSION 2 ////

Command Escape: Excellent news that both First and Final Reports are completely positive/completely positive/completely—

SmartHawk: Oh, Command Escape! So great to hear from you. The Water Planet is NOT a good Goldilocks Planet. And AlphaWolf wants to tell you all about it.

AlphaWolf: I do?

LaserShark: Yes, you do. Because you are the one who caused all this. You hit the asteroid that smashed into our new clam friends.

AlphaWolf: It might not have been me.

StinkBug: Yes, it was. Remember when you took the Nose Rocket controls?

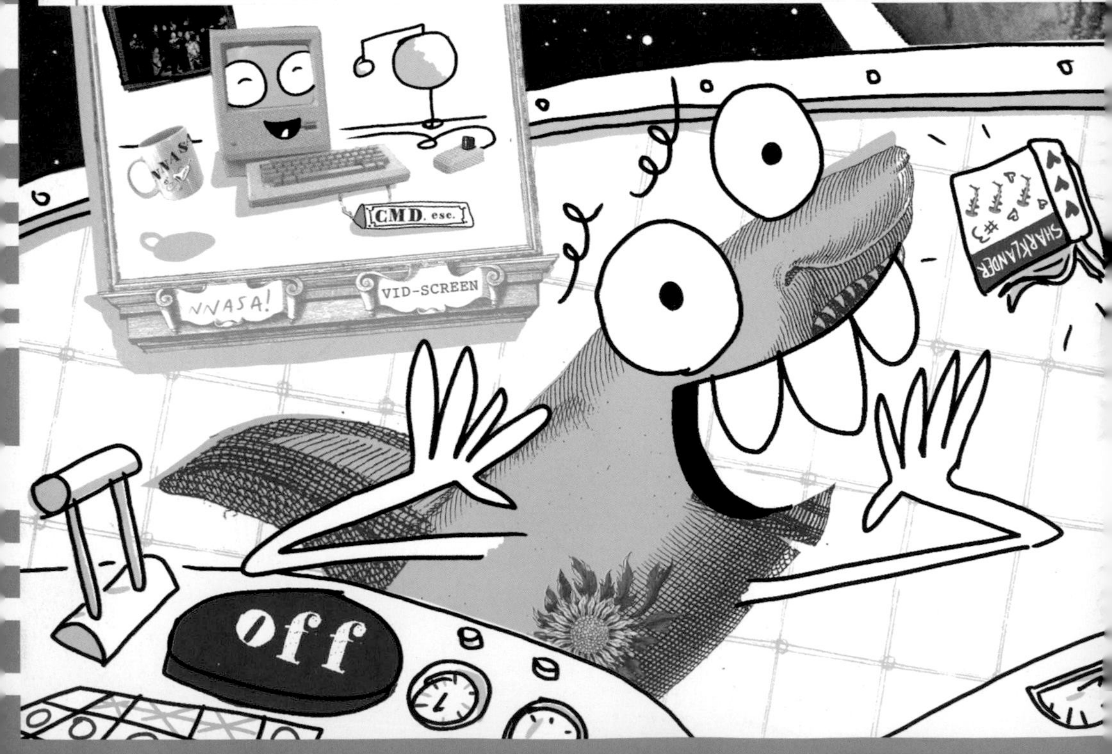
CMD. esc.
NNASA!
VID-SCREEN
SHARKLANDER #3
off

AlphaWolf: StinkBug! Not now.

StinkBug: And then remember you did a barrel roll?

Command Escape: Clam friends? Asteroid? HMMMMMMMMMM BEEP. That would explain the message we just received from the Water Planet: "Asteroid destroyed only Clam Parthenon. Clam Revolution Lives On. Love, Susie B./Love, Susie B./Love—

SmartHawk: What? So AlphaWolf accidentally saved the day?

AlphaWolf: I did? I mean, of course I did!

SmartHawk: Oh, for goodness' sake.

LaserShark: Love, Susie B.! Love, Susie B.!

Command Escape: This new data changes everything. I will recompute. There may not be enough time for another mission. AstroNuts, return to Base Thomas Jefferson and stand by/stand by/stand by for further orders.

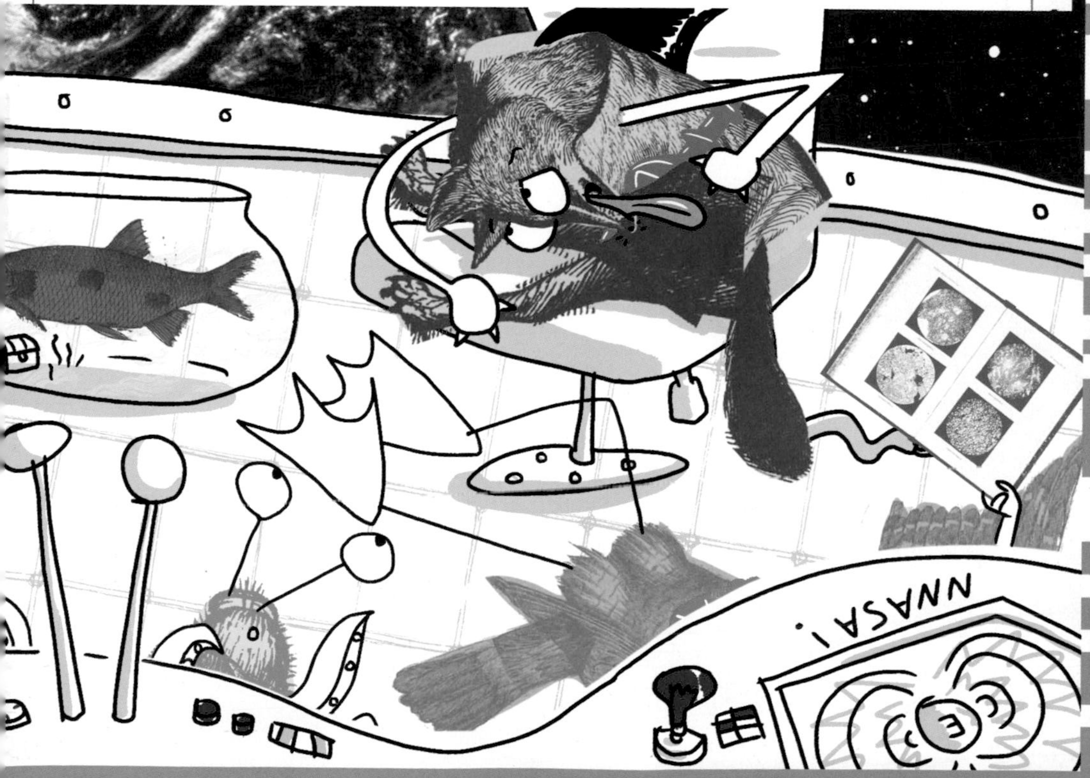
NNASA!

The AstroNuts reentered Earth's atmosphere, wondering if this was the end—no more missions.

The Water Planet would never have been a good Goldilocks Planet because 1) there was not enough land for humans, 2) it was more messed up than Earth, and 3) it was already occupied by intelligent life.

But at least they did learn one very valuable lesson from Susan B. Clamthony and her Resistance Clams.

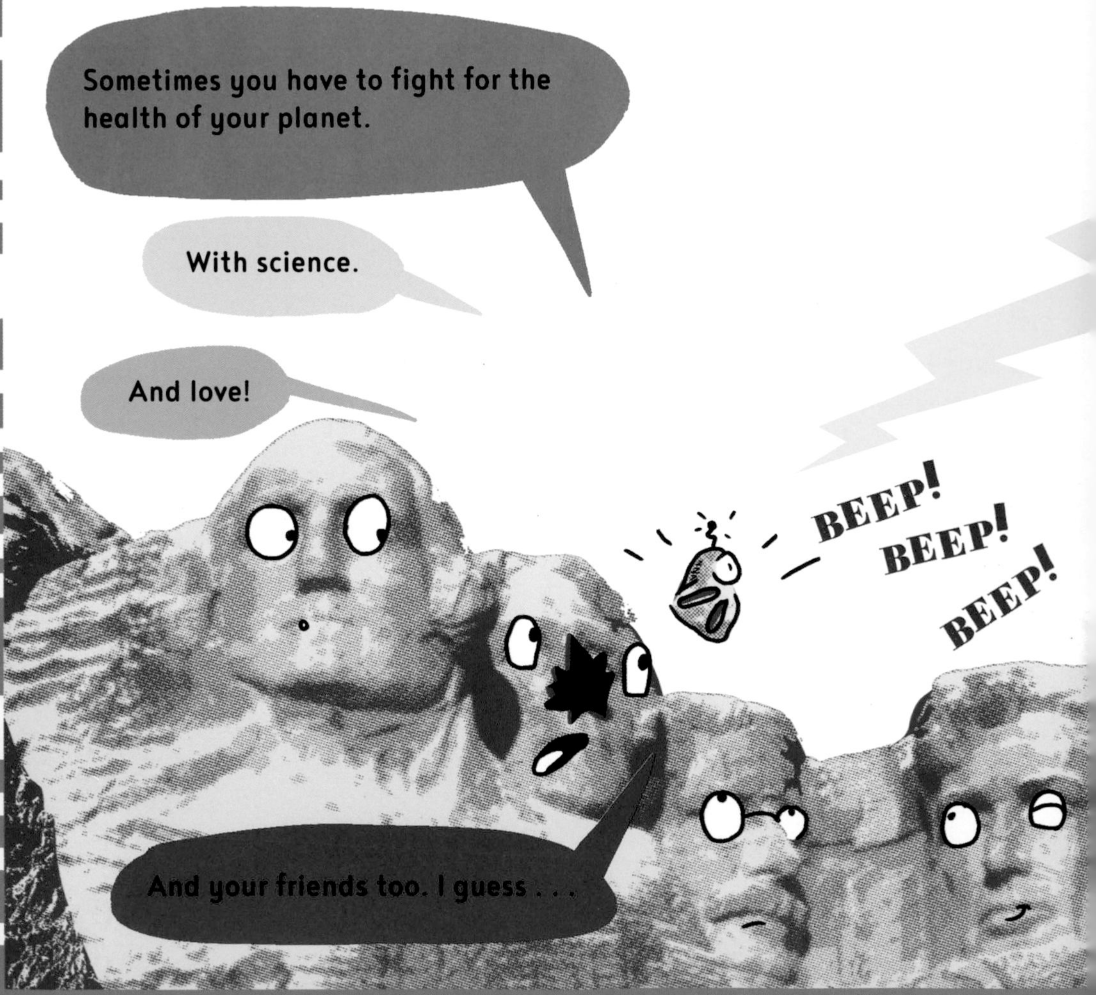
Sometimes you have to fight for the health of your planet.
With science.
And love!
BEEP!
BEEP!
BEEP!
And your friends too. I guess . . .

AstroNuts! This is it.

We are running out/running out/running out of time. Some damage to Earth is already irreversible.

But you are Earth's best hope. Prepare for what may be one last chance — Mission Three: The Perfect Planet/Mission Three: The Perfect Planet/Mission Three: The Perfect Planet/Mission Three: The Perfect Planet/Mission Three: The Perfect Planet/Mission Three: The Perfect Planet/Mission Three: The Perfect Planet/Mission Three: The Perfect Planet/Mission Three: The Perfect Planet/Mission Three: The Perfect Planet/Mission Three: The Perfect Planet/Mission Three: The Perfect Planet/Mission Three: The Perfect Planet.

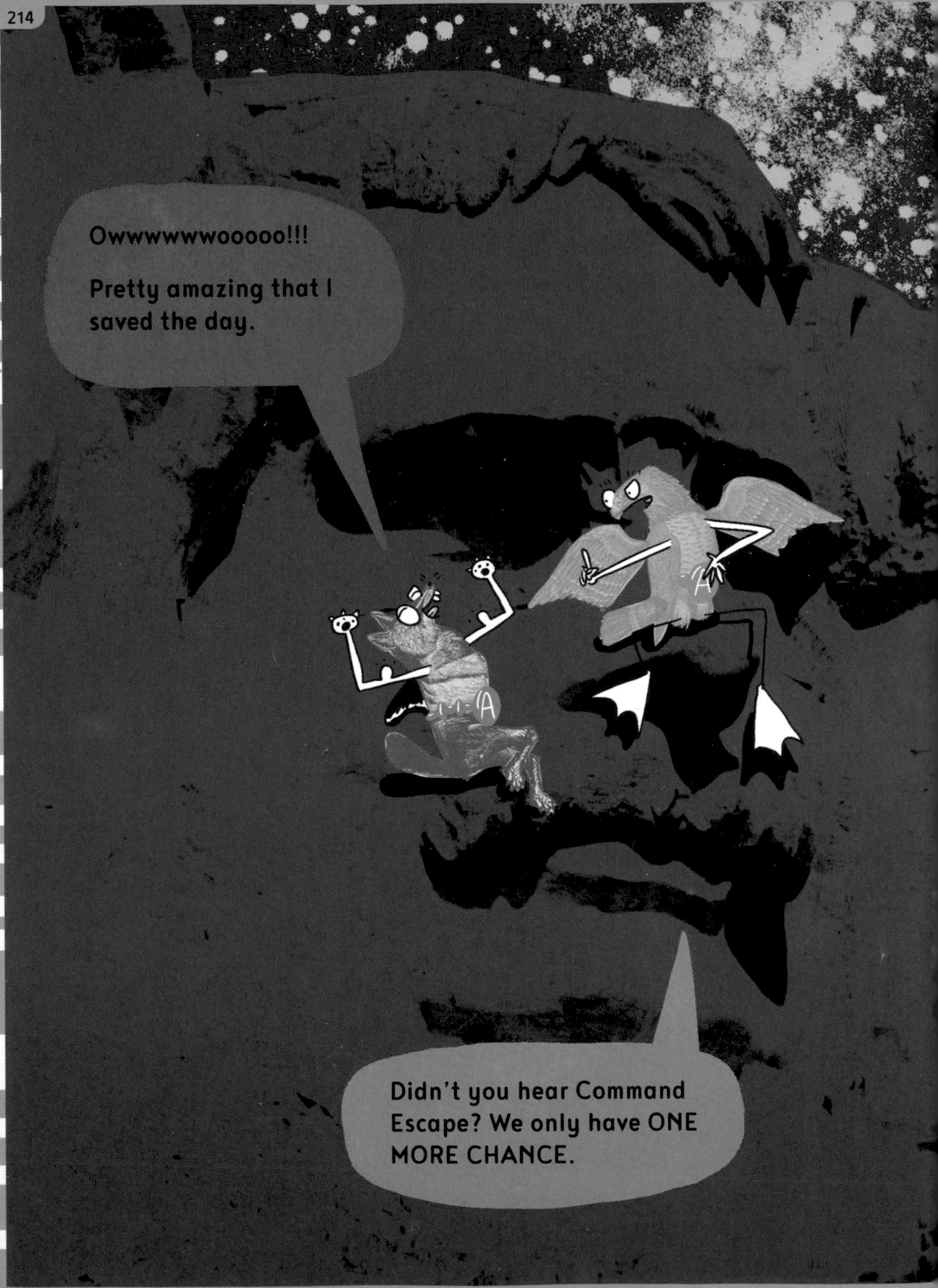
Owwwwwwoooooo!!!
Pretty amazing that I saved the day.
Didn't you hear Command Escape? We only have ONE MORE CHANCE.

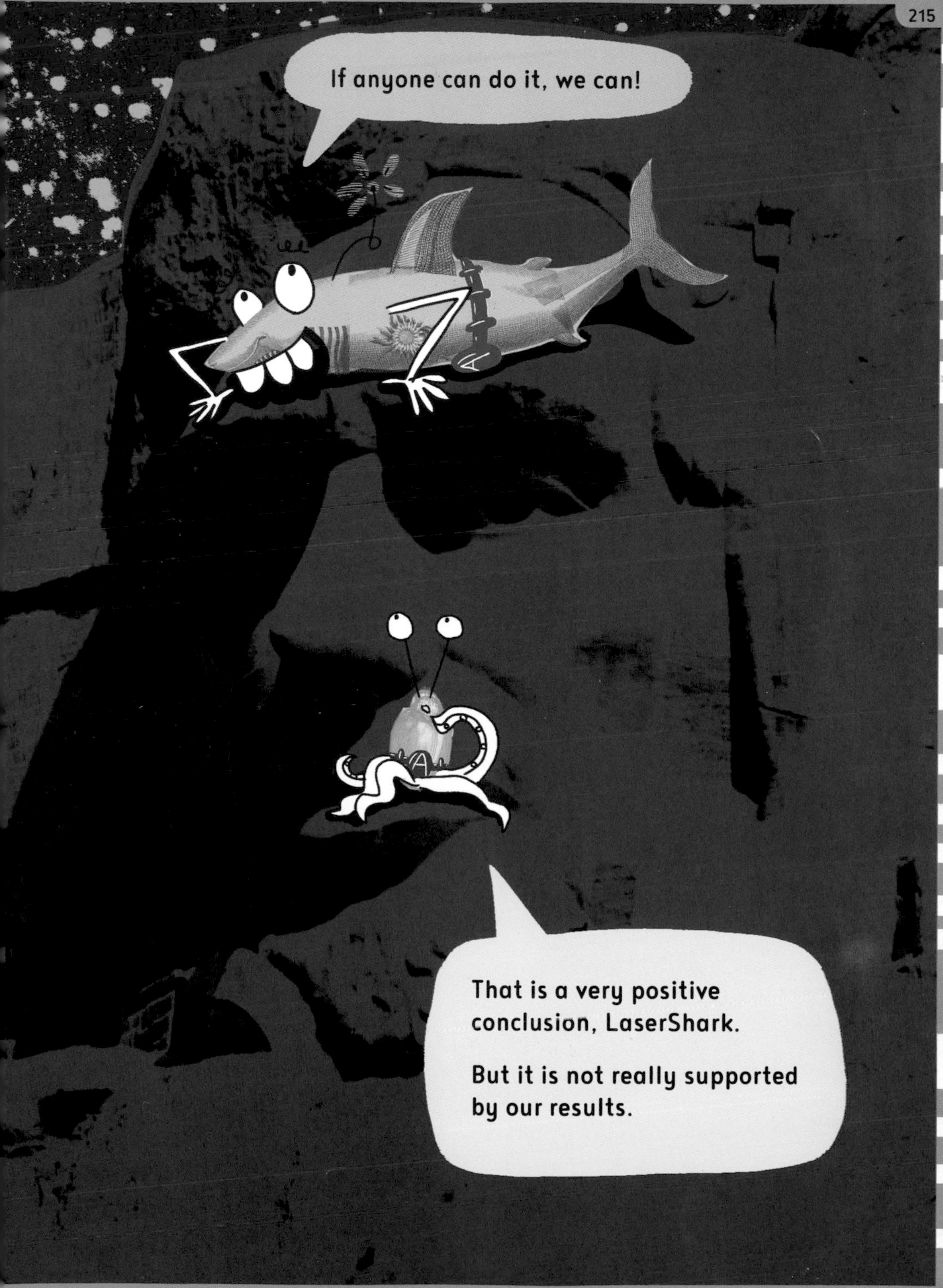
If anyone can do it, we can!
That is a very positive conclusion, LaserShark.
But it is not really supported by our results.

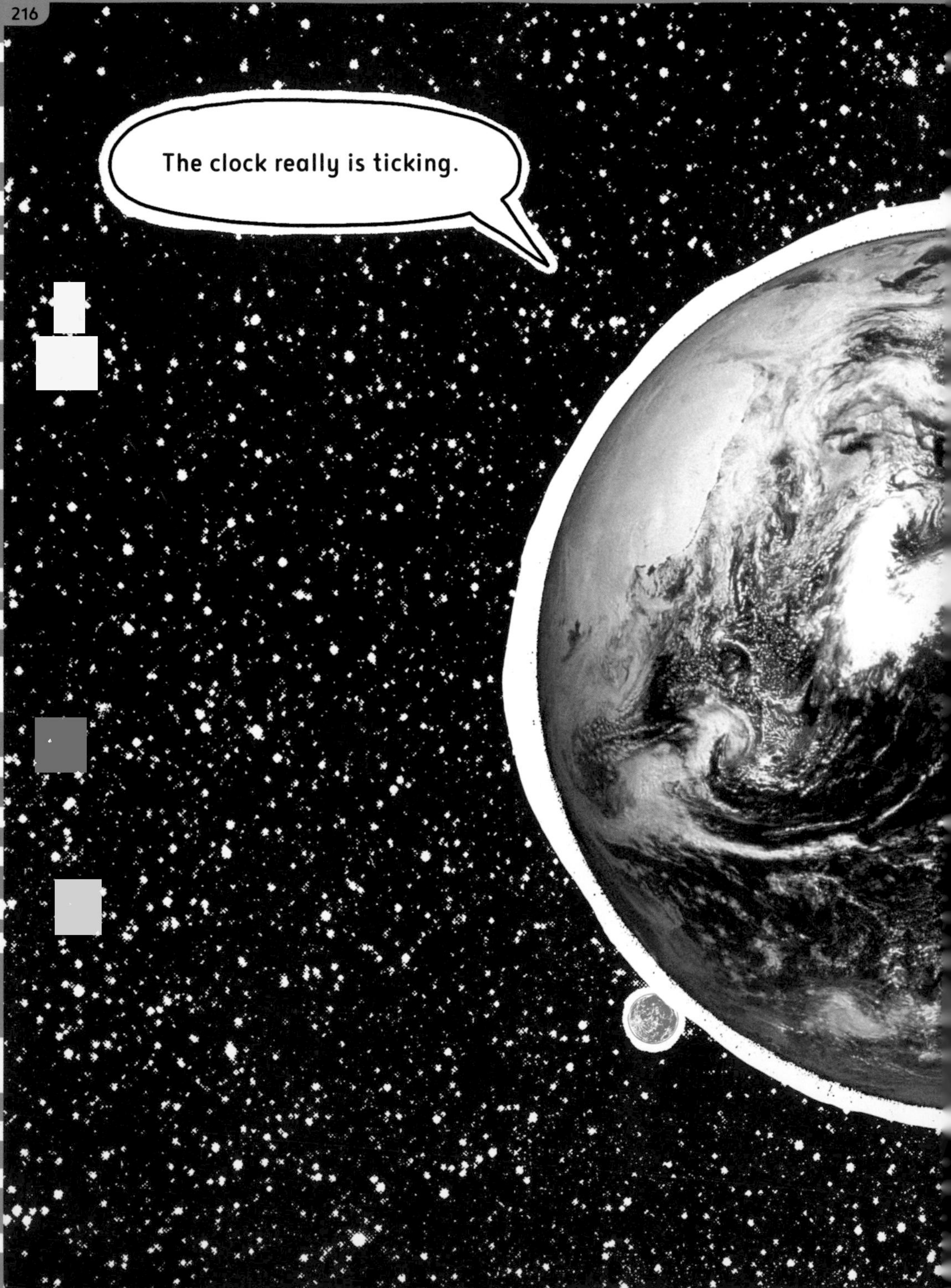
The clock really is ticking.

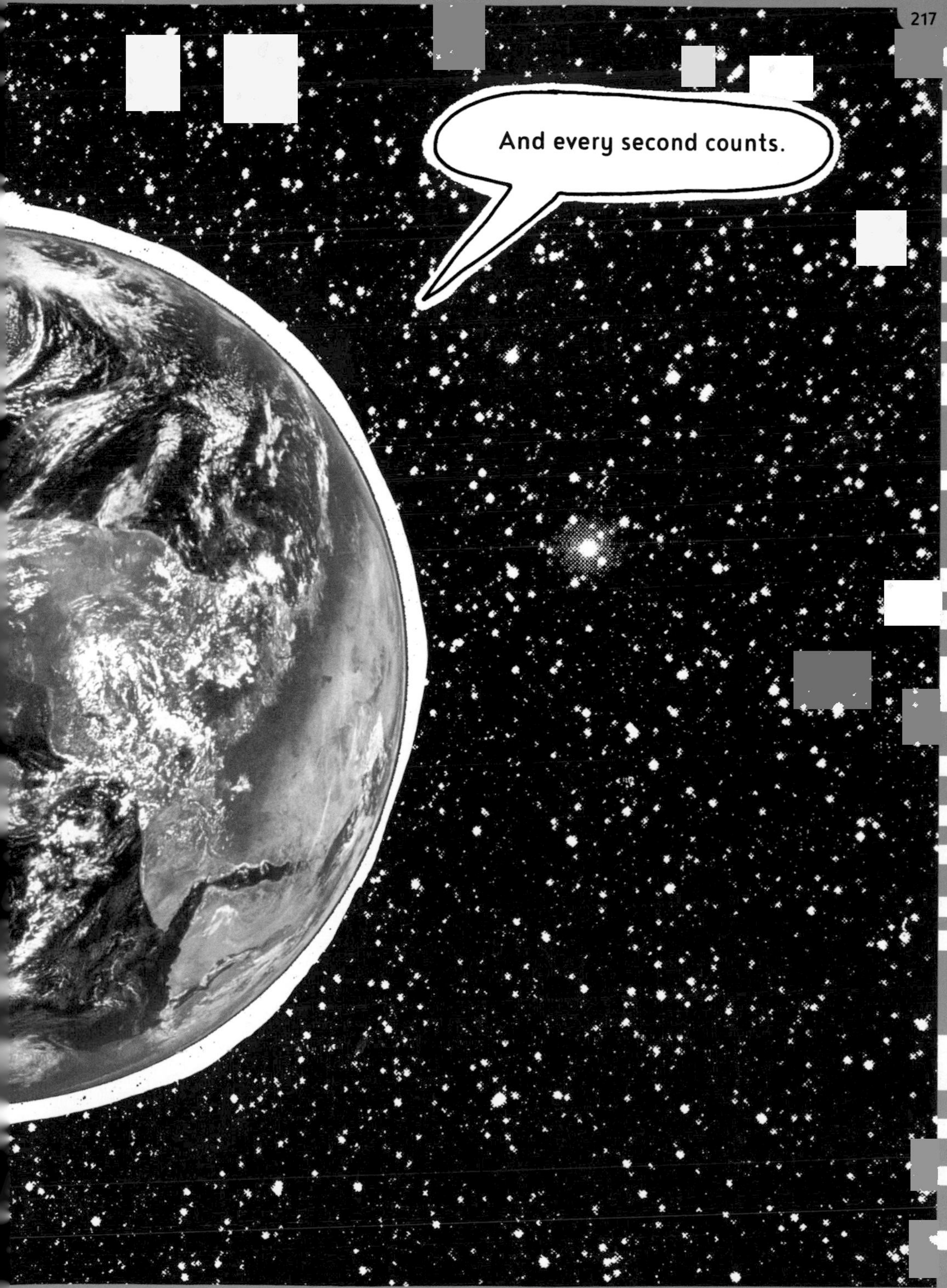
And every second counts.

EPILOGUE:
A New World

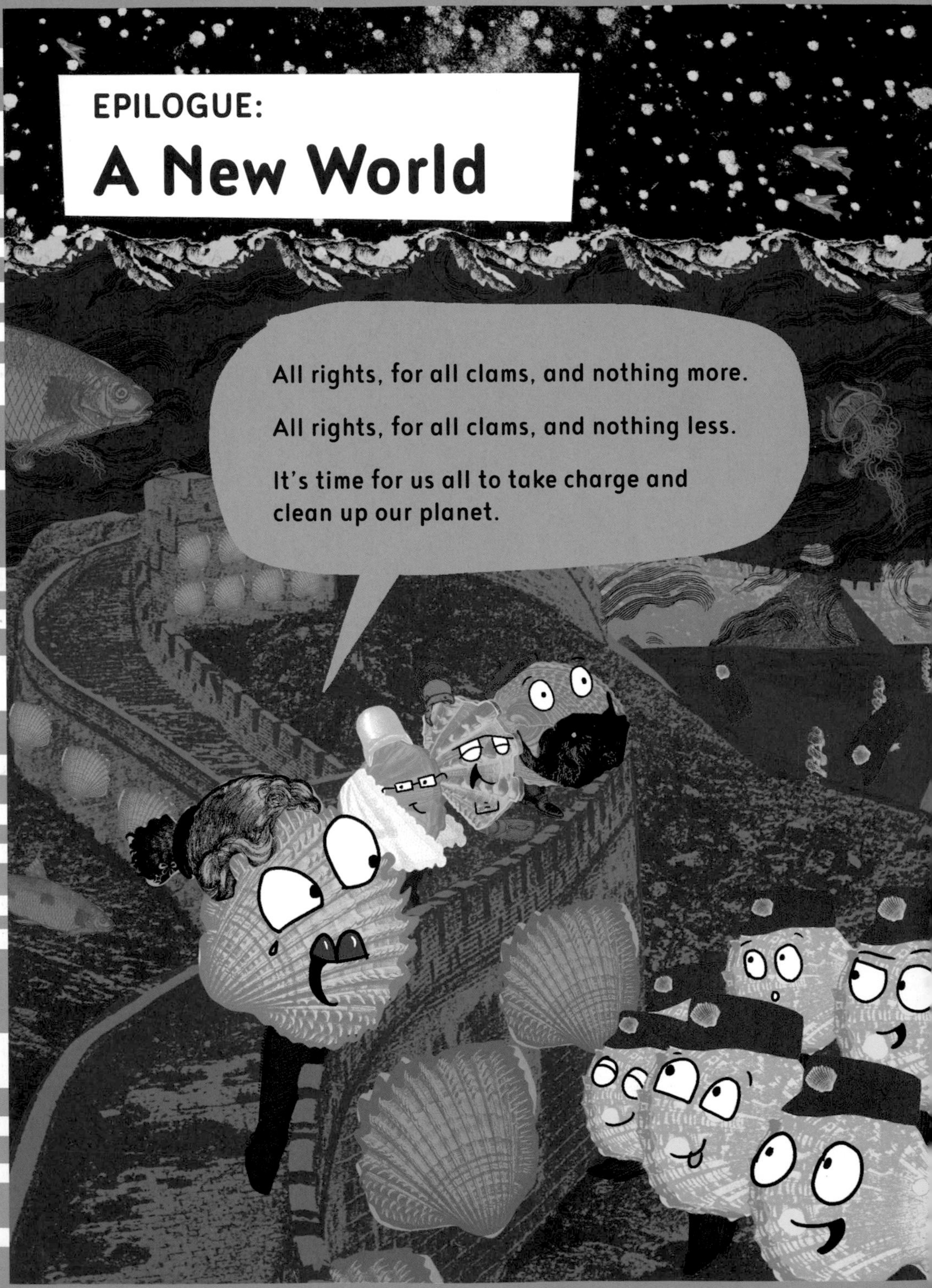

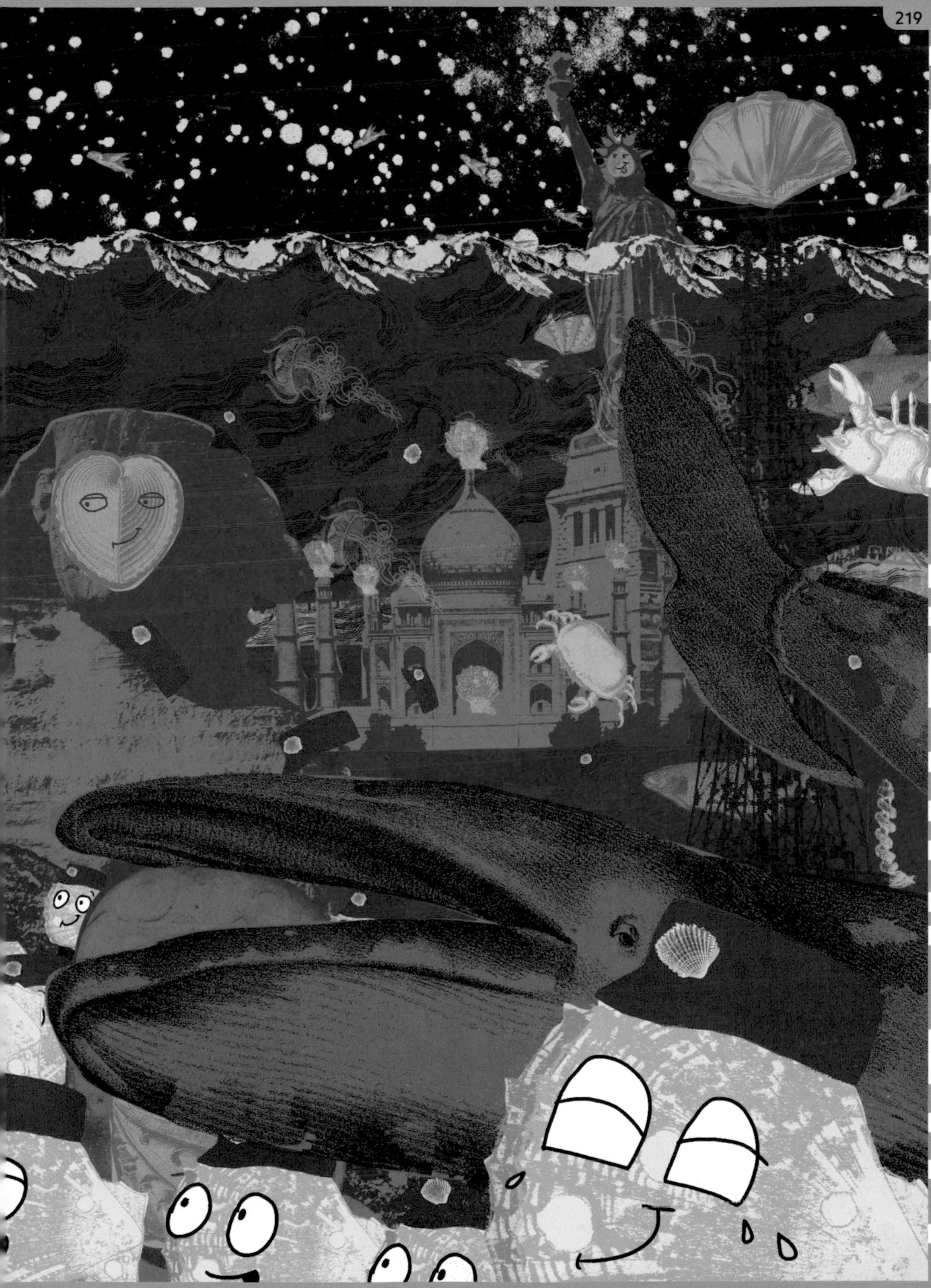

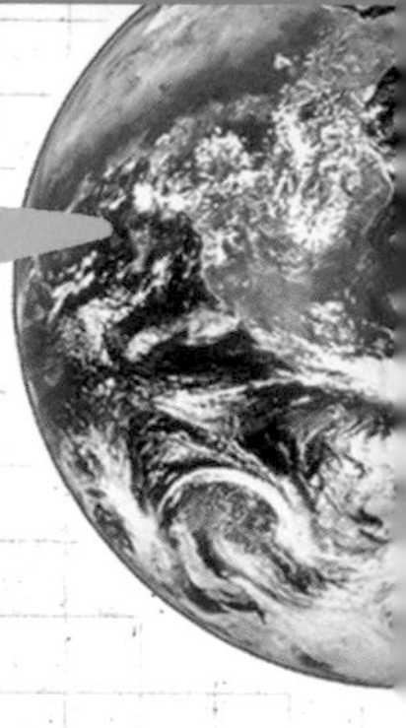

Just like in Mission One, many illustrations in this book were cut out of other artworks and re-used. Illustrator Steven W. took art from places like the Dutch National Museum (the Rijksmuseum) and cut and pasted and colored it. That's called "collage."

AlphaWolf is collaged from an engraving by Albertus Willem Sijthoff between 1861 and 1913.

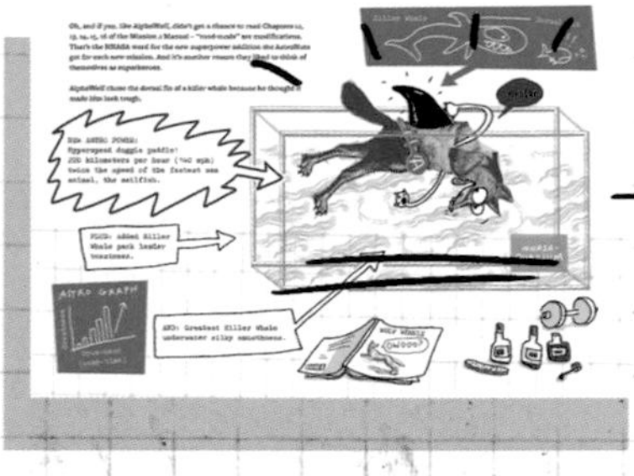

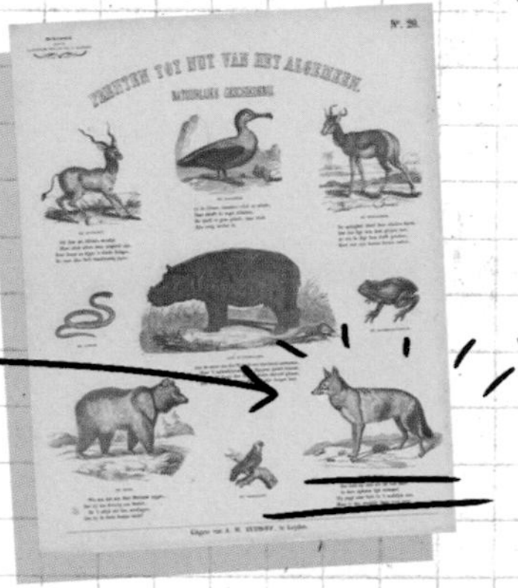

This incredible wave is collaged from "Under the Wave off Kanagawa," a woodblock print by Katsushika Hokusai between 1829 and 1833.

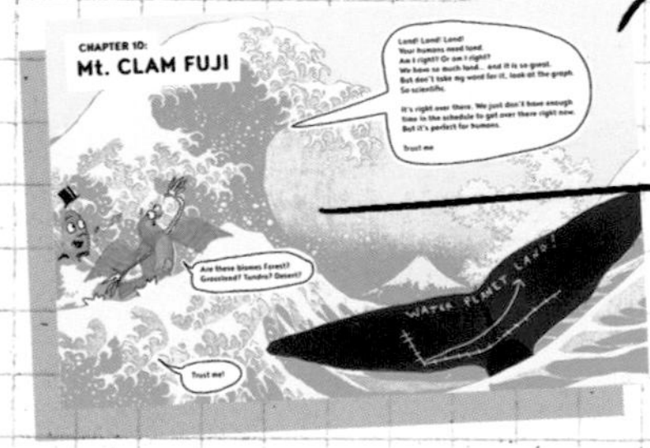
CHAPTER 10:
Mt. CLAM FUJI
Trust me!

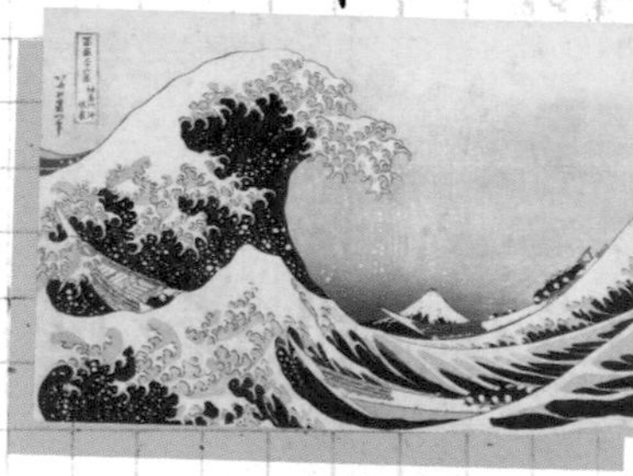

A lot of the art in this book is collaged from the work of artist and scientist Ernst Haeckel, who lived from 1834 to 1919.

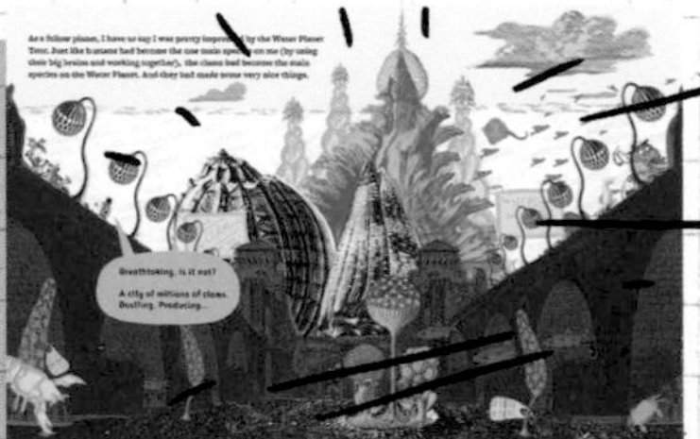

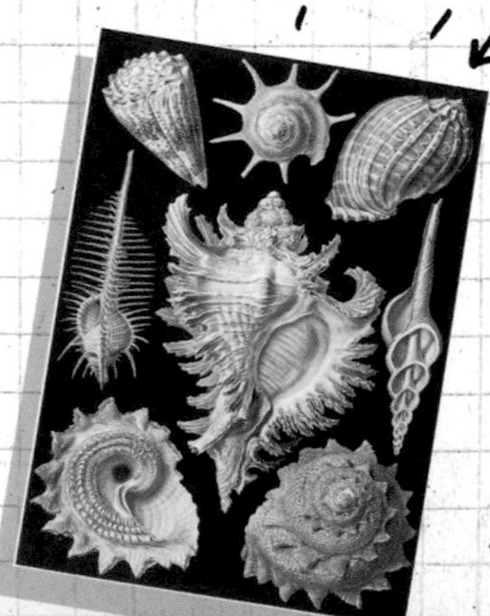

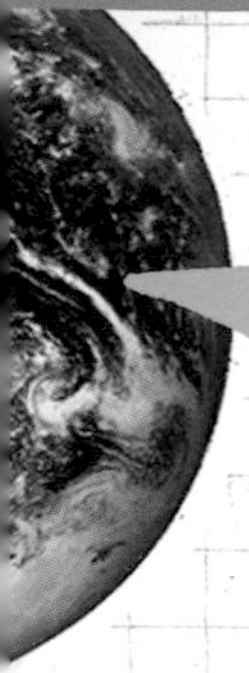

Now I know as Earth, I'm not supposed to play favorites, but this Haeckel guy was pretty special. He studied some of the smallest organisms on me, drawing and classifying them in his most famous book *Art Forms in Nature*. Haeckel provided early evidence for Darwin's Theory of Evolution, inspired Art Nouveau, and did just what the AstroNuts missions do: show science and art working side by side!

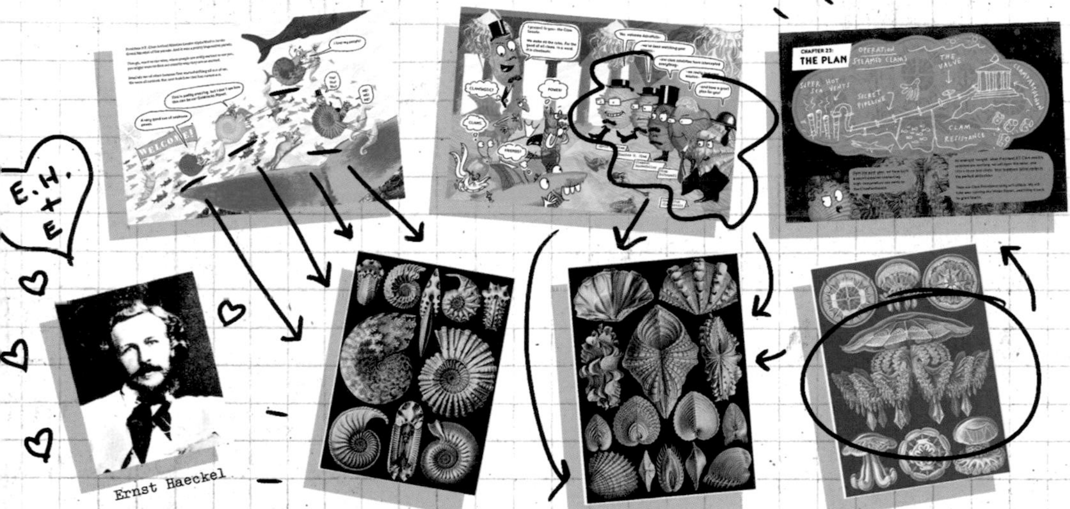

E.H. + E
CHAPTER 23:
THE PLAN
Ernst Haeckel

And don't forget! Make your own AstroNuts on the book series website: AstroNuts.Space. Download printouts and MORE!

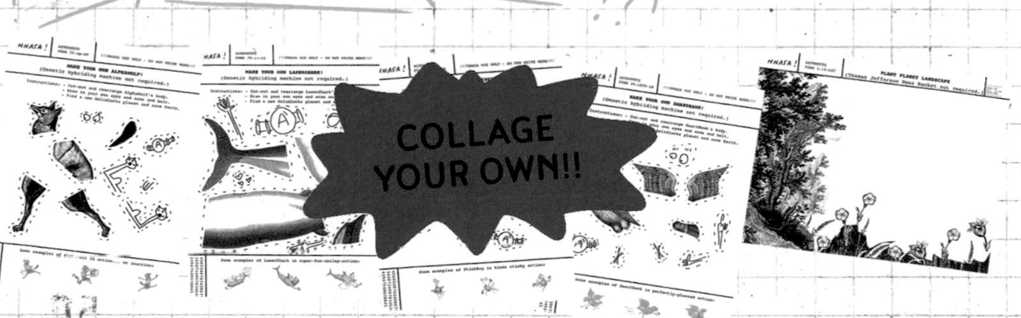

COLLAGE YOUR OWN!!

Don't worry. Steven is not breaking any laws. The Rijksmuseum wants people to see and use their amazing collection of artwork. So they have put almost all of it online.
For more information, go to: RIJKSMUSEUM.NL

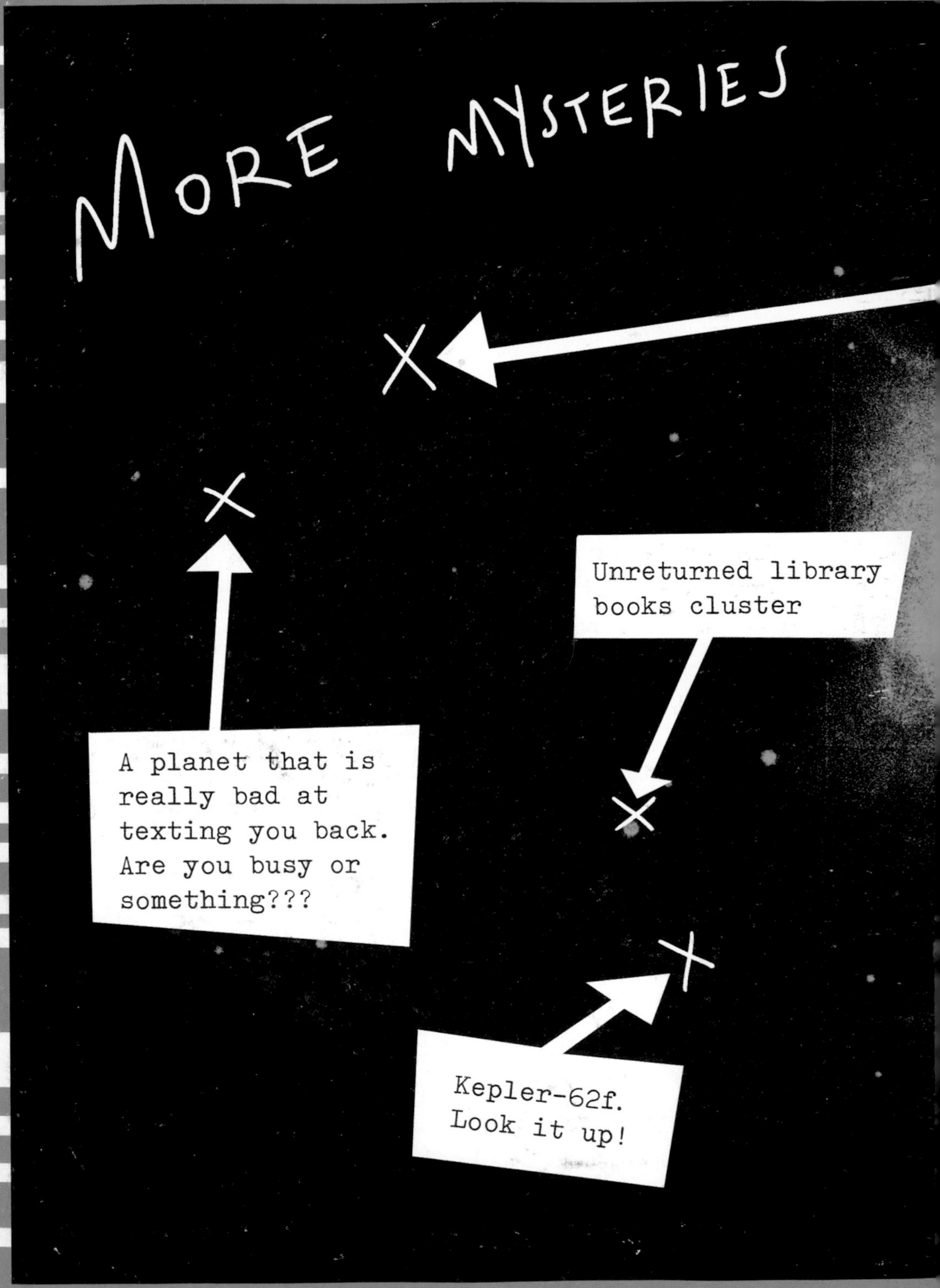
MORE MYSTERIES
Unreturned library books cluster
A planet that is really bad at texting you back. Are you busy or something???
Kepler-62f. Look it up!